"YE HAVE CAPTURED MY HEART, LASS."

How many years had Flanna waited to hear such words? As a woman, she had longed for love. But she was the Flame now, and words like that would only destroy her.

"I must go back to my people," she whispered. "I am their leader. They need me."

"Ye are a woman," Roderic murmured. "I need you."

He leaned closer. She could feel the steady beat of his heart, could feel herself falling under his spell.

Yet she had vowed to protect others. She could not go back on her word.

"Flanna," he breathed, leaning closer.

"Nay!" she gasped. "I am not Flanna. I am the Flame."

"Ye are a woman, and ye are mine—"

Other **AVON ROMANCES**

Highland Flame

Lois Greiman

AVON BOOKS ◆ NEW YORK

HIGHLAND FLAME is an original publication of Avon Books. This work has never before appeared in book form. This work is a novel. Any similarity to actual persons or events is purely coincidental.

AVON BOOKS
A division of
The Hearst Corporation
1350 Avenue of the Americas
New York, New York 10019

Copyright © 1996 by Lois Greiman
Published by arrangement with the author
Library of Congress Catalog Card Number: 95-94932
ISBN: 0-380-78190-5

First Avon Books Printing: March 1996

AVON TRADEMARK REG. U.S. PAT. OFF. AND IN OTHER COUNTRIES, MARCA REGISTRADA, HECHO EN U.S.A.

Printed in the U.S.A.

RA   10   9   8   7   6   5   4   3   2   1

To Cindy Hartwig,
who, with a couple of ratty fur coats,
could make a dancing bear.
Thanks for being the best sister a
little girl could possibly hope for.

Highland Flame

Prologue

The year of our Lord—1497

"**S**he is still the verra image of her mother."

With red-rimmed eyes, Arthur MacGowan stared at Flanna and she stared back, amazed at the changes four years had wrought in this man she had once thought invincible. His face was ghostly white. His breath rattled harsh and loud in the darkened room.

"Ye had hoped she would sprout a red beard like yers?" asked Troy Hamilton.

"Dunna mock me! I am still laird here!" shouted the old man. But his words were reedy, and the fist he raised as a symbol of power shook with weakness. "Aye." He nodded once, letting his arm fall to his velvet coverlet. "I am still laird here, and I am dying."

For the first time in a long while, Flanna felt her hands tremble. She clasped them more tightly as memories rushed in on her. Memories of a small girl holding a shattered mirror and crying. But she would not cry now. Not this time.

"Whether she is the image of her mother or nay, she is yers," Troy said. "Like the acorn is the oak's, she is yers. And yer heart knows it."

"My heart!" The old man laughed, but the sound gasped into a cough. By the light of the single tallow candle, Flanna could see that the spittle at the corner of his mouth was flecked with blood. "My heart, like all those I trusted, has betrayed me."

1

" 'Tis ye who has betrayed, MacGowan. First the mother and then—"

"Dare ye criticize—" shouted the old laird before a spasm stopped his tirade. He squeezed his eyes shut and grappled at his chest for a moment before lying still. "Aye, ye would," he whispered finally. "Few others have dared find fault with me. And though we are but distant cousins, we were like brothers for many years. But all is behind me now, Troy. All past." His head moved weakly from side to side on the pillow, and when he opened his eyes they were bright with unshed tears. "Would that I could call back the days and start anew. Mayhap I could right the wrongs. Mayhap I could gain my lady's love."

"Ye had her love," Troy murmured. "But it couldna survive yer jealousy."

The bloodshot eyes closed. "What of her bairn?"

Troy was silent a moment, then in a voice as dark as the room he said, "He, too, died, as ye well ken. Buried in Bastia beside his mother."

"Scotland's lad buried in foreign ground," murmured Arthur. "How old would he be now?"

"It has been twelve years since her death and his."

The old man opened his eyes. Even now, Flanna could see a hint of the old rage in them. Even now, she could remember her sobs as she beat on the lid of the trunk that imprisoned her while she was being sent to France. She had begged to be let out, begged to know what she had done wrong. She had vowed to be good, to be the perfect daughter if only he would not send her away, if only he would cherish her again.

"Ye have counted the years?" the MacGowan asked, his tone suspicious.

"Ye still wrong her," Troy rasped. "Soon ye shall have ta face her again, and ye still slander her name."

"Dear God!" The old man turned his face into the pillow. "I could think of na other woman even when I was in another's arms. Why did she na age? What pact did she make with the devil to draw men's eyes ta her,

ta make them want her? Even ye, me faithful friend . . ."
He stopped again, gripping the coverlet in gnarled hands
and fighting for breath.

"Have I brought the lass from France after all this
time only ta hear yer accusations again, old man?" Troy
asked.

"I am dying," the MacGowan croaked. "My people
need a leader. Ye ken well why I called ye here."

"I will not marry," Flanna said. Her tone was tight
and abrupt in the still air of the room. She hadn't thought
she would have the power to force the words past her
fear. But suddenly it seemed as if she were not herself.
Instead, she stood apart from the scene, watching the
straight, tall figure beside the bed, hearing the iron-cool
steadiness in her voice, and marveling at this woman
who was nothing like the terrified girl she knew herself
to be. "Whoever he is, I will not marry the man you've
chosen. Not even to give the clan MacGowan a leader."

The room was silent for a moment as the old man
turned his gaze to her. "So Troy, ye have na told her
why I called her here."

"There are things she must hear from her sire and
none other," Troy said.

The old man nodded and motioned her closer.
Strangely, foolishly, Flanna thought, she obeyed.

"Ye think ta defy me wishes again?" he asked.

Flanna didn't answer. Indeed, she feared she could
not, for terror gripped her in a clammy hand. But she
fought it down and managed to raise her chin.

"So ye hate me, lass." The words were not a question. "I offered ye a chance for happiness. Yer mother
said ye were na meant for the life of a convent. She
begged on her knees," he murmured as though even
now he could see her, "and so I negotiated a marriage
for ye. 'Twould have been a good match, but ye refused.
Why?"

Flanna didn't answer. Long ago, shame had tortured
her, causing her to refuse to give him her reasons. Perhaps pride kept her quiet now. Or perhaps it was merely

that she knew her answer would matter little.

"Why?" Arthur demanded again, but in a moment he gritted his yellowed teeth and swore. "Ye need na say, for I ken the truth. Ye shunned the match I found for ye because ye had already taken a lover. Ye were determined ta disgrace me just as yer mother had. But this ye willna refuse!" Suddenly, he grasped her wrist. Flanna winced but her body moved forward of its own volition and her gaze remained hard and cold on her father.

"So!" said the MacGowan. "There is na longer a woman's softness in ye. Na longer tears. They have been replaced by fire in yer eyes, lass. Fire!" the old man croaked, then suddenly released his hold. "And it is good, for ye willna longer be a woman. Nay, ye will rule my people in my stead. Ye will be the Flame of the MacGowans."

Chapter 1

The year of our Lord—1499

The night was as black as the sins of the Forbes. Thunder rumbled an ominous warning. Mist rolled up on silent, invisible wings. But the Flame's stallion carried her through it, his rapid hoofbeats muffled by the wet heath, his pale, dappled body shrouded by the swirling mists.

A hillock rose before them, and they raced heavenward. At the knoll's crest, Flame straightened. Below them, the castle of the Forbes was wrapped in the protective, swift-flowing arm of the river for which it was named. Bathed in the silver light of the three-quarter moon, it looked like a mystical citadel with its roots planted in the mists that roiled about it. Here was a place of magic, where pearl-horned unicorns might cavort amidst the revered Sidhe of yore.

"By the saints," Flame murmured. Fear mingled with awe in her breast. It was not too late to turn back. She sat erect, barely breathing. Perhaps Troy had been right, mayhap this was a fool's errand. But the Forbeses' sins were many and damning, and she could avoid vengeance no longer.

She would not turn back. She was the Flame of the MacGowans, sworn to protect her people. And although the Forbeses were formidable adversaries, they would surely pay for their betrayal, for she had planned her revenge well and carefully.

5

Curling her fingers into Lochan's mane, Flame touched her heels to the stallion's sides. Without further encouragement, he leapt across the hilltop and toward the castle. The drawbridge was down. Flame pressed Lochan onto the heavy wooden timbers and pulled him to a halt. Although the portcullis stood as protection against the outside world, the bridge beneath them had been lowered as tangible evidence of the Forbeses' all-consuming arrogance. How dare they pillage her land and kill her clansmen, then think themselves safe from retribution?

Anger and fear surged within her. "Let me in!" Flame's voice sounded shrill and frantic to her own ears, just like the voice of the simple, terrified lass she pretended to be.

No answer. Beneath her, Lochan fidgeted, rattling his bit.

"Please, for pity's sake, let me in," she pleaded again. Her words were louder now, but her tone was no less desperate. " 'Tis help I come ta beg."

Through the beaten, iron grills of the portcullis, Flame saw a flicker of light. She held her breath, waiting, feeling dried sheep's blood crack across her knuckles as she tightened her fingers on the reins.

A gnarled figure stepped forward, nearly hidden behind the metal squares. "Who comes to the gate of the clan Forbes?" The gruff voice was barely audible above the rush of the water below.

For a moment, a wave of terror held Flame silent. She was desperate for this mission to succeed. She could no longer pacify her people with words of peace, and her leadership was being tested.

"Who's there, I say?"

"Please." She forced uncertainty from her mind and pushed the word past lips stiff with dried blood and fresh fear. "I need help."

The guard raised a lantern, casting a hesitant light on her. "We let none save our own enter these gates past day's light,'' he said, squinting into the darkness. "Come back in the morn."

"Nay, I canna!" Flame called.

"And I canna let ye enter, lass, so take yerself to yer home until the dawn," ordered the guard, turning away.

"But me sister! She will surely die before the break of day."

The man turned back. "What's that ye say?"

"I have heard of the miraculous wonders worked by yer Lady Fiona. Please. I come to beg her mercy."

The lantern was lifted, though it illumined little more than the guard's woolen cap and heavy, downswept brows. "What be yer name, lass?"

"Cara of the McBains. Yer allies. For pity's sake let—"

"Who rides with ye?"

"I come alone. Please sir. If she dies . . ." She let her words choke to a halt as her mind searched for chinks in the armor of her plan. She could not fail.

The lantern lowered, then, "I shall let ye enter, lass, though I canna promise assistance."

The creak of the rising portcullis scattered Flame's thoughts and seemed to speak of her death. She sat unmoving, trying to force her muscles to do her bidding, trying to capture the renowned courage of the Highlander. But she was only a trembling girl come to do a warrior's job.

The protective grill rose above her head like the iron teeth of a ravenous monster. Safety called from the shadows behind her, but Lochan dragged the reins through her fingers and stepped forward, undaunted.

His hooves rapped against the thick timbers and then against the hard-packed soil within the confines of the dark courtyard.

"Ye say yer sister's taken ill?" asked the gnarled guard, lifting his lantern again and squinting up toward her. "Jesu!" he rasped, "what has happened ta ye?"

" 'Tis me sister's blood," she lied. "I must see the lady of the hall."

The guard remained mute, then nodded sharply, not drawing his gaze from Flame's face as he spoke to his unseen partner. "Finlay, take the lass ta the lady."

"But—"

"Na buts, man, or our Fiona willna forgive the delay, babe or na babe." There was a moment's pause, then, "Hurry it up now. Canna ye see she be in great need?"

It was only a short distance to the hall, and yet Lochan's footfalls seemed to go on forever. It took all Flame's courage to dismount and leave the stallion's protective presence behind her.

The huge door groaned as the man called Finlay dragged it open. Flame's knees trembled as she stepped into the room. Against the wall, a hound rose and whined, treading on its companions and pulling at its tether. Its shadow stretched, wavering in the fickle light cast by ensconced tallow candles.

"Finlay?" A man's voice broke the silence. Flame gasped, darting her gaze to the speaker who appeared suddenly in the dimness. "Be there trouble?"

"The lass begged entrance," explained Finlay. "Said she must see the lady."

"Fiona? Why?" The man drew nearer, seeming to grow as he approached. "Step into the light, lass," he ordered, but before she could force her legs to obey, he drew a sharp breath and halted. "Gawd's wrath, what has happened to ye?"

"I be fine," she whispered, her voice weak. Who was this man and why was he here? She had come for Fiona and none other, for the lady was known for assisting those in need no matter the danger to herself.

"Fine?" Without warning, he reached out, grasping her arm in a firm hold and pulling her toward the candles' wavering light. "What foolishness is this?" He grimaced, searching her face for the source of the blood. "Ye are in need of ministering. Come lie down," he commanded, but she pulled sharply from his grasp.

"Nay! I canna stay."

He scowled at her. Flame swallowed her fear and concentrated. Whatever this man's name, he was tall, strongly built, and spoke with authority. But he dressed as any Highlander might, in a simple saffron shirt and earth-toned plaid. He was only another guard, she assured herself. For the Forbes brothers always rode with their warriors. Surely they did so tonight, for Flame's men had started a blaze large enough to be seen from Normandy. She had smelled the smoke from where she had hidden in the woods, had watched the Forbeses race from their gates toward the fire her men had set to attract them. She had known they would go in large numbers, for the notorious brigand band roaming the countryside was becoming bold and ruthless enough to alarm even the great Forbeses. She had watched them leave, had waited in the shelter of the trees until the last man had vanished into the night.

"I must go!" she said, remembering her mission, her careful planning. Glancing about, she hoped to spot Fiona, but the only other people in the hall were clustered fast asleep near the long-dead fire.

"Must go? By the sins of auld horny, ye mustna, lass, for ye've been badly wounded."

He reached for her again, but she drew back with a jerk. "Nay. I have had na but a prick. 'Tis me sister's blood ye see."

His scowl deepened as he tried to decipher her wounds by the fickle light. "What say ye? Tell me this tale," he ordered, then clenched his jaw and swore vehemently. "Was it the brigand band?"

For the first time, Flame looked him straight in the eyes. The warriors would return soon, and she must be far gone. "Nay." Her voice was soft but even." 'Twas na brigands."

"What then? Tell me that I may pass the word to Fiona."

Such caring in his voice! Flame narrowed her eyes, trying to discern his thoughts, but there was no time. "Me sister and me were foraging in the woods. We were hungry. There's verra little . . ." She pushed a sob up her throat and let her eyes fall dramatically closed for a moment. "There's verra little since the death of our parents. 'Tis just she and I, and I . . . I dunna ken what I shall do if she . . . Please!" she said, reaching forward to grasp his pale shirt in her bloody hands. "Please, dunna let her die."

"There now, lass, hush." To her surprise, he didn't pull her grimy fingers away, but held her steady by her shoulders. "Dunna fret. If there is ought ta be done, we shall do it. But ye must rest and tell me the whole tale. What is it that has happened to yer sister?"

Flame raised her gaze to the solemn face before her. His was a well-sculpted visage, lean and fair with heavily lashed eyes set deep and far apart. His hair was the color of barley straw and hung to his shoulders in thick waves. But that knowledge gave her no clues to his identity. "We were huntin'," she whispered, holding his gaze with her own and feeling her body tremble in his hands. "We heard a noise. I wanted to run. But me sister, she is so brave. And we were verra hungry. She thought it to be a hare or somethin' na more dangerous. Something we might snare and cook. But . . ." With a sob, she pulled her fingers from his shirt and dropped her face abruptly into them. "We didna ken it was a boar. Dear Jesu! We didna ken." She lifted her gaze again. Tears swelled in her eyes. "I will repay ye in any way I might," she vowed breathlessly, placing a hand upon his. "Please, if ye will only have pity on me, me laird, and . . ."

"Hush, lass. I will do what I can, though I am na the laird."

"Nay?" She blinked rapidly, finding her vision blurred by tears. It was said that Laird Forbes had hair as black as a crow's wing, while this man was crowned in gold. She must place him, assure herself of his insignificance. "But . . . surely ye must be of royal blood, for ye be so strong and . . ." She saw the hint of a smile lift his lips at the flattery. And his eyes were dark blue, Flame realized suddenly.

"I fear I am but yer average untamed Scot, lass," he said softly. "Hard of head and soft of heart." She could hear the smile in his voice now, though she lowered her eyes and refused to lift them.

"Yet I will do what I may. Finlay, I will be bringing the lass's sister here. Tell—"

"Here?" Flame drew back with a start, her gaze flying to his. "Nay. Ye cannot. I mean . . . ye canna!"

His sharp gaze stabbed her. "Why?"

"Surely the journey would be too dangerous for me sister!" Dear Jesu! She must dissuade this man from coming, for she did not want to be the cause of his death. "She's . . . she's badly hurt. I managed to get her to a broken stable. There I built a fire, and by that light I could see . . . the wounds." Her voice cracked into a sob. "She canna be moved."

"There now, lass. I have carried the wounded many times afore this. Even Lady Fiona would assure ye of me ability to do so. All will be well."

"Nay!" Flame repeated. "The lady must come with me. Ye must convince her of the necessity of all haste," she said.

He shook his head. "Fiona canna leave Glen Creag, lass, for she is still abed. I am here to make certain she does na overtax her strength on some errand of mercy as she is wont ta do. Though I was na happy ta be left behind for so light an injury as mine."

"She is . . . abed?"

"With her second babe," was the answer. "Just birthed. She canna leave. But ye have me promise to bring yer sister to her with all due speed."

"A wee babe?" Flame asked. Her plans were crumbling around her like so many grains of sand, leaving her on precarious footing. "But . . ."

"I see yer concern, lass," said the other, taking her hand gently in his own. "But I tell ye true, Fiona Rose must await our return here, for if harm should befall me brother's wife, Leith would wear me hide as a mantle and me teeth as an amulet."

The world creaked to a grinding halt. Air became trapped in Flame's lungs. She could feel the blood drain from her face. "Laird Leith is yer . . . brother?" she whispered.

"Aye." The corners of the blue eyes crinkled again. "He is that, lass, and though he acts the wee kitten beneath his Fiona's hand, we Forbeses are na always so gentle as we appear."

Not so gentle! "Then ye are . . ." she began, but her voice failed her completely now.

"Roderic Forbes, lass. And ye?"

Damnation! He was Roderic Forbes, one of the men she had vowed to make pay through their lady's abduction. She had been so certain he would have left with the other warriors . . . and that Fiona would have accompanied her. "I . . . must return to me sister," she murmured, trying to pull away.

He held her still, his expression somber. "Aye. We will ride together. Finlay—"

Flame reached out without conscious thought, tangling her fingers in his voluminous sleeve again. "Please, sir. I dunna wish to bother ye, and I have heard of yer lady's kindness. Surely—"

"The babe needs her, lass."

"But surely there be another who nurses the wee one."

"Nay. The lady cares for her own and willna leave him."

Flame remained silent, watching the man before her. She was not a small woman, but he was much larger. For one shameful moment she felt all courage fail her. Then she remembered his betrayal. The Forbeses had vowed to be their allies, but instead they had chosen to raid her herds and torment her people. The wounds of the herd guards had been grievous enough. But Simon's death had steeled her will. Only the devil's own would slay a peaceful messenger. For a moment, Flame remembered Simon's raucous laughter, laughter that had been replaced by his widow's mourning keel.

"Then ye must come," she whispered.

"Aye. I will," Roderic said. He held her gaze for a moment before lifting it abruptly to the man behind her. "Return to yer watch, Finlay. With me brothers gone we canna neglect the gate."

"Roddy? Be there trouble?" A sleepy-eyed lad of twelve or so years approached on silent feet. He stopped at Roderic's side, watching him from beneath a tousled mop of flame-bright hair.

"Aye, Roman. The lass's kin needs Fiona's ministrations. I go to bring . . ."

But the boy was already hurrying toward the door with a sheepdog at his heels. "I will fetch Mor."

Roderic nodded. "And ready a mount for the lass."

The door closed behind Finlay and Roman, but Flame barely noticed their exit, for her attention was caught on Roderic's words. She would not leave Lochan Gorm, for the stallion was her friend and prized possession. "I have me own horse, me laird."

"Have I na told ye I am na laird?" Roderic asked.

"I . . ." He stood very close and the seconds ticked away. "I have me own horse," she repeated uneasily.

"Aye, lass, but yer beast is bound to be weary. A fresh mount will speed our journey."

"Nay! It would not!"

He cocked his head slightly, studying her. "Mayhap yer animal be made of iron?"

She had sounded too haughty and too well educated. "Nay," she said more softly now. Was he laughing at her? Anger welled up, but she tamped it carefully down. "Of course na, me laird. He is but flesh and blood as any other steed."

"Then the decision is made. Ye will ride a Forbes mount."

"But . . ."

"Hush. What be yer name, lass?"

She watched his eyes, momentarily forgetting to breathe. "Cara," she said softly, "of the McBains. Me sister waits in a shelter just to the south of Forbeses' land.'' She let her eyes fall closed and added in a whisper, ''If she yet lives.''

Flame could feel his warm gaze on her face. ''Come,'' he said abruptly, and leading her toward the table where he had sat, lifted a pewter chalice and pressed it into her hands. ''Drink. Nay,'' he said, preventing her unspoken refusal. ''Dunna argue, for yer sister waits and ye'll need the strength ta ride a Forbes steed.'' His eyes seemed to smile, and though she took no time to try to decipher his mood, she heard the boast in his voice. ''We grow our horses large indeed at Glen Creag. And ye must ride like a seasoned warrior this night.''

Holding his eyes with hers, Flame took the warm cup. She lifted it quickly, draining the potent liquid in one unending quaff.

''Be ye ready to ride now?'' she asked, handing back the goblet.

Roderic glanced from the chalice to her face. ''Already ye *drink* like a seasoned warrior.'' He raised his fair brows in amazement.

''Be ye ready?'' she repeated.

''Aye. If ye can walk, lass, I be ready.''

Turning, she strode quickly for the door. Thumping the empty chalice to the table, Roderic hurried after her.

The air outside felt heavy with humidity and anticipation. Lochan nickered and appeared from the darkness, a pale shadow in the night.

Behind her, Roderic cleared his throat. ''So this be yer . . . steed?''

Flame placed a hand to the mane she had intentionally muddied, letting her emotions flow easily through that simple touch. Lochan tossed his head. ''Yes. He is mine.''

''Well . . .'' Roderic said hesitantly. ''I am sure he's a fine ride, lass, but Roman comes even now with our mounts. Yer animal will be well tended until our return.''

''No.'' She spoke softly without turning toward him. ''I will ride me own. I thank ye for yer generosity, but

I am but a simple maid, me laird, and . . .'' The lad stopped a pair of gigantic mounts nearby. They shuffled their heavily feathered feet restlessly, laying back their ears and turning white-rimmed eyes toward Lochan. The smaller stallion rumbled a low challenge and danced sideways at the length of his reins.

Flame pulled him nearer. "I am but a simple maid," she repeated, "and surely couldna control such a powerful beast as ye offer."

"Fear na, lass. I will see that na harm befalls . . ." Roderic began, but before he could finish his promise, Flame had vaulted onto Lochan's bare back.

"Me sister," she reminded him breathlessly. "She canna wait. And Lochan knows the way even in the dead of night."

"Verra well then, lass. Ye say yer sister waits at our southern border?"

"Aye."

"Then we should reach her just afore dawn," he said, speaking to the lad now. "Though the return trip will be slower, look for us three hours or so past first light."

"Could I na go with ye, Roddy?"

"I wish that ye could, lad. For I would feel safer with ye at me back. But we canna spare a single man ta-night." Roderic's teeth shone in the darkness as he spoke, and the boy's back seemed to straighten with pride at his words. "I am placing the safety of all here in yer hands until me return, for I know ye can do a man's job."

Roman nodded solemnly, then unbuckled a scabbard from his hips and handed it quickly over. "I have brought Neart, for ye canna go unarmed with brigands about."

Roderic reached for the long blade, then fastened it to his own lean waist. Flame's heart seemed to stop in her chest. She had hoped to bring the Forbeses' lady, not an armed warrior, but she could not turn back now.

" 'Tis a blessing ye are, lad," he was saying. "Put

Skene back and make certain Fiona be prepared for our return.''

The boy nodded and Roderic mounted his waiting stallion.

It was only a short distance to the castle's front entrance. With a word from Roderic, the portcullis was raised and the horses trotted over the wooden bridge. The big stallion's footfalls were cadenced and ponderous, Lochan's were quick and light.

With a single word of farewell, the iron grill was lowered. Night stretched out before them, welcoming Flame with dark, reaching arms. Lochan pressed into a gallop of his own accord, swallowing the leagues with his long, sweeping strides. Above, the beleaguered moon found an opening in the tattered clouds and shed its mercurial light across their winding trail.

Gnarled, mist-heavy bracken grabbed at Lochan's hooves, but he flew through it. He knew the destination and Flame was certain he would not fail her. She laid a hand to his neck, feeling his strength. Cresting a hill, she gazed downward. The glen below was wreathed in shadow and cloud. Flame loosened the reins, letting Lochan choose the course into the sea of fog where the tumbled remains of a stable would lie shrouded and silent.

Mist lapped at their legs like a swelling tide.

All would be well now. Flame consciously slowed her breathing and tried to ease the tension from her muscles, but worry and fear held her in a tight grip. All would be well, she assured herself again. There was no one to stop her. It was only a little farther. A hundred rods or so and . . .

From nowhere, a dark arm reached from the shadows. Flame screamed and jerked sideways. Lochan spun wildly away, nearly losing her. But the arm drew back of its own accord, sweeping upward on outstretched wings and materializing into a hunting owl. It was a bad omen. Flame straightened on Lochan's back, but failed to breathe. Someone would die this night.

"Lass!" Roderic was beside her in an instant, grabbing Lochan's rein and pulling him to a halt as Flame remained unmoving, staring into the mist toward their destination. " 'Twas but a owl. Are ye unhurt?"

She swallowed convulsively. "Aye. I am fine."

"Ye're shaking." His hand moved from the rein to her arm. Even through the damp woolen sleeve, his fingers felt warm and strong. For a moment her will weakened. "Come. Ye can ride with me."

"Nay," she breathed.

"I willna hurt ye."

"Nay," she repeated, lowering her eyes. " 'Tis just a wee bit further till we see me sister and..." She turned her gaze to Lochan's mane and trembled.

"There now, lass." Roderic straightened but let his hand remain on her arm a moment longer as if to support her. "Dunna fear. I think I see a bit of light through the mist. Yer sister, she is there?" he asked, squinting through the fog. "Just ahead?"

Flame nodded, unable to find her voice, but forcing herself to remember her reasons for revenge.

"Ye must na punish yerself further, lass. I will go in alone and bring her out. Ye need na look upon her wounds until Lady Fiona has mended them."

Against her will, Flame found his eyes in the darkness. They were shadowed and deep. She caught her breath. Her lips parted. She had not thought to find kindness in this man. She had not wished to. The truth trembled to spill forth from her lips, but the anguish of her people stopped her words. She nodded slowly.

The warmth of his hand dropped away. In a moment he was gone, swallowed by the darkness and rolling mists.

Flame sat immobile, every muscle taut. Beneath her, Lochan half reared, pulling at the reins.

"Roderic," she whispered, but loyalty to her clan held her steady. Whether she wished it or not, her people depended on her, needed her strength. Lochan pulled again and Flame loosened the reins, letting him trot forward.

The broken structure of wood and stone appeared out of the earthbound clouds. Roderic's horse stood alone, his saddle empty.

Slipping from Lochan's back, Flame hurried toward the abandoned stable. The doorway was a golden square of light in the darkness. She rushed through and halted as her heart hammered against her ribs.

A fire burned low. Seven of her men occupied the stone enclosure. One leaned against the far wall, holding his arm.

"Praise the saints!" Troy rumbled. "We heard yer scream and feared fer yer safety."

Flame tried to speak, but her throat was too tight, her attention too riveted on Roderic Forbes.

He stood very still with his arms pressed against his back. Troy loomed over him, his hawk-sharp eyes visible above his captive's head as he bound Roderic's wrists.

Flame watched, finding no words. A narrow rivulet of blood trickled down Forbes' forehead. His sword was held by Gilbert, one of the warriors who surrounded him in a grim half circle.

" 'Twas wondering . . ." began Roderic—his tone was smooth, but his gaze was hard and cold in the flickering light thrown from the fire behind him—"which of these bonny maids be yer sister, lass?"

Chapter 2

"I'll show ye a bonny maid, ye blackhearted devil!" snarled Bullock, stepping forward. His face was red and his body, as stout and squat as the animal for which he was named, was stiff with rage. In his meaty fist he held the handle of his sword in a deadly grip. "Me claymore will give ye a kiss ye'll na soon forget."

"Cease!" Flame ordered. Although her knees felt weak, her tone was sharp and steady as she stepped forward. "There'll be no bloodshed here tonight."

"Na bloodshed?" Bullock scoffed. "Ye should have told the Forbes that afore he cut Shaw."

"Shaw!" Flame breathed. Realizing finally why that stalwart warrior had been so silent and still near the wall, she turned rapidly. "Are ye badly hurt?"

"Nay, me lady." Shaw was a young man, quiet and brave. Clutching a bloody arm and looking pale, he straightened. " 'Tis fine I am."

"He's sorely wounded!" said Nevin. His back was rigid, but his face looked pale as he turned from the sight of the other's wound.

"What were ye thinking?" Bullock asked Flame, still holding his huge claymore at the ready. "Ye were ta take the Lady Forbes. 'Tis what we agreed."

Control lay in the balance. Flame stood very still, assessing her men's moods, debating her next move. Doubt assailed her, but for eighteen months she had been their leader, winning their trust and loyalty by painful

19

increments. She could not back down now, for the MacGowans had no love for cowards or fools.

"*We* agreed!" Flame lifted her chin. If she faltered now, all would be lost. Her clan would be in dissension and the Forbeses would sweep down upon them and wipe her people from the craggy face of Scotland. "Could it be that ye forget who ye be talking to, Burke MacGowan?" she asked, using Bullock's Christian name as a reprimand. "Do ye forget whose father was laird for more years than ye have lived? Do ye forget who ye chose as yer leader?"

No man spoke.

"Do any of ye forget?" she asked, raising her voice and looking at each warrior in turn. "Do ye forget that ye swore vengeance against the Forbeses? Do ye forget who risked her skin to deliver one of their own into your hands?"

Bullock dropped his gaze and let the point of his claymore dip to the grass at his feet. The fire crackled, spewing living embers toward them and their prisoner. "Me apologies, me lady."

Flame drew another deep breath, feeling her hands tremble and crossing her arms quickly against her chest, lest her weakness be noticed. "Are there others here who question my judgment?"

"Nay," said several voices.

"Nay, lady," said Nevin. "One Forbes be as good as the next. Though Fiona is said to be a healer and could have done much to aid our kinsmen instead of slicing the arms of the few warriors remaining to us."

Flame's resolve faltered as her gaze hurried back to Shaw's injured arm. Blood seeped between his pale fingers, soaking his sleeve. The sight of it made her stomach turn, another weakness to be dealt with—and hidden.

"William." It took all her self-control to keep her tone steady as she addressed the quiet warrior who stood nearby. "See to Shaw's wound. As for our prisoner—"

"Prisoner?" Roderic's tone was laced with caustic

humor. Not for a moment had his gaze left her face. "Surely such a motley lot as ye dunna plan ta keep a Forbes captive among ye."

"Aye!" Bullock stepped forward aggressively, though the top of his head barely reached Roderic's shoulder. "That we do. Until yer laird pays in full for the damage he has done the MacGowans."

Roderic turned his arrogant gaze to Bullock's face, though his hands were bound and the rivulet of blood still coursed along his eyebrow and down his left cheek. "So ye be the MacGowans." Slowly he turned his attention to Flame. "And ye be their . . . lying witch?"

"Damn ye!" Shaw swore, lurching from the wall.

"For that ye'll forfeit yer tongue!" vowed Bullock, whipping his claymore upright as the others crowded around him.

But Flame grabbed the double-edged sword from Bullock's hand and swept forward. Tilting the tip up to meet Roderic's throat, she pressed it just beneath his jaw.

"Shall I kill him, lads?" she asked softly.

Roderic's head was tilted away from the blade, but his eyes showed nothing but disdain.

"Shall I kill him? Or shall I let him live?" Keeping the sword poised, she turned her gaze toward the men behind her. "Shall he live so that we might gain even greater revenge?" she asked, raising her voice. "Shall he live so that we might recoup our losses and show the Forbeses that the MacGowans are not to be toyed with?"

For a moment Flame thought her ploy would fail, but finally Shaw murmured, "Let him live, for surely he will wish himself dead when his brother pays the ransom and vents his fury over the losses."

"Aye," muttered Bullock reluctantly.

"Aye," agreed Nevin in his soft voice. " 'Tis best ta let their sins go unavenged, though Tate will never use his right arm again, and Simon's widow and wee ones will miss him dearly."

Flame gritted her teeth. Nevin's words, as usual,

served to salt open wounds more than soothe them. She felt her own temper rise with her men's at the reminder of their great loss. Simon had been the MacGowan's spokesman, a loyal man who had died too young at the hand of the Forbeses. With an effort, she controlled her anger, for she could not afford the luxury of raw emotion now. "Will one dead Forbes bring Simon back?" she asked softly, as though she truly pondered the question in her own soul. "Will it return our horses and our stock?"

"Nay." Though angry color still stained Bullock's cheeks, he saw the wisdom of patience. " 'Twill be a slower vengeance, but 'twill be sweeter."

Thank God for Bullock. The sword was beginning to tremble in Flame's hand but not because her arm was frail. "Are we all agreed then?" she asked quietly, eyeing each man in turn.

There were nods of concurrence and a few mumbled words.

"Good. Then we have no more time to waste. Bullock . . ." She handed back his sword, tip first. "I trust ye to guard the prisoner. William, ye will see to Shaw's arm. Nevin and Gilbert, ye will keep lookout." For the first time, she let her gaze slip weakly to the huge warrior who stood behind Roderic. "Troy, I will see you outside," she commanded, then turned rapidly away.

"Ye dunna mind if I sit down, do ye?" asked Forbes from behind her.

Flame turned back, barely able to make that simple effort for the fatigue that threatened to overcome her. "Be ye so weak ye canna even stay on yer feet, Forbes?"

He slowly canted his head at her. "Mayhap yer beauty makes me feeble," he suggested quietly, his eyes deadly cold. "Or could it be yer senseless prattle?"

She wanted nothing more than to give in to her anger. Instead, she ordered, "Let him sit. And keep him quiet."

Turning stiffly, she hurried through the door. Outside,

the air was still and heavy. She closed her eyes and breathed deeply to steady her nerves.

"Lass?" Troy's voice was little more than an earthy rumble in the darkness as he exited the ceilingless walls of the broken stable.

"Here," Flame answered. In a moment she could see the shadow of the old warrior's towering form.

"So . . ." He stopped before her, gargantuan arms akimbo. "Ye have taken a Forbes."

Her uncertainty and worry had turned to bone-numbing weariness. "I do not wish to discuss that now."

"Lass—"

"Nay!" Her tone was sharper than she had meant to make it. "How long do ye think the MacGowans will accept a leader who does not seek revenge? We have stood the losses for as long as I will allow. I said I would take a Forbes, and take one I have."

Troy shook his head. " 'Tis na just *any* Forbes ye have taken, lass, 'tis Roderic the Rogue."

"I do not care if he be a rogue or a lap pet or the devil himself!" she spat.

The old warrior was silent for a moment, then, "Ye will care, lass, for he is na only Leith's brother, he is one of the fighting trio. 'Tis said none can best him in a scrap."

Flame drew herself up. "I did not think ye scared so easy," she said, but Troy only snorted.

"Save yer clever words for the lads, Flanna Mac-Gowan, and remember this, 'twas I who knew ye when ye were still in swaddling and na bigger than me arm. 'Twas I who saw yer tears in the French convent and brought Lochan to ease yer loneliness."

The air left Flame's lungs, and she dropped her gaze. "What have I done?" she whispered.

" 'Tis a fine time ta ask that now, lass," rumbled Troy, but his anger was already dissipating.

"Lady Fiona had a wee babe," she murmured, finally

raising her gaze to Troy's stoic face. "I could not take her from him."

He shook his head. "I shouldna forget that ye be a woman first," he murmured.

"What?"

" 'Tis nothing, lass."

"What shall I do now?" Flame whispered, feeling herself shake again. "I did not plan to take him."

"But ye felt a need to prove yerself the better man?"

"Kindness has gained me little," she said softly. "Boldness serves me better."

Troy removed his bonnet and ran splayed fingers through thick, gray hair. " 'Tis true that a Highlander has little respect for weakness, lass."

"Or kindness." She turned her face away.

Troy shrugged, still watching her. "Some think weakness and kindness be the same thing."

Flame tightened her jaw and shifted her gaze back to meet his. "As do I," she said.

Troy's expression was inscrutable, though he watched her for a long while. "Then why did ye na let them kill the Forbes?"

"It would have gained us nothing but a dead body."

"Then mayhap there is some purpose for kindness after all."

Flame tried to think of some rebuttal, but she had found long ago that parrying words with Troy Hamilton was a fool's endeavor. She exhaled softly. "What shall I do, now?"

"The tide has gone out and taken us with it. There is little we can do but hold on to the flotsam and try to keep our heads above the waves."

Flame gritted her teeth. Weariness threatened her balance. "For pity's sake, Troy, speak plain this once."

"Ye were set on taking a prisoner and take one ye have, lass. 'Tis nothing ta be done now but ta hold the rogue ransom and pray there be a MacGowan or two unmaimed when the storm passes."

Flame stood immobile, trying to calm her trembling,

but already one of her own men had been wounded. The thought of others being maimed nearly overwhelmed her. Was this boost to her pride and reputation worth the price they may have to pay? But how many more MacGowans would die if they did not trust her leadership and went their own ways?

"Ye will do well, lass," Troy said.

She tried to nod but failed. " 'Tis a strange thing," she murmured, "but I almost wish my father was here."

"He is na."

"Or my brother," she whispered.

"Gregor be gone, too, lass. And ye be all that's left of that house."

She raised her gaze to his and held her breath. "There are those who think ye should rule."

"I have me own reasons for refusing, and ye have been chosen, lass, for better or worse."

"And what of Nevin?" she whispered. "My uncle's son. Why could Nevin not rule?"

Troy turned his sharp gaze down at her. "Not until the sun fell into the sea would yer father accept his brother's son as his successor."

"My father is dead. And I must choose what's best for the MacGowans."

Troy held her gaze with his own. "And ye would choose Nevin?"

She turned away. "He is intelligent. And he is loyal to this tribe."

"But ye are their Flame."

She swung wildly back, fists clenched at her sides. "Well, I cannot burn forever!" Fear swelled up inside her—fear of being discovered for who she really was— a lass who trembled at the thought of danger and retched at the sight of blood. "I cannot guide them!" she said softly. "My father knew I—"

"Yer father knew nothing of ye," Troy interrupted.

A thousand sharp-edged emotions flared inside Flanna. "Am I not his?" she whispered. "Is that why his love for me turned to hate?"

"Ye are his, lass. Yer only sin was to remind him of yer mother."

She tightened her fists and took a step forward. "Are ye lying to me, Troy? Are ye lying to us all? Ye were her friend even at the end. She would have told ye the truth."

For a moment he was silent. "Ye are his daughter, Flanna MacGowan, though he didna deserve ye."

"And the babe that died with her?" Flame asked. "What of him?"

Troy turned away. "There is na reason ta discuss that, for they are dead now. Surely it canna longer matter."

Flame closed her eyes. "If Gregor had but lived . . ."

Troy snorted and faced her again. "Gregor was never meant ta rule. Gregor was a bonny, broad lochan with the sunlight of his father's adoration glistening upon him. But the lochan goes nowhere, lass. It becomes stagnant while the Flame swells and grows when the storm winds blow."

"I don't know what ye are saying," Flame countered. "I don't know what you—"

"Aye, ye do, lass. Ye ken exactly what I say, for ye have yer father's intellect. Ye have yer mother's caring, and ye have yer own gift with the horse. Gregor had none of these things." Troy sighed again. " 'Twas nearly ten years ago that Gregor was spilled into the water during a raid. Aye, he would have died if Leith Forbes had not pulled him out. It was then that peace was made between them and us. But it has always been an uneasy peace, and sometimes I think 'twould have been better had the Forbeses na fished yer brother from those roiling waters.

"Dunna reprimand me, lass," he said, holding up a hand. "Mayhap if Gregor had died earlier, yer father would have seen what he should have known all along. Mayhap he would have brought ye home the sooner."

Flame stared at him in silence. "I canna lead my people," she said softly.

"Aye, lass, ye can."

"I'm afraid."

Troy nodded once. " 'Tis a brave warrior who admits his fear."

"And I'm tired till death of yer meandering wisdom," she said.

Troy laughed, throwing back his great head for a moment. "Then I will remain silent and let ye think."

Flame smiled sheepishly into the darkness. "Forgive me, Troy. Ye know I did not mean that. My worry makes me spiteful, for I fear it will take more than the little wisdom I possess to guide the MacGowans."

"Aye, lass," Troy said. " 'Twill take the strength of yer will, too. But hear me words. Sometimes it takes a woman ta ken how ta handle a man." He turned slightly, nodding toward the cottage behind him. "And Forbes, he is just a man, lest ye forget."

Flame drew a deep breath, fortifying her strength and staring at the shell of the old stable. "Ye know that ye are throwing me to the wolves?"

"Aye, lass," Troy said, setting a broad hand to her back to propel her toward the door. "But ye must remember . . ." he added, walking beside her. "Even the greatest wolf be afraid of the flame."

"Troy . . ." She stopped abruptly, uncertainty flooding back.

" 'Twas fine work ye did in there, lass," he said gently. "I particularly enjoyed the part with the sword." He smiled into her upturned face while poking his neck with the tips of two blunt fingers. " 'Twould have been a wee bit more believable had yer hand not been shaking like—"

"Forbes!" someone screamed.

Panic flashed through Flame. For a moment, she stood paralyzed, and then she jerked about and raced through the stone doorway. Troy drew his sword and thundered after her.

"Back away!" Roderic snapped. One of his forearms lay tight and hard against Shaw's throat as he controlled him from behind. Near his feet, the tiny faggot of wood that had burned his bonds, still smoked. "You! Bullock! Put down yer claymore and slide it toward me. Gilbert, isn't it?" he asked, jerking his head toward the second man who stood poised as if to fight. Roderic's movement set his singed bonds trembling under Shaw's chin. "Don't be clever, for I have na wish ta kill yer friend."

"If we rush him . . ." Bullock began, but Roderic shook his head.

"Tell them na ta move, lass, or Shaw here willna draw another breath."

Flame took one abbreviated step forward, all attention focused on the pair by the fire. "If we leave now, will ye let him go?"

"Aye, ye have me—"

The whine of a loosed arrow sung of death. Flame screamed and threw herself sideways, trying to block the missile's path, but in an instant Nevin's barb sank deep in Shaw's chest.

Flame froze in stunned horror, watching the feathered shaft quiver in its victim. Shaw's lips moved, but no sound issued forth as he slid stiffly from Roderic's grip.

Behind Flame, Nevin rushed into the doorway. "Dear Gawd!" he shrieked, falling to his knees as he saw what he had done. "Shaw! No!" His voice was a wail and he dropped his bow and cupped his face with shaking hands, but in a moment he lunged to his feet. Yanking out his sword, he charged forward.

"Nay!" Flame screamed. Instantly she grabbed Troy's blade from his hand, and flung herself in front of Roderic. "Nay!" She spun about. Her back was to her prisoner, her legs widespread as she held the heavy claymore in both hands. But Nevin rushed toward her.

There was a moment of breathless silence, then a growl of animal-like rage as Troy swept forward. Grabbing Nevin by the shirt, he snatched him from his feet and tossed him through the air like a hound might fling a rat.

The young man hit the wall with a resounding thud. His sword dropped harmlessly to the grass.

"The lass says nay!" rumbled Troy, turning his huge body to protect the woman protecting Roderic. "Be there others who might dispute her decision?"

"He's dead." William's voice was quiet as he knelt beside Shaw's flaccid body.

"Gawd's truth!" said Bullock through gritted teeth. "There will be an eye for an eye!"

Troy moved with slow deliberation to face this new antagonist. "Are ye willing ta spare an eye, lad?" he rumbled softly.

"Will we let this deed go unavenged?" shrieked Bullock. His sword was drawn, his face contorted with rage. Beside him, Gilbert, too, fumed. "Forbes has kilt one of our own."

"Nay!" said Flame, and though she wanted to sob with grief, she held the sword steady in aching hands and refused to look at the downed warrior's staring eyes. "He has not. 'Twas our own carelessness that caused Shaw's death." She settled her gaze on Bullock, who dropped his eyes in unison with his sword.

"I didna ken Forbes had burned his bonds through," he croaked. " 'Tis me fault. 'Tis I who should have died, na Shaw."

A silence as heavy as the surrounding mists held them before Flame was able to speak again.

"Nay, Bullock," she whispered. "None should die." Stepping forward, she pressed the tip of Troy's sword into the earth and put a trembling hand on Bullock's arm. "We all take the blame. We all bear the sadness. But we have no time to grieve now. I know Shaw was your friend. It will be yer right to see that his body gets safely home."

Drawing a deep breath, she turned. The sorrow that wrung her heart shone in the eyes of her men, but that emotion was a luxury she could not afford. "Bring up the horses," she ordered, "and prepare to ride."

Nevin pushed himself from the floor. "Forgive me, my lady. I did not think . . ." His voice broke and his shaking hands clasped at nothing. "I did not think what

I was doing. 'Tis my fault. I saw Forbes holding Shaw and I only thought to stop . . . Dear God!" he wailed. "I only thought to stop him from harming Shaw, but my aim was faulty." He dropped to his knees again. "And we lose another man to the Forbeses. How many more must die because of them?"

Flame tightened her hands on Troy's sword. "There will be no more deaths this day, Nevin. Rise. We must put our sorrow behind ye. Go see to the horses."

He took a deep, shuddering breath and rose slowly, head still bowed. "Aye, lady," he said, and followed Shaw's gently borne body.

Flame turned slowly. "Do ye hear that, Forbes?" she asked.

Roderic watched her. So she truly was the leader of the MacGowans. He had heard as much but had found it difficult to believe. The MacGowans and the Forbeses had shared a cautious alliance in the years since Leith and Fiona had saved the old laird's heir from drowning. But since then, young, hotheaded Gregor had accidentally lost his life during a raid. The old laird had died shortly after. There were those who said the weight of his grief caused his passing.

"Do ye hear?" asked Flanna MacGowan again, taking a short stride toward him so that she stood even with Troy. By any standards, that warrior was a gargantuan man, with both the solid build and the stoic attitude of a wolfhound.

"There will be no more deaths this day," she repeated more loudly. The hilt of her borrowed sword nearly reached her bosom which was hidden beneath a high-necked gown of filthy, somber plaid. Whose blood was it that smeared her face and garments? he wondered. Surely not her sister's, for the laird of the MacGowans had left no other children or close relatives.

The MacGowans had lost many in the past years. Sickness and disease had taken their toll. Their enemies had surely not aided their cause. And now the clan was depleted and weakened. And yet, led by this female warrior, who could guess what they might achieve? Roderic studied her in silence. She was not a small woman. Indeed, she stood well above many of her own men. Her back was as straight as a newly forged lance and her face was as strong and noble as a conquering king's.

"No more deaths!" she hissed, stabbing Troy's sword into the earth again to gain his attention.

Roderic lifted his gaze to hers and insolently raised his brows. "Be ye offering ta set me free?"

"Nay!" She stabbed the floor again. "I am offering ye your life."

"But I already have me life, lass."

"And I will not take it," she vowed, "if ye agree to go with us peacefully."

"And forfeit the pleasure and glory of trying ta escape? Wouldna that be neglecting me duty as a Scot?"

"Ye will not try to escape!" insisted Flame, stabbing again.

Troy winced. "Please, lass," he said, stepping nearer to pry her fingers from the beautifully engraved hilt of his sword. "Gloir was me father's claymore. And his father's afore him." Lifting the blade, he examined it by the poor light. "It has done naught to deserve yer wrath. If ye need ta vent yer fury, ye have a perfectly good victim before yer verra eyes. Or"—he tested the edge of the blade with his broad thumb, eyeing Roderic as he did so. "Shall I vent it for ye?"

Roderic kept his gaze carefully level, watching the huge warrior with a steady glare. "Come on then, Wolfhound. There has yet ta be a time when a bare-handed Forbes canna best an armed MacGowan."

Troy's brows rose the slightest fraction of an inch. "But I be na a MacGowan, wee lad. I be a Hamilton. And a Hamilton is na bested by any man. And she who he guards is na bested either."

Roderic watched the other warrior for several moments, considering the danger from that front. Troy would be a worthy adversary when the time came, but that time had not yet arrived. He shifted his gaze slowly to Flanna's. " 'Twould seem I owe ye me thanks for keeping yer hounds from me throat," he said. "But 'tis hard ta be grateful since ye be the one who set them upon me at the start."

She raised her chin slightly, looking regal and invincible. " 'Tis less than ye have done to us, Forbes."

"And pray"—Roderic crossed his right arm against his chest to grip the plaid near his brooch—"tell me what imagined sins the Forbeses have perpetrated against the clan MacGowan. And take yer time, lass, for I have na pressing engagements."

"It would serve your purposes well if I were to stand here and remind ye of every crime the Forbeses have committed against us, would it not?" Flame asked. "But I have no wish to be here when yer brothers arrive. Mayhap I should have let Bullock have ye."

" 'Tis too late for regrets now, lass," Troy said. "I fear we have na time ta kill him. I'll need ta knock him on the head and take him with us, instead."

Roderic let his arms drop loosely by his sides, feeling his latent temper swell. He spread and bent his legs, balanced carefully, and waited. "Ye are welcome ta try, Wolfhound."

"Stop it, both of ye. Forbes, if ye say ye do not know what sins your people have done against mine, then come along peacefully, and when we reach Dun Ard, I will tell ye the story."

Roderic remained silent for a moment, watching, evaluating. "I have been known ta appreciate a good tale, lass, na matter how outlandish it might be."

"Then ye will like this one," she said evenly, "for it tells of a powerful clan that preys on its allies. And how the wronged clan exacts revenge."

"Indeed?" Roderic narrowed his eyes. A friendly debate was well and good, but he would not allow any person to spew lies about the clan Forbes—not even a handsome, fire-breathing woman of war. "And what clan—"

"Decide now!" Troy ordered impatiently. "Do we

fight or do ye come along under yer own power?"

Roderic turned slowly to acknowledge the looming warrior again. "Know this, big hound, if we fight, ye will be the one carried out." He shifted his gaze to the woman again. "Yet this tale intrigues me, and I fear I would have ta kill all five of yer men afore I could convince the lass to share her story. And by then I might be a wee bit weary." He raised his brows as if weighing the options. "Mayhap even too weary ta appreciate a well-spun yarn.

"I will come with ye," he decided suddenly, "if ye promise ta give me comfortable quarters and see ta me needs as is befitting, of course." He kept his tone irritatingly flippant.

"Ye ken, lad, I have never favored fair-haired heads," said Troy, thumbing his blade again, "but yers would look fine hoisted upon me pike."

"I'll do it," said Flanna, turning her glance from the doorway where the first glimmer of light showed on the roiling mists. "If ye promise to make no trouble."

"Trouble?" Roderic grinned. "Me?"

"I know just the pike Troy was speaking of," she warned evenly. "And I swear by all that is holy, if ye break your vow to be peaceable until we reach Dun Ard, I will allow him to stick your head upon it."

Roderic remained silent for a brief moment, then, "Ye've a convincing way about ye, lass," he said, and stepping forward, added, "I accept yer gracious invitation."

Chapter 3

The night fled, pursued by the pale, worrisome light of morning. Although the heavy mists hid the presence of the traveling band for some time, it finally abandoned them, too, leaving Flame feeling fretful and exposed in the full light of day. But finally, the muted colors of sunset eased her mind. Darkness followed again.

She checked Lochan's speed. Although he had gone nearly twice the distance of the other horses, he easily outpaced the bigger mounts. Flame placed a hand to his smooth neck, trying to absorb his power, his certainty. He had been her companion for many years, and though Troy often said their relationship was uncanny, it was simply the bond formed between a lonely child and a misbegotten beast.

"Almost there, lass," rumbled Troy, pressing up beside her on his great destrier. "Dunna fret."

Flame turned toward her friend, glad of his towering presence. "What makes ye think I fret?"

Troy scowled at the path ahead. "Lochan be switching his tail like a doused wildcat."

Despite everything, Flame laughed. "We do not share every emotion," she assured him. "No matter what ye believe."

"If the beast could talk ye'd have na need for a voice," he said.

Flame drew a deep breath, knowing Troy was trying to take her mind from her worries. "All is well?"

"Aye, lass," he assured her. "Forbes is causing na problems."

"Already, he has caused enough trouble for a lifetime. Shaw's death will not soon be forgotten. But there is little more damage he can do now," she said. The journey south had given her too much time to think, to dwell on the losses they had sustained at the hands of the Forbeses. "Do not forget that his wrists are bound and his weapons taken."

"Dunna disprize the rogue, lass," Troy warned quietly.

"And what do ye mean by that?"

"I have been hearing tales about the lad's deeds for a long while. I credited them to a good storyteller's imagination. But now that I meet the man, I wonder if they are na true." He turned solemnly toward her. "I say again, dunna disprize his abilities."

"So this be me new home?" asked Roderic.

The moon had risen and shone on the white stone of Dun Ard's square tower. From its battlements, the guards had an unobstructed view of the country round about. The uppermost floor of the interior offered only slightly less of a view, and little more comfort.

"Luxurious quarters indeed," he said, glancing at the bare walls, the stone floor, the narrow windows. "Just as ye promised."

"I did not plan for such a royal visitor as yourself," Flame said. She recognized his sarcasm but refused to be goaded to anger.

"Ah, but of course," Roderic responded. "Ye were expecting Lady Fiona." He shrugged, grinning. "Appears 'tis yer lucky day, for ye got me instead."

Flame watched him carefully. He was a handsome man and glib of tongue. "Ye think a good deal of yourself, Forbes."

"Aye. I do indeed, lass. But . . ." He dropped the grin to gaze at her earnestly. "I only meant that had ye taken the lady, Leith would na rest until there was naught but MacGowan corpses in all of Scotland.''

Flame lifted her chin. ''He values her highly then?'' It was strange to think that a man as blackhearted and arrogant as Leith Forbes might find merit in a mere woman. The thought disturbed her, as did Roderic's direct stare, but she kept her voice steady. Last evening, abduction and ransom had seemed a worthy idea. This morning they seemed like a fool's worst nightmare. If only she had taken Fiona instead of this golden-haired devil, surely Shaw would still be alive and the Lady Forbes would do as commanded instead of questioning her every order and mocking her every move.

''Aye. He values her well.''

''Even above the life of his own brother?'' Flame asked. She had honed that particular haughty tone to perfection, but it failed to prick his pride.

Instead, he chuckled low in his throat. ''I willna lie ta ye, lass. Leith knows me well and appreciates me sword arm. But if the truth be known, he has me spitting image at his side as we speak. When there are twins, one is always expendable.''

Flame narrowed her eyes, searching his words for truth. She, too, had heard tales of Roderic and Colin Forbes. And while word of their devilish good looks and quick wit was never far behind, she had assumed the stories had been embellished. Her assumptions had been wrong.

''There is only one Fiona Rose. And Leith would sooner die than lose her,'' Roderic said. His tone was almost reverent.

Emotion sparked in Flame's heart. It almost felt like envy, an ache for something she would never know. But she wouldn't dwell on that, for she had made her choices long ago. ''If ye have something to tell me, Forbes, say it now.''

Roderic took two strides to the right, placing his shoulder casually against the tower's stone wall. For the first time, she noticed his wrists had been singed during his attempted escape. The rope that bound him now must burn like hell's fire. But guilt was a luxury she could ill afford to entertain.

"I am saying, me brother will pay na ransom for *me*, lass," he assured her.

Flame smiled. "Ye will forgive me if I doubt the word of a Forbes?"

"Me?" Roderic's sudden smile easily outshone hers, she knew. "Indeed, I will forgive ye, lass, for I am that kind. But Leith . . ." He shook his head, letting his smile drop away. "He is na the forgiving sort. 'Twould be best if ye set me free afore ye incur his wrath."

"But did ye not just say he will not care that ye've been taken?" she asked sweetly, thinking she had found a flaw in his reasoning.

"Nay, I didna, lass. I said he would na *pay* ta get me back."

"Then do ye suggest that we simply forget yer sins against us?" she asked.

"Ah, yes." He shifted his weight slightly, causing his brooch to glimmer in the light from the open window. The ornament that pinned his plaid to his shirt was nearly as big as her fist. It was beautifully crafted in a circle of fine silver gilt and set with tiny chips of bloodstone that winked at her from miniature wildcat faces etched into the metal. Though it was lovely, it did not demonstrate the full wealth of the Forbes clan. His modest attire surprised her. "And so we finally come ta the long-awaited tale of how the horrible Forbeses have turned on their allies, the innocent MacGowans?"

"Ye mock me," she said.

"Aye. I do, lass! For we have done naught ta harm ye."

She laughed aloud. The sound was hollow in the echoing chamber. "Think ye that the murder of our kinsmen did not wound us?"

He stared at her with narrowed eyes that reminded Flame of the shiny stones set in his brooch.

"Mayhap the Forbeses have so many men that one

life seems insignificant. But we MacGowans count every life precious."

"Gawd's wrath, woman!" Roderic stormed suddenly, taking a quick step forward.

Troy moved closer against her side, but Flame only raised her chin.

"I suppose ye deny everything. Even the raids on our stock?" she asked.

"Yer stock?" Roderic had glanced at Troy's hulking form before dismissively dropping his gaze back to hers. "Now I ask meself, lass, why would the Forbeses be raiding MacGowan's scraggly herds when their own are fat and prolific?"

She bristled. "Then ye deny it?"

"Aye, I deny it!" he said, his tone hard, his gaze steady.

"And ye deny taking our horses?"

"Horses?" He barked a laugh and raised his fair brows. "Now that ye mention it, lass, I do remember seeing a sway-backed nag wandering free past Glen Creag. 'Twas a limping, one-eyed beast with but a few breaths left in its body. It did indeed resemble that wee stallion ye rode this day. Might that have been the precious animal ye lost?"

Without thought Flame took a quick step forward. Her hands were suddenly formed to fists and her body was stiff with anger.

"Now, lass," warned Troy, "remember the worthlessness of a dead Forbes."

She stopped less than a full pace from Roderic and glared into his face. How dare he slander the very beasts he had stolen, she wondered, but she kept her temper under control and her tone sweet! "Ye are right, of course, Troy," said she. "But I am beginning to question the worth of a live Forbes as well."

Troy chuckled. "It has been a long and wearisome journey, lass. Go now. Eat. Sleep. I meself will take care of our prisoner so that ye might rest easy."

Weary! It was hardly a strong enough word to describe Flame's present state. Never in all her twenty-one years had she felt so worn and frayed.

"Thank ye, Troy," she said, finally pulling her gaze from Roderic's sharp stare. "Ye are right. I must rest."

"Aye, thank ye, indeed," said Roderic, his tone even. "But I fear the lady forgets her vow ta tell me the tale of the Forbeses and the MacGowans." He paused to pin his gaze to her face. "Or did ye lie about that, too?"

She raised her eyes slowly. "I do not lie."

"Nay?" He laughed again. "Then I would send a priest to issue the last rites to yer sister, for she is surely on death's door by now."

Flame nodded in concession to Roderic's verbal prick. "I should say, I lie only to snakes and vermin. And now I tire of doing so. Watch him well, Troy," she said, turning away. "Ye know how slippery these serpents can be."

Roderic awoke at the sound of the door latch being moved. The faint light of morning seeped between the shutters. Sleep had come unbidden, granting unwanted dreams and a stiff neck. He pushed himself to a sitting position and stared at the portal, supported by thick leather hinges. Concentrating, he tried to see what kind of contraption held it shut. But Flanna MacGowan took that precise moment to step into the room and distract him.

She had washed and changed her attire. He had had no way of knowing what a dramatic difference such simple acts would make. Rising slowly to his feet with his back against the wall, Roderic watched her enter.

Her hair was red, not a deep burnt color, but the hue of living flame. It was plaited with a ribbon of white and wrapped about the crown of her head. But it did not lie in quiet submission. Instead, it framed her face in wild, curling wisps of bright color. Her skin was golden as if the sun had kissed it, and her lips were as red and plump as holly berries. But it was her eyes that held his attention. They were as green as stained window glass, clear and bright and luminous. Her tall, statuesque body was garbed in a fine forest green gown struck through with threads of bright yellow.

She drew him like dark magic, transfixed him with her eyes, stunned him with her regal features. There seemed no point in denying his reaction to her. "Ye look radiant," he said softly. "And ye honor me."

For an instant, she stood in silence, seeming very young and quite disarmed. But then she laughed as if able to dismiss his flattery with the greatest ease. "Hardly that, Forbes. It happens that we MacGowans do not live like swine . . . as do some I could name," she said, eyeing his crushed and wrinkled garments.

Roderic raised his brows. So this woman would not bend easily to his pretty words. He smiled, welcoming the challenge. "If ye be referring ta me, lass," he said softly, not taking his gaze from her face, "I would be willing ta accept yer help with me bath."

Her lips parted in obvious surprise. Behind her, Troy rumbled a warning, but she lifted a hand to keep him at bay and recovered quickly. "And I would accept your head on a platter," she said sweetly.

Troy chuckled.

Roderic turned his gaze to that stout warrior and scowled. "Truly, lass, though I appreciate yer presence, I must insist that ye tether yer Wolfhound with the other curs when next we meet."

"By the saints!" growled Troy, taking a step forward, but Flame fetched him easily back to her side.

"Did ye not teach me that a dog only yelps if he has no teeth with which to bite?" she asked Troy, though she still held her gaze on Roderic.

"Aye," the old warrior rumbled. "That I did, lass. But this one is bothersome even without teeth."

"Ye want ta see me teeth, Wolfhound?" Roderic asked. He was a patient man by nature, but fatigue was taking its toll, and he was not accustomed to being bested by a woman's sharp wit. He much preferred being adored. Lifting his wrists, he said, "If so, cut loose me bonds."

"I'd rather cut yer throat," Troy commented.

" 'Twould be the MacGowan way," Roderic said, "ta cut me throat without freeing me hands."

"He surely has a wish ta die," deduced Troy, brows lowered.

"I gave ye me vow ta come peaceably. 'Twas an insult ta me that ye bound me wrists just the same."

Just then the man named Nevin appeared in the doorway, holding a meal apparently meant for their prisoner. Roderic glanced at him momentarily before shifting his attention back to Flame and continuing in a softer tone, "Surely I at least deserve the luxury of eating with some freedom. Unless ye wish ta feed me with yer own hand."

For a moment their gazes held, and to Roderic's consternation he found he was holding his breath. But suddenly a dirk appeared in her hand. It was long and deadly and embellished with a square, blood red stone.

Roderic let out his trapped breath and lifted one brow as she approached him. Eyeing the knife, he said, "Mayhaps we should discuss what ye plan ta do with that thing afore ye come any closer."

She advanced. Troy made no objections, though his brows were beetled over his pale blue eyes.

"Did I say something that particularly offended ye?" Roderic asked. " 'Tis a problem I oft have, I fear. But I am na so much the fool as ta fail ta apologize if I am allowed ta see the error of me ways." He lifted his bound hands as if to placate her and kept his expression solemn. But it was not an easy task, for he had finally nudged her from her quiet self-assurance, and that achievement thrilled him.

She stopped directly in front of him. Their gazes held again, and for one moment he thought she might slip the dirk between his ribs. But instead, she cut the ropes. With one quick slice, his bonds fell away.

"Ahh," Roderic sighed, pulling his arms apart. " 'Tis

kind ye are, lass. Or''—he leaned slightly closer to prevent the others from hearing his words—''could it be ye have cut me free because ye are scairt of being near a *real* man. Feeding me could be verra . . . stimulating.''

She leaned toward him, still holding his gaze. ''Or it might just be''—she sniffed—''nauseating.''

Roderic opened his mouth for a verbal parry. But she was right, he smelled ripe. ''Wolfhound,'' he said, not breaking eye contact with her. ''It seems I've a need to wash afore I eat.''

''He's a cocky one. I'll give him that,'' Troy said.

''Me?'' Roderic raised his gaze to the oversized warrior. ''Surely ye misjudge me. I simply dunna wish ta offend the lady. I didna ask ye ta bring me here. But I am na complaining and willna ask ye ta lug water up those weary stairs. I be more than willing ta go ta yer well.''

''He acts as if he doesn't know that our well has been poisoned, that our people have become ill from drinking it!'' Nevin scoffed.

''It's not safe to drink the water there,'' Flame said, and didn't bother to add that there were those who thought a Forbes had somehow stolen into their bailey and dropped the rotting carcass into the water. It was true that the MacGowans were looking for a scapegoat for all their problems. Simon's death had been the catalyst that had fanned their anger into rage. There had been nothing she could do but retaliate.

''Poisoned?'' Roderic asked. ''Then I'll need ta go to the burn.''

''Ye must think us dull-witted indeed if ye believe we will allow ye outside of these walls,'' Nevin said.

''Nay, na dull-witted atall,'' Roderic argued. '' 'Twas a clever plan ye devised ta bring me here. And ta show me appreciation for a good ploy, I will vow na ta escape before the sun sets.''

''Ye are arrogant beyond words,'' said Nevin, ''to think ye can speak to me lady, for she is all that is good and fair . . .''

"Quiet," Flame said, raising a hand. "Why should we trust your vow, Forbes?"

Roderic straightened slightly, reading the nuances in the room. "Because I dunna lie," he said softly. "Even ta snakes and vermin. But I will escape. Like that." He snapped his fingers. "If ye dunna allow me some freedom."

"Ye would have a hard time getting through me, Forbes!" Bullock said, stepping into the room.

Roderic shifted his gaze to the stout warrior. "Do ye think so?" he asked, smiling. As a boy, he had driven the serious Leith to distraction with his blithe moods and practical jokes. Now, he leisurely skimmed his attention back to the clan's bonny leader. "What say ye, lass, do ye grant me this courtesy as a sign of goodwill or must I leave before we get a chance to become better acquainted?"

"A little freedom is a small price to pay for a bit of the Rogue's goodwill, lass," Troy said softly.

Flame remained silent for one thoughtful moment, then nodded. "All right, Forbes. Ye may wash," she said quietly. "But be assured, I'll be watching ye."

Roderic all but beamed. "Be assured," he said softly. "That's the way I like it."

Chapter 4

Perhaps she was a fool to allow Forbes to go outside the protective walls of Dun Ard, Flame thought. Or perhaps, as Troy suggested, this bit of compromise was well worth the effort. There was something about their prisoner that almost made her believe his boasts about his ability to escape. And something that made her believe his vows not to. It appeared she had learned little about men and their deceptive ways, after all.

But he did need to wash, for there was a narrow band of dried blood running down his forehead and it bothered her, though she knew it shouldn't. Although she planned to make the Forbeses pay for their sins, she was not fool enough to poison the man with their well water. Thus she brought him here.

The Geal Burn twisted and gurgled along in its rocky course beneath the drawbridge. As a child of seven, Flame had spent many hours here. It was a peaceful spot, sheltered from the Highland winds by a rough border of hills that followed the winding course of the fast-flowing stream. Yellow flowering gorse grew in abundance, and bent hazels canopied the rock-strewn water. Long ago, she had climbed one of those gnarled trees and later had hurried to her father to proudly tell him of her feat. She remembered her shock when he had called her a liar, for never in her short life had he wounded her in any way. She had had no way of knowing it was only the beginning.

"What be ye thinking?"

Forbes' question wrested her from her thoughts and reminded her that she was not alone. Troy stood not far away, and Nevin had followed with a hand on his sword. She shifted her attention to where Roderic squatted beside the clear, rushing water. He had rolled back the cuffs of his soiled shirt, exposing broad, golden-haired forearms. He had also scrubbed the blood from his forehead with his bare hands.

" 'Twas thinking ye are slow indeed at washing," she lied.

He smiled, showing straight, white teeth. Water dripped down the dimple in his right cheek. " 'Tis good ta know ye be thinking of me atall." He turned away, glancing about. " 'Twas thinking meself that this be a bonny spot. Did ye play here as a wee lass, Flanna?"

"I am called Flame," she reminded him.

Roderic twisted toward her so that his back was to the water. He wore the traditional plaid of the clan Forbes with unspoken pride. It was made of muted browns and greens and rose higher as he moved, showing a bit more of his muscular thighs. His knees were bare, of course, and he had removed his deerskin boots to reveal his corded, powerful calves. "Why? Flanna is yer name, is it na?"

His jaw was broad and clean-shaven, his eyes blue as the heavens and deep set. And . . . Damn! She had lost the course of their conversation. He smiled again. The expression did nothing to clear her thoughts and seemed to speak of his own elevated opinion of himself.

"Why do ye prefer ta be called Flame?" he repeated, as though he perfectly understood her inability to concentrate while in his presence.

She lifted her chin. She was not some blushing lass who would swoon at the merest show of his dimple, and damn him for making her feel like one. " 'Tis the name me sire gave me."

"Indeed?" He watched her closely. "And what of the name yer mother gave ye?"

Flame remained absolutely still. It had been a long

while since she had allowed herself to think of her mother. For such thoughts promoted a softness she could ill afford.

"Flanna be a bonny name," Roderic said softly. "Seems a shame ta leave it behind."

Flame sternly reminded herself to think clearly, to remember who he was, to realize his ploy. The brothers Forbes were not known for their foolishness, but for their savvy. And this one . . . This one had hair as gold as sunlight, skin dark as a hawthorn's bark, and eyes so blue they could enchant an angel.

But the Flame of the MacGowans had no illusions. She was not an angel.

"Are ye trying ta distract me so that ye can escape?" she asked, keeping her tone light.

"Nay. If I were trying ta distract ye, lass," he began, quickly setting his fingers to the brooch that held his plaid to his shoulder, "I would remove me shirt."

It all happened very quickly. Suddenly his brooch was undone, and his chest was bare.

She blinked. Behind her, Troy rumbled low in his chest.

Roderic's gaze failed to leave hers. "Here, Wolfhound," he said, tossing the soiled shirt to the huge guard. "Make yerself useful and see that this gets cleaned. And, Nevin, bring me meal. 'Tis a bonny day. I wish ta eat outside."

Troy strode forward and casually retrieved the garment, but Nevin remained as he was, his back straight.

"I take me orders from me lady. Not from the man who killed me kinsmen. I would sooner die on me own sword than take your orders, Forbes."

"Bring me food first," Roderic said.

Troy looked down at their prisoner and shook his head. "Shall I drag him back ta the tower for ye, lass, or shall we let him crow out here for a wee bit longer?"

Flame smiled up at her faithful old warrior, and for a moment Roderic could imagine her as a child. Even now, firelight wisps of hair curled down to caress her face. As a babe that hair would have been kitten soft and loose. Her eyes would have twinkled with merriment, and she would have giggled as her father tossed her in the air.

Strange, he thought, that the sight of such a warrior woman made him think of children.

"He has promised to be good," she said now, glancing quickly in his direction. "Can we take ye at your word, Forbes?"

"Aye." Roderic nodded once, feeling unusually sober. "Me word is as good as me blood, lass. If I say I will stay, I will stay. If I say I will go, I will go. But this day I willna escape."

Their gazes held for several seconds before she turned back to her guard. "Then let him stay, Troy," she ordered quietly.

The Wolfhound drew nearer. The earth all but shook beneath his footfalls. Not far from Roderic's squatting form, Troy bent. "I have a wee bit of wisdom ta impart with ye, lad. 'Tis the toughest shell that yields the softest yoke. Hurt her, and I'll test me blade on yer bonny neck." Straightening, the huge warrior slapped Roderic's shoulder as if they were the best of friends. Then he turned his attention to Flame. "Young Mary has gathered some early berries, and I've na seen Haydan for some days, lass. With yer permission, I thought I might bring him the fruit and the news of the day."

Roderic scowled. What kind of man would threaten him with decapitation, then blithely speak of berries and news? This Dun Ard was a strange place.

"Go, and tell Haydan I will be there shortly."

In a moment, Troy had turned away, and they were left alone with only one glowering guard.

"Ye may bring his meal, Nevin." Flame said.

"Nay!" Nevin's tone was harsh. Roderic watched Flame turn in that direction.

"What say ye?"

"My apologies, lady. But I cannot bear to see ye with his kind. Let me guard him, for your life is worth

a thousand of my own and I would sooner cut my heart
from my chest than see thee hurt.''

This Nevin was a dramatic one, Roderic thought. But
Flame's expression softened.

"I appreciate your concern, cousin. But I think I am
safe enough for the time being.''

"Do not trust him, lady. Do not sit too near. Indeed,
ye should return to the comfort of your rooms and let
me see to his needs.''

"That will not be necessary," she said.

So Nevin was her cousin, Roderic thought, but approaching footsteps captured his attention. A young
woman drew near, carrying a bucket in each hand. She
had wide, brown eyes and a full mouth. "Me lady," she
said before dipping her attention momentarily to Roderic.

He smiled. "Hello, lass. What be yer name?''

She shifted her gaze rapidly to Nevin and back. "Marjory . . .'' She faltered, uncertain. "Sir."

"They call me Roderic.''

Marjory shifted her gaze nervously to the water and
tossed one metal-bound bucket in, but there was no way
for her to fetch it back without wetting her shoes.

It seemed perfectly natural for Roderic to wade into
the burn to fill and retrieve it for her. Marjory eyed his
bare chest and blinked as he handed her the filled pail.

Roderic smiled. He loved women and women loved
him. 'Twas an agreeable arrangement. " 'Tis a bonny
day. What happened to yer wrist, lass?''

She pulled her arm back so that her sleeve could cover
the discolored skin of her wrist. " 'Tis nothing. I but
fell, sir . . .''

"Roderic," he corrected, and taking the second
wooden bucket from her, filled it in the same manner.

"Thank ye," she breathed as her hand touched his.

"Me pleasure, Marjory.''

She nodded, glanced quickly at Nevin, then turned
and hurried back to the castle.

Roderic watched her retreat for a moment, then waded
through the burn to crouch before the lady warrior. Wa-

ter reached halfway to his knee. "Ye MacGowans are na such a bad lot."

"I'm sure we're all very grateful to have earned your good regard," Flame said dryly.

Roderic chuckled, pulling up one knee to settle an elbow upon it.

Flame's gaze flitted quickly to where his plaid was displaced, and he watched, noticing her disconcerted expression. 'Twas not his fault he was good looking, he thought and almost smiled.

"Yer people are na so much different than me own," he observed. "Each making his life the best he can. 'Tis a shame I canna stay longer."

For a moment she said nothing, but when he turned back to her, her brows had risen, and her green eyes looked cool enough to frost glass.

"Do ye plan to leave us soon then, Forbes?"

"Aye." He did smile now. He had seen a good bit of the world, from London to Madrid, and found that each place had its share of bonny lasses. Some were aloof and some were shy, but this woman had a combination of both attributes that intrigued him. "I dunna want ta go," he said, "but I fear I canna wait about for Leith's arrival."

"Nay?" She still held the jeweled knife with which she had cut his bounds. His gaze settled on it momentarily.

"Nay," he said regretfully and shrugged. "For ye see, I am a man that doesna like strife. Oh, I enjoy a friendly brawl as well as the next Scot, but I dunna like to see any man shed his blood for na good cause. Much as I would enjoy acquainting meself with ye and yers, I canna await me brother's coming."

"Indeed?" There was a strange tone to her voice, and when he turned to her he saw that her lips were pressed into a bonny pucker as though to prevent a smile from escaping.

He didn't guard his own expressions so jealously. "Indeed."

"And how, may I ask, are ye planning to escape? The stairs are the only exit from the tower and they will be well guarded."

He watched her in silence. The sun had found its way from behind a bubbly cloud and cast its golden light on her. Surely this lass had always basked in sunshine, he thought, for she was the only daughter of the old laird. She must have been the very light of his life.

"Unless . . ." She tilted her head slightly, but did not drop her gaze before his. "Unless ye plan to break your word and attempt an escape even now."

"I dunna break me word, lass. And if I ran I would lose this chance ta speak ta ye."

She watched him with an unwavering stare and he found himself wondering about her thoughts.

"Have ye sent word ta Leith already?" he asked.

"No. I have not."

" 'Tis tempted I am ta stay a wee bit longer then. Mayhap long enough to help dig a new well for Dun Ard."

"I am indeed relieved," she said with no sincerity.

"And I am flattered that ye are relieved."

"But tell me," she said without pause. "Why do ye feel ye must leave before yer brother's arrival? Is he so blackhearted that even ye fear him?"

"Leith?" Roderic didn't attempt to hide his surprise. "Mayhap that be a question ye should ask Fiona sometime, or young Roman. They could better tell ye of the state of his heart. But nay," he continued. " 'Tis na fear that forces me ta leave. 'Tis me regard for human life."

"So long as yer brother agrees to our demands, we will harm none of ye."

For a moment Roderic remained in stunned silence, and then he laughed. He couldn't help it, for it was a beautiful day, and he was spending time with a bonny lass with a sporting sense of humor.

"Why are ye laughing?"

"Yer pardon, lass," he chuckled. "I thought ye made a jest."

She raised her brows, and he straightened slightly, watching her and clearing his throat.

"I see that I was mistaken. But ye see, lass, 'twas na Forbeses' lives that I fear losing. 'Twas MacGowans'."

Anger sparked in her eyes. "The Forbeses will return what they took from us," she said stiffly. "And ye shall remain here until they do."

"Which will make me stay verra short indeed, since we took naught."

She gripped her dirk harder in her slim fingers. "And ye say ye do not lie!"

They stared at each other, both angry now. "I dunna, lass," he said softly, "and I say I willna wait for me brother's arrival."

"I say ye will!"

Her obvious anger made his own decline. He liked watching her face when she was riled. 'Twas almost a pity she didn't still have Troy's sword to stab into the earth. It made her look all the more dangerous, like a Viking maiden, flame-haired and fiery-willed.

"And I say I can escape that tower afore two more days pass."

Despite her anger, her tone was smooth when next she spoke. "Do all ye Forbeses have such fantastic imaginations?"

"Na. Just me. Would ye like ta make a wager?"

"I do not wager."

"Ahh." He shrugged. "But I wager a good deal— with those who arena scairt ta do so."

Her jaw tightened. "What is it ye would bet?"

"What is it ye would give me?"

"I begin to wonder if your brother could be foolish enough to want ye back."

Roderic laughed. "I didna say I expect him ta hurry, lass. But we lose track of the important topic. What would ye wager?"

"Nothing."

Roderic shook his head with a frown. "I have heard the MacGowans were indeed tight-fisted. But I didna realize to what extent. Let me sweeten the pot a bit. If I lose I will"—he paused, thinking—"I will give ye Mor."

"Yer steed?" she asked in surprise.

He nodded. "Aye. He is a hearty, well-trained mount and has sired fine bairns. What do ye say?"

"Would ye think it a sign of doubt if I asked what I would owe if ye won?"

"Nay. I would think it a sign of wisdom. And seeing yer hesitation, I will ask nothing of earthly value." He scowled, thinking. "If I win . . ." He dropped his elbow from his knee and straightened from the waist before lowering his voice to make certain his words would reach no other ears but hers. "If I win ye must assist me in bathing sometime."

To his disappointment, she didn't blush. Instead, her cheeks seemed quite pale and her lips even brighter than usual. "Come now." He watched her carefully, feeling somewhat insulted by her expression of horror. " 'Tis na so bad as all that. 'Tis only a bath. Surely ye have assisted men afore."

She didn't argue or agree. Neither did she speak, and Roderic found himself wondering how quickly Nevin could impale him upon his sword should he reach out to shake her from her trance.

"Lass?" he questioned gently. "Are ye well?"

"Aye," she said. "Ye are the one who is ill."

Roderic chuckled. "Nay, lass. I have never felt better. Na that that means I can escape yonder tower," he hurried to add. "Indeed, ye have assured me I canna, which surely gives ye an excellent chance of winning a fine steed."

She remained mute, staring at him.

"Come now, lass, I would offer ye more, but ye did na give me a chance to take much with me when I left Glen Creag."

Flame said nothing, and in that moment Roderic

praised himself for baiting the hook well. Only after seeing Dun Ard did he realize the poverty of the MacGowans. And only now could he understand the value she would place on a stallion of Mor's quality.

"Come, Flanna," he urged again. "The steed will be yers free and clear with me vow na ta attempt ta retrieve him."

He could almost see her internal struggle. He was a handsome, tempting man, and she probably felt she couldn't trust herself in such a situation.

"What say ye, lass?" he whispered. "I swear na ta do anything ta compromise yer innocence unless . . ." He smiled. "Unless ye canna control yerself."

She blinked. Bright color had finally returned to her cheeks, making her look young and angelic and awed.

"Dunna be scairt, lass," he crooned.

"And ye would be . . . naked?" She leaned forward to whisper the words to him.

Good God, she was a bonny thing. "Aye, lass, I would," he breathed. "What say ye?"

"What can I do but agree?" she murmured huskily. "For ye are such an . . ." She leaned closer still and placed a palm to his bare chest. Heat radiated from her touch and he nearly closed his eyes to better appreciate the exhilarating sensations. But suddenly she shoved him backward with a mighty heave. Droplets splashed in every direction as his buttocks hit the water, and when he had swept his wet hair from his eyes, she was standing dry and regal upon the shore. "An arrogant bastard who has already forfeited his steed." She pivoted away but turned back in a moment. "Oh," she added, "ye can thank me later for helping ye bathe."

Chapter 5

They would all pay. But she would suffer the most. The Flame of the MacGowans—the whore of the MacGowans! Aye, she would pay the dearest price. For she had cost him the most. But he must not let anyone suspect his intent. He must keep his bloodlust at bay, for he had planned too long and too carefully to be foolish now. He would watch and wait, and soon all would be his.

By the time Roderic returned to the tower, someone had brought in a straw-filled pallet, a small, rough-hewn table, and a rickety chair. They were the only pieces of furniture that now graced his lofty prison.

Lying on his back, he stared up at the lead sheeting of the ceiling and determined that Flanna MacGowan was not a normal woman. Normal women did not become leaders of unruly Highland tribes. They did not ride out in the middle of the night to kidnap a member of an allied clan. And they did not push him in the water. He shifted uncomfortably, but his sodden plaid was still firmly belted to his waist, reminding him of the humiliation of returning to his tower room dripping wet. Nevin had laughed out loud and related the entire episode to Bullock as they barred the door of the tower room. And though Flanna had controlled her humor, he could see the emerald spark of laughter in her eyes.

No, she was not a normal woman. She was haughty and aloof—and so damned alluring he ached for . . . No!

He was *not* attracted to her even though she had skin like fine satin and . . . God's wrath, he had best leave before he made a complete fool of himself. Rising quickly, Roderic strode to the door. "Bullock?"

There was a moment's delay, then, "What be ye wanting, Forbes?" The guard's tone was tight. These people didn't like him much, it seemed. A pity, Roderic thought, but something that couldn't be helped since they wouldn't be meeting again after tonight.

" 'Tis cold I am, and tired. Might ye fetch me a blanket that I could sleep?"

"Why should I get ye anything, Forbes?"

"Well now . . ." Roderic stared thoughtfully at the heavy timbers that kept them apart. Being wrapped in wet wool had a tendency to make him irritable and the guard's attitude wasn't helping any. "Because I am yer prisoner, held for ransom and dependent on yer good graces," he said, remembering his manners.

"I have na good graces toward bastards."

Roderic scowled at the door. He was determined to be polite, but the other was insulting his father, and his mother, too, for that matter. Therefore, there seemed little reason not to bait this insolent MacGowan. " 'Twas wondering, Bullock, how is it ye came by yer name. 'Tis because of yer build or is it yer intelligence they refer to?"

Roderic thought he heard the man growl, but the portal remained closed. "I am tempted ta kill ye. But a thieving Forbes is na worth me effort."

Roderic deepened his scowl. The man had not only insulted his heritage but had accused him of thievery. Still, Roderic made certain his tone was patient, for there was no need to be rude when starting a brawl. "So ye, too, think that we Forbeses have stolen yer horses?"

"Aye," came the growled response. "I saw ye with me own eyes. The mighty Forbeses take great pride in their colors and dunna hide their plaids, do they now?"

"So ye saw the Forbeses' tartans?" Roderic asked. "How many warriors? What night was this?"

The door swung open with surprising speed and Bullock strode in. His face was red with rage and his fist wrapped about a spear.

"I tire of yer feigned innocence, Forbes. Are ye such a coward that ye canna even admit yer deeds?"

Roderic remained very still, forgetting his quest to learn the truth. Rage was a fool's defense. He took a deep, calming breath and watched Bullock's eyes. "Do ye call me a coward, man?"

"Aye," came the gritted response, "that I—"

Good sense told Roderic to remain as he was and let the anger flow over him. Hot blood told him to strike.

Feigning a left-handed blow to Bullock's chin, Roderic struck his right fist in the other man's belly. The man was built like a castle wall. Still, he bent slightly and in that instant, Roderic swept an upper cut to his jaw. Before Bullock fell, Roderic caught him about the neck and pulled his back up against his own chest. In an instant the other's spear was in his hand.

There was a clatter of footsteps as another guard raced up the stairs and skidded to a halt before them, sword unsheathed, eyes wide.

Roderic nodded once. "William, isn't it?" he asked.

William's face was pale when he returned the nod.

"Listen, lads," Roderic began. "I have been wanting ta say 'tis sorry I am about yer friend's death. Shaw seemed a likable fellow."

William's lips moved, yet no words came. Roderic supposed it did seem a strange time for him to voice condolences, considering he held another MacGowan in a death grip even as he spoke.

"Well now . . ." he said, clearing his throat and feeling a bit foolish. " 'Tis like this, I want a blanket and a chance to sleep. And," he added as an afterthought, "I would like me evening meal early. Do ye think ye could do that . . . or will I have ta kill the two of ye?"

William was a middle-aged man, average in both height and weight, but what he lacked in size he made up for in sheer Scottish bravado, it seemed. "Let him go, Forbes," he said. "Ye'll na get by me."

Roderic tilted his head in concession to the man's bold words. 'Twas not an easy thing to hold one's nerve when looking death in the eye. "I appreciate yer courage, man, but ye surely misunderstand me. I dunna mean ta get by ye. I only mean ta have me meal and a blanket. Bullock here took exception to those requests."

"Ye filthy bastard!" croaked Bullock. His thick neck was bent sharply backward. "Kill me then and have done with it. Just as ye did with Simon."

Roderic remained very still, considering every word. "Simon?" he asked softly.

"Gawd!" Bullock growled, breathing noisily and pressing the hard crown of his head against Roderic's chest. "I should have skewered ye ta the wall."

"Who is Simon?"

"Dunna play me for the fool," gasped Bullock, enraged. "Ye are a filthy—"

But before he could finish his insult, Roderic's patience had fled. Tightening his neckhold with a snarl, he lifted his gaze to the other warrior's. "Gawd's wrath! Who is this Simon?"

William glanced at Bullock's reddened face before hurrying his gaze to Roderic's. "He was the herald Lady Flame sent to ask for an audience with yer brother."

Roderic searched William's face for some sign that he lied. There was none. "And?"

"And his horse came back with naught but Simon's head and a note from yer brother, the laird."

Roderic ground his teeth. Beneath his arm, Bullock struggled one last time and went lax. "Gawd's wrath!" he swore and let the body slip to the floor. "Take him out of here!" he yelled, nodding to the limp man and dropping the spear beside him. "And bring me that damned blanket!"

Roderic's evening meal arrived with his freshly laundered shirt and the blanket he had requested. Flame came shortly after that. Her expression was somber and her stance stiff. " 'Twas kind of ye to point out the fact that I should keep two guards at your door at all times," she said.

Her words fell into the silence like a flat joke. Nevertheless, Roderic grinned. "I'm glad ye appreciated me efforts."

"And I'm pleased that ye were not foolish enough to try to escape entirely. I would, after all, hate to inform your brother of your death."

Roderic snorted. "Dunna be ridiculous. Bullock had fallen like a great stone. If I had wanted ta escape all I would have had to do was . . ." He stopped suddenly and drew a deep breath. "I willna let ye bait me anger, lass." Rising from his chair, he paced the room once, then stopped not far from her. "Why did ye na tell me of Simon?"

"Why should I tell ye what ye already know, Forbes?"

Why could she not be normal, he wondered. Normal women did not make him angry, and he didn't like to get angry. He had learned as a child that when anger took control, people died. His father had been a rash man—and long dead.

"Let us assume for just a wee bit that I ken nothing of yer losses," he said.

Flame opened her mouth to refuse his request, but he raised a hand, palm outward to stop her.

"If I had cut off Bullock's breath just a wee bit longer he would be dead. It could be said, lass, that ye owe me for sparing yer men's lives." He held her with his eyes, reading her emotions and watching her expressions. "When did ye send yer messenger ta me brother?"

She was silent for a few moments but finally answered. " 'Twas five days since. 'Twas Nevin's idea. And for once, he and Troy agreed. Most of the men wished to make a raid instead of a peace parley." She smiled grimly. "But I thought surely it was for the best to make an attempt at peace while I could. Simon set out in the bright light of day, carrying no weapons."

Her back was as straight and stiff as Bullock's spear. "His horse came home with a missive from your brother. Oh, and strapped to the steed's saddle was Simon's—"

"I have heard the rest of the tale," Roderic interrupted, turning abruptly away.

"Ye have heard it?" she asked grimly. "Or ye have caused it?"

He pivoted about. "Ye ken little of men if ye think that of me, lady."

"Then I know little of men," she vowed and strode from the room.

Roderic noticed that the lead ceiling of the tower was water-stained. That meant that when it rained, he would get wet. And they had served mutton for supper. He hated mutton, and thus he had two very good reasons to leave. Besides, he had only promised to stay until sunset and it was well past that time.

Scowling at the cloud-shaped stain, he thought about the meat he had stored in his sporran. He would be a fool not to leave, of course. The MacGowans were a hot-blooded clan and dangerous. They hated the Forbeses, and they hated him.

He sat up and swung his feet over the side of his humble pallet. He had removed his footgear some hours earlier and sat now deep in silent debate.

If he stayed he might untangle the mystery that haunted him. Who had killed Simon and sent the note signed with Leith's name? He knew his brother far too well to even suspect him of such a heinous act. But someone had done it, and Roderic needed to know the truth. On the other hand, if he stayed, someone might soon be wondering who had killed him.

Reaching to the far side of his lumpy straw tick, Roderic retrieved his leather sporran and rose. The wise thing to do would be to leave now. The *safe* thing would be to leave now. There was no reason to think he couldn't solve this puzzle from outside Dun Ard as well as from within its walls.

With that decision made, Roderic glanced about the room. The tower boasted one window. It was shuttered and narrow and more than thirty feet above the nearest wall.

But the drop to the stone parapet didn't concern him. Leith had often said Roderic had been born to be an acrobat or perhaps a jester. Approaching the window, Roderic reached into his sporran and extracted the cold hunk of greasy mutton. He rubbed the meat onto the rusty hinges and hook, then silently swung the shutters open. He was halfway home.

Removing his plaid, he slipped a corner of it around a hinge and pinned it in place with his brooch. It was lucky indeed that Flanna had returned his shirt to him, he thought, or he would be roaming about Dun Ard just as his mother had birthed him. Only larger, and stronger, and infinitely more handsome. He smiled as he tied his sporran about his waist. Then, he retrieved the borrowed blanket from his pallet, knotted the thing to the end of his plaid, and tossed the bound woolens through the window. 'Twas a fine night for a prowl, but the MacGowans would owe him dearly—a brooch, a plaid, and his favorite pair of boots.

The sandstone blocks of the tower wall felt cool against his feet as he descended. Something gave suddenly, but whether it was the brooch or the hinge or the wool itself, Roderic couldn't be sure. Still he skimmed downward, unperturbed by the instability of his rope. His first true concern was when the blanket ended nearly ten feet above the walkway he intended to reach.

Roderic scowled into the dark depths. The parapet was perhaps twice the width of his body and sloped downward in both directions. To the left of that and perhaps six feet below was the stone walkway which completed the enormous width of the wall. To the right was a long, dark, and painful drop into death.

Above him, something groaned against his weight.

Probably the blanket, he thought. 'Twould be like the MacGowans to make inferior wool just to spite him.

Taking a deep breath and sending one quick prayer to his maker, Roderic eased to the end of the blanket, swung to the left, and dropped. His feet hit the parapet, numbing them with the force of the impact and throwing him onto the very edge of the walkway, where he clung like a cat on a limb.

A dark abyss stared him in the face. Somewhere far below was the bailey. His toes curled, his fingers clutched at the stone. He teetered forward, and then with a Herculean effort hauled himself back against the cold wall behind him. He lay there for a spell, gasping for breath and listening for any untoward noises from above or below.

No unusual sounds caught his attention, so he leaned his head gratefully back, taking in deep breaths and gathering his strength.

The cool air finally convinced him to get moving. He glanced at his legs. They were mostly bare, only partly hidden by the length of his freshly laundered shirt. 'Twas a shameful way for a Forbes to return to his homeland. Roderic had half a mind to march into Flanna MacGowan's bedchamber and demand the use of a tartan to cover his nakedness. Or perhaps he should simply leave her something to remember him by, to prove he could not only escape but could breach her very chambers and watch her as she slept.

The night was very quiet. From somewhere far away, an owl called. Roderic smiled. Damned if he wasn't tempted to see her just once more. Not because he was attracted to her, but merely to gloat. Easing his back away from the wall, he glanced about. Where would she sleep?

Dun Ard was not nearly so large or so well fortified as Glen Creag. The tower and forward part of the wall were crafted from stone, but most of the remainder of the fortress was made from crude, native timbers, the far side being perched on the edge of an almost unscalable precipice. He had noticed that the kitchen was set on the far side of the bailey and was also made of timber, a fact which spoke of Dun Ard's lack of stone or manpower or both. The broad sweeps of a windmill were not far away. The stable stood opposite where he now rested, which left the keep, the heart of the castle, as the only place where the MacGowans' Lady Flame would sleep.

Roderic rapped his index finger silently against the stone, thinking. 'Twas tempting indeed to wish her farewell, though Leith would have his hide if he knew the unnecessary risks he took. Still, Roderic reasoned, rising to a crouched position, 'twas *his* hide and none other's. Excitement pumped through his veins. Darkness was an old companion, which he loved for its mystery and challenge.

Less than twenty feet from where he had landed, stairs began. Roderic descended them carefully, hugging the wall in the darkness. There seemed to be no upper floor entrance to the keep from the tower, which meant he would have to cross the hall in search of Flanna's chambers.

At the bottom of the stairs, Roderic halted. Through the arched, stone doorway, he could see the interior of the hall. The last efforts of a fire still burned in the great hearth to his right. Gathered about the dying embers was a plethora of scrambled bodies. Someone shifted, muttering in his sleep. Roderic eased back against the wall, debating. Everyone seemed to be unconscious and therefore would cause no problems. But it would take only a single waking man to make trouble.

Roderic shifted to the opposite wall, studying the scene before him again. Not far from where he hid, two men lay side by side. A squashed, deep green bonnet had fallen from one balding fellow's head. A crumpled blanket covered his knees and his partner's torso. An empty tankard rested on its side between them. So these two had shared a draft of spirits and slept soundly because of it, Roderic reasoned, leaning back again. From the wall near the large, front door, a hound rose and growled softly, watching him, her tawny ears pricked forward. A man stirred, mumbled an oath to quiet the dog, and lay silent again.

Taking a deep breath, Roderic considered the dangers. First, he would concern himself with the men, then, with the dogs. What if a MacGowan should awaken while Roderic was padding across the floor toward the stairway? Would he immediately be recognized as an outsider, he wondered, glancing down at his scanty attire. Many men went barefooted, and during the night just as many loosened their plaids to use them as blankets. Still, he was taller than most, and the entire tribe was bound to be edgy after abducting a Forbes. Roderic glanced about to be certain all was still quiet and stepped into the hall. Squatting by the pair of men closest to him, he lifted the green bonnet from the floor and set it upon his own head.

The nearest man snorted and turned, abandoning his shared blanket altogether and flopping a flaccid hand onto Roderic's bare foot.

Roderic held his breath and remained absolutely still. The hall was silent as a tomb and the tawny hound watched him, but not a man stirred.

Seconds ticked by. Forbes held his breath. Perhaps men were awake after all. Perhaps they lay wide-eyed, watching him. Their swords were drawn under their plaids and they were laughing at his predicament. Sweat beaded on Roderic's brow.

Near the fire, someone began to snore, breaking the silence. Roderic forced himself to relax. Assuring himself that all were asleep, he reached out, pushed the hand from his foot, and claimed the blanket for his own.

He rose smoothly, already wrapping the purloined woolen about his hips as he stepped toward the distant stairs. The watchful hound growled again. Roderic spared her a glance, and then, feeling no particular need to hurry, pulled the mutton from his sporran.

Approaching the dogs at a moderate pace, he stopped

not far away, extending a bit of his meal to the tawny bitch that watched him. She stared into his face, unblinking, solemn and large—a careful lass. Roderic grinned and squatted before her. He had met shy maids before and had overcome their uncertainty, but there was very little time now. Behind him, someone grumbled an expletive in his sleep.

Roderic set the meat by the hound's paws and rose. She tilted her long, elegant head and watched him but made no protest as he moved away.

The stairs up which Roderic finally traveled were narrow. He made his way quickly, his bare feet silent against the cool stone. It was very dark in the hallway that he entered. Barely a glimmer of light penetrated the dimness, but he skimmed his fingers along the walls until he felt the rough timber of a door. Putting his ear to the wood, he listened for just a moment before pushing it quietly open. The tenacious light of the moon through a window showed him rows of barrels and little else.

He moved onward again, his hand grazing the plastered wall until his toes bumped something soft. A feminine voice mumbled a complaint, and near his feet the woman shifted upon her pallet. Roderic held his breath. Of course. Flanna would have a maidservant outside her door. And thus, he knew he had finally arrived at his destination.

Ever so carefully, he leaned over the maid and set his hand to the door latch. It creaked softly beneath his fingers. The woman on the pallet sighed and turned. Roderic froze, not breathing.

An eternity followed, but finally the servant's exhalations could be heard again, soft and cadenced. Stepping over her, Roderic balanced himself between the mattress and the door to ply the hinges and handle with his impromptu lubricant once again.

Only when the flap of his sporran closed over the mutton for the third time that evening did Roderic set his hand to the handle once more. It turned soft as thistledown beneath his fingers. The door eased inward on silent hinges.

He was through in an instant. He pushed the weighty portal closed behind him, stepped smoothly inside, glancing this way and that. 'Twas possible Flanna would retain another servant on this side of the door. But if such was the case, he saw no one on the floor near the huge bed that occupied the room.

It was draped with curtains that were drawn back at the corners, letting in the night air. So Flanna Mac-Gowan was not a lass to become easily chilled, Roderic thought. Indeed, she must be quite a hot-blooded maid. Walking stealthily toward her bed, he kept his attention focused on the form in its center.

The narrow window opened on the night sky not far away, gracing the room with errant moonbeams. They flooded through the window like liquid silver, falling across the mattress and onto the smooth, regal face that rested on a fat, goose-down pillow.

Her hair was loose. Roderic eased a bit closer, drinking in the image. Her lips were parted, her left hand rested beneath her soft cheek, and amidst the tangled blankets, one pale leg was visible from her thigh down.

God's truth, she was a bonny lass. If only he had met her under different circumstances. If only she had not lied to him, kidnapped him, and hated him. But such was not the case, and thus his life now hung in the balance, for surely if he were found in the sanctity of her bedchamber, his life would be forfeit.

He must be crazed to be here. He must truly be out of his mind, he thought, and turned to leave.

But just then she sighed in her sleep, shifting restlessly and drawing her bare leg closer to her chest.

Roderic turned back, noticing how her narrow ankle was turned just so, how the slim muscles of her calf curved gracefully, how the smooth, pale flesh of her thigh . . .

Drawing a deep, careful breath, Roderic rethought the situation. Perhaps he didn't have to leave *immediately*.

It would be several hours yet until dawn's first light.

From the far side of the door, Flanna's maidservant snored, startling Roderic from his reverie.

What the devil was he thinking? Of course he had to leave, and he had to leave now, before it was too late. But ... his gaze skimmed to Flanna's face again. She was very lovely. It seemed a shame not to say goodbye. In fact, it seemed a shame not to smooth his palm down the length of her fine, bared leg, to feel her stir beneath him, to kiss her gently awake.

Good God! What was he thinking? Yes, she was lovely, but she was not some humble milkmaid who might awaken and swoon at his nearness. Nay, she was the kind who mesmerized him with a glance and a touch, teased him with a few breathy words, then pushed him into the burn. It was humiliating, and yet ...

She had such fire. She was the Flame. And the Flame drew and entranced him for he had never met a woman who matched him wit for wit and parry for parry, who could ignite his senses so that he forgot the danger. But flames burned, he remembered suddenly and turned away, forcing himself toward the far side of the room. He should never have come here, but her cool assurance that he could not escape had provoked him into proving how wrong she was. So, as long as he was here, he would leave his mark somehow, let her know he had watched her sleep.

Silently, he moved toward the far wall. There was a small writing desk there. Upon its surface, he could see a scroll of parchment and a quill. Perfect. He would leave her a note. With one quick glance toward the bed, he uncurled the parchment, letting his gaze fall to the bottom of the sheet.

Leith Forbes! The name was written in dark, sprawled letters and seemed to jump from the page at him. Roderic sucked in his breath and skimmed to the top of the text. But the darkness masked the rest of the missive.

God's wrath! So this was the note that had returned with Simon's head. But it couldn't have been penned by his brother. And yet, the signature resembled Leith's sprawling script. Rage filled Roderic like high tide at dusk. He turned rapidly toward the bed, wanting to shake the lady awake and demand an explanation. But in that moment, she gave a small cry.

He stopped in his tracks, reason flooding back. From the bed, Flame whimpered and rolled to her side, pulling her knees to her chest and clutching the blankets to her. She looked very small suddenly, like a frightened child.

A nightmare? he wondered. Was the Flame of the MacGowans frightened despite her usual haughty demeanor? But why wouldn't she be? She had lost all of her immediate family at far too young an age. She had inherited the leadership of an unruly, hot-blooded clan. She had sent a man to make peace with those who were supposed to be her allies and had received her kinsman's severed head for her efforts.

She whimpered again.

Roderic scowled, clutching the note in his hand. Damn it to hell. He could not leave!

Chapter 6

$\sim\!\!\sim\!\!\bigcirc\!\bigcirc\!\!\sim\!\!\sim$

Despite his late-night excursion, Roderic rose with the dawn.

Flame arrived shortly after. Her legs were encased in brown, supple leather. Her saffron shirt was belted at the waist and fell in soft folds halfway to her knees, and at her side was her ruby-studded dirk.

Roderic glanced at her, tried to adjust his breathing and said, "You've doubled the guard." Flame watched him as if waiting for his comment on her attire. But he refused to act shocked. Intrigued was the word to fit his mood more closely. " 'Tis na fair."

"Step back!" Bullock ordered gruffly. Behind him, William, Gilbert, and Nevin looked on. "Step away from the lady."

Roderic shrugged and did as told. Nevertheless, he grinned at her from against the wall. Why did she wear such an outlandish costume? Mannish, some might call it. But the simple saffron shirt caressed her bosom and the leather hose hugged her lower regions. Manly was not the term he would use for it. "How am I ta escape when there are two men at me door and no other way out?"

She watched him closely. Her expression was regal and self-assured, and yet past the polished veneer he sensed fatigue, as if she hadn't slept well. That fact reminded Roderic of his nocturnal visit. He remembered how she had looked in the pale light of the moon, how she had whimpered in her sleep.

It had been difficult to leave her, but he had, taking the parchment with him. In the first rays of morning light, he had read the ghoulish letter over and over. It was short, concise: *I am sending this—a-head, so that ye may know that the Forbeses do not parley with MacGowan filth. Leith Forbes.*

He could imagine Flanna's expression when she had seen her kinsman's severed head and read the missive. But it was not just the murder that would have worried her. It was the fact that the note was written in blood and contained a sick play on words. *I am sending this— a-head . . .*

What kind of man would kill an innocent herald, then compose a sinister joke and blame the deed on another. And why? But the most haunting part of the entire message was the seal that had once held it closed. Stamped into the hardened wax was the image of a wildcat that looked very much like Leith's own seal!

Roderic curled his hands into fists and reminded himself to remain calm. Had someone stolen his brother's seal? Or made a copy of it? He would find the true villain. And the villain would die.

"I told you at the outset that you would not escape Dun Ard," Flame said.

He watched her eyes. They were entrancing, wide, vividly green and filled with a thousand emotions that he could not quite fathom. "So ye did, lass," he murmured, then pulled himself from her eyes to notice the breakfast that had just been delivered. "Am I ta eat alone?"

"Did ye mayhap think that the MacGowans would be falling over each other for a chance to eat with a Forbes?"

It fascinated him that she could banish her doubts and fatigue behind her emerald eyes and meet his gaze full force.

"I had considered it," he said.

She turned away, but he softened his tone and added,

"I am accustomed to the company of me family and friends. In short, I am lonely."

She looked back over her shoulder at him. A queen should look so proud, he thought, and pressed on.

"Might ye na share me trencher?"

"Nay," she said simply and turned away.

"Please" he said softly. "I would speak with ye for a spell. Mightn't ye have a seat?"

"Nay," Nevin warned. "Do not risk it, lady. I know these Forbeses, for my father, bless his soul, used to sell them his wares. They are a crafty lot."

Roderic almost laughed. Four well-armed warriors guarded her. Each man looked hearty, able, and more than willing to cut him into bite-sized morsels should he raise a suspicious finger to her. Still, he was flattered by their worry and glad he had made an impression. "I willna harm her," he vowed. "Ye have me word of honor."

No one moved. Roderic could not quite resist a grin. "What could I do against four guards?"

Bullock shuffled his feet and reddened, probably remembering his disgraceful failure to guard Roderic on the previous day, but Forbes had no need to salt old wounds.

"Yesterday ye werena prepared for me foolhardy attempt at escape, for ye knew I wouldna leave alive," he said. "Be assured that I know ye willna be caught unawares again. Dunna worry. Surely she is safe with me."

Flame nodded once at her men, then turned toward Roderic. All four guards stepped inside, spread their legs, and gripped their weapons.

The room was painfully silent. "Must ye glare at me?" Roderic asked, addressing the guards. "I am na about to devour yer Lady."

"Touch her and ye'll na live long enough ta regret it," Bullock warned.

"Bullock does not oft suffer being made a fool of," Nevin added. "He has some pride."

Roderic watched Nevin before shifting his gaze to Bullock. The stocky warrior's face reddened, the flames of his anger fanned by his companion's reminder of his shame. But Nevin's emotions were not so easily read, though he seemed intelligent and spoke as if he had been well educated.

Drawing his attention from the warriors, Roderic sighed and motioned Flame toward the only chair. "Be seated, lady."

She remained standing where she was. "What is it you wish to speak to me about?"

Roderic moved to the wall nearest her and let his gaze draw in fresh perceptions. Her shirt was laced at the throat with a single narrow strip of leather that was knotted at the bottom, weaved through the holes and tipped with a small cone of pewter that rested against her left breast.

He sighed mentally. 'Twould truly be pathetic to be jealous of a bit of metal.

"What did you want to—"

" 'Tis about Leith," Roderic interrupted, wrenching himself from his reverie and snapping his gaze back to her face. "Have ye sent a herald to him yet?"

It was a poor choice of words, for Simon had been a herald and Simon had been decapitated. Roderic had no wish to remind her of that just now, especially since he had recently stolen the note from her room and she was bound to eventually wonder what had happened to it.

"No." Her answer was cool and reserved and did nothing to shed light on her true thoughts. "I have not."

"Then I would like to send a message of me own."

"And why would I allow you to do that, Forbes?"

"Leith is a stubborn man." Roderic let that statement lay in the silence for a moment. "But he is still me brother. And while 'tis true that for a time I thought I might escape this fortress, I see now that I was wrong. I wish to send him a message saying that I am well and that I wish for na blood to be shed. In essence, I wish to recommend that he comply with yer demands."

"But ye do not know what our demands will be."

"Would I appear petty if I admitted that I think me own life ta be worth whatever price ye ask?"

She pursed her lips. They were full and berry-bright. "I will bring ye a quill," she said and turned to go, but he stopped her again.

"Please stay. There is na rush. I would ken, what *are* yer demands?"

"Ye cannot repay all ye have taken from us, for Simon was a good man and well loved," she said, staring at him from her regal height. "So we but ask for enough goods to ease his widow's burdens and help restore Dun Ard. And, of course, for the return of our stock."

It was no use denying that the Forbeses were at fault until he could prove the truth. And yet he longed to proclaim their innocence, and could not stop himself from asking, "What stock might that be?"

Anger sparked immediately in her eyes. Roderic cleared his throat and tried to look disarming. He took some pride in his innocuous expression. "I mean, what stock, exactly. Ye'll want to be precise."

She drew a deep breath and slipped into the chair. Grace robed her like a velvet cloak. "Ye have taken at least a score of our cattle that were fattening in the glen."

He waited in silence for her to continue.

"More than a dozen sheep were lost or killed."

Beef and mutton were mainstays in the Highlands, but Roderic was beginning to know her mind. "And the horses?"

He saw the anger in the tightening of her lips. "Fourteen steeds are missing, five fine mares, and nine young stallions."

No way in hell would the Forbeses give up fourteen of their valuable mounts to atone for a sin they did not commit, thought Roderic. But he nodded, as if agreeing with her right to have them. "Then ye want them all replaced."

"Nay!" She stood abruptly, nearly knocking over the chair in her haste. "I want those same animals back."

"The sheep?" he asked, knowing he was being contrary.

"Not the sheep! The horses!"

"But perhaps they have been sold. Or perhaps . . ." Roderic took a step toward her, though he knew he should not. He knew he should play along, draw out the facts.

Near the door, the guards tensed and raised their weapons.

"Or perhaps the Forbeses didna take them," he suggested quietly.

"Your plaids were clearly identified during the raids!" she countered and leveled her gaze on his. "Ye took them and ye shall return them. Those exact animals."

"But one cow is pretty much the same as—"

"I dunna mean the . . ." She stopped and narrowed her eyes as if wondering if he was baiting her. Her language changed ever so slightly under duress. It became softly burred. Roderic wondered now about her childhood. Had she spent time abroad? England perhaps? But no, no father could allow such sunshine to leave his life. "I do not mean the cows," she said more slowly. "I mean the horses. We will have our horses returned and will accept replacement for the other livestock."

She really was too attached to those horses, Roderic thought. "I assure ye that the Forbeses steeds be a good deal finer . . ." he began, then mentally grinned as he changed his course and waited for her anger. He couldn't resist trying to rile her. "I mean to say, the horse ye call Lochan is na verra . . ." He waved his hand vaguely.

"Come along!" Her order was brusque and brooked no argument.

"Me?" He motioned toward his own chest, as if surprised by her demand.

"I said, come."

Roderic glanced at the guards, tried not to grin, and shrugged. "As ye wish."

Pivoting on her heel, she stalked toward the door. Roderic followed at a respectable distance. He saw the guards' dubious glances at one another and felt no compunction to cause them alarm by doing something foolish.

Her legs were long and her strides quick as she hurried down the narrow, stone steps. Once in the bailey, Roderic took a deep breath of the fresh air and hurried after her. They must seem a strange convoy indeed, he thought—the MacGowan Flame, their notorious prisoner, and four guards, hurrying along as if auld horny himself were on their trail.

Two maids were tending the herb garden beside the kitchen.

"A bonny morning ta ye, Marjory. And to ye," Roderic greeted.

"Be ye coming?" demanded Flame from the door of the stable.

Roderic nodded and solemnly lengthened his strides until he stood before her. "Ye are so impatient, lass," he said, speaking for her ears alone. "Could it be ye already miss me company?"

She raised her chin a mite. Her jaw was firm and her luscious mouth pursed. It was almost incongruous in her neatly sculpted face. "Few have been granted this opportunity."

He paused a moment, still studying her mouth before leaning closer. "Indeed? And which opportunity be ye speaking of, lass?"

"Few outsiders have seen our horses."

"Ahh." He shrugged noncommittally and settled a shoulder against the stone wall of the immense barn. "I have seen many horses. But *ye,* lass . . ." He lowered his tone. "I've never seen anything quite like ye."

For just a moment she appeared distracted, but then she pulled her dignity about her and opened the door. Roderic followed with a grin. Disarming the Flame was proving to be a difficult but enjoyable task.

The pungent redolence of the barn greeted him. It was a scent he had grown to love as a child. As small boys, he and Colin had delighted in hiding in the loft and scaring the old horse master from his wits as they plummeted from their secret spots in the hay above.

From a dark stall, a horse trumpeted a challenge and banged his door. Another called in more congenial tones and then another.

"Good morn, Lochan." Flame's voice was soft as a blue-gray head reached above a half door.

"Ahh," said Roderic, stopping not far from her to cross his arms and notice the softening of her tone. How would it feel to have her speak to him such? "So this be the poor, wee beast that carried ye ta Glen Creag."

"Poor beast indeed!" Flame said and whistling a shrill, distinctive call, swung the stall door open.

Lochan Gorm thundered into the aisle like a streak of blue lightning.

Tail raised and proud, refined head held high, the stallion was an impressive sight. But Roderic was not quite ready to admit as much. "At least they've freed him from the mud and burrs that bedeviled him on our first meeting," he said, but at a sound from his mistress, the animal charged.

Roderic had barely enough time to press himself back against the timbers before Flanna whistled again. The lithe steed skidded to a halt, but his yellowed teeth were bared and not a full hand away.

Roderic had seen what an enraged stallion could do to a man. Not daring to breathe, he eased to his left. Lochan tossed his silver mane and flattened slipper-shaped ears against his neck. His eyes were rimmed with white as he stalked his prey.

Not far away a two-pronged fork hung between pegs on the wall. Roderic shuffled a few inches closer. If he could but reach it he might have a chance of surviving the day, but just as he prepared to lunge for the thing, Flame whistled again.

Lochan's ears came up. The wild expression left his night black eyes and his head dropped as he turned away.

Air returned to Roderic's lungs. Beside him, the guards chortled at his fear, but he had little time to notice, for his heart still thundered in his chest. He placed a hand over it, not attempting to hide his obvious reaction.

The guards' laughter grew louder. "I thought ye called him a poor, wee beastie," chuckled Bullock.

"Well now . . ." Roderic grinned and drew a noisy breath. He was not above seeing the humor in this situation, although it would have been considerably funnier if it had happened to someone else. "I find that when one is attacked by a crazed stallion, it matters little if he outweighs me by five times or a hundred. 'Tis the lunacy in the beast's eyes that—"

"Lunacy?" Bullock chuckled, nodding to the beast in question.

Lochan stood like an old cart horse now. One hip was cocked and his head drooped peacefully against his mistress's chest.

Flame raised her gaze to Roderic as she straightened the gray's foretop.

"Lady," Roderic murmured in amazement, "tell me how ye did that."

She smiled. Gone was all reserve, he realized. Her eyes were shining with pride and humor, and her body was relaxed. "Mayhap Lochan simply detests the smell of ye."

Roderic chuckled and shook his head. "That couldna be the cause, lass, for I recently bathed. Surely, ye remember, since ye were kind enough ta assist me. Nay," he continued, " 'tis me own thought that the lady transferred her feelings to the horse."

She laughed. It was a bright and bonny sound. "That is an opinion I've heard voiced before. But ye are wrong, Forbes. 'Tis naught but training that makes him act so."

"Nay," disagreed Troy from the doorway. "In truth, she be half horse herself."

"Truly?" asked Roderic, eyeing Troy as he approached. "Which half?"

There were a few reluctant chuckles from the guards. Nevin smiled, too, and said, "I but wish Simon and Shaw were here to enjoy this humor."

Roderic watched the smile die on Flame's lips. Damn Nevin for always reminding them of the MacGowans' losses. It had been like the first breath of spring to watch her smile, to see her worries drop from her for a moment. And Roderic was determined to make it happen again. With that thought, he strode over to the stallion that could so easily have killed him. It was obvious now that there was nothing to fear, at least not until the lady lost her temper.

"Tell me true, lass," he said, standing not far away and gazing at the pair. "How do ye do it?"

"With time and patience any steed, or . . ." A stallion trumpeted angrily from a closed box stall again, interrupting her words with the harsh challenge. "Or any steed but Bruid," she said, nodding in the direction of the stallion that had just screamed. "Most any horse could learn what Lochan knows. Though the brawny brutes will never be so quick and supple."

"Ye jest."

"Nay." Her expression was somber when she turned toward him, and for a moment Roderic felt his breath stop in his chest. Flanna MacGowan was always beautiful, but now she was stunning. "They are living, feeling beings. Not so unlike ourselves. All they want is to be lo—" She stopped abruptly and turned her attention back to the fine-boned stallion.

"All they want is what?" Roderic asked softly.

" 'Tis just training," she said. Her tone was suddenly stiff. "Nothing more."

And love, Roderic thought. She had meant to say that horses, like people, wanted nothing more than to be loved, but such would show weakness. He scowled mentally. Who was this woman that she would need to seek affection from a dumb beast? But, he corrected himself, perhaps *this* beast was not dumb, for he seemed nearly to share her thoughts and had somehow gained her trust enough to press his head against the softness of her bosom.

Some would find such a relationship eerie, he supposed, but some did not know Fiona Rose, his brother's wife. If Fiona could talk to a wildcat, there was no reason to be surprised when Flanna spoke to horses.

"So ye yerself have trained him?" he asked now, watching her face closely.

She remained silent for a moment. "Lochan and I have known each other for a long while."

It wasn't easy for Roderic to pull his attention from Flame's face, but there were now five of her clansmen staring at his. Perhaps it would be wise to hide some of his interest. He turned his gaze toward the stallion. "How is it ye came by such a steed?" Now that the burrs and mud had been removed, Lochan's coat had the silver sheen of a finely crafted sword. Though he wasn't tall, his legs were long and straight. There was no fat on this beast and every line of him showed beauty and grace.

"He was a gift to my father," Flame said simply. She watched Roderic as he walked behind Lochan. Had she been mistaken, or was there a glint of admiration in his eyes?

"Barb breeding," he deduced, studying Lochan from his clean limbs to his wide-set eyes. "Produced through centuries of meticulous, desert breeding. Your father must have been well pleased."

Flame watched him carefully. She hadn't originally planned to frighten him with her stallion's maneuvers. It was Forbes' patronizing attitude that had caused her to fling the stall door open. But neither had she expected him to so rapidly admit Lochan's fine quality. Few did, for in these days of weighty armor and weapons, only the large destriers were coveted.

"My father favored sheer might above all else. The laird of the MacGowans had no use for such a small steed. I acquired Lochan when he was but a colt."

She could feel still Forbes' thoughtful gaze on her face. "Your father must have valued *you* greatly," he said, but his tone was very soft, as if he voiced a question, "to give you such a fine gift."

"So, Forbes," broke in Troy, squeezing his huge body past Lochan's and interrupting their conversation, "the wee beastie scared ye?"

"Nay," Roderic said, turning toward Troy, "na atall."

He was lying, Flame thought, but he didn't seem to care that they knew it. What kind of man could best her guards one instant and so easily disregard his own fear the next?

"At Glen Creag, our steeds greet us in just such a manner every morn." Mischief glinted in his eyes. " 'Tis a daily occurrence."

Troy snorted, but there was the trace of a smile on his lips. "I see wee Lochan hasna scared that glib tongue from ye at the least."

"There are those who say I will be dead first," Roderic admitted.

"Mayhap that will happen when the lass shows ye her other pets," Troy suggested.

"I await the introductions with baited breath," Roderic said.

Flame watched the exchange. Was there comradery of a sort developing here? Or was it antagonism. It was difficult to tell. Only a few days ago, her men had screamed for justice, had insisted that they make the Forbeses pay. But now they seemed intrigued by Roderic, cautious and sometimes fearful, but also amused and impressed. 'Twas like that among her wild kinsmen, she thought. Love and hate were so similar. Rage and respect only a heartbeat apart. She knew that, and yet she resented any admiration they might spare Roderic, for each day she fought to gain a little respect for herself and her leadership. Surely, it was not right or good that he could easily earn what she so desperately wanted.

"Mayhap ye should show him yer other steeds, lady," Bullock suggested.

Flame felt her resentment build. "I have better things to do than entertain prisoners. And so do ye," she said, turning toward her men. They scattered, looking sheepish.

"Hamilton," she said, " 'tis your task to see that Forbes does not escape." Troy was older and not as easily impressed by a glib tongue—she hoped. "If ye have need of me I will be on the green."

She could feel Forbes' gaze on her back as she turned to go. Lochan followed her of his own accord. Horses thrust their heads over half doors as she passed. She heard Lochan stop to stamp and squeal a challenge, but she refused to turn around. She could not bear to meet Roderic's gaze, for somehow she was sure he would see who she really was, a small lass still begging for acceptance. He would know how she struggled for the smallest smidgen of respect. He would know her every weakness.

Roderic watched her go, saw Lochan trot after her when she whistled. Never had he met a woman with her strength.

"So even a hound will drool after a princess." Troy's words broke into Roderic's reverie, and he realized suddenly that the huge warrior had been watching him very closely for some time.

"What the devil are ye talking about, ye half-brained Wolfhound?" he asked irritably. Why could he not be spared five minutes alone with the lady? He had felt, for an instant, that he was very near to learning something important about her. Something that would shed some light on who she was.

Troy snorted. "There are men who are wise enough na ta insult me ta me face, lad."

"And there are men with balls," countered Roderic. "I happen ta be the latter."

The big man laughed. "Ye've got grit, I'll give ye that, but have ye got staying power?"

"Have ye come ta test me strength, then?" asked Roderic.

"Nay, I have come ta learn the truth. Why did ye kill her messenger? Why have ye raided her herds?"

Roderic felt his stomach knot. Tension and frustration were building to a keen edge inside him. "Are ye so daft that ye think I willna take offense to yer accusations or are ye hoping for a fight, Wolfhound?"

Hamilton snorted and placed his fists to his hips. Though he was many years older than Roderic, he was also half a head taller and three stone heavier. None of the weight was fat. "Why would I wish ta fight with a wee one like yerself, Forbes?"

"I dunna ken, Wolfhound," said Roderic, sizing up the other. "Mayhap ta rile up yer clansmen when I wound ye. Mayhap, ye are looking ta cause trouble."

"And why would I want that?"

"Ye're not a MacGowan, are ye, Troy? And though ye act like an ally, mayhap ye have some grudge against this clan. Or mayhap against the Flame herself."

Troy's expression had gone very solemn. "Ye've na idea what ye're speaking of, lad."

"She trusts ye," Roderic continued, watching his eyes. "She trusts yer judgment. Why did ye wish to send Simon to speak with me brother? And why send him alone? Could it be ye were planning to kill him yerself?"

The big man's body was tense, his voice low. "Any ideas why I would do that?"

"None atall. Yet."

"Then shut yer mouth, lad, before I shut it for ye. The lass has enough worries without ye adding yer wild tales."

"Afraid I'll tell her the truth?"

"Tell her anything ye want, wee one, just dunna make me do something I'll regret."

"Such as?"

"Ripping yer tongue from yer head."

Roderic forced a laugh but kept his weight carefully balanced lest the huge warrior charge him. "I see I've got ye scairt, Wolfhound. But what of? Of losing her? I've seen the way ye watch her. Mayhap ye think of her as yer own and think I'll horn in?"

Troy tightened his huge hands into fists, but in a moment he loosened them and laughed. "Ye think I'm scairt of yer effects on her, lad? Ye think yerself such a bonny piece that she'll na be able ta keep her wits about her? That ye'll win her adoration?"

"Mayhap."

Troy laughed again. "Well, then, wee one, I'll let her prove ye wrong."

Chapter 7

Roderic followed Troy out of the stable and across the drawbridge. In a matter of minutes, they stood upon a verdant, level sward of land just beyond the roiling Gael Burn. The sun was flirting with the clouds, and the air was potent with the essence of spring. Freedom lay just within the curtain of trees not a hundred rods away.

But Roderic failed to be distracted by any of these things, for Flanna MacGowan was within sight, stealing his breath and igniting his soul with her beauty.

Her steel gray stallion was cantering in place, a difficult maneuver even for the most powerful beast. It was a marvel to see, like sweet music come alive. Then the canter was halted, and with the suddenness of a cat, the stallion leaped into the air, tucking his forelegs beneath his soaring body. And yet Flame remained steady, and on her face was an expression of sheer joy.

Roderic remained transfixed.

"Na man wins the adoration of such a woman." Troy's words were soft. " 'Tis a freely given thing. A gift."

Roderic turned toward the warrior, disturbed by the man's breathy tone. "And do ye own that gift, Wolfhound?"

Troy didn't answer. Indeed, it seemed as if he were far away and unable to hear Roderic's question, but in a moment he shook himself.

"She comes," he said in a louder tone. " 'Tis yer chance to enchant her, Forbes.''

Roderic turned to watch her approach. She rode like a windswept fire on a cloud of gray. Her hair was unbound and floated behind in wild disarray. The simple lad's shirt embraced her bosom. A taut bowstring lay snugly between her breasts to meet the oaken bow that she carried at her back. A quiver of arrows hung beside the high pommel of her saddle but did nothing to impede her steed's fluid movements.

"What is he doing here?" Flame pulled Lochan to a halt and shifted slightly in the saddle as she looked past him to Troy.

"The wee lad wishes ta win yer adoration."

"What?" She stiffened.

Roderic grinned. Damn Troy and all the MacGowan warriors. "I fear yer Wolfhound's imagination runs riot. I but wished ta see ye work the steed." He watched her eyes. They were cool as glass and unnerving, for if the truth were known, he did want her adoration. " 'Tis difficult ta believe ye trained him yerself."

"Because I am a woman?"

Without looking, Roderic could feel Troy's smile. He damned that man again, then reprimanded himself for his tactless words. He was supposed to be charming, he reminded himself. Roderic the Rogue. "Nay lass, because ye are bonny beyond words. I canna understand how ye have escaped wedlock for so long."

"Flattery is a weak man's cheap weapon, Forbes."

"And yers is yer tongue."

They stared at each other in silence. Roderic grasped his plaid where it crossed his shoulder. He was being very charming, he thought sarcastically. "I didna come to exchange insults with ye, lass," he said softly. "But rather, ta share yer knowledge of the horse."

The joyous, carefree expression was gone from her face, and Roderic found that he wished more than anything to call it back. "And pray, why would I share anything with the likes of ye, Forbes?"

Because he was charming and manly and handsome, he reminded himself. "Because . . ." Roderic, tried not to stare at her leg. But no matter where he looked, her sensuality shook his repose. "Because the Forbeses are oft in need of good horses of war. And because we have ties to powerful families who share our need." She stared at him intently. He warmed to the subject, seeing her interest. "With Leith's marriage to Fiona, some ties have been formed in England. And the French are na unknown to us."

Her hands tightened on the reins. Lochan irritably flipped his tail at the increased tension. "The French are not unknown to me, either." There was anger in her eyes. Was it her hatred for him that caused it, or was this emotion for a different reason? "In truth, many of our steeds were brought from that country. So ye see, if we should wish to sell our mounts, we, too, have contacts."

"But how would ye get them there, lass? Have ye the manpower to see their safe delivery to a port? A knight is na a knight without a fine steed. They cost dear and many would kill for them, as ye well ken."

She laughed, but the sound was harsh. "Ye think I do not realize this? Ye think I turn my steeds out to run wild on the heath. Nay! I have them well guarded. But 'tis said the Forbeses like a challenge. 'Twas dusk when ye attacked my men and stole my beasts."

"It was na the Forbeses." He had not meant to argue, for he knew he could not convince her otherwise. Not yet. But the words slipped from him, low and earnest. "It was na me clan's doings."

Their gazes clashed.

"Ye lie," she said finally and urged the stallion away.

Without a second thought, Roderic reached out to grasp her thigh. She halted the gray and stared at his hand. "Were ye planning to keep those fingers, Forbes?"

"Do ye care so little for yer people, then?" he asked, ignoring her threat. "They be all but starving, lass. Yet,

I begin to think yer horses could save them, if ye could but combine yer Lochan's agility and training with the great destrier's size and might. Tell me of yer horses, Flanna. Show me yer steeds. Convince me of the superiority of yer breeding stock, and I will do what I can to assure the return of yer animals.''

"And why would I trust the word of a Forbes?"

Her tone was breathless, as if she barely dared to hope. He was trapped in her eyes, but suddenly a mischievous gust of wind tossed a long lock of her hair over her shoulder and onto his hand. It was as bright as the sunrise and as soft as a smile. For an instant, Roderic's breath halted in his throat, for they seemed suddenly to be connected somehow, bound together by those few fiery strands of hair.

Flame, too, held her breath. Their gazes met with a jolt. Roderic's fingers burned between the heat of her thigh and the softness of her hair. But in a moment, she exhaled sharply and pushed his hand away before straightening. Still, she did not manage to draw herself from his eyes. Neither did she move.

"I swear it on me father's grave," Roderic said solemnly. "Convince me of the superiority of yer steeds, and I will do me best to see that they are returned to ye.''

"Then ye no longer deny raiding our herds?"

"To the contrary," Roderic said. "I am but promising ta see justice done.''

"The word of a Forbes is of little use to me," she said, quickly turning her face away. "For 'twas they who promised to be our allies. And 'twas they that took our stock and killed our kin.''

"I swear it on me father's grave," he repeated.

She turned her gaze slowly back to his. "So be it." Her tone was utterly sober and her expression the same. "I will accept yer word as a sacred vow.

"Troy." She turned to the huge warrior behind him. "Ye are a witness. I will show Forbes our steeds. Ye must make certain he does not escape while I do so.''

"Aye, lass," rumbled Troy. Placing a hand on Roderic's arm, he turned him around. "Do ye promise na ta run off, Forbes?"

Roderic raised his brows. There had been no room for trust between them thus far. Why did the Wolfhound ask for promises now? "I willna escape this day."

Troy nodded once and looked to Flame. "Do I have yer leave to return to the keep, lass?"

"Ye call that making certain he does not escape?"

The warrior shrugged. "Ye have already accepted his sacred vow, lass. And perhaps it is time."

She scowled down at him. "For what?"

"For ye ta trust another. The falcon and the snake both kill, but the falcon does na pretend to be a stick." For one long moment, he watched her, and then he turned away, showing them the immense width of his back as he headed for the drawbridge.

"What the devil did that mean?" Roderic mused.

"It means he's trying to make me crazed."

"Be I the snake or be I the falcon?"

"Ye be the snake," Flame said, shaking herself from her reverie.

Roderic grinned and she caught his gaze. His long hair glistened in burnished waves of gold just as it did in the dreams that had begun to haunt her. A small braid lay on each side of his powerful jaw and his eyes were as blue as the heavens.

"Why do ye hate me, lass?"

It took a moment to find her voice, for his tone felt as warm and soft as sunlight on bare skin. "Because ye are a devil," she murmured. She could almost believe it was true, for surely no one but Satan himself could be so entrancing, so alluring, and tempting.

He grinned a little, and in that moment she wondered if she might not be entirely wrong. If he might not be an angel. But no, if the devil meant to tempt her, he would send a man just like this one. One with a voice like warmed ale. A man with the wit of a scholar and the brawn of a field laborer. But neither men's intellect nor brawn had aided her in the past, for men always found her wanting and turned away.

"Mayhap I be a handsome devil, Flanna. But I assure ye, I am na auld horny himself."

How was it that even his tremendous vanity appealed to her? Was it because he seemed to laugh at himself at the same time he issued self-praise? Or was it simply that she agreed with his assessment? Dear Lord, either way she was a fool. But surely he could not see into her mind. He could not know how he drew her. "Then I cannot trust ye because ye are a Forbes," she said, using the words to remind herself to keep her distance.

"Because I am a Forbes or because I am a man?" he asked.

She did not gasp, though it was a close thing. Had someone told him about Carvell de Laplant, her fiancé? But no. No one knew. No one except Troy. And he would never tell. He had sworn he wouldn't. But . . . Flame stared at the huge warrior's retreating back. He, too, was a man and already he seemed to foolishly trust their enemy. 'Twould be like a man to betray her friendship for the comradery of another of his own sex.

She straightened slowly. "I am an excellent archer, Forbes," she said, changing the subject and finding a threat appropriate for the moment. "Should ye try to escape, ye would not make it to the trees before my barb pierced your back."

"Would ye truly take me life, lass?"

"In an instant."

He raised his brows and kept his gaze on hers. "Have ye na woman's softness?"

"None." It was true, for she had given up her femininity when she had taken the name of Flame and become the MacGowans' leader. Only now did the sacrifice rankle. But she refused to acknowledge the cause.

"Did I na have eyes, I could almost believe ye, lass."

"Don't call me that!"

It was clear that her harsh tone startled him. "What? Lass?"

"Ye may call me Flame or ye may call me Mac-Gowan. Naught else."

"Yer Wolfhound calls ye lass. Why—"

"Ye are hardly like a father to me." Damnation! Why had she said that?

"So the great hound be as a father ta ye?" asked Roderic.

She stared at him, wishing she had never spoken, that his eyes were not so blue, that she had been born a man. "Get back to the stable. I said I would show ye the horses, and I will stand by my word."

"So 'tis Troy that knows ye like none other?" mused Roderic.

"Go!" she ordered. Her tone was sufficiently harsh, but her body felt taut with anxiety. She knew better than to let a man near her heart.

For a moment longer Roderic watched her. Then he shrugged and glanced toward the castle. "Surely ye dunna expect me ta walk all that way." He smiled.

It was little more than a hundred rods to the draw-bridge. Flame scowled, flicking her gaze down his lengthy, well-muscled form. "Ye have little chance of making me believe ye are too frail to make it that far."

His smiled deepened. "Shall I be flattered?"

"Don't bother."

His blue eyes twinkled in the bright morning. "I would be willing to ride pillion."

"Do ye go?" she asked. "Or do I set my arrow to my bow?"

His smile didn't falter a whit, she noticed, disgruntled. It was little wonder her men had already begun to trust the lout. After all, it was difficult to distrust anyone who smiled as much as Forbes did. Surely it showed he lacked enough intelligence to mastermind an escape. Still . . . She watched his face closely. He did not look slow-witted. Indeed, the opposite was true. He looked as sound as any man she had ever seen. In fact, his body looked as hard and lean as . . .

Flame mentally shook her head. She was no silly maid to be seduced by his fine looks. She had learned better long ago. And now she was the leader of the clan MacGowan. The Flame, as they called her, with no time for girlish sentiment or dangerous dalliances. She reached for her bow.

Roderic laughed, lifting a hand and watching her face. "Though I be flattered by yer offer ta show me yer brood stock, I would sooner see more of this steed's maneuvers first. Or canna he do more than hop about like a bunny?"

Flame watched Forbes' expression for just a moment and then touched a heel to Lochan's side. The stallion spun away at the slightest pressure. And then, like a pouncing cat, he leaped into the air, kicking out behind him at the same time. She knew his heels missed Roderic's face by mere inches, and yet she didn't take time to appreciate her enemy's expression. In a moment Lochan was pivoting on his hind legs so swiftly that the world around her was a blur. Coming out of the spin, he leaped forward again and rose on his hind legs to pummel the air with his forefeet. There was a momentary pause . . . and then, with an ear-splitting trumpet, he crumpled to the ground, carrying Flame with him.

Chapter 8

"**F**lanna!" Roderic gasped and rushed forward to free her from the animal's weight. He reached for her, but suddenly she was on her feet. One hand gripped his shirt while her other was wrapped hard and fast about the dirk that poked firmly between his ribs.

"I could kill ye, Forbes," she murmured. "Before ye'd ever know 'twas a ruse."

Roderic stared into her eyes. They were alight with passion and exhilaration. He drew a steadying breath, trying to remember that it was not passion for *him*. "Ye cued the steed to fall?" he asked.

She tilted her head and nodded curtly. "The enemy assumes the horse is wounded and the rider pinned." She pressed slightly harder with the dirk. "Giving me the advantage."

Roderic raised his brows, admiring the ploy, but admiring the woman more. The fire, the wit, the nerve. "But what if the enemy did this?" he asked, and without allowing himself a moment's thought, he wrapped her in his arms and kissed her.

Her breasts were firm against his chest, her lips soft against his—and her dirk sharp against his side. He felt all three sensations, and though his mind demanded that he draw back and spare his life's blood, his arms refused to let her loose. Her heart beat frantically against his. Her body trembled, and he wondered if it was fear or excitement?

He slid his hand up her back, pressing her closer still,

allowing his thigh to slip between hers, feeling the heat of her body as she kissed him in return.

Sweet Mary, she was kissing him! But just as his loins clambered at that realization, she jerked her head back and pressed away from his embrace. Still, he could not let her go, for he wanted her with an all-consuming ache, and he had felt her answering flame. Her eyes were round with shock, her lips kiss-softened and bright as Yuletide berries. But the dirk had not moved. Roderic lowered his gaze.

A droplet of blood had seeped through his shirt, but it failed to hold his interest.

"Do that again," she warned in a quivering voice, "and I'll carve my name in your gizzard."

But he had felt her tremble in his arms, had felt her need as surely as he felt his own. "Lass, I only wish . . ." he began, but the dirk pressed harder.

"Don't do it, Forbes."

It took every bit of control he possessed to release her. He did so slowly and backed away, trying to remember to breathe as he pushed his fingers through his hair. "When does he get up?"

She blinked at him, looking lost.

"Yer steed," he explained, relaxing his muscles one by one. She was not his for the taking. She was not his. But perhaps she wanted to be. Perhaps she lay awake nights thinking of him just as he thought of her. Thinking of . . . God's wrath, his hands were shaking. Roderic the Rogue with shaky hands. He drew a careful breath, reminding himself to be civil lest he fall upon her with all the finesse of an excited hound. "How do ye get him up?"

Her kiss-swollen lips moved soundlessly. Roderic watched them and somehow, foolishly, they drew him. He moved a step nearer.

"Get back," she warned, but her dirk shook as she raised it.

"What are ye afraid of, Flanna MacGowan?" he whispered.

"I am afraid of naught," she said, but her words were quick and her eyes as wide as those of a frightened doe.

He took a solitary step closer, though he knew he was a fool. "If I were na such a gentleman I would insist on proving ye wrong with another kiss."

She raised her chin and her dirk simultaneously. "And if I were not such a gentle woman—" she began, but suddenly, Roderic covered her hand with his own, easily holding the dirk steady between them as he leaned close.

"If ye were na such a gentle woman ye would have kilt me when ye had the blade pressed ta me ribs," he murmured. "But ye did na."

The air between them crackled with tension. Roderic held his breath, for she was very near, her body tense and her lips slightly parted. His pulse leaped and his manhood did the same.

"Surely it would be a sin to kill ye." Her voice was no more than a husky whisper.

He was trapped in her eyes, in her tone.

"Why?" he asked, mesmerized.

"Because I have vowed to show ye my horses before I kill ye," she said suddenly, and drew away with a jerk. "Now get back to the tower, Forbes, before I change my mind."

God, she was infuriating! Roderic padded silently about his dark tower room. One minute she trembled, the next she teased, and the next she threatened. It was making him angry. It was making him crazy. It was making him . . . randy. Heaven's gate, she aroused him.

Finding his pallet with a sigh, Roderic stared at the ceiling. Even after everything she had put him through, the mere thought of her heated his blood. Without trying, he could remember how her soft, leather hose hugged her thighs, how the simple saffron shirt caressed her breasts and her buttocks. But more than that, he could remember the light in her eyes as she rode, the turn of her wrist as she gestured, the sound of her voice when she . . .

God's wrath! He was on his feet in a moment and pacing again. He had acted the fool since the first moment he had laid eyes on her. He shouldn't have trusted her ruse that night at Glen Creag. In retrospect, he couldn't imagine how he could have believed her to be a simple Highland maid, for she had the bearing of a laird and the beauty of a goddess. He should have immediately realized she was not what she seemed. He shouldn't have been duped. He shouldn't have been taken. He shouldn't have kissed her. And he shouldn't have allowed himself to be locked away in this tower again.

He stopped by the open shutters to look down into the darkness below. It was time to go home, but . . .

She had trembled when he kissed her. Was that fear or budding passion? The question still haunted him. Still begged to be answered.

Gripping the plaid near his chest, Roderic stared into the night. He would be a fool to stay much longer. He tapped his forefinger against his brooch. He would be an even bigger fool to go to her bedchamber again. A really big fool. A huge fool. But . . .

He grinned. Leith had often called him a fool.

Suddenly he knew he would go to her chamber. But this time he would not go empty-handed. Hurrying to his simple table, he picked up the quill they had brought him earlier. With that quill he had carefully penned a message to his brothers. In the missive he had begged them not to be hasty. He had assured them of his safety and asked them not to retaliate. In short, Roderic had done everything he had promised Flanna he would do.

But he had also told them he had no way to escape.

Roderic could imagine his brothers reading such a missive. Leith would snort at the ridiculousness of the words. Colin would laugh out loud, for never had there

been a room from which Roderic the Rogue could not
escape.

No. The brothers Forbes would not come to his res-
cue. They would read his message. They would understand his meaning, and they would stay put and bide
their time, risking no lives and allowing Roderic an opportunity to take care of important business. Such as
watering that tiny bud of passion he had felt blooming
within Flanna.

Roderic grinned at the parchment, dipped the quill
into the ink, and began to write.

Flanna lay on her side with her back toward him. The
descent from the tower prison had gone smoothly despite
the rain that wet the stone walls.

Roderic pulled the note from his sporran, and set it
on her pillow. She had been so sure he could not escape.
What would she think when she awoke to find the letter?
He could imagine her reading it. His tender words would
stoke her woman's soul. But he must not forget the warrior in her, for that facet was likely to skewer him to the
wall should she find him in her chambers. Roderic
turned, preparing to leave when he noticed her shoulder
was bare. It gleamed with the luster of a pearl and was
framed by the flaming mass of her unruly hair.

He held his breath, knowing he should leave. But the
castle slept and the sight of the warrior woman drew
him. Ever so carefully, he perched on her mattress and
reached cautiously forward. The tress of hair he touched
was as soft as he had expected. It curled about his index
finger with careless abandon. If only the lass herself
would relax in his presence. But no. She was cool and
aloof, only letting down her guard during sleep, when
she looked like an angel.

Roderic spared a grin for his romantic notions. Yet it
was true. She did look angelic and innocent in her guile-
less sleep. But if she were innocent where men were
concerned, why did she fear his nearness so?

Had some man hurt her? The thought made Roderic's

stomach twist. He knew there would be men who would resent her. They would be the same men who were intimidated by her position and her power. A noise from the far side of the door cut his musings short.

Without a moment's delay, Roderic dropped to the floor and rolled beneath the bed. However, the door didn't open and no other sounds could be heard. Had someone discovered his escape and followed him here? He lay very still, waiting.

"Nevin."

Though it was nearly inaudible he recognized Marjory's voice. There was a whispered protest, but in a moment he heard the soft rustle of fabric and knew the couple was well occupied. Strange, for Nevin did not seem like a lady's man, and Marjory seemed a shy lass. Perhaps he was taking advantage of her. Perhaps Roderic should put a stop to it, he thought, and then nearly laughed aloud at his foolishness. These were not his people, nor was a midnight tryst any of his business. Still, lasses were under the protection of their laird, or in this case, under Flanna's protection. Perhaps he should tell her of the affair. Instead, he lay perfectly still, waiting. Minutes slipped by in utter silence but he could well imagine the couple's activities. Roderic scowled. He had a pain in his back and his imaginings were not making him any more comfortable. The wooden floor beneath him was hard and cold and he was separated from *his* would-be partner by nothing more substantial than a sagging mattress . . . and the threat of death. An oaken knot pressed into his spine. Roderic shifted, trying to ease the ache, but it only moved the pain to his shoulder. He shifted again and knocked his head on the bed's frame.

He knew the moment Flanna awoke. The soft sighs of her breathing ceased. The mattress rustled quietly. He heard her roll over and held his breath.

A half hour elapsed, creaking along by rusty minutes. Was she asleep? He couldn't be sure, but it was unlikely that dawn would delay its advent on his account. He would have to risk an escape before someone discovered he was missing. Suffice it to say the MacGowans would be rather put out to find him creeping about their lady's bedchamber in the wee hours of the morning.

Ever so quietly, Roderic eased to his left. His shoulder slipped past the edge of the mattress. He allowed himself one shallow waft of air and then . . .

"Pity's sake," Flame sighed.

Roderic froze. The mattress dipped. The ropes moaned and suddenly the girl's bare feet brushed his sleeve. He held his breath and squeezed in his arms but dared not move farther, lest she hear him.

On slim, silent feet, she padded across the floor. Roderic allowed himself another shallow breath, scooted a scant inch to his right and stilled, watching her with unblinking eyes.

She paced to the window and opened the shutters. A spattering of rain flitted in. Flanna lifted her hand, letting a few drops strike her palm before hooking the blinds back in place and striding to the fireplace. Only a few embers glowed there. Dear God, please don't let her see the note he had left on her pillow. Not until he was safely back in the tower.

Lifting a poker from its place by the stone hearth, she hefted it thoughtfully in her hand. The thing would make an effective weapon, Roderic reasoned, if she knew he was there. But of course she did not. And so long as she remained standing, he was well hidden.

In perfect unison with his thoughts, she seated herself on the hearth.

Roderic dared not do so much as blink. 'Twas just like her to spite him.

"What am I to do?" she murmured.

It seemed she looked straight at him. But if she did, having men squashed under her bed must be a nightly occurrence, for she showed not the least bit of surprise. Roderic drew a cautious breath. There was a cramp in his lower back, but he dared not move. Finally she turned away to jab at the embers. After adding kindling, she set the poker aside and tucked her bare feet beneath the hem of her voluminous gown.

Light from the rekindled flame danced on the unruly mass of her hair, setting each individual strand to glistening brilliance. Her profile was flawless, sun-touched ivory rimmed by the bright orange of the blaze behind her. Through the sheer fabric of her gown, he could see the curves of the fine form God had given her.

Roderic found he no longer desired to breathe, for even had he allowed it, he wouldn't have been able to draw a normal breath. What leather hose and manly attire had not shown him, the firelight did, and he was entranced. Every movement she made seemed poetic— the way she brushed her hair aside, how her slim fingers lay softly curled upon her knees. Her pale gown was stretched taut over her buttocks. He could imagine his hand settling there, smoothing along that gentle, rounded curve.

Roderic exhaled softly. Heaven's gate, she was a bonny thing, and though she was always comely, seeing her thus cast a different light on his thoughts of her. She was not the steel-hard warrior woman he had thought her to be.

She was a woman with a woman's strengths and weaknesses. And yet she was more. She was a leader with a huge burden to shoulder. A gifted trainer of steeds. A temptress with a fiery temper.

But now she seemed like nothing more than a lonely lass.

The sight of her thus pulled at him, for surely he could help shoulder her burdens. Surely he could help find solutions to the problems that troubled her. And surely he could give her comfort and companionship.

Why not take her in his arms and offer those things?

But suddenly a slight noise startled her. She rose with the grace of a wildcat. Poker in hand, she stalked toward the door.

He wouldn't reveal himself because she would kill him, Roderic remembered. And if she didn't manage the job, her men would gladly pitch in. Gawd's wrath, he must be insane.

Out of his sight now, he heard her open the door with a noiseless jerk. There was a gasp and then a moment of silence before he heard her sigh. "Marjory."

"Aye, lady," came the servant's breathy voice. "I am here."

"Ye look flushed. Was it ye that made a noise?"

There was a moment's delay, then, "Aye, lady. There was . . . somemat in me pallet. Lice," she hurried to add. "There was lice in me pallet. And they were bedeviling me."

Roderic almost chuckled. Lice was not the only devil in her pallet.

" 'Tis sorry I be, lady."

"No need for apologies. I'm just fretful, I suppose."

"Ye canna sleep again?" clucked the maidservant. "Poor thing. So many worries. Can I get ye somemat? A cup of ale, mayhap?"

"Don't bother yourself, Marjory. Sorry to have frightened ye." She paused for a moment, then, "Go back to sleep," she said, but her words were issued from the hall, and already he could hear her feet padding softly away "Don't concern yourself if I am gone until morning."

"Good morningtide, Flanna," Roderic said, not bothering to rise from his pallet. He was tired and irritated. Where the hell had she gone in her flimsy nightgown in the middle of the night? To her lover's room?

For a moment she stared at his legs. They were bent at the knee and bare to midthigh but she couldn't see more. In an instant, her gaze snapped to his face. Her cheeks were pink. Perhaps he had been wrong about the view, he deduced, feeling somewhat better.

" 'Tis early ye come this morning," he said, sitting up and swinging his bare feet to the floor. "I hope ye slept well." God's wrath! Where had she gone? He had stayed beneath her bed until just before dawn, but she had not returned. Frustration made him rise abruptly to his feet and mentally grind his teeth. He had been patient. Hell, he had known her for nearly half a week. Why wasn't she infatuated with him when he couldn't seem to spend a single minute without thinking of her? "What brings ye to me lofty tower? I hope there is na cause for alarm."

"Nay." Her tone was very taut. Last night she had looked young and unprotected. But there was little of the innocent child in the woman who stood before him. "Why should there be?"

"Indeed, there should na," he said with a shrug. "All is right with the world. Or at least . . . all is right within the confines of this tower." He lifted his hand to indicate the small space which was allowed him. Who the hell had she been with? "Why na allow me the freedom of Dun Ard?" The words escaped him before he had time to make them sound charming.

She narrowed her catlike eyes at him. Good God, she was stunning.

"I am becoming restive in this place." Indeed, the thought of her with another man made him want to pace. At first he had thought her cold and unfeeling. Later he was certain she had been hurt and would not allow herself to be wounded again. The knowledge that she was simply not interested in him made him insane. "I'm not used ta such confinement. Even the English are na so cruel as to give their prisoners na leeway. King James was educated and allowed to live at court during *his* captivity. Surely I could, at the least, be given permission ta take me meals in the hall." And learn where she spent her nights. "After all, where could I go? I could never escape with so many eyes watching me," he continued, glancing past her to the men in the hall. "I am getting cramped from lack of exercise." He flexed an arm.

She didn't seem to notice.

He frowned. "I would be willing ta work for the privilege of some freedom. I could dig ye a new well," he said. God's wrath, he would dig from here to London if it would afford him a chance to learn more about her.

"And soil your hands?" For a moment he thought she would laugh at him.

He grasped his plaid near his brooch and pushed back his anger. "They've been soiled afore."

"Truly? When?"

She was mocking him. "Ye ken little of me and mine, wee Flanna. I would that ye'd learn the truth."

She watched him with solemn eyes and for a moment he thought she was questioning her own misconceptions, but instead of voicing inquiries, she turned away. "I have not the manpower to worry over the well at this time. We can continue to draw water from the burn for a while longer."

"But what if ye are besieged. Ye must have fresh water inside the walls."

"Besieged?" She turned smoothly back and laughed. "As ye said, Forbes, my people are all but starving. What do we have that others might covet?"

"Horses," he said easily.

He knew in an instant that he had struck a sensitive chord, for her expression went cold. Did she regret telling him of her breeding program?

He was tempted to soothe her worries, to tell her that he would hurt neither her dreams nor her people, but she wasn't ready to believe him. "I will dig the well," he said. "I need na help. But I do require some activity other than staring at the ceiling of this tower."

"Then ye have not..." she began and stopped abruptly. He waited. "Ye have not..." Lowering her voice, she took three steps forward—"left this place?"

So she had gotten his note and she had thought of him. Did she have a lover she had told? Had he been jealous? Roderic almost smiled. Instead, he forced his brows upward in an expression of innocence. "Mayhap ye think I sprouted wings and went flying about Dun Ard by night. Only"—he laughed, feeling a bit more at ease—"I missed this tower so I came back here to perch?"

For several moments she held him with her eyes, but finally her gaze drifted to the window. "A rider leaves even now with your message for Laird Leith," she said, keeping her tone perfectly steady. "I thought ye might wish to know."

"Aye." Roderic nodded, watching her. He wished she would not look out that window, for he thought he might have bent one of the hinges on his hurried flight up the plaids. He had lain for a long while under her bed, and though he had told himself he merely waited to make certain Marjory slept, he knew he awaited Flanna's return. "Me thanks. But ye have na answered me regarding dining in the hall."

She flickered her gaze briefly to him before turning her attention away and striding to the window. "And why would a Forbes wish to be pressed in among the MacGowans?" she asked, gazing out toward the distant kitchens.

Roderic shrugged, trying to rid himself of his tension. From where he stood he could see now that the hinge was indeed bent. "'Tis a fault of mine," he admitted blithely. "I like people."

Flame scowled, not turning from the window. "Even MacGowans?" she asked, placing a hand on the shutter.

Roderic pinned his gaze on her fingers. They were inches from the crooked hinge, and now he thought he could see a frayed thread of brown woolen caught upon a splinter nearby. "It be difficult ta say whether I like MacGowans or na, lass, since I've been granted so little opportunity to mingle with them."

She remained silent, still studying the world outside before absently closing one shutter.

"And, too," Roderic added, hoping to distract her, "our meeting was hardly of the most pleasant nature. After all, ye did lie ta me from the verra start. Ye did . . ." Her hand had moved on the listing shutter. "Ye did take advantage of me trusting spirit. 'Tis true, lass," he rambled on. "It didna enter me head that such a lovely maid as yerself might seek to play me for a fool. Might even"—he waved wildly and shook his head, trying to draw her attention—"even seek to hold me hostage."

She turned to watch him, and for a moment he lost his breath, so grand and proud did she look against the dark backdrop of the stormy sky.

"I fear 'tis another fault of mine," he murmured, finding his train of thought. "I be forever misjudging women." Never had he misjudged a woman. Not until he had met Flanna. But now he was making a habit of it. "Must be me lack of experience."

Hand still on the shutter, she turned a bit more toward him. "I think ye be the one playing *me* for a fool, Forbes."

"Me?" He tapped his brooch, feeling honestly offended. "How so?"

"Forgive me if I do not think ye gained the name Rogue because of the time ye've spent playing flute for the sheep."

"In all honesty, lass," he said, feeling a bit better for the reminder of the name his kinsmen had given him, "I have a gift for quieting sheep."

"And for quieting women?"

He raised his brows at her. Thinking her jealous would definitely improve his frame of mind.

"I would guess ye have tossed more innocent lasses than I could count," she said.

He dropped his hand to his side and canted his head. "Tossed?" he asked, his tone sober as he straightened. "Nay."

For a moment there was a flash of something in her eyes. "Nay?" she asked. "Ye are saying ye would not . . ."

He watched her closely. The young lass was back, uncertain, innocent, and more beautiful than the heather on the hills. He took a step nearer. "What?"

"Are ye saying ye would not"—she faltered, groping

for the correct words—"dishonor . . ." Her gaze turned nervously to her hand, and suddenly her body became stiff.

In profile, he could see her scowl as she plucked the snagged thread from the shutter. It was brown—as was the plaid of the clan Forbes. She turned abruptly, holding the yarn between her fingers. Her expression had gone hard, he noticed, but he kept his own blithe as he watched her.

"Yours?" she asked softly.

He shrugged, trying to disavow his tension. "Mayhap."

"How did it get there?"

He shrugged again. He was ready to offer an innocent explanation, but looking into the deep intelligence of her eyes he knew such would never work.

So instead he made his expression very sober and stepped nearer. " 'Tis like this. I wished ta escape. Indeed, I jumped ta the window. 'Twas a tight fit but I squeezed through. Then I"—he scowled, thinking—"I knew I couldna jump so far below," he said, hurrying to the window to stand beside her and gaze down at the wall beneath them. "So I . . . removed me plaid." He nodded, as though thinking his story quite clever. "I took off me plaid and tied it to"—he glanced quickly about—"to that hinge. See there. 'Tis bent from me weight." He was very close to her now.

Her face was smooth as marble and showed no expression other than cool disdain. "So ye crawled down your plaid?"

"Aye."

She raised her brows, causing a single wrinkle to appear in her forehead. The Flame of the MacGowans would age well, Roderic deduced, if she were afforded the opportunity to age at all. If she were not killed raiding or feuding. She would not go to fat but would keep the tone of youth and vitality for many years. For she was royalty in spirit as well as in blood.

"But your plaid was not long enough?" she asked,

playing along with his story. "So ye climbed back up to await your breakfast?"

"Nay," he said and grinned. "I dropped down." He glanced at the wall below and grimaced. "Though, 'twas a frightful long way, I managed to hit the wall."

"Aye?" She tilted her head at him.

"Aye."

"And what did ye do once ye got there?"

"Oh . . ." He shrugged casually. "I jumped down to the bailey."

"Ye didn't even bother taking the stairs?"

"Nay." He shook his head, making a disdainful expression. "Thought I, if I can manage ta hit the wall, tis certain I can hit the earth."

For a moment the flicker of honest amusement lighted her eyes and teased her lips. "Truly?"

He stared at her, entranced, before finding his voice. "Nay. I lie, lass," he said softly. "But I dunna lie about this—I had nothing ta do with Simon's death. And neither did me people."

She watched him in silence before drawing a deep breath. "Promise ye will not try to escape."

It would be so easy to become lost in her eyes. "Why would I wish to?" he asked.

"Promise me."

"This day I will na escape."

"Bullock, Forbes will be free to roam Dun Ard and take his meals in the hall henceforth."

"Aye, me lady."

"But keep an eye on him."

"Aye, me lady."

"And Bullock," she added, turning abruptly, her back straight as a lance as she stared first at Roderic and then at the window, "bind the shutters closed."

Chapter 9

The bitch still lived. Forbes should have killed her. He should have slit her throat with her own jeweled dirk and fled. But he had failed. Even when he had been left alone with her, when he had been given every opportunity, he had failed. Instead, he had kissed her. And the bitch had kissed him back, like a hound in heat.

So she was falling for the cur's charm, was she? Well, all the better, because when Forbes died, she would mourn, and then she would follow him to hell where women like her belonged.

"Has anyone seen me bonnet?" asked an aging fellow with a balding head.

"Anyone seen me tartan?" growled another.

Roderic ignored the questions as did the others at the table, for 'twas the third night in a row they had asked the same. Only Roderic knew both items were safely hidden beneath his humble pallet in the tower.

"So it be true that Lady Fiona Forbes be the verra daughter auld Ian MacAulay lost as a babe?" asked old Alexander. He had a marked shortage of teeth and was usually the first to seat himself close to Roderic during meals, for he loved a good tale as well as any man there.

The hall was busy this evening. The balding fellow and his companion moved off, mumbling about thieves in their midsts. Warriors and servants and roving hounds mingled. 'Twas the fourth day Roderic had been allowed in the hall, but still he hadn't learned anything about

Flanna's nocturnal whereabouts. "Aye," he said in answer to the old gaffer's question. "Fiona is Ian Mac-Aulay's daughter. And me brother, Leith, has the scars ta prove it."

There were chuckles from his circle of listeners. " 'Tis said she be a feisty thing," commented someone.

"Feisty?" Roderic raised the drinking horn to his lips. In the past days he had come to know these people. In fact, he had stood elbow to elbow with a few, heaving a shovel or pick. Digging a well in the rocky earth of Dun Ard was not a simple endeavor, but it did relieve some of his roiling frustration. "Nay. A wildcat is feisty. Lady Fiona is ... dangerous."

More chuckles greeted his words. There were few traits the Highlander appreciated more than spirit. "But is she na a healer?"

Roderic canted his head, then stabbed a piece of venison from a nearby trencher. " 'Tis truth I tell ye, lads," he began, then paused for effect as he held the meat high. "Were Fiona here, she could breathe life into this buck's lungs."

Groans of disbelief greeted his words, but Roderic pulled his most offended expression and continued. "Dunna doubt me words. The beast would stand upon this verra table, complete with hide and hair and a full rack of antlers."

The groans grew in volume, generously peppered with chuckles. The MacGowans did not resent Roderic's propensity to stretch the truth. In fact, if their demeanor toward him was any indication, they believed his vow that he had nothing to do with Simon's death and the loss of their stock. But if they did, they were not yet willing to set him free. Only to listen to his tales and delay further judgment. "Gawd's truth," he lied glibly.

The chuckles turned to laughter, and not a person turned away. Leith had oft said Roderic could entrance a snake if given a couple mugs of ale and a few viable lies. He grinned and drank again. The MacGowans, it seemed, were not so different from the Forbeses. Less prosperous, less prolific, but with the same zest for life and the same proud spirit.

"And I suppose the lady's beauty rivals the splendor of the sun," said someone.

Roderic lifted his gaze from his horn. " 'Twould take the multitude of stars and the moon itself ta so much as dim her glory. Her eyes . . ." He lifted his hand, palm upward. "They are like two jewels so rare that none can afford their value. Deep as Loch Ness and just as mysterious, they are. And her hair . . ." He sighed dramatically. " 'Tis rich as winter berries and burns with its own light. Aye," he said with a shake of his head. "When Lady Fiona is near, na fire need be lit, for her beauty warms the hall like a thousand blazes."

"Woe ta us!" someone said loudly. "For if Laird Leith knows yer feelings for his lady, he will surely leave ye here forever."

There was laughter from every listener. Roderic, too, chuckled. Lifting his horn to the speaker, he nodded in concession. "Set in plenty of supplies, lads," he said. "Winter comes early and I like ta eat well."

"Lock up the lasses," someone warned. "If Roderic the Rogue be staying."

"Nay," called another. "Methinks we need na fear, for he says there is none to rival his sister by law and the Rogue Forbes seems fair smitten by her."

"Smitten? Mayhap," said Roderic, finally letting his gaze rest on Flanna. She sat upon a high-backed chair at the center of the hall. Although the benches around her table were filled, she spoke to no one. "But I didna say there were none ta rival her beauty."

"Merely that the moon and stars could na."

"Aye," Roderic conceded. "But far be it from me to think a lass is na more inspiring than the constellations."

"Dare touch that inspiration, lad, and the Flame will burn yer fingers off," warned old Alexander, leaning close and nodding toward the lady of the hall.

Roderic drew his gaze from Flanna to settle it on the old man's weathered face. "Ye think so?"

"Aye." The old one nodded. "She be our flame, and too hot for the likes of ye."

"Now get back, lads," said the maid called Effie as she tried to push her way through the mob with a fresh pitcher of ale. "Canna ye let Forbes eat in peace for a moment's time?"

"We be discussing important business here," complained a nearby warrior.

"Aye, I ken what be important ta ye men," she said, then gasped as someone's hand found her well-padded bottom. Though she tried to look angry, there was a spark of humor in her eyes. "Ye most likely be discussing which lass has the softest bum."

They chortled in response before a man named James spoke up. "If that be the question, I would be the one ta ask, for the maids have a weakness for me."

Several men groaned. Someone threw a bit of venison at him. It caught in James' beard, and he picked it out with a chuckle and ate it.

"And whose would ye say would be the softest, Forbes?" asked Alexander.

"Softest?" Roderic mused, not shifting his gaze from Flanna's back. "Perhaps 'tis firmness I desire. The firmness of a rider's seat."

"Dunna even think about her," warned James, anger sparking in his eyes. "She is na for the likes of ye."

"Nay." Nevin slipped onto a bench, holding a mug and scowling thoughtfully. "But I fear she is na for any man."

"What do ye mean by that?" asked James.

Nevin's fair cheeks colored, and he quickly took a quaff of beer. "I have already said more than I should."

"What are ye talking about, lad?" Alexander asked.

"She is a brave woman," Nevin said quickly.

"Na one said she was na," James reminded him.

"And I would give my life for her," Nevin said. "I would fight any man who would say she should not rule the MacGowans, any man who would say it is not a woman's place. That we are not men enough to choose a true laird, that we are laughed at by the other tribes.''

Around the table, the men were suddenly quiet.

"I am na laughing," Roderic said.

Nevin stared at him for a moment, then pulled his gaze away.

"I worry about none of that," Nevin continued. "It is good that she leads us. But what of an heir? Should she not have a husband?"

"And what makes ye think she willna?"

"Because she prefers her stallions," said Nevin.

"Damn ye!" James swore, rising to his feet.

But Nevin had already gone pale. "I did not mean it like that. Sweet mother of God, I but mean she spends so much of her time in the stable. I've seen nothing to suggest any . . . sinful acts with her steeds. Truly . . ." He seemed to be trying to convince them, and yet the flush on his normally pale face suggested the opposite. "I've seen nothing."

No one at the table spoke. But not far away someone laughed, accentuating the silence. James found his seat.

Effie cleared her throat. "Well, 'tis a lot any of ye know," she said, "for 'tis said the Flame has chosen her kindling."

"What?" Alexander asked.

Effie leaned close as she poured a bit of beer into the old man's horn. "She has a suitor."

"What?" Nevin said, looking up quickly. Marjory started at the sound of his voice and glanced up from where she poured a drink for her lady several rods away.

"How ye be knowing this, Effie?" James asked.

"Was bound to happen," said old Alexander.

But despite his words, every man there seemed relieved, as if they thought Flanna's independence somehow unnatural. As if they thought she had no desire for a man. Obviously, none of them had ever felt her tremble beneath his hands. That thought made Roderic feel slightly better, but he reined in his optimism and concentrated on Effie's next words.

"Marjory told me," she said.

"Her maid?"

"Aye."

"And what did she say? Who be the lad?"

Effie drew herself up, enjoying her importance. "I am thinking I have already said too much."

"Devil take it!"

"Tell us, lass."

"Verra well," agreed Effie, eagerly leaning nearer. " 'Tis said there was a love note on her pillow some days past."

"Nay! On her pillow?"

There were hushed denials and arguments.

" 'Tis true." Effie nodded smugly. "Marjory saw it with her own eyes before the lady snatched it away."

Roderic allowed himself a single sigh of relief. So Flanna's suitor was himself. Still, that did not explain her nocturnal whereabouts. But if she had a lover, she must keep him well hidden indeed.

"I dunna ken who," Effie whispered. "But if I had ta place me bets I'd put me coin on Troy."

Troy! It took all of Roderic's self-control to keep from jerking to his feet and screaming the man's name out loud.

Old Alexander had no such inhibitions. "Troy!" he cackled softly. " 'Tis daft ye are. He's auld enough ta be her da."

The toothless way he said it made a few men chuckle. Roderic was not amongst them. Neither was Effie.

"Aye, but he's still a virile man, and there are them who like their men well aged."

"Nay," argued someone. " 'Tis Bullock she favors."

"Burke?"

"He's a right braw lad."

Bullock! Roderic steamed in silence. Good Lord, not Bullock. He had a fat neck.

"Bullock would be a fine choice for the Flame. Their bairns would be as braw as the oak. Dunna ye agree, Forbes?" asked Alexander, turning to Roderic. But Roderic had risen to his feet. "Forbes?" he said. "Where ye be going?"

Roderic didn't answer, for Flanna was within his sight and anger was in his soul.

She didn't look at him as he approached her table.

He remained silent a moment, soothing his temper. "Good eventide," he said to the side of her head.

She turned finally, showing in her cool emerald eyes that she had been well aware of his presence for some time.

"Might I sit and share a few words?"

"As ye can see, all seats are taken," she said, nodding toward the far end of her table.

"Aye," he said, "but I have important issues ta speak of." Had she met someone in the dark of the night? Didn't she know that he lov . . . lusted after her? Hadn't she read his note? Of course he hadn't signed it, but he had thought she would hope it was from him. Perhaps, instead, she had shown it to her lover. Perhaps they had even laughed over it.

"Such as?" she asked.

"Such . . . such as?" he repeated, losing the trail of their conversation.

"What did ye wish ta discuss, Forbes?"

"Ahh," he said, trying to sound thoughtful. Heaven's gate, he was acting like a love-smitten, knobby-kneed lad. " 'Tis . . .'tis a matter of some import."

"So ye have said."

"And should be spoken of in private."

"I believe my people have a right to hear words that may affect their lives."

Despite his anger, Roderic could not help but admire her. She was as regal as a queen, filled with beauty and intelligence and a caring she kept carefully hidden. In short, the MacGowans did not deserve her, for they did not appreciate her as they should. They thought her unnatural. More interested in her stallions than men, indeed! What a ridiculous notion. But he could make them see her value, if he were her husband.

God's wrath! He was losing his mind! He would have to be a pain-loving dolt to wish to tie himself to any woman who called herself the Flame.

"Say what ye've come to say," she ordered.

Who is your lover? He almost asked the question that hounded him. But good sense and the desire to remain alive stopped him. " 'Tis about a cistern." Good God! A cistern? Sometimes it seemed that his lips were possessed when he was near her. Even he could not guess what they might say next.

"A cistern?" she asked. Those around her table had gone absolutely silent. Every man there watched him. He used to have some pride, Roderic reminded himself. Where had it gone?

"Aye, a cistern. If properly designed, ye could draw water on every floor of Dun Ard."

Beside her, Troy rose to his great height, and Roderic could not help but think the man looked disgusted. " 'Tis truly a personal matter ye have ta discuss with her, Forbes," he murmured and then he said more loudly, "Take me seat."

Roderic did so, but the quiet that surrounded them was chilling. Close at hand, several warriors rose and left in rapid succession.

"Is it me?" Roderic asked.

Flanna toyed with her roasted ptarmigan before finally raising her gaze. "Nay, Forbes. I have promised to sell three trained steeds to the MacGraw. It seems my men do not approve of my decision to deliver them myself. They think it unbecoming of Dun Ard's lady. They did not say whether it was unbecoming of their leader. Mayhap they forget I am both." She watched him carefully.

Despite himself, Roderic smiled. She was a rare one, and he would not insult her intelligence by pretending things were different than they were. "Mayhap 'tis yer manly attire that they find disconcerting," he said quietly. "It could make them feel less like men."

Her eyes met his in sudden, brilliant shards of green. "And does it make ye feel less manly, Forbes?"

"Nay," he said on a soft breath, feeling the impact of her presence to the depths of his soul. "Ye make me feel more the man." For one instant it seemed there was no one on the earth but the two of them. But in a moment, she turned her gaze to her trencher.

"Do ye know how to construct a cistern, Forbes?" she asked. Her tone was suddenly cool, as if she had felt none of the heat between them. What would it take to penetrate her defenses, to have her trust him? But, in truth, that was not all he wanted. He wanted *her*, he realized suddenly. He wanted her in his arms and in his bed, true. But he also wanted himself in her thoughts. He wanted to know she dreamed of him and only him. And yet, it seemed as if she could dismiss him out of hand.

" 'Tis said ye have chosen a lover," he whispered, needing to draw her attention back to him.

It worked. Her sharp gaze snapped to his. "How dare ye?" she gasped.

Roderic kept his gaze pinned to her face. It was suddenly pale. He had been a fool to say the words, of course. And why had he? He was a master at this game of seduction. What made him act the dolt now? "Shall I take that as a denial?" he asked softly.

"Ye can take that and shove—"

"Is Forbes bothering ye, me lady?" asked Nevin.

"Nay." She didn't look up as she said the word. "Do not concern yourself."

Nevin's narrow hand trembled near his sword, as though he were afraid to lay his hand on the hilt, but there was a passionate light in his eyes. "The lady is not interested in the likes of ye, Forbes," he said. "Say the word, lady, and I will find the courage to run him through."

Roderic rose without thought. "Do ye wish ta try?"

Flame jumped to her feet, and pointed to Roderic's chair. "Sit!" she demanded, then drew a deep breath, calming her tone. "I said he is not bothering me, Nevin. Go."

The quiet sensitivity in Nevin's eyes was momentarily replaced by a fierce light. But it disappeared in an instant, and he turned away.

With a soft exhalation, Roderic sat. If he was going to continue challenging men to duals, he should at least obtain a sword first. He must keep his head, literally and figuratively. But the MacGowans' Flame had a way of making him say and do things far out of character.

"Tell me I was wrong," he said when she found her chair.

"Ye have more nerve than brains, Forbes," she said. "If I chose I could kill ye here and now."

"Tell me ye've taken na lover."

"Why?" she asked hoarsely.

"Because I can think of naught else when ye are in the room." It was a direct quote from the note he had left on her pillow. Her face went pale as freshly fallen snow.

"It was ye?" she whispered, her expression unreadable.

With everything in him, Roderic longed to say yes, to admit that he had breached her bedchamber, had watched her sleep, had seen her fine body kissed by the gentle light of the fire. "Me what?" he forced himself to ask instead.

She swallowed and pushed her hands under the table. To keep him from seeing them shake? Roderic wondered.

"Yes." When she raised her eyes again, every emotion had been deftly wiped from her face. "I do have a lover, Forbes," she said.

Roderic remained perfectly still, though his heart pounded in his chest. "Who is he?"

" 'Tis none of your concern."

"But I am concerned," he said, his voice a hoarse whisper to his own ears. "For I think that in yer heart ye are mine."

She rose rapidly, nearly unsettling her heavy chair. "Your vanity far exceeds your wit," she hissed. "I say

I have a lover, and he leaves me little time to think of any other.''

Frustration rushed through Roderic like an unchecked fire. "Aye, lass, and 'tis rumored his name is Lochan Gorm," he whispered, leaning close.

In a heartbeat, her hand gripped his shirt and her knife pricked his throat.

A woman shrieked. Men jumped to their feet. Somewhere near at hand, a pitcher dropped, splattering ale in every direction.

"It will be a pleasure to kill ye!" she growled.

"Flame!" someone yelled.

"Roderic," a woman gasped.

"Lass," Troy rumbled from behind her. "Are ye ta kill him now?"

"Mayhap?" She spoke through her teeth as she pressed the blade against Roderic's throat. "And why na?"

"Because we dunna want Forbes' blood defiling our hall."

"Damn the hall!"

"Lass." Troy's hands were on her arms now. Though Roderic didn't shift his gaze from hers, he knew the Wolfhound was trying to urge her away. " 'Twould be a waste of a good hostage."

" 'Twould be a waste of me time ta let him live."

Roderic kept his attention riveted to her face. "Rarely have I seen anyone react so violently to a *lie*," he suggested.

She pressed the blade harder against his throat. "By all that is holy, he wants to die, Troy."

"Then make him suffer, lass. Disappoint him," the Wolfhound soothed. "And let him live."

" 'Tis only a matter of time before ye are mine," Roderic whispered.

The blade shook against his throat before she yanked it away. "Take him to the tower!" she ordered. "Or feed him to the hounds."

*   *   *

Within the silent confines of her bedchamber, Flame paced. Roderic. How *dare* he say the things he had? She stopped to stare out her narrow window. Even now her hands shook.

So the gossipmongers were stirring. Even now, after she thought she had gained some loyalty. But who was she fooling? She was no laird, no chieftain, no great ruler. She was a woman. But not a whole woman. She had given that up. And for what? To please her father? But no, she had realized the futility of that long ago. She had become the Flame because the MacGowans needed her, and because she needed them. She had become the Flame to gain acceptance. But how could they accept her as she was? She was neither a woman nor a man. Neither a laird nor a peasant. She had to be more than all of those, bigger and better and different, without being too different.

There had been a time not so long ago when she had thought she could be like other women. She had dreamed a simple dream, believing, for a while, that she could be loved and cherished by a charming man. But the man chosen for her had proven himself to be less than charming and far less than honest, for he had said he adored her. The truth had shamed her to her soul. For all along, he had loved another.

Flame stared into the abyss of the night outside her window. The memory still made her want to hide as she had after her father had struck her for the first time. But cowering beneath her bed had aided her no more than her tears. And, in truth, Carvell's betrayal had forced her to stand up to her father. And though her legs had been quaking with fear, she had done so, and refused to marry her betrothed. She could remember her father's rage as if it were yesterday. Even now, she could feel his fists slam into her. The pain had echoed in her skull like distant drums. But before she had lost consciousness, she had told herself that the sins he hated her for were not her sins, but his own. So why did she still feel she must repent?

From somewhere far away, an owl called. The sound carried well in the still air. It had been just this kind of night when a small girl had climbed sick and shaky from a trunk to blink at her first sight of France. Her tears had dried and she had made a vow to be a better child. Not an evil thought would enter her mind, not a cruel word would pass her lips. She would be tractable and soft-spoken until her father would come for her. He would take her in his arms and beg for her forgiveness.

But he didn't. In fact, she had not seen him again for nearly ten years, and then only when she refused to marry. It seemed her betrothed and her father had been cast in the same mold. But that did not mean that all men were alike. 'Twas possible that a man could deal honorably with a woman, was it not?

Without meaning to, she moved to her bed. The note was there, under her pillow.

Slowly, she withdrew it and smoothed it against the white linen that covered her bosom. Pretty words. That's all they were, and yet . . . it had been a long while since she had felt like a woman.

There were tears in her eyes. They were hot and they stung, but she refused to let them fall.

It was probably just a hoax. No one could truly believe the words that were written on the parchment. No man thought her more beautiful than the heather on the hillock. There was not a man in Dun Ard who was left speechless by her presence.

But someone *had* been here only a few nights before. Someone had penned the words, slipped into her room, and watched her sleep.

The small hairs at the back of her neck stood on end. The reaction should be caused by anger, she knew, or at least by fear. But it was neither. The reaction was caused by the titillating realization that someone had stood in the dark, mere inches from her. He had thought her beautiful and had not hated her for it. Perhaps he had dreams of holding her in his arms. Perhaps he had seen past her men's clothing into her heart. Perhaps he had seen the fear and loneliness there. Perhaps he was Roderic.

Dear God! She turned quickly from the window, gripping the note. She was being a fool again.

But no longer. She would rip the parchment to shreds. Crumpling the letter in her hands, she prepared to do just that, but her fingers would not tear, her heart would not completely give up hope, though she knew she should.

Loneliness ripped at her soul, but there was someone who would listen and care, and tonight she needed him. Cramming the parchment back under her pillow, she hurried from the room.

The hall was quiet now. All the tables, but the one at which Roderic sat, had been stored against the walls. Men lay scattered about the room, asleep in the rushes and covered with their plaids. The hounds were tied at one wall. The tawny bitch he called Bonny watched him. To his right, William lay with his face squashed against the rough-grained wood of the table.

"Ye are na such a bad sssort, Forbes," Bullock said. His chin was propped precariously on the heel of his hand and his eyelids were at half mast.

"And ye are a terrible dice player. Ye owe me another drink."

Bullock failed to respond. His lids had fallen closed, but one popped open suddenly. "Did I thank ye?"

"For what?"

"For na killing me."

"Nay."

"Ahh," said Bullock before changing the subject with the clever speed seen only in one badly inebriated. "Have ye noticed that the lady Flame has eyes like emerald lochans?"

Roderic tightened his fist. Could it be that *Bullock* was Flanna's lover? he wondered, but in a moment he discarded that notion. It was far into the night. What man would choose to spend time with his comrades instead of with Flanna if he had a choice?

Bullock was not her lover. But was there someone else? Was she with him even now? Roderic slipped his gaze to the top of the steps.

"Promise ye willna escape this night, Forbes."

Was she holding someone in her arms? Was she giving her lovely, sensuous body to another even as he gambled with an intoxicated guard?

"Forbes."

"What?"

"Promise."

Roderic turned toward Bullock. Slumped over the table as he was, he looked nearly as broad as he was high. "Why should I promise now?"

"Because I am drunk. Prraps ye didna notice."

On the contrary, Roderic had noticed. In fact, he had spent most of the night causing it. "I promise."

"Ahh." Bullock lifted his mug in a sort of salute. "Ye are a good . . ." he began, but before his statement was finished, his head fell to the solid table with a resounding thump.

Roderic watched him. "Bullock?"

No answer.

"Ye are a good man, too," he said, and rising to his feet, hurried across the floor and up the stairs to Flanna's room.

Chapter 10

*S*o they laughed at Forbes' jests, admired his boldness, welcomed him into the fold. The fools! Had
they already forgotten Simon's gristly head? Had they
so easily forsaken their vows for revenge? They would
need a reminder. A poignant reminder. And what would
be so poignant, or so sweet, as Flame's head severed
from her body. Yes. Another loosed head would renew
their bloodthirst.

Marjory slept beside her mistress's door. The sound
of her breathing was soft and even. Roderic stood for a
moment, hand on the latch. He was being a fool. If he
had retained any pride, any good sense, he would march
back down those stairs and leave Flanna MacGowan to
her own diversions. After all, he was Roderic the Rogue
of the proud Forbes clan, admired by men and adored
by women. Why should he concern himself with a
haughty lass who dressed like an outlandish man and
rebuffed him at every turn, whose very hair glistened
with tempestuous life. True, her face was like flawless
marble and her figure as firm and smooth as a fine stat-
uette. Her wit was as sharp as the tip of her dirk and . . .

Jesu! Roderic swore silently and pushed the door
open.

The chamber was empty!

God's wrath! Not again! His temper suddenly boiled.
Could she embrace another when *his* touch ignited the

121

flame in her? When she was meant to be in his arms? He had to find her, and he would.

Before the foolishness of his decision dawned on him, Roderic was storming down the hall, jerking open doors to peer inside. Storage barrels, baskets of wool, and silent looms peered back.

Another door was pushed open and . . .

"Stay back!" a small voice quavered.

Roderic remained very still. The room was lit by a single candle. It washed yellow light about the tiny chamber, illuminating the narrow lad who faced him with a dirk and a countenance as pale as death.

"Wh-who are ye?" he whispered. The knife shook when he spoke.

Roderic drew a calming breath and let his gaze skim past the boy to the still form beside his low pallet. It was Flanna. Her lovely body was covered with a bright green tartan and her face was peaceful as it rested upon the edge of the boy's mattress.

So this was where she came in the deep of the night. Relief washed over Roderic like a warm evening tide.

"I said . . ." The lad's voice quavered again, but he tightened his unsteady grip and took a step nearer. "Who are you?"

"I am Roderic, of the Forbeses."

The boy's gasp was surely loud enough to wake the dead, and yet Flanna slept on. Roderic let his attention drop to her again. God, she was lovely and she was not in another's arms. But why was she here? He took a step forward to see her more clearly, but the boy brought up the dirk and spread his skinny legs. They were bare below his white nightshirt and looked as frail and knobby as a felled myrtle branch.

"You'll not harm her, Forbes. Not so long as there is br-breath in my b-body."

Roderic forced himself to contain his smile. Surely such a gallant heart should not be mocked, he thought. "I willna harm her," he said. "But may I close the door so that we dunna disturb her maidservant?"

The boy's hand shook visibly and his eyes were so large in his pale face that Roderic feared he might faint. "Why are you here?"

"I come looking for yer lady," he said and nodded casually toward Flanna, but his mind was racing. Who was this lad to her? Could it be that he was her son? A love child? Or a child of shame, born out of wedlock, forced upon her by rape? 'Twould explain much of her distrust of men.

Rage mingled with questions within Roderic, but he quieted his emotions. Easing his hand to the door, he closed it silently while watching the wide, falcon-steady eyes of the lad. "I will hurt neither ye nor her, young Hawk."

The dirk shook again, and the lad's face showed his uncertainty. "My name is not Hawk."

His hair was as black as a raven's wing, making his narrow, sharp-boned face appear very pale, and his light blue eyes seem almost silver.

"What be yer name, then?" Roderic asked.

The boy pursed his lips, and in that moment he reminded Roderic of Flanna. "'Tis Haydan. Haydan Boudreau."

"Boudreau? Then ye are na the lady's . . . relation?"

The boy looked surprised. "Nay. I but wish I had a spark of her flame. But I do not. Why have you come?"

"Because I worried for her welfare."

"You?" The lad could not have sounded more shocked if Roderic had proclaimed himself to be the devil incarnate.

"I mean her na harm, wee Hawk."

Haydan's brows lowered slightly. Intelligence was etched hard and clear on his face. "Why do you call me that?"

"Because ye have the heart of the prince of the skies."

"You mock me." The words were spoken with pride, though Roderic could hear the pain behind them.

"Nay. I dunna."

"Do not judge my mind by the size of my form." He spoke like a scholar and yet the top of his head would barely reach Roderic's lowest rib.

"I dunna. And neither do I confuse fear for cowardice."

"Are they not one and the same?"

"Nay," Roderic said. "Fear is borne of intelligence and caution. Cowardice is borne of a weak heart."

The dirk lowered slightly as the lad perused him. "The physicians say that I *have* a weak heart."

"The physicians are wrong."

"How do you know?"

"Because a lad with a weak heart would have awakened the lady and begged her to protect ye from a monstrous Forbes."

The slightest shadow of a grin lifted the boy's mouth. "Are you a monster then?"

Roderic shrugged. The boy looked weak enough to collapse. Such an event would surely cause him great shame. "If I am, I am a weary monster. Do ye mind if we sit so we might finish this discussion?"

"I see no reason to think you would be more dangerous seated than standing."

Roderic smiled and found a spot with his back to the wall. "And ye would be less dangerous," he said, nodding to the pallet.

Though his knees shook, the boy remained standing. "I have your word that you will not harm her?"

"I swear it on my father's grave," Roderic assured him.

After a moment, the lad seated himself on the edge of the mattress. He pulled his nightshirt over his bony knees and watched Roderic's face. All was quiet.

"She does not speak of you to me," Haydan said finally.

"Does she speak ta ye of other things?"

"Yes. Everything."

It seemed rather pitiable to be jealous of this frail

child, and yet perhaps it was not. "So this is where she comes when she canna sleep?"

The boy let the dirk droop to his lap as he turned to gaze at the lady on his floor. "I am usually awake and I would give much to help shoulder her burdens," he said quietly. Never had Roderic seen love shine more brightly than it did in this lad's eyes.

"Then be content, young Hawk," he said. "For ye have obviously done that, for she wouldna sleep so peacefully if yer words had not soothed her mind."

"Words!" The exclamation was scornful and surprisingly emphatic. " 'Tis all I offer, when I would take a sword and . . ." He stopped and drew several heavy breaths as if even that simple task was difficult. His lips turned a grayish blue and his throat convulsed as he struggled for air.

Mercy made Roderic wish to rush forward and help him, but mercy also held him back. For the lad needed to retain some pride.

After a few moments, a bit of color returned to the boy's face. His breathing became less labored and his muscles relaxed.

"My father was the laird of the Forbeses," said Roderic as though their conversation had never been interrupted. "He had great problems to ponder, great decisions to make, yet when he was weary he would oft come to me, though I was no more than a wee lad."

"Why?" asked the black haired Hawk.

"Because I would tell him of me day."

"Was your day so interesting then?"

Roderic smiled. "Nay. But I be an accomplished liar."

The boy laughed, and for a moment all tension left his face. "Tell me a lie, then, Roderic Forbes."

No one had ever accused Roderic of being short on words. Nearly an hour had flown by before he wound up his tale. "And so the saying—the meek shall inherit the earth—but the sneak shall inherit a first-rate pair of horsehide boots.''

Hawk laughed uproariously, but in a moment the laughter turned to choked wheezing.

''Haydan!'' Flanna awoke with a start. She turned her frantic gaze to the empty pillow then jerked it toward the door. Her gasp was just loud enough to be heard over the boy's tortured breathing. ''Forbes! Why are ye here? What have ye done?'' she demanded. Scrambling forward, she wrapped an arm about the boy's shoulder. ''Haydan, relax now. All will be well,'' she promised, but the wheezing turned to wracking coughs. Still, she held him and crooned until the fit finally ceased and the boy was able to draw breath normally. ''There now.'' Her voice was gentle and though she smiled down at the lad, Roderic could see the worry, stark and deep, in her emerald eyes. ''Were ye slaying dragons in your dreams again, lad?''

''Nay,'' said Haydan and lifted his gaze to look into her eyes. In that instant, the scene was etched in Roderic's mind—the lady warrior, soft and kind as she cradled a child against her breast. ''Forbes told me a tale. It made me laugh.''

''Dragons seem to be safer than laughter for ye, *mon amie*,'' she said softly, and though a smile tilted her lips, there was a catch in her voice. ''Ye'd best sleep now.''

''Mayhap 'tis diversion he needs more than sleep,'' Roderic suggested.

Flanna lifted her gaze to his. ''Mayhap ye wish to entertain us by telling what ye have done with your guards?''

Roderic shrugged. ''They were sleepy,'' he said simply and changed the subject. ''The lad needs a healer.''

She opened her mouth as if to reprimand him, but the boy interrupted.

''He calls me Hawk,'' he said weakly.

''Hawk?'' She turned her attention to Haydan, and then with a gentle touch she swept back a shock of midnight hair from his forehead.

"Yes," the boy whispered. "For he says I have the heart of a falcon."

"The heart of a . . ." she whispered and lifted her face to Roderic's. In that moment, he saw her confusion, as though an enemy had just offered her a priceless gift. "A falcon?"

"He says there's a difference between fear and cowardice."

" 'Tis true," she said softly, still holding Roderic's gaze. "But now ye must sleep, *mon amie*."

Haydan eased out of her embrace and scooted across the pallet to push his legs beneath the covers. Flanna rose to her feet.

"My lady?" The boy's eyes were already closed.

"Yes?"

"Hawk . . . it sounds a bit like Haydan. Does it not?"

"Indeed, it does," she murmured. For a moment longer, she stared at him before opening the door and stepping into the hall.

Roderic followed. "Should we na douse the light?"

Flanna closed the door behind them. "Nay," she said and offered no more.

"But he might knock it from its stand and ignite the chamber."

"He's scared of the dark!" she whispered, turning rapidly toward him. "He is scared. Can ye understand that? Have ye ever truly feared anything, Forbes?"

"Aye, lass, I—" he began, but suddenly her fingers gripped his shirt front and her lips found his in a kiss that trembled with emotion.

Shock stopped Roderic's breath in his throat, but in an instant, she pulled away and ran down the hall toward her own chamber.

The next morning Roderic sat at his usual table in the hall, half listening to a much-exaggerated tale. Why had she kissed him? he wondered. Where was she now? Had she already broken the fast, or had she not yet arrived?

It had been a strange night. He had not bothered waking his guards but had returned to the tower on his own. Still, sleep had been elusive, for Flanna's image haunted him. He longed to go to her room and watch her sleep, to see her face softened in slumber, to see her defenses down and her hair spread like a blazing halo around her. But it would avail him little.

What he must do was to speak to her, to learn more about her, to touch her and kiss—No! He didn't need to kiss her. He needed to apologize for being a cad, he needed to woo her and . . . God, he needed to kiss her.

But she didn't trust him, and it wasn't just because he was a Forbes. It was because he was a man. He knew that much. But he needed to know more. And he suspected Haydan could tell him.

Roderic let his gaze skim to Effie. She bore a trencher in one hand and a mug in the other. An idea sparked in his mind. He stood abruptly and crossed the hall to speak to the maid.

In less than a minute, he was in the lad's narrow room.

"Good morningtide," he said, trencher in hand.

"Roderic." The boy looked up from the book that lay on his coverlet.

"Ye read?"

"Yes. Since long before I came to Scotland."

Roderic approached the bed. "And where are ye from, lad?"

"Bastia in France."

"And yer mother, does she still live there?"

The boy was silent for a moment. "Who takes and never apologizes, gives and never rejoices?"

Roderic settled himself onto the pallet. To a bedridden boy, riddles would become like precious pearls. "The English?" he guessed foolishly.

The lad smiled but shook his head. "Death. It takes life and gives heaven."

"Is your mother in heaven then, lad?"

"Do you believe there is a heaven, Roderic the Rogue?"

"Where did ye hear that name?"

"From Effie. She says the lasses are agog at your good looks."

"Of course they are. Did she na mention me charm? Or me astounding strength?" Roderic asked, leaning closer.

Humor sparkled in the boy's intelligent eyes. "I wonder, do ye laugh at yourself or do you think yourself so marvelous, Roderic Forbes?"

"Which do ye think it be?"

The boy canted his head. "I think it is both," he said.

Roderic laughed aloud. "And I think ye are clever far beyond yer years."

"My mother is dead."

The boy's mind changed track with the speed of a winter gale. Roderic hurried to keep up.

"I am sorry."

"Some say she was a whore and that I was her punishment."

God's wrath! Who would say such a thing! "And some say there isna hell, but I say those that told ye thus are bound ta feel its flame, young Hawk."

Roderic thought he saw tears in the boy's eyes, but in a moment they lifted.

"My lady," he murmured.

Roderic turned. Flanna stood in the doorway with a trencher.

"I . . . I didn't know ye had brought Hay—Hawk's meal."

The sight of her stole his breath and his thoughts, for she looked young and vulnerable again, as if she had been caught caring for the lad when she should be out roaring orders and wielding a sword. Roderic scrambled for something to say to beat down the barrier that just now seemed to be crumbling between them. "Mayhap we should call him Black Hawk, the Great."

"Nay," piped the scrawny boy from his pallet. "Haydan, the Hawk of the Highlands."

Roderic watched Flanna's gaze lift to the lad's. The

caring there was painfully obvious, though she hardened her tone and tried to disguise her sentiments. "Ye should eat, young man."

"But I am not hungry."

"Ye must eat."

"True," said Roderic, turning to the boy. "What warrior can ride on an empty stomach?"

"The Hawk of the Highlands will sooner fly than ride," said the lad quietly.

"What? Ye have na steed?"

"He cannot ride," Flanna said quickly. "It makes him wheeze."

Roderic shrugged, still looking at Hawk. "Women have been known ta make me wheeze. It doesna mean I avoid them."

Haydan laughed.

"Troy needs to speak to ye, Forbes," Flanna said. Her tone was suddenly cool.

"Troy?"

"Yes. Immediately."

Roderic rose. "Verra well. Ye eat, Black Hawk and I will teach ye ta handle Mor."

"Mor?"

"Me stallion."

"And is he so great as his name implies?"

"Greater."

"Better than Lochan?"

Roderic opened his mouth, then snapped it shut and leaned close to Hawk's ear. "The lady already resents me, lad. I am trying to reverse the trend," he said and winked as he drew away and raised his voice. "Nay. Na steed is as great as Lochan Gorm."

"Forbes!" Her tone was frosty now.

"Aye. I am coming."

The door closed behind them. Side by side, they strode down the hall.

"What be Troy wanting?"

She stopped and turned on him very suddenly. "Ye will not promise Haydan what ye cannot deliver?"

"What?" he asked, shocked by the tears that welled in her eyes.

"He cannot ride!"

"Why?"

"Because he is dying!"

"Dying? He's small, true, but he's only a child and—"

"He is twelve years of age and the physicians cannot help him."

"Twelve?" Roderic repeated. The lad looked to be nine, maybe less.

"Aye." She seemed calmer now and clasped her hands in front of her. "I but wish for him to reach thirteen."

"Then ye canna treat him as if he's already dead."

For a moment he thought she would strike him, but she did not. Instead she pivoted on her heel and hurried away down the stairs to the hall.

"Flanna," he called, cursing himself for a thousand kinds of fool and rushing down the steps after her. The sorrow in her eyes had made him desperately want to solve her problem, but once again he had acted the fool. What was it about her that brought out the barbarian in him? "Flanna," he called again. Faces turned to watch him hurry through the crowded hall. "We need to talk."

She turned to him. Gone was the tender lass. In her place was a woman whose heart could not be touched by the injustices of this world. "No, Forbes," she said coldly, "we don't."

Chapter 11

The hall was absolutely silent as every person present watched them.

"Troy," Flanna called, "I will be riding on the green if—"

Roderic needed to be speak to her, to apologize. But not here. Not now, with a hundred ears hearing his words. "I wish ta try one of yer renowned mounts," he interrupted her, thinking of no other way to seize her attention. "If ye are na ashamed of them."

She turned toward him, her gaze sharp with anger and disdain. "If ye think to goad me with that feeble prick to my pride, Forbes, think again. I gave up shame long ago."

What did that mean? he wondered, but she was already turning away, and he had to draw her back. "But I am na convinced of the superiority of yer horses."

"And ye imagine that I care?"

"Has me brother agreed to yer demands, then?"

Her jaw tightened almost imperceptibly.

"Nor will he," Roderic said, his voice softer now. "Leith will na pay for me return, lass."

"Then mayhap we will be forced to kill ye."

"'Twould be the act of a fool, Flanna MacGowan," Roderic said. "And though ye have yer faults, ye are na a fool."

She turned away after a moment. "I'll be on the green," she repeated to Troy, but Roderic stopped her again.

132

"I swore I would see yer horses returned if ye convinced me of their worth," he said. "I canna be assured of their value until I ride them."

" 'Twould be good ta get him from the castle."

Flame scowled and turned at Troy's words. The Wolfhound stood close beside them and shrugged apologetically.

" 'Tis the men, lass, they get nothing accomplished while Forbes is spinning yarns. Na ta mention the women." He scowled. " 'Twould be good ta have him gone for a wee bit."

Roderic scowled. Since when did the Wolfhound take his side? he wondered, but now was not the time to spit on a helping hand. "I wish only ta see what ye do with yer stallions." Damn! Bad wording, he thought, remembering the horrid things he had accused her of earlier. "That is ta say, I but wish ta watch . . ." He stumbled, seeing her expression grow frostier by the moment. "I mean, they seem ta love ye so . . ." He winced outwardly now, seeing no hope of hiding his unusual clumsiness. "Well, Wolfhound, how are ye ta save me from her this time?" he finally asked in exasperation.

If Roderic wasn't mistaken, there was a light of laughter in the huge warrior's eyes.

"Methinks I will let ye blather on, lad, and see how she decides ta kill ye in the end."

Roderic sighed and found her gaze again. " 'Twould be a kindness to make it quick," he murmured tonelessly. If ever he had bumbled a plea, this was the time. 'Twould serve him right if she did kill him. No one who acted as idiotically as he did of late deserved to live. And there wasn't a chance in hell she would ride with him.

"Come along."

Roderic raised his brows, certain he had misheard. "What?"

"Come along," she repeated and turned away.

He followed in her wake but not so close that he could not admire her movements. She walked like no other woman in the world. But hardly did she walk like a man. Nay. There was a lithe smoothness to her movements, an easy, catlike grace that spoke of strength and control.

"Why do ye truly wish to ride?"

She had stopped and turned. Roderic halted and felt a hound's wet nose bump the back of his bare knee. Raising his gaze abruptly to Flame's eyes, he damned himself for not concentrating. She distrusted him already. There was no need to compound the problem by ogling her at every turn.

But he couldn't help it.

"What?" he asked, feeling more foolish by the moment.

"I said, why do ye truly wish—"

"Ahh," he interrupted, remembering her question. "I wish ta see for meself how yer steeds move."

"Ye wish to escape," she countered dryly.

Roderic took a deep breath. He was past the age of being smitten like a lovesick calf. Gawd's wrath, he was six and twenty years of age. "Nay," he denied softly. "I wish ta apologize."

The morning was very still. Not a breath of air stirred. They stared at each other.

"For what?" she murmured.

"For the things I have said."

"Ye called him Hawk, and ye made him smile," she said softly and disappeared inside the stable.

Roderic hurried after her. Close at hand, a giant hoof thudded against a wall. Bruid's deep-throated trumpet echoed in the dim building, but all Roderic's attention was on Flanna.

"And so ye would forgive the unforgivable for one brief glimpse of Haydan's smile."

"He is but a child," she whispered, "who has done nothing to deserve his plight." There were tears in her eyes again.

"Flanna," Roderic whispered, stepping forward, but she held up a hand.

"Ye have my thanks, Forbes. Don't ask for more."

"Flanna," he repeated, but she had already turned away.

"Ye will ride the bay in the next stall," she said. Her tone was hard and cool again. "Know ye how to saddle yer own beast? Or do the mighty Forbeses have squires to do such lowly tasks?"

Silence settled over the stable.

"Well?" she asked, finally emerging with Lochan. But Roderic already had Cam saddled and was watching her.

"Why do ye hide yer kindness behind chilly words and hard expressions?

She strode quickly past him, refusing to answer. "Mount up if ye're coming along."

Roderic caught her arm. "I promise na ta escape this day. In case ye be worrying."

Flame stared at him. He was less than two feet away. His eyes were as blue as a Highland Harebell and his mouth tilted like that of an enchanting boy's—or like a scheming demon's. Nay, she was not worried he would escape. She was worried he might not.

The truth hit her like a blow. Even in her own mind, she hadn't admitted it. But now she saw it as fact. She had been a fool to bring him here. She had been a fool to think the MacGowans might extract vengeance upon the powerful Forbeses. And she was a fool to believe she might attract him as he attracted her.

"Do ye think ye could escape my arrows even if ye tried?" she asked, hoping nothing was revealed in her expression, hoping her tone was sufficiently haughty. But in her mind's eye she saw every dream that had haunted her nights of late, every shameful, lusty image that seared away her facade and revealed her true self. A girl in a woman's body, crying for love.

He stared into her eyes, and though she was certain he could see into her quivering heart, she could not draw away.

"Nay. I dunna think I can escape ye," he murmured. His mien was absolutely sober. His gaze held her in a steely clasp. She dared not breathe, lest she reveal all. It took every bit of strength she had to force herself to move past him and through the door.

The drawbridge wasn't far away. It lowered with no more than a nod to the guard there. Lochan's footfalls sounded hollow against the massive planks. Cam's thudded after, but in a moment the bay destrier thundered up beside her. Forbes' adopted hound romped ahead.

They rode side by side, past the green sward where she usually worked her mounts. For today she needed to breathe, needed to feel sheer speed beneath her.

The rugged country of the Highlands swept past them in varying shades of greens and tans. The earth was awakening to the call of spring, bursting forth in buds and blossoms. Heather dotted the hillsides, ever green and pungent. The air was warm against her face, easing her worry and softening her mood.

Miles sped by beneath their mounts' flying hooves. They spotted MacGowan stock, sheep, goats, cattle. In a quiet lea, sheltered by a grove of slow-budding oaks, they found a herd of horses.

Flame halted Lochan on a hill's crest to stare down at the scene. Powerful mares lowered their heavily maned necks to graze upon the sweet spring grasses. Newborn foals lay flat out upon their sides or pranced about their dams and reared on sturdy hind legs.

Flame remained silent, absorbing the scene into her soul and trying to forget her trouble, but he would not be silenced.

"I have been wondering," Forbes began. "Were ye trying to prove yer steed's stamina, or were ye trying ta escape from *me*?"

Three men guarded the horse herd. She could see their bright tartans from over five hundred rods away. Though the MacGowans had no particular pattern they called their own, the clan was partial to a deep green weave. " 'Tis the sea kelp that makes Lochan swift and hardy. That and the barb breeding," she said, stroking the steed's silken neck absently. He shook his wavy mane

and tossed his head to trumpet at the mares in the valley.
"Cam, yer mount, has only seen four summers. But he
is Lochan's lad and has inherited some of his sire's ability. I would match his endurance against the best of the
Forbeses' aged stallions.''

"I would know, lass, has there ever been a question
ye have actually answered?" Roderic asked.

She turned to look at him. It was a foolish act, for his
eyes were just as blue and his features just as perfectly
chiseled as when she had first met him on that dark,
frantic night at Glen Creag. But now he was even more
frightening, for in his eyes she not only saw strength and
daring, but kindness and concern. She could not let those
qualities draw her, for she knew the pain that would
follow. Even her father's eyes had once shown concern.
"Why would I wish to escape from *you*?" she asked,
careful to keep her tone stiffly controlled. "I think ye
forget which of us is the prisoner.''

"Do I?" Roderic watched her closely. Too closely.
Though she tried, she couldn't hold his gaze. With a
nudge of her heel she turned Lochan away, but in a
moment he was beside her again.

"Tell me of young Haydan, Flanna. What is he to
ye?"

"Haydan?" she asked and nervously turned toward
him, only to find that he still stole her breath. She faced
forward again, trying to steel her resolve. She was the
Flame and had vowed to remain so as long as her clan
needed her. There was no room in her life for softness.
"Troy has elderly relatives in France. Some years ago
they took in a sickly bairn whose mother had died of
the pox. When I was in Bastia, he brought the lad to
meet me.''

"So ye have spent some time in France," he said.
"And a good deal of time, judging by yer accent.
Why?"

She had the good sense to keep her gaze straight
ahead now. But she knew he was watching her intently.
He would be sitting very straight upon Cam's back, and

his unusual height would exceed hers by several inches. " 'Tis good to see foreign lands."

"Was it for yer own protection? Yer father, was he worried for yer safety?"

Nay, she thought, her father was the greatest threat to her safety. But she would not let the memories disturb her. She wouldn't think of the stifling darkness of the trunk, the frantic pitching of the ship that carried her from her homeland.

"I could not blame him for coddling ye," he said. "If I had a daughter I might do the same."

She drew a deep breath and told herself to simply agree with his guesses. He didn't need to know the truth. But hard memories beg to be shared with someone who might care. And though she tried to deny it, Roderic Forbes seemed to be that type. She couldn't dismiss the kind words he had spoken to Haydan, neither could she forget the tears of hope in the boy's eyes. Yet, she'd be a fool to trust this man, for he was charming just as her father had once been, just as her fiancé had seemed to be, and she was too weak.

Flame held her silence with an effort. Up ahead, a winding ribbon of trees sheltered a craggy valley. Through the lacy new leaves she saw the frequent wink of sun on the brook there.

"I only wish to know the circumstances," Roderic said softly. "For I admit, I dunna understand it."

"I am sure there is much ye do not understand, Forbes."

"Although 'tis true that ye test a man's patience, it still baffles me."

She turned toward him. Their gazes struck like flint against steel, sparking on impact.

"How could he let ye go?" Forbes breathed.

"I assure ye, it was no great hardship." She tried to keep her tone utterly casual, as if the topic was of the least importance to her.

"I canna believe that," Roderic said, his voice very soft.

"Well 'tis true!" Emotion made her hands shake as did her voice. Lochan stopped as she faced Roderic breathlessly. "He sent me to a convent, and finally negotiated a marriage for me to a handsome and charming man named Carvell. We were betrothed for many years. But in the end . . ." She faltered. In the end, he, too, had turned from her in disgust. "No vows were spoken."

"Ye were betrothed?"

Damnation! She had said far too much. She should never have mentioned Carvell. Feeling like a babbling fool, she urged Lochan into the trees that lined the sparkling burn.

"Surely na man would let ye go after ye vowed ta wed him," Roderic said, pressing up beside her.

"I assure ye," she said, finding her tone was blessedly steady, though she fought a terrible battle to keep it so, "he was glad to see me gone."

"Nay." She could feel Roderic's gaze on her face. "Couldna be true."

"And why, pray tell, would ye believe such foolishness?" she murmured.

Again their gazes caught. But there was no clash now, only a soft melding of thoughts.

"Because ye are what ye are, lass."

"And what am I?"

"Ye are all that is good."

She shook her head and turned away, but he caught her hand, pulling Lochan to a halt.

"Ye are kind and good. But ye are more, Flanna. Ye are strength and wit and fire, able to hold control and loyalty in the verra same hand."

"Loyalty?" She shouldn't share such a discussion with him, she thought. She should be nothing but self-assured and haughty, but she found she couldn't hold that demeanor with him, especially now, when doubts assailed her from all sides.

He watched her closely. "Ye inspire loyalty, lass," he breathed.

She was being pulled in by the sweeping undertow of

his gaze. Everything in her longed to ask if *he* could be loyal, if he could love her and cherish her. But she wouldn't allow such weakness. "My men——" she began, turning her face away.

"Yer men," he interrupted, drawing her gaze back to him with his husky tone. "Aye, they, too, are loyal. But they wait ta see if ye will stay and stand the test of fire. And they await yer praise."

"What do ye mean?"

"Yer warriors would jump from the battlements if ye but gave them a kind word."

"Since when were the Scots softened by gentleness?"

"Since the beginning of time, lass," he said, holding her gaze. "Ye are a fine leader, but it wouldna hurt ye to offer a bit of encouragement."

"To them or to ye?" she asked breathlessly.

His hand felt strong and warm upon hers. "I need na encouragement, Flanna, and I warn ye now, if ye were mine I wouldna let ye go till the heavens ceased ta be."

The air left her lungs in a painful rush, and though she tried with all her might, she found she lacked the strength to pull her gaze from his.

"And when ye look at me like that, lass, I would gladly give me life ta call ye mine."

Flame jerked herself back to reality. Words of adoration were cheaply bought, she reminded herself, and jumped from Lochan's back to squat by the water's edge. "You're talking foolishness, Forbes," she said.

"Why do ye deny yer womanhood?"

"Because I must rule," she said. "Because I've no time for——"

"Nay," he said softly. "Because ye dunna believe in yerself. Because ye've been hurt. Tell me of him."

She hadn't heard his approach. Startled, she let the water slip between her fingers and jumped to her feet.

"Lass." He reached for her arm, but she stepped quickly back, bumping into Lochan's shoulder as she did so. "Ye tremble."

"I do not."

He remained as he was, watching her with narrowed eyes. "Aye. Ye do. But why?"

"Why are ye here?" The words rushed out of their own accord.

The shadow of a grin tilted the right corner of his mouth, teasing a dimple into his cheek. " 'Tis a wee thing called abduction, lass. Surely ye dunna forget."

"I mean, why are ye *here*?" Her tone was choked. Panic threatened to drown her senses.

"Here?" He pointed to the earth at their feet and took a step nearer. "Because ye are, lass."

His magnetism was a tangible thing, drawing her in, pulling her under, promising things she did not deserve and would never have. " 'Twould be a fine time to escape," she whispered.

"Ye'll na escape me, lass."

"I meant *ye*," she breathed.

"And why would I wish ta escape when ye are near? Even yer men know that I have na wish ta do so, for see, we are alone."

Her heart was pounding. 'Twas a foolish thing to be afraid of words, she knew. And yet, his were frightening. Frightening and so exhilarating that it made her chest ache. "Why?" It was the only word she was able to force from her lips.

"Because ye draw me. Against my will, against my better judgment, ye draw me."

Though she searched for words, all she could do was stare at him.

"Come, lass," he breathed. " 'Tis a bonny day and yet ye search for rain in the cloudless sky. Why look for trouble when it is na there? Come, let us sit for a spell and talk of life."

He turned his broad back and strode to a rotting log, where he sat with his shoulders to its loose-barked expanse and gestured for her to join him. His dog Bonny trotted over to sit adoringly beside him. He placed a gentle hand upon her head but kept his gaze on Flame's. "Have I ever done ye harm?"

She didn't answer, but he shook his head as if she had.

"And never shall I, lass, for 'tis sure ye have been harmed enough."

How did he know how she felt inside? "And what, pray, do ye mean by that?"

He shrugged. "Ye hide behind strange clothing and haughty expressions. Why, but to keep men at bay?"

"An interesting theory," she said.

"Aye. Isn't it? Why na sit here beside me and pierce it full of holes?"

She nodded once. There was no point in denying that he drew at some indefinable thing deep within her. There was also no point in admitting it. Tossing the reins over Lochan's neck, she allowed him to graze unencumbered, then strode across the short distance to the log. Slipping her bow from her shoulder, she placed it in the grass before boldly taking a seat beside Roderic.

Their sheltered spot beside the burn was quiet but for the chatter of rushing water. Despite Flame's attempt to act nonchalant, she felt stiff with tension, but Roderic took a deep breath and propped his elbows upon the log.

"I wait," he said, finally turning to look at her.

"I have a lover." Her words came suddenly and sounded utterly ridiculous, like a ghost story in the bright light of day. To her amazement, he didn't grin. Instead, he remained motionless, holding her with his eyes.

"So ye have told me." He turned his attention back to the burn. "And I ask meself, who might the lucky man be?"

" 'Tis none of your affair."

Breaking off a piece of rotting bark, Roderic tossed it easily into the garrulous waters. "But still I wonder." His eyes found hers again. The depth of them was breathtaking. "Does he tell ye yer hair glistens like rubies in the firelight? That he longs for yer slightest touch? Does he say that when ye ride he envies Lochan so that he can hardly speak?'' His voice was husky as he leaned slightly closer.

"I have a lover!" she gasped.

"Aye, lass," he breathed. "But do ye have a friend?"

"A friend?" Her voice wavered.

He lifted his hand. His fingertips touched her cheek, stroking it gently. Against her will, her eyes fell closed. The quiver from her voice seeped through her body. "A friend be the best kind of lover, me thinks," he said softly. "Someone ta confide in. Ta share words and more at the day's end."

She swallowed. An image appeared in her mind. An image of Roderic the Rogue, stretched lean and masculine upon her bed. In her mind, his chest was bare and his touch was feather soft against her arm, but their words were of everyday things, of hopes and labors and needs.

No. She did not have a friend like that.

"Tell me what has made ye the woman ye are," he murmured.

"Bad blood." She said the words quickly and opened her eyes. "My father's blood, though even on his deathbed he doubted that I was his."

"Nay." Surprise showed clearly on Roderic's face. "Surely yer own sire did not deny ye. Surely ye were his pride."

"His pride?" She watched him for a moment, before turning to the burn. "No. He was a . . . jealous man."

His fingers stroked down her throat and stopped there. "If I had a wife with yer beauty and fire, I, too, would cherish her."

"Cherish her!" Emotion exploded in that single word. "He did not cherish her. He accused her of adultery, when he gladly admitted his own dalliances! He struck her!" She was breathing hard and clasped her hands together now to steady them. "He locked her only daughter in a trunk and sent her to France, because he could not bear to look upon her face. Sent her to live with nuns whose love for God far exceeded any love they might spare for a small Scottish girl who could not speak their language.''

"Sweet Jesu, Flanna! 'Tis truly sorry I am.''

She had to drop her gaze from his face, for there was caring there. The kind of caring she had longed for until she thought she would die from the need. But she needed it no more, she reminded herself. "I don't mourn his actions,'' she said. "I only mourn the years I spent hoping to win back his good favor.''

"Ye have a wondrous ability ta love, Flanna.''

"Love!'' She nearly spat the word. "I did not love him. I hated him! I hated him with every drop of my blood for sending me away.''

"And ye would have forgiven him all if he had but opened his heart and brought ye home.''

Though she hated to admit it, she knew he spoke the truth, for she had imagined that very thing a thousand times. "But he did not,'' she whispered.

"Because he was a fool, Flanna, and not worthy ta call ye his child.''

"Mayhap he saw into my heart,'' she whispered. "Mayhap he knew of my evil thoughts.''

"And what evil thoughts did ye harbor, lass?''

"I was a jealous, spiteful child. I did not like sharing Father's attention with Gregor, who was four years older and could run faster and ride better. I remember wishing he was gone, that he would simply disappear and not come back.''

"And ye think that for that evil thought ye deserved ta be sent away, lass?'' Roderic's voice was very soft, and his hand, when it gripped hers, was strong and steady.

"Men—people,'' she corrected, focusing on their hands and refusing to look into his eyes, "seem to see the true me and back away.''

"There is naught **but** good in ye, lass.''

"Nay, there—'' she began, but he shushed her with a finger to her lips. "I once told Leith I hoped the wolves would come and devour him. Then I'd find his remains and take his footwear. Gawd I loved those boots. In fact, I stole them from him three days later.''

She raised her gaze breathlessly to his. ''Ye must have paid dearly.''

''Dearly? He threw me in the burn, boots and all. But he didna lock me in a trunk and send me away, Flanna. No one in his right mind would do such a thing. 'Twas na ye, lass, that was at fault. 'Twas yer father. Ye were his daughter, the Flame. He should have cherished ye.''

It was difficult to swallow. ''Hardly was I a flame then. I was naught but a scrawny girl with unruly hair and fidgety fingers.''

Roderic gently stroked those fingers now. ''Gawd must have seen the foolishness of locking such beauty away in a convent and sent ye back to yer homeland.''

She watched his hand caress hers and tried to deny the shudder that shook her. ''My mother felt I was not suited for the cloistered life. She must have loved me well enough because she swallowed her fear and humiliation and begged my father to find me a husband.''

Roderic gently lifted her hand in his and stroked her palm with the index finger of his opposite hand. How could such a simple touch stir so many feelings?

''And?'' he asked softly.

'' 'Twas said Carvell and I would make a good match. And I was fool enough to think him besotted with me.''

''Ye found him with another,'' Roderic guessed, his voice quiet. ''And yer pride wouldna let ye be betrayed as yer mother had been.''

''Nay,'' she said, unable to stop the word. ''Not as my mother had. 'Twas not a woman I found Carvell with, 'twas his cousin Jacque.''

Flame saw the shock on his face and waited for the rejection. Now he would see what she truly was—a woman so unnatural that she could not even tempt her betrothed away from another man. Not a woman at all, perhaps, but a mistake of nature.

''Flanna,'' he murmured, gripping her hand firmly in his own. ''Some men are fools, but some are . . . odd.''

He said the word as though he could not possibly fathom the idea. " 'Tis sorry I am that ye've known both kinds.''

For a moment, she looked into his eyes and found she couldn't speak, but she had to keep her bearing, remember that he was a man, and not to be trusted. "I was sorry, too, when I told my father I would not marry him.''

"Surely he didna want ye ta, na after he knew of the man's perversion.''

She could remember the moment as if it were yesterday. "It was late in the evening,'' she said softly. "I walked into the garden to get a bit of air, and there was Carvell, kissing . . .'' She shook her head and mentally turned away from the image that had branded itself in her mind. "Shame is a strange thing. It settles into your very bones and will not let go.''

Her words slipped into silence. Beside Roderic, Bonny rose to her feet and pitched her ears forward.

" 'Twas na yer shame but yer betrothed's,'' he murmured. "And yer sire's. Surely ye know that.''

She lifted her gaze to his face. "Sometimes one does not feel in one's heart what one knows in one's head.''

"And sometimes one's heart insists on doing what one's head deems foolish,'' he murmured, and leaning forward, he kissed her.

There was no thought of resisting him, for he was right. Sometimes, no matter how hard she tried, she could not deny her heart.

His lips were warm and firm, undemanding, yet persuasive. Her breath caught in her throat. Her heart hammered in her chest. She had fallen under his spell, was bound by the tenderness of his touch. Bonny growled, but the world had retreated. There was only Roderic with the gentle hands and quiet understanding. Only Roderic with his ready laugh and quick wit. But in an instant he pulled away. He turned his leonine head, making the tendons stand out in hard relief against his broad throat. She sat immobilized, mesmerized by his stark masculinity and failing to notice the sound that issued from the woods behind her. But suddenly, he reached for her and she was tossed like a bit of dry chaff to the far side of the log.

Chapter 12

❧◦◦⟨⟩◦◦❧

"**W**hat?" Flame gasped. She struggled to rise, but Roderic's hand was atop her head, pushing her back.

"Stay down!" he commanded, but his words were mixed with an arrow's whirring approach.

She heard the sickening sound of it striking flesh. For a moment he faltered, but then he vaulted over the log to crouch beside her.

"Dear God," she breathed, "ye're hit."

"Stay down. Where is he?" He continued to peer over the barrier into the woods.

"Roderic," she breathed, feeling faint. "Ye're—"

He crouched lower and turned to face her. " 'Tis the first time ye've used me Christian name, lass," he murmured, offering her a wry smile. " 'Tis a bonny thing to hear from yer lips."

"There's . . . there's an arrow protruding from your arm," she breathed.

" 'Tis just a flesh wound," he said and reaching across his chest, snapped the arrow in half. "There now. Does it look less gruesome?"

"Dear God!" she moaned.

"Who was it?"

"What?"

"Did ye see anyone in the woods?"

"Nay."

He scowled. Except for her dirk, they were weaponless. Although her bow rested close at hand, the arrows were behind Lochan's saddle. "Is there one or more?"

"More," she said.

He looked at her in surprise. "How do ye know?"

"I heard noises off to the right. The arrow came from the left."

A smile flirted with his lips again. " 'Tis quick ye are, lass."

"I'm not completely bereft of sense," she said, and garnering all her courage, peeked over the top of the log.

"Gawd's wrath!" he swore, dragging her down to cover her with his own body. "Then prove yer wit and stay put."

"*Ye* looked over," she argued.

"I'm a man."

"And I'm a woman."

He gave her a full smile. "Dunna think I havena noticed, lass." Her breast was crushed against his chest as she lay on her side beneath him.

"Get off me."

"Ye must flee."

Courage and pride had flooded back to her with surprising force. " 'Tis MacGowan land," she hissed. "I will run from no one."

"And ye willna be wounded," he argued. "Na while ye are under me own protection."

"Hardly am I under your protection, Forbes! Do not forget that ye are my captive," she said from her crushed position beneath him.

"Nay. I willna forget. But me bonny tower room is looking more and more appealing. Might we not return there to discuss me capture?"

She scowled, trying to push him aside and rise. "If I could just reach my bow . . ."

"Ye willna."

She deepened her scowl. "I'm an excellent archer."

"Death would change that," he murmured, easing off her to glance furtively about. "And I'll na risk it."

"They will not chance harming me."

He turned quickly toward her, his expression sharp. "Ye know who it is then?"

"I have no idea. But they will not harm the leader of the MacGowans."

He snorted, then turned his gaze to the right. "If ye whistle, will yer gray come or is that a stable trick only?"

"He'll come."

Roderic nodded absently, glancing over her head to peer into the woods. "I tied the bay. Ye'll have ta ride alone."

"And leave you?" she gasped. "Ye must be daft."

"Do ye imagine I *want* to stay here? Fly ta Dun Ard as fast as ever ye can. Dunna look back." His expression was somber as night. "If ye can, send yer warriors for me."

"Ye have lost your mind," she breathed. "I will not leave without ye."

"Dare I hope ye care a wee bit, lass?"

"Of course I care," she breathed. His lips were inches from hers when she spoke again. "I've never had a prisoner before."

"Gawd's wrath!" he swore, drawing irritably away. "Call the horse and be ready to flee."

"Nay."

"Ye will," he gritted.

"I won't."

"Heaven's gate, ye are stubborn." Easing upward, he hurried another glance over the log. An arrow whizzed out of the woods almost directly to their left and quivered at a sharp angle into the log. "Jesu! They be circling around. We have na time ta argue. Ye will go."

"Not without ye."

"Yer gray canna carry two with any speed."

Dragging her legs from beneath Roderic's heavy form, Flame crouched in the shade of the log. "Ye sorely underestimate the quality of my stock. And ye will ride with me."

"I tell ye we have na time for this," he complained.

"Then come along!" she ordered, and grabbing his wrist, she whistled.

Lochan appeared in less than a heartbeat, skittering out of the brush near at hand.

"Come!" Flame ordered.

"Jesu!" Rising, Roderic swore and then tossed her into the saddle.

Arrows came from opposite directions now.

"Ride!" Roderic yelled, slapping Lochan's rump and jumping back.

The gray leaped into a gallop, but in an instant, Flame circled him about.

"Not without ye, Forbes!" she screamed back.

An arrow twanged, quivering into the earth at his feet.

"Come or my death will be on your hands," Flame challenged.

There seemed to be nothing he could do but obey or risk her life. In an instant, his foot found her stirrup. He felt her hand on his back, urging him behind the saddle. Lochan jumped, nearly tossing him to the ground. Roderic grappled for a grip, finding Flame's waist and almost pulling her down with him. He balanced on one foot. An arrow twanged from its bowstring.

"Go!" Roderic roared. Deadly missiles hissed past his ear, and then they were running.

From behind, they could hear men shouting. A stallion trumpeted. Hoofbeats thundered after them.

Roderic held tightly to the saddle's high cantle and looked over his shoulder. He could see nothing through the thicket from which they had fled. A mile sped beneath Lochan's hooves, but suddenly five steeds emerged from the copse ahead.

"Turn. Into the brush!" Roderic ordered, but Flame held her mount on a steady course.

"Praise be!" she breathed. " 'Tis Troy. We are saved."

The MacGowan warriors thundered up.

"What happened, lass?" Troy rasped.

"We were attacked by the burn."

"How many?"

"Two or more."

"Bullock, escort them back to Dun Ard. The rest of ye come with me!" ordered Troy.

"I'll come, too," said Roderic.

Troy turned to him. "Be ye daft? Ye have an arrow in yer arm."

"Aye," said Roderic, "and it has made me a bit peeved. I will return to the burn."

But suddenly, Flame's dirk was placed to his chest as she twisted toward him.

"Ye are wounded," she said softly. "But ye will not die—unless it be by my own hand."

Looking down into her eyes, Roderic saw nothing but absolute sincerity.

"Ye've a way with words, lass," he said, and Flame turned Lochan toward home.

"How is your arm?" Flame stood in the doorway of the tower room. Forbes was stretched out on his back with his left hand resting beneath his head and his right hand lying limply at his side. The arrow had been removed. Marjory had cleaned the wound and bandaged it in white linen, but the cloth was stained red at its center. Bonny's long nose rested on his bare chest as she mourned her master's injury.

Propping himself on his elbows, Roderic grinned at her. Bonny sat up with a sigh. "It hurts like the verra devil, lass. But," he said, lowering his voice, "perhaps if ye kissed it . . ."

Flame shook her head and advanced, trying to hide her relief. "I see ye have not lost your questionable sense of humor, Forbes."

He sat up, swung his feet to the floor, and chuckled softly. "Think ye that I jest?"

She felt her cheeks warm with the impact of his gaze and cursed herself.

"How is he?"

"Troy!" Flame said. "Are ye unharmed?"

"Aye, lass." Troy Hamilton stepped into the room and set a hand to Flame's arm. "I am fine. Dunna worry for the bear when the hare is being chased."

Flame smiled. "Even the most powerful bear can be snared," she said.

"Did ye find them?" Roderic asked abruptly.

"Nay, I didna," Troy said.

"Mayhap that is because one of them is in this room."

Silence settled in with sudden stillness.

"Are ye accusing me, lad?" Troy asked, quickly dropping his hand from Flame's arm to stride toward him.

"How did ye find us so quickly in our time of need, Wolfhound?" Roderic asked.

Troy's huge hands formed to fists, but in a moment he drew a deep breath and loosened them. "Watch yer mouth, lad," he said softly, "or the next time yer tongue runs wild . . ." The shallowest hint of humor lighted his expression. "I'll let her kill ye."

" 'Twould be simpler than seeing ta it yerself," said Roderic.

"Aye," nodded Troy, "but na so satisfying."

"Be that a challenge?"

"If ye—"

"For pity's sake! Stop it! Both of you!" ordered Flame. Striding up, she pushed between them. "I swear, the two of ye are possessed. Why do ye snarl at each other when there are others to blame?"

"And how do ye ken it wasna he that tried ta kill us?" asked Roderic, nodding toward Troy.

"Us?" Troy echoed harshly. "Were ye a target, too, lass?"

"Nay," Flame denied. "They tried to kill Forbes only." She turned her gaze on him. "And who would not?"

"We dunna ken if they attempted to injure her," Roderic said. His tone was unusually sober. And thinking back to their time by the log, Flame realized that even under the most deadly of circumstances, Forbes had seemed all but jovial. It was only one of a hundred irritating qualities about him. "But the fact remains," he continued, "she could have been wounded as easily as I."

"Is that true, lass?" Troy asked.

" 'Twas Forbes that was wounded, not I," she reminded them.

"So ye say ye found nothing?" Roderic asked.

"Nay," Troy said, drawing himself from Flame's gaze with a sigh and sweeping off his woolen bonnet. "Nothing but crushed grasses. Na even a spent arrow."

"Did ye search the woods, the moist earth? What of footprints to give us a clue to their identity?" asked Flame.

"Nothing, lass. Me apologies. 'Tis as if they vanished. But who else could it be but the brigand band?"

"What brought *ye* there, Wolfhound?"

Troy turned slowly toward Roderic. "The afternoon was wearing on, and the lass was with ye. I thought mayhap she had come to harm."

"But ye found her so easily." Roderic did nothing to hide his suspicious tone. "And it was ye who wished for us to ride together."

"I be a patient man, Forbes," said Troy "But ye stretch me limits." He turned away. "Lass"—he sighed, looking into her face—"ye have aged me greatly this day. 'Twould ease me mind if ye would walk with me to the hall."

Flame glanced at Roderic then placed a hand on the huge warrior's arm. "Sleep, Forbes," she said, turning away. "I'll send Marjory in the morning with more herbs for yer wound."

The door closed behind them.

"Gawd's wrath!" Roderic swore aloud and ground his teeth in vexation. Why did she trust that hulking warrior and still doubt *him*? Could Effie have been right? Was she in love with Troy? And was it possible that he was the one who had attacked them by the burn?

Turning on his heel, he paced and slammed his fist against the wall. It hurt. "Damn it to hell!" he growled. Questions bedeviled him. He paced again. Bonny paced with him, matching him stride for stride, her claws clicking on the wood floor as they circled around and came back to the center of the room.

Finally, exasperated, Roderic seated himself on the lumpy straw tick. "What am I to do?"

Bonny rested her nose on his knee and gazed into his face. Sighing, he stroked her satiny ears. " 'Tis nice ta be adored," he murmured, grinning. "Still, I have always preferred women with less . . . fur."

The hound neither blinked nor appeared disappointed by his peculiar taste.

"But for now 'tis good ta have yer company." He lay back on the mattress until darkness settled in.

By midnight he was pacing again. Having tired of her beloved's restlessness, Bonny stretched out in the middle of the tick, apparently undisturbed by the lumps or Roderic's fretfulness.

Thoughts of Flanna consumed Roderic. He ached to see her again, to make sure she was safe. But he had come close enough to losing his life at the burn, and if the arrow was intended for him, he had best be cautious and stay put. But what if the arrow was meant for Flanna instead? What if her life was in danger?

He had to see her, if just for a moment. Silently, Roderic positioned the furniture upon the mattress and crept up the teetering back of the chair to remove the loose ceiling tile. Finally, he was once again skimming noiselessly down the hall toward Flame's private chambers.

Beside her bed once again, he watched her sleep. The moon cast its mercurial light through the open window and across her regal features. Time drifted on. He was a fool to be there, of course. And he was a fool to stay. But the day's events tormented him. Seeing her safely asleep was not enough. He had to solve the mysteries that haunted him, for what if the brigand's arrow had struck *her*? And what if it had not been the brigand band at all, but someone else? Someone who wanted to see her dead? One of her own kin, perhaps. He had accused Troy to fluster the massive warrior, but in truth Troy seemed to care for her. Still, it was not unheard of for a clansman to pretend loyalty, then make an attempt on his leader's life. If not Troy, then who? Easing noiselessly onto the mattress behind Flanna, Roderic allowed himself to touch her hair. Who would gain the most from her death? That was what he needed to learn.

She sighed in her sleep and tossed an arm atop her blanket. The Flame was restless tonight. And why not? Roderic thought. She had a failing abduction, a hot-blooded clan, and an attempted murder to consider. Or was it something more personal that disturbed her? Loneliness, perhaps, the need for a gentle touch in the dark of night? 'Twas possible, of course, for despite her bold words she did not have a lover. He knew it was true, for there was not a man alive who could have her once and not give his life to spend eternity by her side. And there was no man here. No man but himself.

With that thought, Roderic leaned slowly forward, drawn against his will. Her hair was as soft as a goose's down and smelled like sweet lavender. Her skin, too, would be soft, her lips warm and welcoming. He leaned closer.

She moaned. Roderic jerked back.

Employing every ounce of discipline he possessed, Roderic forced himself from the bed and toward the door.

"Haydan, why be ye awake?" Marjory's words were whispered from the far side of the door

Behind Roderic, Flanna moaned and rolled to her back.

"I could not sleep."

Flanna bent a knee. Roderic stared at her, frozen in place. She was on the edge of waking. He could sense it, and yet, he could not leave the way he came.

The window glared at him. Flitting soundlessly to it,

he peered out. It was a long and precipitous climb to the bailey below.

"The lady is sleeping. We should let her sleep."

"Marjory?" Flame awoke with a start.

He had been caught! Execution would be lenient compared to what he would endure.

"Marjory?" she said again, and suddenly she was on her feet. But instead of threatening his life, she was moving toward the door. "Is something amiss?" she called and opened the heavy portal.

Roderic heard Marjory's apologies, but he delayed not a moment more. He squeezed through the window, gripping the ledge with clawed fingers and searching for footholds with his bare feet.

From above, voices continued, but it was all he could do to cling to life and his precarious hold. Inch by inch, he eased downward. Just a little farther and he would reach the thatched, slanted roof below, and from there it would be an easy drop to the ground.

But just then, he heard a gasp from below. "Who goes there?" someone yelled.

Suddenly, an arrow whirred through the air. There was no time to lose. Pushing off with his hands and feet, Roderic dropped to the narrow roof beneath him.

Timbers creaked and groaned. Thatch scattered, but already he was running, skimming along the slanted roof.

The archer yelled again. Another arrow flew. With one silent prayer, Roderic propelled himself from the thatch and into the air. Darkness swelled around him. The earth was solid beneath his feet There was no time to delay.

Ahead the door to the hall waited. It was the last place they would search for him. It creaked open beneath his hand. He drew a deep, steadying breath and slowed his pace.

A man near the dead fire sat up. Roderic could barely make out his dark form in the single, flickering light of the wall sconce. "Someone yell? Thought I heard something."

"Seems a wildcat tried ta dine on our geese." Yawning, Roderic walked into the hall. "He'll na try it again, but it will take the cooks half the day ta roast the stringy bastard."

"Aye," sighed the man, then, wriggling about in the scattered reeds, he lay back down. " 'Tis too bad deer dunna long fer goose. 'Tis venison I prefer."

Without halting, Roderic strode through the far door. Once out of sight, he was running again. Down the dark passage. Up the stairs. The tartans he had left hanging from the tower roof groaned beneath his weight. Perched atop the castle, Roderic's fingers felt numb with tension as he untied the woolens and tossed them inside. Balancing the lead ceiling tile atop his back, he launched himself onto the mattress below, but he had left the chair atop the table when scrambling from the tower.

How he managed to hit all the furniture and Bonny, too, Roderic would never know. The hound yelped, the chair clattered to its side, and the table skittered from the mattress and onto the floor.

In less than a moment, the door burst open.

Bullock stood bleary-eyed in the entrance, holding a torch high and blinking. "What the devil is going on, Forbes?"

"Dear Gawd!" gasped Roderic, letting his eyes go wide. "Me thinks I attacked Bonny with the chair."

Behind Bullock, Gilbert hurried forward, looking little more rested than his partner.

"What's the ruckus about?"

"Attacked the hound with the chair?" asked Bullock, shaking his head. "Have ye taken leave of yer senses, man?"

Roderic managed a chagrined expression. Luckily, his versatile plaids had fallen on the far side of the mattress. They could not be seen from the guards' vantage point. He hoped. " 'Tis sorry I be ta disturb ye, lads," he said now. " 'Tis me awful dreams!" Swinging his feet to the floor, he called to the hound. She wagged her tail and advanced cautiously. " 'Tis a terrible thing to molest me only friend in the world," Roderic said, setting his hands to Bonny's head. "Ahhh," he sighed, looking mournful and hoping against hope that they would not, in their drowsy condition, question why the table, too, had been moved. "I am only grateful that I did meself na harm."

"Harm?" Bullock looked all but ready to fall over from fatigue. It must have, indeed, been a wearying search they had performed by the burn.

"Dunna concern yerselves, lads. 'Tis fine I be. And so long as I be unhurt, Leith willna seek vengeance. After all"—he grinned—"abduction be a time-honored tradition for us Scots. Why, I recall once when I was only ten. Or was I nine? I forget now, 'twas so long ago. In fact, it might be that I had only seen eight summers for Frances had just arrived. Ahh, Frances. I remember him fondly. He was—"

"Go ta sleep, Forbes," ordered Bullock, turning away.

"And try na ta kill yerself," mumbled Gilbert, following him.

Darkness settled in. Roderic drew a deep, steadying breath and reached to the far side of the bed to shove his blankets and stolen cap beneath his pallet. His lungs felt as if they would burst from exertion. Who had been in the bailey? Had they recognized him? Would they yet come? He forced himself to lie down.

"Is he safe?"

Roderic heard Flanna's gasped words, but forced himself to remain as he was.

"Who?" Bullock's question was groggy.

"Forbes!" she snapped. "Is he there?"

"Of course, me lady."

"Let me see."

"We only just checked him."

"Open the door!"

"Aye, me lady."

Sitting up, Roderic blinked into the torchlight. She was dressed in nothing more than her nightgown. It was voluminous and billowing, and yet it seemed he could see every curve of her body.

"Flanna"—he couldn't stop her name from coming to his lips—"ye shouldna appear such before the likes of . . ." He managed a hard-won grin. "Us."

"What happened to the furniture?"

Roderic blinked at her, gathering his wits with all due speed. " 'Tis an embarrassing tale, lass."

"Why?" Her tone was sharp, her face pale, and her hair a wild mass of flaming curls.

" 'Tis bad dreams I have, lass. They make me act—"

"When did ye move them?" she interrupted.

He rose to his feet. Only the great length of his shirt kept him from complete nakedness. "Has something alarmed ye, lass?" he asked softly, approaching.

"When did ye move the table, Forbes?" she breathed.

He shrugged, trying to look confused. "I dunna remember, lady. It must have been done during me sleep. 'Tis true. Ye can ask Bullock there. I be a fitful sleeper at best."

Although she didn't turn toward the guards, Bullock spoke up. "He has startled us in the past, lady."

"And ye checked on him?"

"Aye."

"And he has always been here?"

Both guards looked immediately confused. "But of course, me lady. Where else?"

Lifting her torch slightly higher, Flame scrutinized the walls of the enclosure before skimming her gaze to the ceiling. He saw her attention rivet there and held his breath. Foolishly, he noticed that her throat was very slim and smooth as she stared upward.

But in a moment, her attention turned back to him. "Why?" Her tone was very husky and quiet.

"Yer pardon, me lady," Roderic said, forcing himself to breathe. "I dunna ken what ye—"

"Yer words by the burn," she whispered. "Ye've never seen my hair in the firelight. Unless it be by *my* fire in *my* chambers."

He shrugged. Gawd she was beautiful beyond words. She was clever and resourceful and she needed him, though she did not know it yet. "I fear I still dunna ken—"

"Take out the table," she ordered suddenly. "And the chair."

Chapter 13

*H*e had had the bitch in his hand. How it galled him to fawn over her, to pretend she was truly a leader, that she had the right to that position. For years he had carefully schemed, and he had been so close to victory. Close enough to taste her blood. But the bastard Forbes had moved just in time to take the arrow in his arm. He had planned it so perfectly. She would not have died immediately. Indeed, she was to remain alive until he lifted her head from her body. And Forbes was to watch—and die later, by her arrow.

But his plans would yet pay off. Forbes was becoming increasingly infatuated with the bitch. He was taking greater and greater risks. Soon he would go too far, and some MacGowan warrior would take offense at his liberties, for they treated the bitch as if she were a sacred goddess instead of the whore she was. Just as every woman was a whore.

Soon, very soon, she would die. The MacGowans would accuse Forbes and tear him to shreds. After that, blood would spill in earnest—both Forbeses' and MacGowans', and he would be there to pick through the bones.

The morning crowd in the hall was noisy and restive as they discussed the events of the previous night. Everyone knew someone or something had been seen clinging to the stone wall of the keep. Old Alexander, who had been wandering outside to answer a call of

162

nature, swore he had seen an unidentified man running across the roof, and had shot arrows at him. Roderic gazed about, keeping his expression innocent.

He had been busy this morning, cautiously questioning his guards and others in an attempt to formulate some guess about who might have attacked them by the burn. Thinking he could perhaps learn something from the arrow Marjory had taken from his arm, he had asked the maidservant to have a look at the bloodied weapon. But it was already gone, tossed from the window into the river. Her cheek sported a purplish bruise that she had said was caused by a fall in the dark. He supposed her restless night was the reason for her distraction. Nevin should take better care of his lady, Roderic thought, and wished with all his heart that he had the opportunity to take his own advice.

He turned his gaze to Flanna, where she sat near the center of the room. She was safe, he assured himself. Bullock was with her, and though he was hot-tempered, he was loyal and stalwart. Wasn't he? God's wrath, he could trust no one and should be beside her himself even now.

In fact . . . He rose smoothly, unable to stay away.

"Now I understand why you came to the tower last night," he said. "I heard of the disturbance."

She turned slowly toward him, striking him with her jewel-bright gaze. " 'Twas nothing to concern yourself with, Forbes."

Truly, she took his breath away. " 'Tis na what I heard, Flanna," he murmured. "They say someone may have been attempting to reach yer chambers."

She let the silence stretch between them as she studied him. " 'Twas most probably only vermin of some sort."

Did she know it had been he? Had she felt his gaze on her? Did she think of him standing there, watching her in the dark of the night?

She rose abruptly, pushing her heavy chair from the table.

"Where are ye going?" he asked.

Again she smote him with her eyes, but in a moment she turned silently away.

Without hesitation, he strode after her, and she stopped at the door to turn and look at him once more. "Where do ye think ye're going?"

He smiled down into her face. "With ye."

She smiled back. "Nay."

He shrugged, hoping to look disarmingly charming, or at least, harmless. "I am yer guest. 'Twould be a sin ta mistreat me."

"And how would it be to get ye killed by my own carelessness?" she asked abruptly.

Her expression was suddenly sober. Roderic drew a deep breath and sternly forbade himself to touch her. "Na so bad as getting yerself kilt, lass."

He heard her sharp inhalation and wondered what it meant. But in a moment she was her usual self again—controlled, cool. "Bullock," she said, looking past him. "I will be on the green. Make certain Forbes stays safely within the walls of Dun Ard." She turned to go, but Roderic reached out and grasped her elbow in an unplanned movement.

She glanced at his hand, then at his face, and slowly raised her brows.

"Ye willna go without me, lass," he warned.

"Indeed?" Her tone was haughty.

"Indeed."

"Trouble, lass?" rumbled Troy, approaching Roderic from behind.

"Aye." She nodded once. So cool and perfect were her features that they might have been chiseled in purest marble, or in ice. "It would seem Forbes has a wish to die."

Whether she was threatening him or protecting him, Roderic wasn't certain. Nevertheless, he kept his grip steady and his gaze on her face.

"Methinks ye neglect yer duties, Wolfhound, if ye let her leave these walls unescorted. Or could it be ye dunna mind if she dies?'' Turning, he looked into Troy's strange, pale eyes.

"I tire of yer accusations, Forbes," he said quietly.

"I asked about ta find out who would gain the reins of control if Flanna died," Roderic said evenly. "It seems ye would be a likely one ta rule, Wolfhound."

The big man nodded slowly. "I be her father's cousin."

"Hence, ye have a great deal ta gain," Roderic said. "And hence, ye are the most likely culprit."

Unidentifiable emotion sparked in Troy's silver gray eyes. "Thus ye have decided ta save the lass from me. But Nevin is her father's nephew. Bullock was fostered by the auld laird himself. Who is ta say who might reign if the Flame was doused? Will ye protect her from all of us, Forbes?"

"If there is a need," Roderic said, and drew his hand from Flanna's arm. "And I believe . . . there is a need!"

For an old man, Troy moved with admirable speed. Suddenly, he clenched Roderic's shirt in his huge fist. Behind him, Bonny growled, but Troy ignored the hound and hissed, "Then cease skulking about in the dark like a thieving scoundrel and do somemat!"

With his fists poised for a blow, Roderic tried to decipher Troy's words. "What?" he murmured, hesitating, but Troy merely shoved him away and turned toward Flame.

"Despite Forbes' wish to die, I again vow ta keep him safe, lass, inside these walls and out," the Wolfhound promised. "Be assured he will yet live when night falls upon us."

Flanna rode across the drawbridge on a great black stallion with a mincing gait. Roderic went on foot, followed by Troy, who was followed by thirty or so warriors on horseback.

They gathered on the broad, green sward as Roderic stood to the side and watched. Troy placed his back to a gnarled, lone oak and said nothing. Left to his own devices, Roderic watched Flanna ride and felt that now-familiar lurch of his heart.

Her hair was unbound and blew like windswept fire. Her face was smooth and somber, her hands steady.

Not only did she ride the dark stallion Dubh as if she were a part of him, but she tutored her men at the same time. She seemed to watch every equestrian team, to command and critique every miraculous movement they made. Never in his life had Roderic seen such feats performed on horseback. And it was all orchestrated by Flanna MacGowan.

She didn't seem like a woman who needed protection. And yet, without trying, he could remember how she looked when she slept. He could remember her slim body, curved and soft. He could remember her face, kissed by the firelight, and he knew that whether she wanted protection or not, he would give it, for she stirred something deep inside him.

"Ye'd do well ta think with yer head instead of with yer nether parts," rumbled the Wolfhound.

Roderic drew his gaze slowly from Flanna. "What the devil does that mean?"

Troy turned his great, shaggy head. The feather in his tam danced in the morning breeze. "Ye made a bloody big target against the wall, Forbes. Tis lucky ye are ta still be alive."

Roderic narrowed his eyes. Now was a time for caution if ever there was one. "Is there meaning ta yer words?"

Troy lifted his weight from the oak with a snap. "Though ye are acting the fool, Forbes, I am hoping ye are na."

"I, too, am hoping that, Wolfhound."

"Then use yer head," he said, "or lose it."

Roderic stared at the huge warrior, but Troy had turned his attention to the riders and refused to say more. Had the Wolfhound recognized him on the side of the keep? And if so, why didn't he tell the others?

Nothing was certain except that Roderic must guard Flanna with his life.

The day passed slowly, for though Flame usually enjoyed her training sessions, Roderic's presence disconcerted her. Regardless of where she was or what she did, she felt his gaze on her at all times. And when she could no longer ignore his stare and would turn to him, he would smile that heart-stopping smile and shatter her concentration. Why did he insist on being there? Why didn't he attempt to escape? Had it been he who was found creeping down her wall like an unearthly cat? And if so, how had he gotten there? An eerie feeling crept up her spine. Was the letter from him? But no. It didn't matter, for she had no time for such things.

She turned the black stallion toward her men, trying to concentrate. But still the thought of Roderic disturbed her. She could imagine him in her chambers, watching her, touching her hair, leaning closer to . . .

For pity's sake, she had to get control of herself before she became just like the hound that followed him everywhere and couldn't bear to be out of his sight. She had to gain control, for her clan's sake, and for her own.

Evening was nearly upon them when they made their way back into Dun Ard. It was time for the second and last meal of the day. The riders were weary as were the horses. Flame led the company into the stable. Lochan greeted her with a reproachful nicker for her inattention. Bruid's trumpeted call was not so musical. Men and horses filed past to their respective stalls. Laughter and easy banter drifted to her ears. If there was any place in the world where she belonged, this was it, for the stable usually allowed her peace of mind. But as she turned to lift the saddle from her mount, her gaze fell on Roderic. He stood in the aisle, his back against a wall, his attention pinned on her.

She scowled at him as her contentment fled. He smiled back.

"Might I care for yer steed, lass?" he asked, still grinning.

She gritted her teeth. Her nerves felt raw from his constant attention. "I always care for my—" she began, but suddenly a door burst open and a giant gray beast thundered into the aisle, trumpeting a challenge.

"Bruid!" Flame shrieked, frozen in place. Her mount knocked her to the earth as he pivoted toward his rival. Ears pinned back and teeth bared, he reared, towering over her, hooves thrashing. She raised her arm with no hope of sheltering herself from the blows. But suddenly she was plucked from the floor and snatched away.

"Flanna!" Roderic gasped, holding her in his arms.

Behind her, two stallions screamed and clashed, but she could see nothing but Roderic's face.

"Are ye hurt?" he breathed.

She couldn't speak, couldn't lift her gaze from his eyes. Worry was etched there. Worry for her. His arms trembled.

She opened her mouth to answer the emotions she saw in his eyes. But Bruid screamed again, snapping her from her trance.

"Nay," she yelled. Breaking free of Roderic's grasp, Flame launched herself toward the thrashing stallions.

"Flanna!" Roderic roared and leaped toward her to grasp her by the shirt and toss her out of harm's way.

"Nay!" she cried again, terrified for the horses' safety, but just then Roderic threw himself into the fray.

Grabbing Bruid's head collar, he tried to drag the horse to a halt. But the stallion was enormous and enraged, and he reared again, whipping Roderic into the air like a stubborn autumn leaf.

Men stood immobile and transfixed as they watched in horror. From Flame's spot on the floor, every incident seemed to be played out like a scene upon a stage. She saw the stallions rear in slow motion. Saw Forbes lifted from the ground. It almost seemed as if she saw herself rise. Saw herself propelled forward to grasp Dubh's headstall and drag him around. From nowhere, Troy appeared, lending his weight as he, too, pulled at the black.

Bruid crashed his forefeet to the earth and finally men swarmed forward with hay forks and loose timbers. With shrieks and threats, they drove the great stallion backward. Leaning into the gray's shoulder, Roderic forced the beast around and back into his stall. Gilbert thudded the door closed behind, opening it only far enough to allow Roderic to slip back out.

But for wild trumpeting and the thudding of hooves, all was silent.

"I've said a thousand times we should be rid of the beast," Troy said. "How did he get loose?"

Roderic turned toward the old warrior, his hand still on the door. "The latch has been tampered with."

The two men's gazes met with a clash and held. Flame watched, barely noticing when someone took Dubh from her.

"Nay!" she said, striding forward. "Ye were both on the green. No blame can be cast."

"'Tis na true," Roderic said. "Someone is ta blame."

Troy said nothing.

All stood immobile, watching, listening.

"'Tis enough," Flame said, turning abruptly on shaky legs. "The entertainment is ended. 'Twas an accident and nothing more.

"Magnus, make certain Bruid's stall is mended. Ye others, see to your mounts then go to the hall." She tried a tentative smile, though she wondered if it looked ghoulish and frightening more than soothing. "Go fetch your meals. We cannot have the great MacGowan warriors so famished they grow weak."

The men seemed to shake themselves from their trances as they watched her.

"My lady!" gasped Nevin, rushing into the stable. "I heard a commotion and feared for your life." Bruid crashed his hind feet against his stall, and Nevin jumped and veered sideways. "The beast got loose!" he gasped, shifting his gaze from the shattered latch to Flame's face. "Sweet Mary, ye could have been killed."

"I am fine," she said.

"But, lady," Nevin said, his voice choked with emotion, "ye are as pale as death. Ye must go rest after such a fright."

She managed to laugh. "I assure ye, I am fine."

"Where have ye been, Nevin?" Roderic asked.

Nevin turned slowly to Forbes. "You!" he said, his voice a growl. " 'Twas you that caused this."

"He was on the green all day," Magnus said.

"But what of before?" Nevin asked. "Who watched him while ye were saddling your mounts?"

No one spoke.

"Lady," Bullock said, "I should have watched him myself ta make certain he caused na harm. But ye are unhurt?"

"Aye. I am unhurt. 'Tis time for the incident to be forgotten." Though Nevin and Roderic still eyed each other, it was easier for Flame to smile now, for perhaps Forbes had been right. Perhaps these men were loyal to her. They were certainly concerned. And perhaps they would appreciate her praise. "I am unharmed. 'Tis a fine job ye did with Smitty today, Bullock." His chest seemed to swell. Her knees felt steadier. "And Bryce," she called, "no one has handled Dana better."

By the time the warriors made their way to the hall, they were chatting and laughing again. Even Nevin had lost his pallor.

"Come and eat, lady," said Bullock, filling the doorway with his great bulk. "We canna allow our leader to become famished, for who would tame the beasties for us wee men?"

Flame laughed as an unfamiliar warmth spread through her. Comradery was a strange feeling. Was it caused by her simple compliments to the men? Should the credit go to Roderic's suggestion? "I will be along shortly. I only wish to spend a moment or two with Lochan."

He nodded and turned to follow his friends.

Only a few warriors remained with their mounts now. Troy and Roderic stood in the aisle, watching her.

"Go eat," she said softly.

"Nay," they said in unison.

She scowled first at Roderic then at Troy. "What is the matter with ye two?"

The men remained silent.

" 'Tis fine then. Starve if ye like." Turning her back to them, she spoke a few words to Lochan and stroked his face. Behind her, her protectors watched. Flame remained as she was, trying to find the peace that the stable usually granted her, but there was no peace to be found with these two men lurking about in her wake. She moved on, stepping into Dubh's stall.

He was beginning to calm down, but a large patch of hair had been torn from his neck. A swelling as large as her fist protruded from his shoulder. She set a hand gently to it. "Dubh," she said reproachfully, "ye should know better than to scrap with the likes of Bruid. But . . ." She sighed, not looking behind her at the men who hovered at the stall door. "So is the way of men, I suppose." She moved closer, appreciating the stallion's warmth, his solid presence. Her fingers touched the muscle of his cheek before running down the powerful neck and back to his wounded shoulder.

From the doorway, Roderic held his breath. He couldn't pull his attention from her hands. They seemed so small and delicate against the huge animal's body. They seemed so gentle and tender. And there was nothing he wanted more than to feel that tenderness against his own skin.

"Aye, ye look and ye dream," rumbled Troy in his ear. "But do ye have the stones ta act?"

Roderic turned irritably toward the speaker. "What are ye yippin' about now, Wolfhound?"

Troy shook his head in disgust. "Chance is lek a bird." Lifting one huge hand, Troy gripped it into a fist. "Tek it now or it will fly."

"Gawd's wrath! What is that supposed ta—" Roderic

began, but Troy raised his voice and shifted his gaze to Flanna.

"Please come, lass," said he, "while the lad makes up his mind."

Outside the tower, lightning flashed like golden pitchforks across the ebony sky. Thunder cracked. Roderic paced. He should be with her. He should be guarding her. He should surely not be here, confined to this high stone Hades. But he doubted whether the MacGowan warriors would allow him to sit at the end of Flanna's bed as she slept.

Roderic paced again. Storms made him feel edgy. The thought of Flanna in danger made him feel violent.

And there was danger. But from where did it come? Who was the culprit?

Chance was like a bird, Troy had said. What the devil did that mean?

Who had shot the arrows? Who had tampered with Bruid's latch? He had to know. But he did not. And so he must keep her safe. But neither could he do that.

And so . . .

He stopped abruptly. Bonny's wet nose bumped his bare leg. He glanced at the shutter. It was boarded up. He looked at the ceiling. Without the furniture, it was far beyond his reach. The door held the only possibility of escape.

But how? Glancing desperately about, his gaze fell on the hound. She smiled adoringly up at him.

It might work. He squatted down and stroked the dog while he studied the dark outline of the door. It *would* work. He would leave—tonight. But he would not leave alone.

Chapter 14

❦

Beneath the plaid, Bonny wagged her tail against the straw tick. Roderic whispered to her, stroking her face and pulling the woolen over her head.

Thunder shattered the stillness but very little light invaded the room.

He stroked the hound's face again, waiting for the quiet to return. In the darkness, he checked the tautness of the plaid he had tied around Bonny's neck and run beneath the mattress. It felt solid enough to hold her for a few moments at least.

Sending a silent prayer to his maker, Roderic reviewed his plans. When all was ready, he rose.

Taking a deep breath, he waited a moment and shrieked, "Nay!" in a terrified tone that fairly shook the roof. In a moment, he was flying silently across the room to press his back against the wall beside the portal's hinges.

There was the sound of someone bumping to wakefulness, and then the door burst open.

"Forbes!" Bullock called. Through the crack between the door and the wall, Roderic could make out the broad warrior's form. Though his features were sleepy, his sword was drawn.

Diffused light fell across his tousled hair and onto the bright MacGowan tartan that covered the lumpy mattress. Beneath the woolen, Bonny wriggled wildly.

"Forbes!" Bullock called again.

173

"What is it?" Gilbert gasped, pressing in beside his partner.

" 'Tis Forbes," Bullock snorted, his tone calmer now as he shook his head. "Another of his damnable dreams I would guess. Ye stay here. I will shake him awake."

Roderic tensed. Bullock strode forward.

Bonny wiggled. The plaid fell aside, exposing her long, furry head. Bullock gasped at the same time Roderic threw his weight against the portal, slamming Gilbert against the wall.

There was a shriek, a gasp, a curse, and a howl. But suddenly, Gilbert's sword was in Roderic's hand, and Gilbert's back was pressed against his captor's chest.

No one breathed.

Bullock raised his arms carefully, sword tilted downward. "The hound took yer blanket?" he guessed cautiously. "And ye want another again?"

Roderic granted him a grin for his humor. "I fear me complaint is more serious than that tanight, lads," he said.

"Ye want fresh bandages for yer wound?"

"I must leave," Roderic said.

"Good riddance ta ye," gasped Gilbert. "May auld horny himself go with ye."

Roderic's smile increased. "Will ye never believe that I had nothing ta do with Simon's death?"

The room was silent for a moment. " 'Tis a strange one ye be, Forbes. That I say."

"Well, I didna," said Roderic, and moving quickly, he shoved Gilbert away.

He crashed forward, nearly ramming into Bullock, who steadied him with his hands.

Upon the mattress, Bonny slipped from her woolen tether to bound across the room to the door.

"And neither will I harm yer lady if ye do what I say."

Thunder rumbled like a feral growl through the heavens. Lightning crackled. In the scattered light, Roderic could see the guards' faces pale.

"Nay." Bullock shook his head and carefully hefted his sword. "Ye willna harm her for ye willna touch her, Forbes."

" 'Tis sad I am ta worry ye," disagreed Roderic gently. "But she will leave with me. I only ask that ye do me bidding, so that she may remain safe. Promise ta keep quiet."

The guards' mouths fell open in unison.

"I will tek your word as yer bond," he said solemnly. "If ye promise na ta call for help until the dawn, I willna harm her in any way."

Thunder crashed, followed by stunned silence.

Bullock watched him with narrowed eyes. "I dunna think ye will harm her anyway, Forbes," he said softly. "Or else why go through the effort of saving her from Bruid today?"

Roderic canted his head in concession. " 'Tis the truth ye speak, Bullock. I couldna harm her. But I tell ye, if ye vow ta keep still until morn, I will see her safely returned ta ye. If na . . ." He shrugged. "The Forbeses have the power ta hold her forever."

" 'Twould be better for us if ye bumped us on the head and tossed us from the window," said Gilbert. "For when the others find her gone, they will surely do worse ta us."

"The others is the reason I am taking her, for I know na who she can trust. But I have a message for the Wolfhound. Tell him that if he had any sense, he would have had ye guarding the Flame instead of guarding the Rogue. And tell him"—he grinned, feeling the exhilaration of impending freedom wash over him. "Tell him that I wish it had been he guarding the door. For it would have made na difference. When Roderic the Rogue decides ta leave, he leaves." Thrusting the sword beneath his belt, he gripped his plaid near his chest and drew a deep breath. "Do I have yer vow of silence?"

"Aye." Their acquiescence came reluctantly, but it came.

"Good lads. I willna forget your cooperation." Without shifting his gaze from the two by the mattress, Roderic retrieved his boots and backed away. In a moment, the door was barred behind him.

Bonny laughed up into his face. Thunder cracked again. Roderic shoved the tops of his boots beneath the strap of his sporran. They dangled against his backside, leaving his feet bare and silent. Stealth was a necessity if he hoped to live out the night.

Silently, he moved down the stairs. The hall appeared much the same as always in the dim light. With a signal from her beloved, Bonny sat at the bottom of the steps and waited as her master slipped across the hall.

Marjory again slept before her mistress's door. Wasting no time, Roderic stepped over her and lifted the latch. The shutters were closed against the wild weather, and the fire had burned down, leaving the room steeped in darkness. He made his way to the draped bed. His heart was beating rapidly now. Whether it was caused by his own furtive mission or Flanna's proximity, he wasn't certain.

Memories of seeing her abed numbed Roderic's senses. He wished he had time to delay, to wake her slowly. To stroke her hair and soothe her, for though she seemed the fearless leader of the MacGowans, she was a woman at heart, soft and fragile and sweet.

"Move and you'll wear my dirk between your ribs." Her words came from behind him and were spoken through gritted teeth in a low and angry voice.

"Lass?" Roderic questioned, remembering, a bit belatedly, that sometimes she was sweeter than others. "Is that ye?" he asked, turning slightly.

"Do not move if ye value your life."

He did and found that her dirk was just as sharp as the last time he had encountered it. It was placed between two ribs about halfway down his back. 'Twould be an ugly wound if she but thrust a bit harder.

Roderic shook his head gently. "Nay, lass, I wouldna even consider moving. I may never move again. In fact, if ye like, I could—"

"Shut up!" she said, thrusting the dirk a bit harder against his back.

He nodded once. "I could do that, too."

Thunder crackled, then rumbled to silence.

"How did ye escape?"

"Well . . ." Roderic cleared his throat. He had been quite clever really and didn't mind relating his exploits to an appreciative audience. "I—"

"How did ye get past Marjory?"

He opened his mouth to speak again.

"What the devil are ye doing here?"

"Which of those would ye like answered first, lass?"

"Ply me with your glib tongue and I'll feed ye to the hounds, Forbes."

"Most unsavory. Are ye fully dressed?"

The knife was pressed in earnest now and she gripped his hair in her other hand. "Why are ye here?"

"Is it the truth ye wish for, lass?"

"The truth or your death."

He nodded once. "The truth is, I couldna keep meself from ye any longer." He paused, expecting her to speak, but she did not. "Every moment away from ye is torture. Each night is an eternity. Yer presence is me very breath." Raising his arm, he gripped his plaid over his chest. "The very beat of me heart."

Silence echoed in the room.

" 'Twas ye that left the note?" Her voice was low and husky.

"The truth again, lass?" he asked softly.

"The truth."

He turned carefully to glance over his shoulder at her. "Aye. 'Twas me."

"Ye lie?" The knife had slipped away a bit. She pressed it harder, but now Roderic wondered if he felt it tremble slightly. "There is no way ye could have escaped the tower. Not alone. Who aided ye?"

"Yer beauty aided me. None other."

"Ye lie!"

Roderic arched his back away from the knife and

grimaced. "Well, that I do, lass. But na at this moment. I had na aid. For me desire for ye canna be bound. Na matter how thick the walls or how high the tower."

"Do not speak to me in the deceitful tongue of the gallant knight. I have heard the words before."

He did not mean to turn. In fact, he had every intention of remaining immobile, of not frightening her. But the thought of her in another's arms was unbearable and suddenly he twisted about. While managing to avoid the blade, he gripped her wrist in his hand.

"But ye heard them from the wrong man," he breathed.

She ceased her struggling and stared into his eyes. "Why are ye here?" she whispered.

Lightning crackled, but whether it occurred beyond the walls or inside this very chamber, they could not have said for such was the intensity of their touch.

"I am here for ye, lass."

Beneath the simple, saffron shirt, her breasts rose and fell with each rapid inhalation.

Every good intention slipped away, every fine sense of self-control and good sense. Despite it all, he kissed her. Her lips met his in a hard clash of emotion. Against his chest, he could feel the warm crush of her breasts.

Dear Gawd, she tasted like heaven and felt the same. Moving his hand onto her back, he moaned and pulled her closer and let his kisses slip to her throat. "Lass," he groaned.

"Roderic!" she gasped, trembling.

"Lady?" Marjory called, knocking at the portal.

Their eyes popped open. They stared at each other from mere inches away, finding sanity with a jolt.

"Lady?" Marjory called again. "Are ye well?"

"I leave tonight," Roderic whispered. "And ye will go with me."

Flame's lips parted soundlessly.

"Lady?" Marjory's tone was distraught now.

"There has been a bit of trouble in the stable," Roderic called in a voice he hoped did not sound like his own. "Lochan is unwell."

"Who's in there?" Marjory gasped.

"If ye play the game with me, none will be hurt," Roderic whispered. "Otherwise, I can guarantee naught."

Flanna's body was very stiff in his arms.

"Do ye hear me?" he asked, easing the dirk from her fingers.

"Do not fret, Marjory," she called. "Lochan but kicks at his belly. Gilbert came to tell me."

Roderic nodded his approval, then turned her about and nudged her across the floor toward the door. It opened silently beneath his hand.

"Me lady?" Marjory questioned.

"Sleep," Flame ordered. "I will be back soon."

"Aye . . ." The maidservant sounded dubious but did not move from her spot near the door.

Roderic tilted his head downward, hoping his borrowed bonnet would hide his features. The steps were cold against his bare feet. The hall was typically quiet as they stepped into it. From the stairwell opposite them, Bonny whined. Roderic motioned to her and she came, bounding joyously through the dried rushes with the stealth of a crashing herd of swine.

Roderic winced.

"Lady Flame?" grumbled William, sitting up near the dwindling fire. "Is somemat amiss?"

She was silent for a moment. Roderic squeezed her arm in warning.

" 'Tis only Lochan's disquiet. I go to soothe him."

"I will come with ye. 'Tis na a fit night."

Roderic squeezed harder.

"Nay," she said quickly. "In truth, I couldna sleep anyway. I need some time alone in the stable. Go back to sleep."

"Ye are sure?"

She nodded.

"As ye wish," William said, and lay back down.

They moved on as a single unit, with Roderic walking close behind her. "Verra good, lass."

She didn't respond.

Outside, fat drops of rain splattered against their faces. 'Twas a wicked night to escape, thought Roderic, but he had gone too far to turn back now.

The stable door creaked open. Even within the confines of the bailey, the wind gripped it so that Roderic struggled to pull it closed.

Bright torchlight greeted them.

"Lady!" Three men rose abruptly. Dice tumbled to the blanket beneath them. "What brings ye out? Who—?"

"Dunna move!" Roderic warned, gripping Flame's arm from behind. "Na if ye dunna want to see her hurt."

The men froze. "Forbes!" gasped one. "How—?"

"Though I would be glad ta relate me cleverness," began Roderic, "I fear there is na time. For I must leave and yer lady will go with me."

"Over me own dead body!" gritted one warrior, grabbing a nearby sword.

"Nay," Roderic said, slipping Flame's dirk from his belt. "Over *her* dead body."

Not a soul moved.

"Verra good. I need a horse readied. You, with the bonnet. Fetch a mount," Roderic ordered.

The man moved stiffly away. Taking a rope from a peg on the wall, he opened the stall door and latched the lead on to the steed's head collar.

"You," Roderic said, nodding to the next man in line, "get the saddle and . . ."

But suddenly the stall door was swung open. The first warrior ducked behind it and came up with his bow already bent. An arrow whizzed past Roderic's head. Roaring with rage, he pushed Flanna behind him and swung his sword at the lantern on the wall.

It flew from its peg, landing on the woolen blanket and plunging the stable into darkness.

A man yelled and sprang for him. Not wishing to kill anyone, Roderic swung his fist. It thudded against a skull. A body fell. The loose horse skittered down the aisle. Grasping Flanna's arm, Roderic yanked her nearer and grabbed the stallion's flying rope.

In an instant, they were outside. "Get on!" he rasped.

Flame moved toward the horse, but suddenly her elbow caught him in the side and she pivoted away. He dropped the sword and grabbed wildly for her with both hands. His fingers tangled in her hair. She stopped with a shriek of pain, but now his hand found her wrist and he yanked her forward, grabbed her by the waist, and tossed her aboard the stallion's back.

Aided by pumping excitement and the sure knowledge that he had only one chance to escape with her, Roderic swung up behind. Gripping her tightly, he forced the steed into a gallop.

"Let down the bridge," he roared.

"Who goes there? What be yer business?" gasped a gnarled voice.

" 'Tis yer lady's life!" growled Roderic. "Let down the bridge or she dies."

The bridge creaked downward. Behind them, men yelled and swarmed across the bailey.

"Gawd's wrath!" Roderic swore. Thumping his heels against the stallion's sides, he forced the steed back into a gallop. The bridge had not yet reached the opposite shore, but the great beast thundered up, reached the end, and launched itself from its summit to the earth below. Its hind feet hit the rushing burn. His knees buckled, throwing his riders onto his neck. Roderic gripped the mane, holding Flame tightly against his body and urging the stallion to his feet.

"Let it down! Down!" someone yelled.

But in an instant, the stallion found his footing and flew into the night.

Chapter 15

Darkness rushed past them. Roderic's arms entrapped her as he held the stallion's reins in both hands. She should have fought harder to remain behind. She should have clawed and kicked and screamed, but he had kissed her, had spoken gentle words, and a thousand emotions had clouded her judgment, a thousand confusing thoughts had rushed upon her. Thoughts of his strength, his smile, his laughter had dazzled her. But it was the images of him dead on MacGowan soil that had decided her. He could easily have been killed by the burn. Dun Ard was not safe for him, and so she had come with him, had aided his escape, and in so doing, had abandoned her clan. 'Twas a woman's weakness that had brought her here. 'Twas a Flame's strength that would take her back.

"Stop the horse," she ordered.

"Surely ye jest," rasped Roderic, pressing their mount to greater speed as he glanced over his shoulder.

"Ye are safe now," she said, wrapping one hand in the mane. "Let me go."

"Nay." They crashed through a darkened woods, finally emerging in a clearing, but the world was little brighter there, for the clouds seemed to hover around their very ears.

"Ye do not need me anymore," she said. "I have served my purpose for ye."

"Hardly, lass."

She stiffened in his arms. "What do ye mean?"

He pulled the stallion to a shuddering halt and looked behind them as lightning illuminated the world once again. Their faces were very close. His thighs were hard behind hers, and his arms felt strong and warm.

"I mean . . . ye have captured me heart, lass."

How many years had she waited to hear such words? As a child in a cold, gray convent, she had wept for strong arms to hold her. As a woman, she had longed for love. But she was the Flame now, and words like that would only destroy her.

"I must go back," she whispered. "I am their leader. They need me."

"Ye are a woman," he murmured. "I need ye."

Warmth suffused her. What would it be like to be loved, cherished, protected? All her life she had wanted those things.

He leaned closer. She could feel the steady beat of his heart against her arm, could feel herself falling under his spell.

She had vowed to protect others. She could not go back on her word.

"Flanna," he breathed, leaning closer.

"Nay!" she gasped. "I am not Flanna. I am the Flame."

"Ye are a woman," he breathed, "and ye are mine—"

"Nay!" she shrieked and slammed her elbow into his side. She felt the cartilage between his ribs bow beneath the impact, but there was no time to consider the damage. Taking advantage of his loosened grip, she threw a leg over the stallion's neck and launched herself from his back.

Flame hit the ground on all fours. Behind her, Forbes hissed an expletive of wrath or pain. In an instant she was on her feet and running. Five rods away, the woods towered up to meet her, but already she could hear Cam's snort of surprise as Roderic thumped him into a gallop. His great hooves thundered against the earth, echoing in her ears, and suddenly he was beside her.

"Flanna!" Roderic rasped. "Stop this. Stop!" he in-

sisted, but she was nearly to the woods. Just a little farther and she could slip among the trees where the huge
destrier would have to slow. 'Twould be so simple to
hide there.

"Flanna!" Roderic yelled again. "Oh hell!" Though
she didn't see him, she knew the moment he propelled
himself from the horse's back. She twisted away with a
cry.

His fingers clawed at her back, throwing her off balance. She shrieked again. He hit the earth with a thud
and a groan, but managed to grab her leg.

She fell with a snarl, kicking and fighting until she
hit the ground with a lung-crushing jolt. Stunned and
speechless, she lay motionless and in that moment he
grappled his way up her prostrate form.

"Gawd's wrath, lass," Roderic rasped. "What is the
matter with ye? I'm na going ta hurt ye."

Every inch of her squashed body ached. She gasped
for breath.

"What were ye thinking? Ye could have gotten yerself kilt."

"Me?" she rasped. The single word sounded as if it
had been scraped from the bottom of her boot. "Ye are
the one who would kill me!"

"Nay, lass. What be ye talking about? I willna hurt
ye."

"Won't hurt me!" His very presence threatened the
Flame's existence, and if the Flame was killed, Flanna
would be all that was left. And Flanna was painfully
vulnerable. "Won't hurt me," she said again, breathing
more normally now and trying to calm the frantic beat
of her heart. "Ye threatened to kill me!" Inches away,
Bonny planted herself beside Roderic and thumped her
tail.

"Oh, lass." Absently, he stroked a strand of hair from
her face. "That was just fer yer men. Surely ye didna
believe such dramatics."

No, she had not believed his threats, and there lay the
problem, for her heart could not afford to trust him.

"Let me go," she ordered, but the command was hopelessly breathy. "Let me go before—"

"Why would ye wish ta go after all I've done for ye?" he asked. Even in the darkness, his crooked smile was devastating.

"Done for me?" she asked, trying to be angry.

"Aye. I have saved ye from the villain who would kill ye."

"He was trying to kill ye, ye braying—" she began, but suddenly his hand was clasped over her mouth and his body pressed more tightly to hers.

"Shh," he hissed.

Out of the darkness, a score of horses thundered down upon them.

Flame tried to scream, to call for help, but before she could do so much as manage a squeak, the riders had sped past.

Roderic slipped his hand from her mouth and grinned. "Sorry. But that might have been the villain himself."

"You're the villain, ye vile—"

But his hand was clasped to her mouth again. More horses galloped up.

"Can ye see any sign of them?" someone yelled.

"Nay! Damn Forbes' black heart to hell!"

She watched that same black-hearted Forbes grin into her face like a smug gargoyle and listened as this new band of horses thundered off.

"Sorry," he said again, easing his hand from her face for a second time. "But we canna risk being found. The villain could be anyone. Even yer most trusted warrior."

"They'll find us," she said stiffly. "And then your heart will be—"

This time it was not his hand that covered her mouth but his lips. They moved upon hers with firm, slow warmth, taking her breath and her senses. His heart thrummed against hers. His fingers slipped along her neck, stroking her gently as they moved into her hair. One of his heavy thighs lay between hers, and the heat of his body seemed to sear her to her very soul.

"Pierced," he murmured, drawing away to gaze into her eyes.

"What?" It was the best she could manage.

"Me heart will be pierced," he said softly, then kissed the corner of her mouth, her cheek, the point of her chin. "It will be pierced by yer beauty."

She blinked, trying to marshall her senses.

"Pierced by yer beauty, trapped by yer eyes, and healed by yer love," he whispered.

She swallowed hard. This was ridiculous. What kind of fool would believe the words of a man who had abducted her at knifepoint? "Pierced by my arrow more likely," she rasped. Her voice hardly trembled at all. "Let me go."

"I canna, lass," he said, but his words were little more than a breath of air against her cheek.

"Ye don't need me any longer." Panic rose within her. She hoped it was caused by her capture and not by the feelings that flooded through her.

"On the contrary, Flanna." He touched her hair again, sweeping gentle fingertips through it. "I have needed ye from the moment I met ye."

She forced herself to laugh. "As ye have needed every other woman ye have seduced."

His expression was suddenly very somber. "Nay, na lek that atall," he said, and leaned forward again.

She scrunched back into the soggy earth beneath her. "They will return."

He looked slightly disoriented. "Who?"

"My men."

"Oh." He sighed and caressed her cheek with the back of his fingers. "I dunna think so, for the steed ran on." His lips touched the corner of her mouth, sweeping a wave of heat through her system.

"He'll soon stop!" she gasped, trying to push away. "They'll see he bears no riders and turn back."

"He'll run on till he finds the mares," Roderic corrected softly and gently kissed the edge of her jaw.

She shivered beneath his touch. "Don't do that."

He drew away ever so slightly. "Why?"

"Because I don't like it."

He questioned her with his eyes. "Because ye are scairt," he corrected gently.

Employing every bit of strength she possessed, she drew her pride about her. "Not of ye, Forbes," she said haughtily. "I will never fear ye. Ye cannot make me."

"I am sorry if it seems that I have tried."

"If ye let me go, I will not let them find ye. Ye will have safe passage back to your homeland." Two raindrops hit her face with sharp force. For the first time, she noticed the wail of the howling wind.

"And what of yer safety?" he asked quietly.

" 'Tis none of your concern."

Rain spattered against them with a sharp, regular cadence now, pinging off her leather hose and burning her face.

"I have made it me concern, lass," he breathed and kissed her again.

All good sense was lost in the shock of his caress, the feel of his hand in her hair, his thigh beneath hers. The assault numbed her. She was left breathless when finally he drew away.

"Correct me if I am wrong, but I think it is raining," he said.

No, it was pouring, coming down in great gray sheets of liquid ice, but she saw no reason to state the obvious.

He peered over her head, squinting into the rain. " 'Twill be a long night, lass," he murmured. Slipping from her body, he set one hip to the ground and grimaced in pain. It seemed she had somehow wounded him. "And ye are such a delicate thing," he said sardonically. "I hope ye be up ta the challenge."

His voice sounded very casual, as if he had not just seared her senses to ash. She struggled to sound the same.

"I am certain I can manage anything ye can, Forbes."

*   *   *

Four hours later, Flame wished she had never spoken. Nay. She wished she had never been born.

"Are ye well, lass?"

Every single fiber of her body ached. "Yes." It seemed they had been walking forever, scrambling through the pelting darkness for a nightmarish eternity. It had given her far too much time to think, to remember that she was no more than his prisoner, and though he could kiss her until her mind turned to sap, she must return to her people.

But just now they stood in a ramshackle crofter's hut. Or rather, she stood, he stooped, for part of the roof had fallen in, allowing them only an abbreviated, sloping space in which to escape the weather that howled outside. "I am fine," she said and shivered.

He scowled at her and arranged a few soggy, scattered boards to cover the doorway. The gloomy light of pre-dawn seeped in between them, allowing her to see his expression. "Nay ye are na," he said.

"Ahh." Rain dripped from her hair to slide chilling fingers down her throat and beneath her shirt. She raised one brow and shivered again, though she forced herself to ignore it. "So ye are an expert on women's well-being as well as women in general."

"Aye." He grinned. Although he couldn't straighten his neck completely in the cramped quarters, he looked disturbingly content. "I am that."

She turned away with a snort, although *away* meant merely turning her face into the dank corner.

"Tek off yer clothes."

She swung about so quickly that the muscles in her neck cramped. "What?"

His grin increased. "Tek yer clothes off?" he said, as if it hadn't been he who had suggested it the first time.

"Ye must surely be feverish!"

"Better that I be feverish than that ye be. Get out of those wet clothes, lass, and let yer skin dry," he said, moving toward her.

"Touch me," she warned, "and ye die."

She hadn't expected him to laugh, but he did. Settling onto his haunches, he threw back his head and laughed till he cried.

She glared at him. It did no good. She gritted her teeth and swore through them. And then, when it seemed the uproar would never end, she thumped him on the chest with her foot. He tumbled onto his buttocks, letting his legs sprawl out in front of him. The laughter finally turned to chortles and the chortles to silly, sporadic hiccups of glee.

"Ahh, lass." He wiped his eyes with the backs of his fingers and shook his head. "Ye are so serious."

She glowered at him.

He chuckled again. "Soaked to the skin. Shivering lek a wet hound." He patted Bonny as if apologizing to the cur for comparing the two. "And still as haughty as a queen." He paused and shook his head as he grinned at her. "But even a queen has to remove her clothes sometime."

She tried to sharpen her glare but it felt as if her muscles were frozen in place.

His expression sobered. "If I said please?"

"Ye are crazed."

"I dunna wish ta tek the clothes from ye by force."

Flame raised one brow and smiled at him. "And I do not wish to kill ye," she said sweetly.

He chuckled again, then sobered. "And what do ye think would happen if ye died of a fever?"

She scowled at him. "I think ye would hustle away to hearth and home and the arms of a woman more foolish than I."

"Well, ye are wrong, lass. I would sit and mourn yer passing, until yer warriors came ta slit me throat ta avenge yer death."

His eyes were deep and entrancing. It would be very nice to believe she saw concern in them. "I am not going to die," she assured him evenly.

"I willna hurt ye," he murmured.

But he would. He would reduce her to the quivering

lass called Flanna MacGowan. He would make her trust him, make her love him, and when he saw her true self, Flanna MacGowan would die again, and the Flame would no longer be strong enough to take her place. A spasm of cold shook her from head to foot, causing her goose-bumped skin to ache. Still, she could not admit her weakness. "And what of ye, Forbes? I suppose ye do not feel even the slightest discomfort?"

He shrugged noncommittally.

"Of course not," she said. "And tell me, is that because ye be a Forbes, or simply because ye are a man?"

He studied her carefully. There was not even a hint of laughter in his eyes now. "Is it the truth ye wish for, lass?"

" 'Twould be a welcome change."

"I be so cold I canna feel me fingers. I think me left kneecap is frozen and 'tis a grave possibility that I broke me ribs when jumping from the horse."

Surprised by his candidness, Flame opened her mouth to speak, but he held up a hand and continued.

"The muscles of me legs are knotted up lek the trunk of a windblown oak. Me back hurts lek the verra devil. And me wet plaid has worn me skin raw."

"Then mayhap *ye* should take off *yer* clothes."

He paused only a moment, "If ye wish," he said, and put his hand to his belt.

"What are ye doing?"

"Taking a lady's advice," he said.

"No." Her tone sounded panicked to her own ears.

"Think about it, lass. We be miles from any sort of comfort and we be soaked ta the skin. We could at least share the heat of our bodies."

She drew a sharp breath. "I will not risk that."

His hands stilled. "I wasna speaking of risk, lass," he said, his tone befuddled. " 'Twas speaking of sharing our bodies' warmth and nothing more."

She backed away a step. Her shoulders bumped the wall behind her. "I have nothing to share with ye."

"I think ye misjudge yerself, Flanna."

"Nay, tis ye that misjudges. I know men, Forbes."

"Do ye? And who have ye known that makes ye such an expert?"

"Do ye forget that I lead the MacGowans? That the warriors listen to my—"

"Nay, I dunna forget, lass. But I speak of a more personal nature. As a lass, as a woman, who have ye known?"

She knew exactly what he meant. "My father . . ." she said.

"Ah yes, yer father," Roderic said softly. "Yer father who couldna bear the sight of ye for ye reminded him of the woman he loved but did not trust."

She could not speak, but with all her heart she wanted to believe that was the only reason for her father's abandonment. With every fiber in her, she wished to believe she was worthy of love.

"And Carvell. That charming gallant who chose a man over a woman's tender charms."

Flame turned away, unable to meet his eyes. "Why did they hate me so?" she whispered. "Am I so detestable?"

"Nay, lass," he said softly. "Ye are all that is good and fine."

She shook her head. "I am my father's daughter, Forbes, make no mistake. And he . . . He . . ." She swallowed, knowing she should say no more, but finding she couldn't stop the words as dark memories echoed in her skull. "He was incensed that I refused to marry. I think for a time he went mad, for as he beat me, he called me by my mother's name, Cecelia."

"Gawd's wrath!" Roderic swore, rising abruptly to his feet, his fists clenched.

She shrugged, drawing a deep breath and steadying her voice. "I think he wished to kill me. But as ye see, I did not die, for I am a fighter."

"Like yer sire."

She nodded once.

"And for that ye despise *yerself*."

"He chose me to be the leader, Forbes. He could have chosen his nephew. But he did not, for Nevin is but the son of a kind, lowly cloth merchant. He is intelligent and sensitive. Surely, in my father's eyes, he was not fit to rule."

"So ye think ye were chosen because ye are like yer sire? Because ye are cruel and merciless."

"Mayhap my father knew me better than I knew myself."

"Yer father knew ye na at all," Roderic rasped, and taking a step forward, touched her cheek with his fingertips. She was caught in his eyes, lost in that blue, steady gaze. "But I see ye for what ye are."

"And what is that?" she whispered.

"Soft and strong, naive and wise, caring and fierce. 'Tis a woman ye are, lass."

"Nay." She forced the word between stiff lips. "I am the Flame of—"

He lifted his hand from her cheek to stroke a finger against her lips. Lightning flashed through her being.

"There is na reason ye canna be both the woman and the Flame, lass," he murmured.

Heat diffused every fiber of her body. Desire sparked in her breast and blazed outward, setting her afire. But she had heard a man's pretty words before, only to find that that man was no better than her father. When she had found Carvell with his lover, he had threatened her life if she told his secret. But it was not his threat that had kept her quiet. It was her shame. Drawing her shoulders up, she pulled herself from his embrace with an effort. "I will not be a pawn, Forbes. Not yours or any man's," she whispered. "I will not be stroked and petted and tossed aside at your whim."

"Ye devalue yer own worth, and my intelligence, lass. I am na the kind ta toss treasures aside."

His eyes offered caring and honor and all the things she longed for, but she could not accept, could not trust.

"Ye lie," she whispered.

"Do I? Then touch *me*, lass. Stroke me and pet *me*. And when ye are through 'twill be yer decision if I am ta be tossed aside."

Chapter 16

❦❦

"Ye say I can pet ye and leave ye," Flanna said. "But the world does not work that way, Forbes. Do ye not know that women are the weaker vessels? Scripture says it is so. And therefore—"

" 'Tis na the strength of the chalice that determines its worth," Roderic interrupted softly. "Indeed, 'tis the delicately crafted vessel that is most cherished."

"But we are the ones that must bear the burden of childbirth."

"Some consider it a great blessing, lass."

"My mother died in her travail," she said. "Shamed, despised, and exiled from her homeland."

"Is it childbirth ye fear then, lass? Or is it something else?"

He was so very near. So large and powerful and alluring. So frightening.

"I fear nothing," she lied. "But I am—"

"Then ye are na afraid ta kiss me?"

A thousand feelings exploded within her. Her chest felt suddenly tight. "Nay," she breathed. "I am na afraid. I am merely uninterested."

His smile tilted only one corner of his mouth, and when he touched her face, his fingers were as light as falling snow. She shivered. "Now it is ye who lies, lass."

His hand slipped slowly along her jaw and down her throat. Against her better judgment, Flanna closed her eyes.

194

"Ye are scairt." His fingers flowed around her neck and into her hair. His words were no more than a breath in her ear. "Ye are afraid of what ye feel for me."

"Nay," she denied, but again she shivered.

"Then kiss me, lass, and prove it."

She opened her eyes, breathing hard. His face was tilted down toward hers, his high, broad cheekbones sharply chiseled, his eyes intense. She was a fool. She was weak. She kissed him.

Lightning struck her lips and sparked through her at the gentle caress. But in a moment, he moaned and pulled her closer, pressing her hard against him as he ravaged her lips. A thousand suppressed emotions jangled in her head, confusing her, titillating her, frightening her.

She shivered violently, quaking with cold and heat and denied longing. Roderic's hand slipped downward, over her jaw, her throat, the thundering pulse that raced between her collarbones.

"Heaven's gate, lass!" he rasped. "I need ye."

"Nay!" She broke frantically away from his embrace. He took a step nearer, but she flattened herself against the wall with her heart beating like galloping hooves.

He stopped only inches from her. "Please, lass," he pleaded. "I need . . ." he began, but he watched her carefully and finally drew a shaky breath. "I didna mean ta frighten ye."

"Ye did not." The words sounded pathetically untrue to her own ears.

Roderic smiled and ran splayed fingers through his wet hair. "Truly?" His hand trembled and he laughed. "Well, ye scared the hell outta me, lass."

She said nothing. Never had she felt such rampaging emotions. Carvell had charmed her, had flattered her, and she had imagined herself as his bride, as the mother of his children. But this was entirely different. This was a desire so primitive that it seemed to shake the very foundations of the earth.

"Ye may na believe this, lass, but I'm usually

quite"—he chuckled, seeming to be laughing at himself—"sane."

God forgive her. She wanted him right here, right now, and damn the consequences. "Truly?" Her breathing was still harsh. "Ye couldn't prove it by me," she said and shivered.

"Me apologies, lass. I am usually a patient man. I dunna often lose control."

"Should I be flattered?"

He raised one brow, and in that moment he looked very noble and aloof. "Aye, lass. Ye should. Now take off yer clothes."

Her mouth fell open, and he laughed out loud.

"So ye think ye've but to kiss me once and I'll beg for your favors?" she asked, aghast.

" 'Tis usually how it works."

"Ye are a conceited, braying—"

"And ye are freezing," he interrupted. "Take off yer clothes, lass, and I'll . . ." He skimmed his hot gaze down her saturated form where her clothing clung like a second skin. "I'll . . ." She braced herself against the onslaught of his eyes. "I'll start a fire," he said, before turning stiffly away to rummage about for dry kindling. After a few moments, he took a flint from his sporran and sparked a tiny flame into the scraps of wood he had found. Adding a small bit of a stool leg, he fanned the flame.

Flanna moved closer. Her eyes were huge in her pale face and her hands trembled as she stretched them toward the fire. He turned away, still lacking control and forcing himself to think of something other than how she felt in his arms.

Outside, thunder rumbled again and though the wind had decreased, the day grew no brighter. There would be little hope of finding dry timber beneath the flint-gray sky.

Roderic searched the interior by the light of the feeble fire. He found bits of twigs, fragments of broken crockery, and then, buried beneath the tumbled stone of what had once been a fireplace, he uncovered a blanket. Dust wafted from the small, tattered plaid in billowing clouds as he pulled it from the debris. Its color was indistinguishable, but it was mostly dry.

He rose to a stooped position and raised his gaze. Flanna caught it. Emotions sizzled.

Roderic drew a deep breath and reminded himself that despite the heat that seared his nether parts, she was cold and scared. "If I vow na ta look, will ye take off yer clothes and wrap up in it?"

She shivered.

"I willna compromise ye, lass."

She blinked at him, and for one wild moment he hoped she would beg him to do just that.

She didn't.

"Despite what ye think of men, me word is good."

An eternity passed before she nodded. "Turn around."

He did so. In a moment, he could hear her soggy boots drop to the earth. Her shirt followed. His manhood throbbed. Imagination, he mused, was a wonderful, if excruciating, thing.

"Ye may turn back, now." Her voice was small.

She was wrapped from head to foot in the ratty woolen. It was just wide enough to circle her body one and a half times, he noticed, and he saw how she held it together at her bosom with a white-knuckled grip. He steadied his breathing and managed a grin. "Ye look bonny."

"And ye lie," she said, louder now.

"Nay." He retrieved her soggy garments, and straightened them by the fire. The leather hose felt soft and slick. "I dunna."

"Then ye are blind."

"Na that either," he assured. He straightened as best he could, and then began loosening his belt buckle.

"What are ye doing?"

"I am cold and wet and weary, lass. And I am removing me plaid."

"Nay!"

He chuckled. It was good to know his impending nudity disturbed her, for indeed 'twould be a sad thing to think she simply didn't care.

"Ye mustn't take off your clothes," she breathed.

"Ahh, but I must, lass," he disagreed. "For I, too, am cold."

"But"—she glanced frantically about as if looking for a rock to hide under—"there are no more blankets. Ye'll only get colder."

God she was beautiful. Every fiber in him was singing with the thought of being near her. He loosened his sporran and belt with a couple quick jerks and in a moment, his heavy, soaked plaid was in a pile on the floor. Her gaze flitted to it before snapping abruptly back to his face.

Roderic unlaced his shirt with numb fingers, then he dragged its wet length along his shivering skin. In a moment he was stark naked and colder than ever.

Her eyes were huge and vibrant green. All traces of the haughty lady fled as he stepped toward her.

"What are ye doing?" Her words were no more than a whisper. "Ye promised."

"I promised na ta look. I didna promise na ta touch," he said, and snatching the blanket from her hand unwrapped her far enough to press himself up against her. She could feel every inch of his naked, rock-hard form, the heavy strength of his thigh as it brushed hers, the bulging curve of his arm against her breast. Desire unfurled within her like a blossoming rose.

"I do not want ye," she lied, shaking violently.

"Na even a little?" he murmured, looking into her eyes.

"Nay. Never!"

"Ye dunna long for me touch?"

Dear God, she would sell her soul for his touch. "Nay."

He turned and leaned closer so that his chest brushed

against the aching nub of her rigid nipple. "Ye dunna dream of my kiss?"

Every night. "Nay," she breathed.

His eyes smote her with blue flame for a moment, and then he shrugged. "As ye wish," he said, and turning away, dragged her along in the cocoon of their shared plaid and sat down in front of the fire.

There was nothing she could do but plop down beside him. Thus, they sat side by side before the weak blaze, staring into its crackling center. Her left side was pressed against his from thigh to shoulder. Roderic repressed a grin. She felt as stiff and cold as a slab of ice.

"Flanna?"

She jumped at the sound of her name, and he turned an innocuous gaze to her.

"I must add a bit a kindling to the flame. Ye willna faint if a bit of me bare arm is exposed, will ye?"

A flash of color returned to her cheeks. "I assure ye," she said through clenched teeth, "I could not care less if ye pranced naked as an owlet from here to Edinburgh."

His laughter was gently mocking. "Ah, 'tis a poor liar ye are, lass," he said, and reached for the kindling.

"I assure ye, I do n . . ." she began, but his movement had forced the blanket to fall from his chest and her attention caught there.

Roderic froze. Their gazes melded as he drew a sharp breath. "I willna hurt ye, Flanna. Ye could surely chance a touch."

"I—I told ye, I have no desire to . . . touch ye."

He smiled, not taking his gaze from her lips and losing himself for a moment in his own thoughts. "Would that I felt the same, lass," he said with a sigh and stretched out on the ground beside the fire.

He heard her gasp of dismay as the blanket was stretched tight between them. Probably, the filthy woolen was tugged from her grasp and threatened to expose any manner of interesting body parts, Roderic deduced. It took a good deal of self-control to keep from looking, but Roderic managed to remain facing the fire, and finally closed his eyes. 'Twas going to be a long, cold, wearisome day.

Roderic was not sure what had awakened him. Thunder rumbled softly. Breakfast would be waiting in the hall below, he thought. But he was still tired and his feet were cold. He tried to pull them under his blankets, but something weighted down the woolens.

He opened his eyes only to discover he was not at Glen Creag, nor in his tower room. He was not in a bed, and his muscles ached. The hut he occupied was very dark. It smelled rather like wet wolfhound, and something warm and soft was pressed against his back.

Please God, don't let it be a dog, he thought. It was then that he realized one slim arm rested across his waist. Not daring to move, he mentally assessed the rest of the situation. Someone breathed softly against the back of his neck. His right leg was bent at the knee and pulled up slightly. His left leg was straight. It was the third leg that intrigued him. It was cradled between his, and if he wasn't mistaken, warm, soft breasts were pressed up against his back.

Roderic stared at the dying embers of his pitiful fire, barely daring to hope. Either Bonny had changed a great deal or . . .

The slim arm moved. Roderic held his breath as the third leg was drawn upward. Instead of lying with comparative innocence between his, it settled with firm conviction against his buttocks and . . . other things.

Heaven's gate!

He drew a ragged breath. Hot desire sparked at the point of impact and scampered off in every direction, galvanizing his system.

Behind him, Flanna sighed softly in her sleep and snuggled closer.

Oh God! He had promised not to compromise her. What did that mean exactly? Since at this very moment he was lying naked with her, he could only assume he had been referring to copulation. Gawd's wrath! 'Twas an idiot's promise if ever he had made one!

But no. Wait. He was thinking with his nether parts. There were a thousand things a man could do without actual fornication.

Her fingers moved, brushing softly against his abdomen. Roderic sucked air through his teeth and let himself absorb every vibrant sensation, the feel of her breasts as she shifted, the rasp of her coarse pubic hair against his backside.

She moaned again and shifted restlessly. Her hand moved more swiftly, patting him tentatively, as if searching for familiar landmarks, first his abdomen, then his hip.

He knew the moment she awoke. There seemed nothing more practical than turning on his back and saying, "Good morningtide."

"What are ye doing here?" Her voice was weak, her eyes very wide.

Roderic tried to grin, but her nearness was taking its toll on his devil-may-care attitude. Still, he did his best to maintain his position as The Rogue. "The question is, lass, what were *ye* doing?"

Her mouth opened, but no words came. She tried again. "I thought . . . I didn't. . . . I was cold," she said, finally settling on a haughty tone.

"Ahh." Despite the throbbing ache of his desire, Roderic could see how the situation might be considered amusing . . . if he tried really hard. "Ye were na trying ta seduce me then?"

"I . . ." She shook her head, looking very young in her present state of disarray. While he slept, she had apparently unplaited her hair. It was mostly dry now and haloed her face and shoulders in brilliant, auburn curls.

He could not resist touching it.

"I . . ." she tried again.

His fingertips stroked her ear as he pressed a few fiery wisps behind its delicate curve.

She shivered. "I wasn't." Her voice was no more than a whisper.

He watched her eyes. "Ye weren't what?" he asked, letting his fingers sweep back to her scalp and then down her long, elegant throat.

She swallowed. He felt the movement beneath his fingers and let his hand slip to the soft hollow between her collarbones.

"I wasn't trying to seduce ye," she whispered.

"Yer heart beats as fast as a captured fledgling's," he murmured, feeling her life thrum beneath his fingers. "Perhaps ye didna think ye had to."

She blinked and swallowed again. "Had to what?"

"Seduce me," he whispered, unsure whether he was answering her question or begging for her attention. The look in her wide, emerald eyes made him realize that she, too, was uncertain.

He sighed. "I be as harmless as a wee babe, lass."

"Forgive me if I doubt ye." For just a moment her gaze slipped to his naked chest.

"Dunna doubt. Touch me and I will prove it."

She was holding her breath and doubting, he knew. But finally her hand moved.

Her fingers were as light as a spring breeze against his unshaven cheek. "Ye see?" he murmured, remaining very still and not allowing so much as a grin. "Soft as a bairn's behind."

"Hardly that," she whispered, but her tone was hoarse. Her hand remained where it was.

"Ye could"—his body felt as tight as a bowstring as he waited—"move lower. I dunna bite."

" 'Tis not your teeth I fear."

Roderic grinned. "I willna do that either, lass."

She searched his face for honesty, and apparently she found it, for her hand slipped slowly lower, over his throat and down the center of his chest. Now it was he who shivered.

Startled, she lifted her gaze to his face. He shrugged apologetically. "I canna control all me impulses."

For a moment he saw raw desire etched in her regal features, but she lowered her eyes quickly and drew her hand away.

" 'Tis na right that ye despise yer own longing." Reaching out, he gently lifted her chin to look into her eyes.

"Would ye have all of Scotland mating like wild beasts?" she asked.

"Nay. Just us. Sorry," he apologized quickly, but in that moment he realized she was neither offended nor shocked.

Indeed, the faintest shadow of a smile teased her lips. It enchanted him, for Flanna MacGowan smiled all too little. Placing her palm flat against his chest, she said, "Ye are a strange man, Roderic Forbes."

The look in her eyes made his upper half feel light and his lower half heavy. "Aye, lass," he rasped, remembering to breathe. "That I am."

"Why are ye here?"

"Have ye forgotten the abduction yet again?"

His attempt at levity did not divert her. Her hand slipped to the right, over one pectoral. She felt the hard muscle leap beneath her fingers. "Why am *I* here?" she whispered. "Why do you keep me here?"

The slow breath he drew sounded ragged. "Because ye would get soaked outside?"

She watched him in silence.

"The truth again, lass?"

"Aye," she said.

"I keep ye here because ye are the verra star that lights me night. The sun that warms me skin. There is na another like ye, Flanna MacGowan."

It would be so easy to be lost in his eyes, in the warmth of his words. So foolishly simple. But she was not a fool.

"Is it oddities ye search for then, Forbes?" she asked.

"Nay." He shook his head. " 'Tis spirit, and intelligence, and depth of character." He pulled her hand closer and placed it over the steady beat of his heart.

She may not be a fool, but she was lonely, and he touched her soul as none other had.

"Ye know nothing about me," she whispered, reminding herself to be wary.

" 'Tis na true, lass. I have admired yer spirit, suffered for yer intelligence, and witnessed the depth of yer character."

He still held her fingers over his heart, but she no longer had any desire to pull them away, for she had done the forbidden. She had fallen into the heavenly blue of his eyes.

"Ye know nothing of my character."

"I know of a boy named Haydan," he said, and she shifted her gaze away, trying to keep this enemy from touching her soul, but his fingers had left hers and smoothed slowly down the length of her forearm. "At first I couldna understand why ye concerned yerself with him. But now I ken the truth. Yer heart is as soft as yer skin."

She must not cry. Must not show weakness. "He has suffered enough. I but give him an anteroom and a straw tick."

"And yer love."

Fear coursed through her. She must not let him past her defenses. "Ye're entirely wrong."

He smiled directly into her eyes. "I am na, lass. There is na another that champions him as ye do. Even Troy, who is his kin."

"Haydan, too, was a Scot in France. We shared some history. That is all."

"Ye share yer heart," he murmured. "And ye are scairt to admit it."

"He had no one else to see to his welfare," she whispered, desperate to prove she had invested no emotion in the child called Haydan, but Roderic's eyes called her a liar. "He was alone." She was weak, so hopelessly weak and there seemed little point in denying it. "As am I."

"Nay," he murmured, and leaning closer, he kissed her.

The shock of the caress shook her entire being. It soared through each vein and tingled every nerve ending. Somehow his arms were wrapped about her body and she was crushed to him, breast to chest, thigh to thigh. His hand slipped along her spine and she arched against him, feeling the heat of his fingers burn her senses, feeling his hand cup her buttocks and pull her closer.

"Lass," he breathed. "Ye have the heart of a warrior and the form of a goddess."

He squeezed her closer still. Flame felt him throb hot and heavy and upright between them. Against all good sense, she was drawn to that heat and pressed against it. A moan escaped her lips. But it was barely audible over his.

She pushed her hips forward. His tautness tormented her with sweet promise. His kisses blazed a flaming trail from her mouth and down her neck. She moaned again and pressed her head back, arching her back and granting him access to lower regions.

"Sweet Flanna," he murmured. His breath caressed her like a summer breeze and then he kissed her breast.

The breath stopped in her throat. Her body went rigid as she waited, and then he took her nipple in his mouth and suckled.

Sparks of hot desire flashed through her, and she gasped, tangling her fingers in his hair and pulling him closer.

Her knees bent of their own accord and suddenly her legs were wrapped about his hips. She felt the smooth tip of his manhood throb against her moistness and pressed toward it.

"Flanna!" he rasped, pulling his head from his breast to stare at her.

"Please," she whispered, "don't stop."

He closed his eyes. Beneath her hands, the muscles of his back tensed. The hard shaft of his desire throbbed against her. She waited, breathless, needy. He leaned closer and their lips met again.

But suddenly, the wood at the door crashed to the ground.

In one smooth movement, Roderic rolled away and crouched like a besieged lion protecting his mate.

Flame gasped, Roderic swore, and Bonny thumped her tail against the dirt floor and proudly dropped a hare at her beloved's bare feet.

Chapter 17

"**B**onny," Roderic breathed in relief.

With shaking hands and trembling knees, Flame pushed herself to her feet, the musty woolen draped before her. Dear God, what had she done? What had she been about to do?

"Bonny," Roderic said again, "ye startled the verra devil right outta me." Turning slowly, he rose to his feet, finding Flame with his eyes.

She felt sickened by her weakness.

"Flanna," he said softly, "I—"

She lifted her chin a notch and tried to calm her trembling. "I will return to Dun Ard now."

Roderic drew a deep breath and bent his arm against his chest, as if prepared to clutch his plaid in a characteristic gesture. But his plaid was not there and his bulging forearm touched nothing but the mounded firmness of his pectoral. Below that his abdomen undulated in hard hillocks of muscles and below that . . .

She blushed for them both and looked away.

"Flanna—" he began, but she shook her head.

"I will go."

He scowled. "I willna let ye die, lass."

Anger was suffusing her system. Anger at herself for her weakness, at him for his allure. "Do ye think yourself so powerful that ye can decide who lives and who dies. Is that how ye can justify"—her voice trembled for a moment as she raised a hand to indicate their place by the fire—"this?"

"Lass," he breathed, "surely ye dunna blame me for—"

"Who then?" She was the Flame of the MacGowans, had vowed to be strong, and had failed again. Thank God for the hound or she would have been far past the point of no return.

"Gawd's wrath, Flanna. Ye blame me for yer reactions."

"I—"

"Nay," he said, lifting a hand to silence her. "Ye wanted me as I wanted ye. As a woman wants a man. But ye are ta scairt ta admit it."

"I am not," she denied, but her voice trembled.

Roderic snorted and turned abruptly away. With a sweep of his hand, he knocked the remaining timbers aside and stepped into the open air.

Flame watched him go, but in a moment he returned, snatched his plaid from the dirt floor, and marched out again, his backside as naked as his front. She drew a steadying breath. Her hands were shaking. It must be caused by the cold, she told herself and retrieved her shirt. It was damp and made her skin stand up in sharp goose bumps as she dragged it over her arms. Her hose were no better, making her struggle to pull them over her legs.

She shivered within the clammy clothes. Thinking of a fire, she hurried to his sporran, where he had replaced the flint. But reality struck her suddenly. He was gone. This was her chance to escape. They had slept through the day, and night was almost upon them. She must think and take what she could. Sweeping up his sporran and the limp rabbit, she rushed for the door.

"Going somewhere, lass?" He stood in the crooked doorway, big as life and just as irritating. His arms were full of firewood and his chest was bare.

She careened to a halt, losing control of his sporran, which tumbled to the ground as she scowled at him. "Home," she said, trying to recall some dignity.

"With me sporran and Bonny's meal? She will be quite distraught."

Roderic bent his neck and took a step inside. Flame backed away, but as she did so, her gaze fell on the tumbled contents of his sporran. There was a flint, a steel, a dozen other objects that he had gathered from somewhere, and a curling scrap of parchment.

She stared at it for a moment and then bent to pick it up. It felt soggy as she smoothed it open. 'Twas the note regarding Simon's death.

She filled her lungs with air and straightened her back to stare at him. "Ye stole the Forbeses' missive from my chambers."

His jaw tightened. "It was na written by me brother."

"How, then, do ye explain the presence of his seal."

"Someone must have duplicated it. 'Twould na be such a difficult task. I have asked meself who might have seen the seal and realized that anyone who has done some traveling might be the culprit. Troy mayhap or—"

"Damn ye!" she swore suddenly and swung the hare with all her might and rage.

The flaccid rabbit hit Roderic squarely in the face. He staggered backward in surprise, spitting fur from his mouth, but she was already streaking through the door. Not looking back, not thinking, she raced for the nearby trees.

"Flanna!" she heard him roar, but anger and panic propelled her on. "Gawd's wrath! Flanna!" he yelled again, and sped after her.

She could hear his footfalls as he followed her but dared not look back.

"What the devil!" he rasped. He was nearer now, gaining on her.

Her lungs felt as if they would burst.

"Lass!"

Dear God, he was right behind her. His fingers grazed her back. She shrieked, and in one unplanned movement, swept a branch from the earth and swung.

It whizzed with incredible speed, bare inches from his face. He careened to a halt.

"Gawd's—"

"Don't come near me!" she panted. "Or next time your head will be forfeit."

"Lass," he soothed, one palm stretched pleadingly outward toward her.

Dear God, she had almost hit him in the head. She swallowed hard and tightened her grip. "I don't want to kill ye."

"And I dunna wish ta be kilt. So why na drop the branch and we'll talk."

"We'll not talk," she said. "I'll leave."

"Why?"

"Why? Because the Forbeses have raided my herds and killed my kinsmen, and now ye have the gall to blame your deeds on others. To pretend my own people may have . . ."

Her words sputtered to a halt and she swung her branch with all her might. He ducked, grabbing the stick, and she fell with him atop her.

"Get off me!" she shrieked.

"Na until ye settle down and tell me what has riled ye so."

"Ye abducted me!" she stormed.

"As ye did me."

"Ye threatened me."

"As ye did me."

She scowled, feeling the anger drain from her. "Ye hold me against my will," she murmured.

"Again the same," he said and gently smoothed a strand of wild hair from her face. "What has truly angered ye, lass?"

She opened her mouth to speak, but no words came.

"Could it be that ye know I am right? That ye realize it wasna the Forbeses who have caused yer problems, and so ye must cast the blame elsewhere, perhaps on yer own kinsmen?"

"They are my people," she whispered. "I would give

up everything I have, everything I am, for them. I could not bear it if they turned against me again.''

His fingers skimmed the upper curve of her ear. ''The MacGowans havena turned against ye, lass. But perhaps *someone* has. That doesna mean there is something wrong with ye or yer leadership, only that there will always be those who cause trouble, who are filled with hatred.''

''They're all I have,'' she whispered.

He skimmed his fingers along the edge of her jaw. ''But ye could have more, Flanna.''

It was difficult to breathe when he looked into her eyes. ''Why did ye leave the note on my pillow?'' she whispered.

''Is it so difficult ta believe that I meant what it said?''

''Yes,'' she breathed, ''it is.''

''Damn yer sire, and damn the Frenchman,'' he said softly, and rising to his feet, pulled her toward the crumbling hut.

The rabbit was slow to roast, for the wood was damp and the fire fragile. The meal tasted like the very substance of life, but it was too small.

When darkness closed in around them, Roderic rose to his feet. ''Are ye ready?''

She found his gaze with her own. ''Ye are not going to allow me to return home?''

''Nay.''

''The MacGowans have no wealth. Ye've seen that with your own eyes. You'll get nothing for me.''

For a moment, she thought he would comment. Instead, he reached for her hand and pulled her into the darkness.

They traveled all night. It rained sporadically but hard, wiping out any tracks she might hope to leave behind.

Morning found them near a noisy little burn. The sun had risen some hours before and after fighting its way through the looming, dark clouds, had forced its bright radiance on a saturated world. It felt lovely against

Flame's face. Seating herself on a rock near the burbling water, she pulled her boots carefully from her feet. They were blistered and raw.

"Why did ye na tell me ye have blisters?" Roderic asked.

She held her breath and plunged her feet into the stream. The contact burned like the very devil. Gritting her teeth, she waited until the sharpest edge of pain passed. "They're *my* feet."

"Stubborn," he said and wading into the water, took her ankles in his hands.

"What are you doing?" she gasped, trying to pull them free.

"Stubborn!" he repeated irritably as he squatted to examine her blisters. The rushing water reached his knees, soaking his boots as it washed past. "Ye are surely the most stubborn lass in all the world. Why did ye na tell me ye were hurt?"

"And what would ye have done if I had, Forbes?" she asked. "Carried me all these miles on your back?"

He raised his brows and grinning, leaned closer. "Mayhap I could pretend ta be yer beast of burden. Ahh . . . even better. I will be Lochan, with yer legs wrapped tight about me and yer hands—"

"You *are* a beast," she said, and pushing with all her might, shoved him backward with a foot to his chest.

He hit the water with a shuddering gasp of surprise. His plaid floated about him in billowing waves of browns and greens.

For a moment Flame sat perfectly still, watching in stunned silence, and then she laughed. Perhaps it was the sheer, aching fatigue that made her silly or perhaps it was simply him, lying in the stream, immobilized by the shocking cold, that she found amusing.

Whatever the reason, she laughed until her sides hurt, until she was doubled over on the rock and tears streamed down her face. Dear God, she thought, still hiccupping, he would be angry now, for men did not like to be made to seem like fooks.

She lifted her gaze and caught his.

He remained perfectly still, watching her, and for a moment, she wondered if he had died from pure shock right where he sat.

"I have never seen ye laugh."

She giggled and wiped her nose on the back of her hand. "I have never seen a Forbes make such a splash."

"Indeed." He lifted a corner of his mouth into that devastating grin that was distinctly his own. "I must make a funny sight. But methinks it would be more amusing yet . . ." He rose slowly. Water dripped from every inch of him. "If you joined me."

He made a grab for her, but she shrieked and fled her perch on the rock.

Bonny barked. Roderic roared and gave chase. But Flame's feet were blistered and bare. At the top of a grassy knoll, he caught her easily and swung her into his arms.

She shrieked again, but his lips were suddenly very near, his smile mesmerizing.

" 'Tis glad I am ta ken I amuse ye, lass," he murmured.

Her chest felt tight and her head light, but she concentrated hard and managed a scowl. "Put me down," she ordered.

Nodding once, he let her feet slip to the ground. She backed away, and bumped into something hard and solid. Rough bark pressed into her back, and now Roderic's arms locked her in as he leaned his weight against the tree.

"I could be even more amusing," he said, leaning closer.

She pushed at his chest, trying to free herself before the frantic, exhilarating thrill of his nearness crushed her senses. "I believe ye tried that yestereve." Her tone was blessedly steady, despite the fact that her skin burned where his arms touched her, and her heart thundered in her chest.

The grin slipped slowly from his face. Drawing a deep

breath, he watched her eyes and said, "About yester-eve . . .'Tis sorry I be."

She blinked once, certain she had not heard him right, but he braced his feet a bit farther apart and took a deep breath. It made his nostrils flare, and even that slight motion fascinated her somehow.

"I am na usually known ta be so far from control."

"Not known?" she asked. "Does that mean ye are usually fully in control when ye rape women or—"

"Still afraid ta admit yer desire, lass?" he asked, leaning closer still.

She pressed into the oak trunk, wondering how long it had been since she had drawn a breath. "Ye flatter yourself, Forbes."

"Do I? Then let me flatter ye as well, lass." His hand ran down her waist to caress her hip. "Ye have the firmest behind and the softest lips I have ever—"

"Look!" she squeaked, turning her head away. "Is that a cottage?"

His gaze didn't move, though his lips lifted into a sardonic grin. "Ye are indeed a slippery one."

"It is . . ." she began, but when she looked at him, her breath stopped in her throat. "A cottage," she finished, striving to strengthen her tone. "Look for yourself."

Hemming her in with his palms against the tree again, he turned his gaze downhill. "Where are we?"

She followed his line of sight and tried to think of something other than the intensity of his eyes, the tantalizing tilt of his lips. And though it was difficult to estimate how far they had traveled in the dark, she concentrated hard. The wee lochan to the right looked familiar. Mayhap that was still on MacGowan property. The cottage, however, was not, of that she was sure. "Lamont land, I would guess."

He sighed. "I, too."

"Our rivals," they said in unison.

He grinned at her, and though she knew better, she grinned back.

"Do you suppose they'd feed us before they kill us?"

Roderic shrugged. "If they're Lamonts, 'tis hard to guess. Unless . . ."

For a moment, she thought she saw a twinkle of mischief in his eyes, but he pushed away from the tree and turned abruptly away. "What?" she asked suspiciously.

"I dunna ken for certain where we be. Therefore, I canna guess how we might be greeted in yon cottage."

"Surely chancing it would be better than starvation."

Roderic shook his head and nodded surreptitiously toward the hound that sat happily at his feet.

Flame scowled. "Surely even a Forbes must feel the burn of hunger."

"Aye, I do," Roderic all but whispered. "But I dunna wish ta hurt Bonny's feelings." At the sound of his voice, the hound gazed longingly into his face and thwapped her tail against the bracken. "Aye, lass, 'twas a delectable meal ye brought us. Never have I had finer. Is it na true, Flanna?"

"Ye are a strange man, Forbes," she said.

He tsked at her and grinned. "And ye dunna appreciate the hound."

"Not true," she argued, squaring her shoulders to head back to the stream for her boots. "I would sooner be lost with the hound than with ye."

When she turned, boots in hand, he was still standing near the tree. But one fist was planted on his lean hip while his opposite hand rested on Bonny's sleek, narrow head.

"I am quite insulted," he chided.

" 'Twas my intent," she assured him, picking her way barefoot through the heather.

"Where are ye going?"

"To the cottage."

"Going ta tell them ye are the Lady MacGowan? Mayhap ye could ask them flat out if they would like ta hold ye for ransom."

" 'Tis a fine idea, Forbes. But I did not plan to tell them who I am."

"Ahhh . . ." He turned to follow her course downhill. "And I'm certain they willna guess, for there be any number of women galivanting about in leather hose and men's shirts."

"Do ye have a better idea?" She didn't turn to look at him, for she knew the effort it would take to think straight if she did.

"Aye. We shall go to the wee lochan below so that ye may rest and I may decide our next course of action."

"I will not walk all that extra way when I could rest and ye, supposedly, could think right here?" she said, continuing on.

"Aye, ye will, lass."

She did turn now and raised a haughty brow at him. "No, I will not."

"Aye, ye will, lass," he argued again, hands on hips. "And 'tis fer yer own good."

She blinked her eyes and hoped she looked like the sappy, love-infested lass he was used to dealing with. "And tell me, oh great Forbes, how it is for my own good?"

His expression was deadly serious, but his eyes . . .

"I ken honesty is important ta ye, lass."

She could not hold the cheap smile much longer. "And pray tell what that has to do with anything."

"I willna make ye break yer vow."

"What vow?"

He shrugged and pacing up to her, prodded her toward the water. "Suffice it to say that I am ready ta let ye fulfill yer vow and I prefer the warmth of the lochan to the chill of the burn."

Chapter 18

◯ ◯ ◯

Flanna stood frozen like a rock to the earth. A shapely rock, Roderic thought, but a rock, nonetheless. She stared into his face.

He stared back, granting her a carefully benevolent smile. "Dunna bother to thank me."

She said nothing, only continued to watch him with wide eyes.

"Lass," he said, lifting a hand to wave it in front of her face, "are ye alive?"

"I did not agree to your foolish wager. I did not promise to bathe ye," she breathed.

He brightened his smile. "Ahh, but ye did, lass. Ye said . . . and I remember the exact words. 'What can I do but agree?' "

"I was being cynical!" she gasped.

"Ahh. Cynicism doesna become ye, lass. And it was still a wager."

"But . . . but I did bathe ye!"

"Ye pushed me in the burn, lass. 'Tis na quite what I had in mind. And ye well know it," he said and took a step closer.

"Damnation! There was no way for ye to escape the tower."

He chuckled gently, glad to see she was so greatly impressed by his deeds. "On the contrary, lass," he said modestly, "there were several at least."

"But I . . . I can't . . ." All the color had left her face and her voice went soft.

217

"Now, lass," he chided gently. "Ye are too hard on yerself. Ye canna say whether or not ye could scale the tower until ye are driven as I was. Indeed, the trek through the window wasna so very difficult and ye have strong legs." He glanced down at her limbs, admiring their slender shape. "Aye, lass, fine legs they be. And probably able to get ye from—"

"I cannot bathe ye!" she interrupted hoarsely.

He frowned at her for a moment. "Oh. And why would that be?"

She swallowed again. "It would not be . . . decent."

"Again I must beg ta differ, Flanna," Roderic said in a mildly scolding tone. " 'Tis a much honored tradition for the laird's daughter to assist a guest with his bath."

"Ye are not my guest."

"But I was."

"You're not now."

"That's because I won the bet," he said and laughed. "Come now. Ye will feel better once the debt is paid. I can tell ye are feeling poorly for having delayed so long."

She was definitely feeling poorly. In fact, panic was swelling up from her stomach in a dark, stifling tide. What a fool she had been to underestimate this man. But it was so easy to do, for he seemed so harmless . . . most of the time.

Without trying, she remembered the tale William had related to her regarding Roderic's first opportunity to escape. He had grabbed Bullock and twisted the spear from his hand. Rather absentmindedly, he had choked the air from his prisoner before tossing the spear to the floor and storming back into his high dungeon. Who could guess at such a man's moods? Certainly not she. So she turned stiffly away, stumbled toward the lochan, and thought up every possible means she might have to escape.

But no fantastic ideas came to mind and soon she stood before the small loch, staring at it in horror. It was blue-green, still and quiet and seemed to belie her agitation.

"Well, lass," he began, "how shall we—"

"What will it take," she interrupted, turning stiffly toward him, "for ye to forget the foolish wager?"

He blinked. His lashes were incredibly, indecently long, and his expression suspiciously benign. "Forget? I fear I dunna understand, lass. For if the truth be told, I have an outstanding memory. Especially when it concerns matters of such import as—"

"What'll it take, Forbes?" she all but shouted.

The dimmest shadow of a grin flitted across his face. "Methinks ye are becoming overwrought." He leaned slightly closer. "Could it be ye have been anticipating this event more than I knew?"

She didn't slap him, didn't kick him, didn't even swear at him, and for this, she was quite proud. Instead, she straightened her back, filled her lungs with air, and watched him with her haughtiest expression. "The MacGowans are not a wealthy tribe," she said quietly. "But I am willing to pay what I can. What will it take?"

He looked her straight in the eye. "I will take yer firstborn," he said evenly.

Her mouth fell open. Her lips moved. And then she laughed. The sound, however, was a bit high-pitched. "Ye have a whimsical, if rather unorthodox, sense of humor, Forbes."

His face was deadly serious. "And ye are stalling."

"I asked what it would take to change your mind."

"And I answered."

She drew a steadying breath and found her dignity. "I tell ye truthfully, Forbes. I will never bear a child. Yours or any other man's."

For a moment he didn't speak but stood immobile, trying to understand her words. "What foolishness is this now?"

"I am the Flame of the MacGowans, chosen to lead. But I will not bear an heir. My people will have to choose another when my time is done."

"Because ye think yerself such a horrid ruler?" he asked.

"Because I am my father's daughter." Her voice trembled with the words, but she kept her chin high.

"Aye." He scowled and drew himself straighter. "Ye are yer father's daughter. And is that na a terrible thing? For look, ye are so selfish ye would rather give up yer leadership than fight another yer clan has chosen. Ye are so vain that ye dress yerself in simple garb so that yer people can fare better. Ye are so evil that ye strive ta keep peace even though ye think we Forbeses have grievously sinned against ye. Ye are so vindictive that ye saved me life when yer warrior would have taken it." His voice had dropped to a whisper, and he stepped forward to touch her cheek. "If yer blood is tainted, lass, any child would be honored ta be so poisoned."

His words and nearness sent a quivering warmth through her. How long had she longed for tenderness? How long had she craved kindness?

"There may be others more fit to rule than I," she murmured, trying to keep her head. "Nevin is intelligent and kind."

Roderic stroked a finger down her cheek. She tried not to tremble. "Have ye looked into his heart and found purity, then?" he asked. "Or do ye simply judge yerself so harshly that others look better by comparison?"

"But Nevin—"

He slid a finger gently over her lips, stopping her words before skimming along her jaw. "Do na tell me of Nevin, lass, for I trust no one where ye are concerned. Especially na one who might rule if ye were dead."

"He is loyal to me and the MacGowans."

"Mayhap, but yer own children would also be loyal, and they would have yer fire." His fingertips drifted lower. "And yer heart and yer beauty." A flame of desire sparked in the trail of his touch.

Flanna felt the kindling of her long-dry passions. Temptation lured her, numbing her good sense. But she fought her own weakness and pulled back with a jolt.

"Nevertheless"—her voice cracked on the single word. She clenched her fists at her sides—"I decided long ago that I would bear no man's child."

"Ye only say that because long ago ye had na met the right man."

"Could it be that ye are speaking of yourself?" she guessed blithely.

He grinned. "How is it that ye have guessed?"

"In my fairly vast experience, 'tis a man's favorite topic," she mused. "But ye must think yourself a particularly miraculous lover if ye think ye can change my mind."

"I dunna mean ta seem immodest, lass, but miraculous is na a word unheard by these ears in the dark of night."

"And are ye familiar with the word 'vanity' as well?"

"Aye, lass," he said with a laugh. "I have heard that one, too. And now that ye've had some time ta relax, are ye prepared to assist with me bath?"

"No, I am not."

"And what of yer vow?"

"I did *not* vow! And, too, we were within the safe confines of Dun Ard where I would have been well protected from—"

"And what about me own protection?"

She stared at him.

"Do ye na think I worried that ye might attack me own person? Especially once ye have seen me"—lowering his head, he stared at the ground and made a crescent shape in the sand with the toe of his boot—"unclothed?" Peeking up through his lashes, he looked for all the world as if he were trying to blush.

She thumped him on the chest with a good deal of force. "Ye are a braying ass!"

His mouth fell open in apparent surprise, but he failed to stop his chuckle. "I was but trying ta act humble, for I thought ta please ye."

"Well, ye failed miserably."

"Humility is a new endeavor for me, Flanna. Surely I will improve in time."

"Were I ye, I wouldn't plan to live that long."

He chuckled again. "I see ye are truly relaxed now. Shall we begin?"

For a moment she wasn't quite sure whether he was speaking of making babies or bathing. "When the clouds rain gold coin," she said to both ideas.

"Now, lass, I am merely trying to help ye fulfill yer vow. 'Tis true," he assured her, apparently noticing her dubious expression. Or perhaps it was her gritted teeth that made her appear skeptical. "I wouldna wish ye ta continue yer life knowing ye have failed to keep a promise to yer fellow Scot," he said, undoing the wildcat brooch from his tartan and shirt. It dropped to the ground. Flame's gaze followed it, then hurried back to his face. But his hands were already on his belt. It loosened with one simple movement. His plaid dipped and followed the brooch.

She took a deep breath and prepared to flee. His gaze settled on her. "Did I tell ye, lass, that I be the fleetest runner of all the Forbeses?"

She swallowed. "I believe ye forgot to spew that bit of braggery."

" 'Tis true," he said. "I can best a steed for twenty rods."

"Luckily, I am not a horse."

He grinned. "Ye wouldna escape."

She licked her lips. "If I . . . help ye bathe . . . will ye let me go?"

"Nay."

"Then why should I do it?"

"Because ye are honest," he said, and grasping the bottom of his voluminous, saffron shirt, pulled it over his head.

Flame gaped in shocked immobility. He stood before her in the broad light of day, every muscle taut and lean, every line sculpted and powerful. Turning smoothly, he marched into the water, leaving her alone on the sand.

Dear God! Flame stared after Roderic, ready to lambast him. How dare he make her feel guilty for not bathing with him? How dare he disrobe before her very eyes? But he had already dived beneath the water. If she hoped to scold him, she would need to follow him, she thought, gazing at the spot where he had disappeared.

But that was ridiculous. Now was her time to escape. And yet . . . all she could think about was that he was naked. Every muscle in his long, tight form would be as sleek as seal skin. And she would have an excuse to touch those muscles, to run her fingers down his hard form and . . .

She shook her head and paced, trying to forget her mental images of him. But when next she turned to the pool, he had surfaced. The water lapped lovingly at his shoulders. His hair gleamed like molten gold in the summer's sun, and every muscle stood out taut and hard, just as she had imaged. In a moment he disappeared again.

Her leather hose seemed to drop from her of their own accord, but when her fingers moved to her shirt, she pulled them away with an effort and waded into the water. It was surprisingly warm. She hurried toward deeper water, for despite her shirt, she felt exposed and jittery. But the pool was much shallower than she had expected. It had not yet reached her waist when Roderic surfaced not half a rod from her.

His eyes matched the color of the water. His wet, slicked-back hair exposed every lean line of his face in sharp detail. A fat droplet slipped lovingly along his jaw to follow a taut cord down his throat and onto his chest. Flame watched its progress.

"Ye came." His voice was husky.

Flame swallowed and tried to think. "Did ye doubt?"

"Aye." He must have been kneeling, for he rose slowly to face her, baring unspeakable parts of his glistening, rock-hard anatomy. "And I was fast running short of ways ta look appealing."

"Mayhap ye should have stood up sooner."

His grin only lifted the right corner of his mouth. She could feel the blood drain from her face.

"I did not mean that the way it sounded."

His brows rose the slightest fraction of an inch. "Of course na, lass."

"I merely meant . . ."

"Aye?"

She stared into his eyes and tried to think of some clever explanation, but she could barely recall her own name. "I have not the faintest idea why I said that."

He tilted his head back slightly when he laughed. Even his neck was muscular and alluring. But he was also dangerous. Flame knew that, and yet . . .

The blush burned her face, but in a moment he reached out to touch her cheek. "I am flattered. Dunna be embarrassed. For I am na."

"Well"—she drew a deep, shaky breath—"ye should be."

He chuckled again. "Do ye always bathe in yer clothes?"

His fingers had slipped to her neck. She stood perfectly still. Water plastered the long shirt to her hips, pressing intimately to places better left unnamed. "Yes. All the time. It saves work for the washing women."

His teeth were incredibly white and straight, the right side of his full lips tilted slightly upward. "How thoughtful of ye, Flanna MacGowan, to worry about the fate of the washerwomen. Did ye ken ye have dried mud on yer nose?"

"Umm . . ." She swallowed, searching for an answer, but his gaze was too intent on hers. She couldn't face him, but neither could she turn away. So she stared at his collarbone and wished she could act like who she was, the lady of her clan. The proud blood of royalty charged her veins. But even his collarbones were beautiful and jangled her senses.

"It makes me wonder where else ye might be dirty." He leaned closer.

"Roderic!" She tried to move away from him, but

either the bottom of the lochan was very muddy or her feet simply refused to leave him, for they were stuck fast in the mire.

He caught her about the waist before she flopped gracelessly into the water.

Their faces were inches apart. All hope of dignity fled.

"Aye, lass?" he said softly.

"Roderic," she said again, but his name was no more than a murmur now.

"Aye, lass," he repeated.

"This was a . . . bad idea."

"I must agree. But it can be easily remedied. The shirt can be removed."

Flame took a slow breath. She wanted to speak, but no sound would come. She tried to step away. His arms loosened slightly, still balancing her but allowing her escape.

"But I can wait."

She wanted to tell him that his hair would turn gray and fall from his head in clumps before she would remove her shirt, but again her lips betrayed her. "All right," they said instead. It occurred to her that the demon Forbes was bent on causing trouble. She should march right out of there, but apparently her knees were also possessed, for she did not even try to back away.

"There's a bit of mud right there," he said, touching her nose. Water dripped from his finger down to her lips. She shivered at the feeling. He grinned, rubbed gently, and dropped his hand to the water before raising it and rubbing again. She could do nothing but stare into his face. "And there." His fingers skimmed to her eyebrow and smoothed with luscious slowness along the ridge. "And there." Her cheekbone felt his touch.

Flame closed her eyes. His hand slipped lower.

"There," he murmured, running one finger along her bottom lip. The shiver took her entire body now, trembling her from head to foot, but already his mouth had captured hers.

She tried to resist, but he was all hard muscle and soft

sentiment. And at this moment, she was all woman. The heat of his kiss seared her senses. The tenderness of his fingers against her cheek abolished her objections, and when he drew away, she felt bereft. But in a moment, he bent and lifted her from the water. She could hear him splashing through the gentle waves, but she didn't look where he took her. For this moment, she wanted only to feel the beat of his heart against her breast, the play of his muscles beneath her hands.

Finally, he bent. She felt her back brush against the smooth surface of a warm rock. He settled her legs into the soft grip of the water and her bottom against the sand. A jumble of age-worn boulders stood here, trapping still, sun-warmed water in their midst.

Roderic settled beside her and then he was kissing her again, half covering her with his torso. Even through her shirt, Flame could feel his muscles flex and shift against her breasts. She should call this to a halt, she knew. Instead, she raised her hand to his chest. Air rasped between his teeth at her touch. Their gazes met and melded. Without her consent, her hand slipped lower. Her fingers skimmed over each rib and onto the taut, undulated plane of his abdomen. Again, air hissed through Roderic's teeth, but he didn't draw away. His lips were slightly parted, she noticed, and his body was as still and rugged as if it were crafted from purest granite.

Curiosity pulled at Flame. Her gaze slipped down his broad throat, over his mounded chest, and lower still.

His desire stood rock hard and upright against his flat belly.

She jerked her gaze and her hand away with a start. "Roderic!" she gasped, sitting upright.

He blinked innocently. "Aye?"

"This is . . . this is foolishness."

"Nay, lass, this is heavenly."

"But I . . ." She was breathing hard. A hundred night raids would be less frightening than this—and less exhilarating. Her gaze caught his, and the intensity in his eyes stopped her breath in her throat. "I . . . I left my hose on the shore," she murmured hopelessly.

"That I noticed, lass."

"And I"—a thousand proper phrases came to mind, but she seemed unable to force a single one of them past her lips—"I don't want to stop ye."

"Forgive me for having na regrets."

"But I must stop ye."

"Nay, lass," he whispered, his expression suddenly serious. "Trust me ta stop meself."

"I do not trust men," she whispered.

He touched her face ever so gently. "I admit that I may have earned the name of Rogue, Flanna. But I have never broken a vow. Trust in me now, lass. Even if ye beg, I will not agree ta mate with ye this day. However, I am about ta remove yer shirt."

She could not stop him, did not want to. The fabric felt wet and soft as he slipped it from her arms and over her head, and suddenly she was as naked as he.

Flame watched his eyes and shivered beneath his attention. Instead of reaching for her, he urged her further into the water. Sand cradled her back. Soft, warm ripples caressed her.

Roderic's nostrils flared and his jaw tightened as his gaze skimmed her body, caressing her breasts, her belly, the length of her legs.

She felt breathless and tight as a bowstring.

"Ahh, ye are stunning, lass. I can hardly believe ye have been saved for me," he murmured. His gaze felt hot on her skin.

She closed her eyes and trembled. Her heart hammered against her ribs. *Do something. Say something*, her mind commanding. "Did I not tell ye I have a lover?"

"Aye, ye did, lass," he murmured, kissing her throat.

"And did I mention the others?" Though she tried to sound flip and confident, her throat felt tight and her hands were clenched to fists in the water.

"Others?"

"Yes. Hundreds."

"Ahh," he murmured and smoothed the backs of his fingers across the high swell of her breast. "So there have been hundreds, have there?"

"Yes. Scotsmen, Frenchmen . . ." She shivered as he brushed her nipple. Against her will, her head dropped back.

"Beggermen, thieves?" he asked.

"Yes . . . those, too," she said and trembled again.

He laughed. The sound was husky and caused something deep inside her to ache. "I dunna mean ta call ye a liar, lass, and though I ken that men are often fools, na man could have ye once and na give his life ta call ye his verra own. Have ye left dead men in yer wake, lass?"

"None to my knowledge," she breathed.

"Then ye were saved for me."

She tried to argue, but his lips were on hers again. They moved with a tender warmth that teased and tantalized. With the fluidity of a wave, his body slipped onto hers. There was nothing more natural than cradling him between her thighs.

Sunshine caressed her skin. And wherever the light reached, his hands reached, too, skimming over the bridge of her nose, the fullness of her bottom lip. Feather soft, his hand drifted along her shoulder. She was breathless with the feelings he evoked. But there was more to come, so much more, for where his hand roamed, so roamed his kisses. Her arms quivered beneath his caresses, but when she drew them toward her body, his kisses only drifted to the side. She gasped at the feel of his lips against the aching tenderness of her breast.

"Roderic!" she murmured, trying to push away, but he only slipped forward onto one hip at her side. Ever so gently, he eased her back and kissed her lips.

"I dare not let myself trust." Her breath brushed his lips. Their gazes fused, azure on emerald.

"Be ye speaking from yer heart or yer head, lass?" he murmured.

"I am speaking from my memories."

"Then let us make new memories, Flanna. Memories we shall na forget for a lifetime." He touched her cheek with tender fingertips. "Memories ta make ye smile."

She wanted that. She wanted the memories he promised. But she was being foolish, and pain followed foolishness. But perhaps he was worth the pain. Perhaps a moment in his embrace was worth anything. She reached out, knowing her hand shook.

The bone in his shoulder was thick, the muscle of his upper arm, bunched and firmly packed. Without breathing, Flame ran her hand down his back. It rippled with power, but he neither hurried her nor stopped her exploration. Her fingers fell easily into the furrow that creased the middle of his back. They ran along that course until the rise of his buttocks. There her fingers spread, smoothing over one tight mound and down the back of his bulging thigh. It was as hard as an oaken bough. Instinctively, she pulled him toward her, aching for closer contact.

Roderic willingly obliged. Coarse, golden hair rasped against her thighs as he dragged his leg over hers. Against her hip, Flame could feel the hard press of his desire and the heavy, twin sacks beneath it.

Reaching up, Flame slipped her free hand behind his neck and pulled him closer. Their kisses were no longer tender but scorching. With a moan, she pulled him back between her legs.

The hard length of his manhood pressed against her. He moaned. With a hand beneath her hips, he drew her closer still. Water sloshed over them, rocking her in its wake. Flame tilted her head into the pool and arched upward. She felt the urgent thrust of desire and pressed against his throbbing heat. He moaned but didn't enter her. She pushed more eagerly and he pushed back until they were rocking together on the waves, breathing hard and trembling with desire. Her shoulders pressed into the sand. His hands gripped her buttocks, pulling upward.

She arched higher and suddenly she felt his mouth close over her nipple. She shrieked against the intensity and thrust her hips wildly against him. Sparks of excitement streaked from her breast to her loins and off in every direction. Desire became pain, relief necessity.

Wrapping her arms about his back, she pulled him nearer still, trying to fill the aching need inside her, to find the utopia that called like a siren's song. She heard his throaty moan again, but took no heed, for an unfamiliar need drove her onward.

"Lass," he rasped, abandoning her breast to kiss her throat, "dunna stretch me limits too far."

She was so close. So close. He pulsed hot and heavy against her nether regions. She arched against him.

"Lass," he moaned again, "I vowed."

"Damn the vows," she swore and dragged him inward.

Their gasps melded. But for the drawing of gasping breath, their bodies halted. He had entered her virgin gates by the barest fraction of an inch. Their eyes were shut, but each glimpsed heaven's door.

Flame's hands moved finally, drawing him closer with a ragged groan. Roderic shuddered, fighting a battle she neither shared nor condoned and raised himself to his hands and knees.

Flame felt paradise slipping away. "Nay!" she gasped, trying to pull him back.

"I vowed," he repeated through gritted teeth.

"But I did not," she rasped, gripping his arms with her nails. "And ye said I could use ye. Use ye and toss ye aside if I wished."

A self-mocking smile twitched his lips, but Flame could see nothing amusing.

"Was that not also a vow, Forbes?"

"Aye," he murmured, straddling her thigh to settle against her, "that it was."

"Then . . ." she began, but already he was suckling her again. "Oh!" she whimpered, thrusting her hips upward. Her desire did not meet the hard answer of his manhood. But it met the solid relief of his thigh. And it would do, for desire was exploding within her, erupting in sharp, demanding waves. She pressed urgently against him time and again, finally gaining the summit of need to fall limply on the other side.

He was there to catch her in his arms. But even through the blur of her tattered emotions, she felt him tremble.

Flame drew a shaky breath finally and tried to sit up. He allowed her a scant inch of room to lever her elbows into the pool's sandy bottom. She couldn't meet his gaze, but felt the sharp penetration of his eyes as he watched her.

She cleared her throat and pushed a strand of dripping hair from her face. His chest was very broad and rose and fell slightly with every breath he took. But finally, she couldn't resist the allure of his eyes and lifted her own to meet his. They shone like twin blue flames. Emotion made his features appear as hard as sculpted stone.

She could feel the sharp evidence of his unfulfilled desire against her abdomen and blushed. "Why do ye look at me like that?" she asked breathlessly.

"Like what?" His tone was husky, his stare as steady as a falcon's.

"Like you'd like to devour me."

The world around them was silent. "If ye dunna ken that, ye are na as smart as I suspected," he said and rose slowly to his feet.

His manhood reached nearly to his navel, hard and erect and still throbbing.

Flame gulped and forced her gaze to his face. He had, then, found no pleasure in their embrace, and so he was angry, she deduced, but she would not apologize, for in the past, apologies had gained her little. Haughtiness served her better. "Fetch my clothes," she demanded.

"Am I ta be yer maidservant then, lass?" he asked.

She nodded once, hoping he couldn't see how her hands shook. "Since ye have taken me far from my own servants, ye will need to serve me in their stead."

For a moment, she thought she saw a hint of amusement light his eyes, but then he bowed from the waist. "As ye wish, me lady," he said, and scooping her garments from the sand, hurled them into the lochan.

Chapter 19

❦❦❦

"What are ye doing?" Flame gasped, rising with a jolt to her feet. The sudden movement caused her naked breasts to jiggle and his loins to throb with need.

Roderic gritted his teeth. "I be saving ye from yerself."

"You're demented!" she rasped angrily and spun toward the lochan, but in an instant he caught her arm. Her wet hair lashed about them both, binding them together for a moment

"Nay, lass," he breathed, finding even the touch of her hair was nearly more than his strained self-control could handle, "I am randy. And ye are verra bonny when ye are"—her eyes fairly sparked green flame—"naked," he finished.

"This was not my idea," she reminded him, trying to pull away. "So do not blame it on me."

"Were I ye, lass, I wouldna do all that bouncing about or there will be more blame to be placed. Lest ye forget," he said, drawing her against his aching body, "I be only a man. Na a saint."

He watched her throat convulse and fear vie with pride in her eyes. Hauteur won the battle. She lifted her chin. "Fetch . . . my . . . clothes."

There was nothing he could do but laugh, for despite it all, her spirit thrilled him. "Nay, lass," he said with a chuckle and backed away a half a step lest her prox-

233

imity be his undoing. "For they would only find ye trouble."

"Trouble?" She yanked at her arm but he held it fast.

"Aye. Ye be too proud for yer own good. Ye would march like a triumphant queen to yonder cottage and demand provisions."

She glared at him. Her hair was slick and shone in copper-bright radiance. The sun stroked her golden face, showing every line, every slope of her features. This was not a pampered young lass with milky complexion and sparrow-light bones. This was a maid born to match a man in spirit and wit and raise bairns to make them proud. This was a woman!

"Now then, lass. 'Tis like this," he said, "though I sometimes canna say why, it would grieve me ta see ye taken hostage . . . unless ye be *my* hostage. Therefore, I canna allow ye ta hie yerself up to the Lamonts' in yer manly garb, for they would recognize ye even afore ye spoke."

Her eyes narrowed as understanding began to dawn on her. "Drag me naked to that cottage and ye'll regret the very day ye were born."

Roderic struggled with his smile and miraculously won. "Nay, lass. Na naked. We have the tartan I found in the broken hut."

"Surely ye do not expect me to march up to that cottage wearing nothing but a blanket."

He shrugged. "If it puts yer mind at ease, lass, I will confess that I, too, am leaving me telltale garb behind."

"I will not share the blanket!"

This time he laughed aloud. "Ye are so fickle, lass. First ye refuse to wear it, then ye refuse ta share it. And ye say ye are na like other women."

She opened her mouth to retort, but Roderic controlled his chuckles and stopped her.

"Though I realize yer appetite has been sated, lass, me own has been stoked to an aching edge." For a moment her gaze dipped, but she darted it back to his face before it had reached its destination. "Take me word for it, Flanna," he all but whispered, "it aches."

Again she opened her mouth to speak, but though he didn't stop her this time, she seemed unable to utter a response.

"Come," he said finally, "surely even the Lamonts will feed two needy travelers who have been set upon by brigands." He tugged at her hand. For a moment, she hung back, but finally she allowed him to propel her along in his wake. It was only a short distance to where their ratty tartan lay in the sand. Dropping her wrist, Roderic picked it up and swung it over her bare shoulders.

Foolishly, he allowed his knuckles to brush her flesh. He drew in his breath with a start, then gritted his teeth and found control. "Ye must quit tempting me, lass."

"I did nothing," she gasped.

Roderic shrugged and loosened his tightly knotted muscles with a good deal of effort. "Ye breathed."

Turning away from her took all the fortitude he possessed, but in a moment, he had tugged his shirt over his head. It scraped along his wet skin and as he struggled to drag it away from his face, he felt her gaze burn his exposed manhood.

"Lass," he said, finally yanking the shirt lower to peer at her above the laces, "I told ye ta quit tempting me," he said, trying to untangle the great length of the thing. Unfortunately, the garment was now wet and stubborn and refused to be pulled down past his waist.

"What?" She gasped and swung her gaze to his, looking like nothing more than a wayward urchin caught stealing eggs.

Roderic eased a draft of air into his lungs and gave up his battle with the shirt. He must not move. He must not fulfill his most fundamental desires. True, she was tempting. True, she was lovely beyond words. But he could not afford to touch her again until his desire had cooled. "Ye're staring," he warned with quiet control.

For a moment, he thought she might flee, or at least deny her actions. Instead, she dropped her chin slightly.

Looking up through her lashes, she asked in a voice no louder than a whisper, "Does it really ache?"

Against his will and better judgment, Roderic stepped forward with a growl.

Her eyes flew open wide. He wrapped one arm about her waist, pulling her closer. The tartan gapped away from the tender swell of her beautiful bosom.

"Lass," he rasped, "methinks ye be intentionally spurring me on."

"Nay." Her stunned disclaimer could not have sounded more honest. "I but"—she blinked—"wondered."

Roderic fought his lusty nature with every scrap of self-discipline he possessed, but it seemed she felt no compunction to assist in the battle, for her body relaxed a whit and she spoke again but only in a whisper.

"Is it always so . . . hard?"

Never in all his life had he wanted anything more than he wanted her, but he had promised to be strong. 'Twas a vow that made his arms tremble and his brow sweat. He stood in immobile self-control, trying to deny his need, determined to fulfill his vow.

"Is it?" she whispered, watching his eyes.

Heaven's gate! She truly *was* intentionally tempting him. But why? Because she wanted him or because she wished for him to break his vow so that she could denounce him as unworthy as all the men in her past? Either way, her goading brightened his mood and fortified his self-discipline. Employing every ounce of control left to him, Roderic dropped his arm and retreated a scant step. "That be for ye ta find out, lass," he murmured huskily, and turning his naked backside to her, bent to retrieve his sporran.

The short walk to the crofter's cottage was silent. Flame could still feel the blush burn her cheeks. What the devil was wrong with her? For pity's sake, hadn't she done enough damage? After all, she had almost allowed him to . . .

Allowed him! Her choice of words made her scoff at herself. She hadn't almost allowed him to do anything. She had almost *begged* him. What a fool she was. What a weak-willed ninny.

And yet, even now, her stomach felt queasy at his nearness. He led the way, forcing a path through the bracken and holding branches aside so that she could follow more easily. She couldn't ignore how the tendons stood out in hard cords in his broad throat when he turned to her. She couldn't still the pounding of her heart when his hand inadvertently brushed her shoulder, and she couldn't help but wish he would stop and . . .

Damnation! She was not some limp-willed milking maid who swooned when a brawny lad looked her way. In fact, she was more likely to spit in his eye. So what was wrong with her?

Flame's gaze skimmed to Roderic again. His damp shirt clung to the shifting muscles of his back. He had finally, thank God, forced his damp shirt over his hips. At least she could look at him and manage to keep drawing air into her lungs now. But he had not donned his tartan. Instead, he had tossed it casually over his shoulder. Her attention settled on the back of his powerful thighs. His clothing, or the lack of it, was the problem, she deduced.

"Lass?" he began, turning toward her.

"It's your clothes!" she blurted, snapping her gaze from his legs to his face.

His brow rose slightly. "Yer pardon?"

She swallowed hard and hoped a large hole would open up beneath her feet. 'Twould be a suiting demise for a fool such as she.

"I said . . ." She tried a disarming smile, but disarming smiles were not her forte. She was better at throwing a dirk and better still at archery. Somehow she doubted if she could best this man at either. "I said, 'tis yer choice."

He scowled. "What is?"

"Whatever ye were about to ask."

"Are ye feeling dizzy?"

She all but sighed with longing as she looked into his face. "Aye, a bit."

Placing the back of his hand to her forehead, he deepened his scowl. "Must be the lack of food."

"Must be," she agreed weakly.

"Come along. 'Tis but a wee bit further." Placing a hand to her back, he urged her forward. "Ye must let me do the talking."

His hand felt like a thousand tiny sparks against the small of her back. She tried to ignore it. "Why?" she asked, attempting to concentrate on something other than his touch.

"Because I'm charming," he said.

She stopped in her tracks and stared into his face. "And I'm not?"

A muscle tightened in his jaw. Vaguely, she wondered if other parts of his anatomy were still tight and hard.

"Look at the man of the house like that, lass, and ye'll find yerself either tossed on yer back or out the door, depending on whether there be a mistress about."

She blinked. "What?"

The jaw muscle tightened a bit more, but he looked away and nudged her forward. "Just keep quiet," he ordered hoarsely and after hiding his sporran and his telltale Forbes plaid in a patch of heather, strode off toward the cottage.

It was very small. A battered barn of sorts listed to the north not far from the house. A shaggy-footed steed and a trio of goats watched their approach. Bonny sniffed at the heady smells and bolted off to explore.

"What be ye wanting?" a gruff voice asked. It took Flame a moment to find the speaker in the shade of the dilapidated barn.

The old woman held a metal-bound wooden bucket in each hand. Her heavy gray brows were beetled over her eyes, and her back was bowed.

"We've come to beg assistance," Roderic said.

"Assistance!" Despite Flame's doubts that the old

woman's eyebrows could drop any lower, they did so, all but covering her eyes. "Well, ye'll find none here. We've nothin' ta spare." Taking a few bandy-legged steps, she began toward the house as if to ignore them.

"Here now, mistress," Roderic said, quickly stepping forward to take the buckets from her. They were nearly brimming with milk. "Surely ye have a brawny son ta carry these for ye?"

"Aye." She scowled up at him from her crooked position. "I've a pair of sons, but both of them thought it more thrilling ta soldier fer the Lamont than ta do a bit of honest labor here.

"Well, so long as ye got them buckets, ye might just as well take them inside."

Roderic turned toward the cottage, but her scratchy voice stopped him.

"By the stars, lad! Ye be half naked! What happened ta yer tartan?"

"Ahh . . ." He twisted slightly toward her, not spilling a drop as he did so. " 'Tis a wee bit of trouble we've had. But 'tis plain ye've had yer share and be needing none of ours."

He turned toward Flame. "Cara, will ye open that door?"

It took her a moment to remember the alias she had given herself upon their first meeting. Grasping her tattered blanket in one hand, she hurried to the hovel to swing the wooden latch from its cradle. The low, slanted portal creaked partway open on cracked leather hinges, then settled firmly into the mud. Tugging harder, she managed to control her blanket while dragging the thing open.

"Just put them buckets down there by the door," ordered the old woman.

Roderic did as told, bending his wide back and showing a bit more muscular thigh.

Three young women in drab gowns drifted to the doorway. Their eyes were wide, their jaws slightly lax as they noticed him. He nodded in greeting. "So these be yer bonny daughters, mistress?"

They were, Flame thought, each as plain as field turnips.

"Aye, they be mine. And a working they're ta be," she said, shooing them back to their duties.

"And na men ta care fer ye?" Roderic asked.

The old woman turned a jaundiced eye up toward him. "Why ye be wanting ta know?"

The right corner of Roderic's mouth lifted in a characteristic half smile. "Maybe I'm thinking ta take ye into the woods and ravage ye, mistress."

Flame froze in stunned surprise. The old woman's eyes snapped wide. And then she laughed, cackling like a laying hen and bending double to slap her thigh.

"Ye're a live one, ain't ye, lad." She snorted raucously. "Me Jamie was lek that." Straightening to the best of her ability, she looked him in the eye and nodded. "Aye, ye're a live one. What be yer name?"

Roderic widened his stance a bit, seemingly unaware that he was scandalously short of clothing. But perhaps he was not unaware at all, knowing him as she did, he was likely using that fact to his advantage, Flame thought irritably. "Me name be Gillie McNaught. And this be me sister, Cara."

Sister! Flame almost opened her mouth to retort, but found that his widened stance had somehow allowed him to press his heel sharply upon her bare toes. She scowled and remained silent.

"And be the two of ye always marching about bare as the day ye were birthed, or be this an exception?"

Roderic grinned again. " 'Tis na me usual way, mistress. Though I admit, on these warm days, such garb, or the lack thereof, has a way of cooling me"—he paused as if thinking something wicked and flapped the bottom of his lengthy shirt—"toes."

The old woman cackled again. Flame gritted her teeth.

"The truth now, lad," ordered the crone. "Afore I needs send me blushing daughters out of hearing."

The grin fell from Roderic's face. "The truth be that the MacGowans are Satan's curs."

The increased pressure on Flame's toes warned her to stay silent, lest she be limping for a week.

"Tell me something I have not said with me own lips, lad," suggested the crone.

"I tell ye this then," said Roderic with a sharp nod. "I was but delivering me sister ta her betrothed when they fell on us. They took everything. Our horses, our provisions." He gestured angrily toward his own scantily garbed person. "Our clothes."

There was a decided twinkle in the old woman's rheumy eye. "And how is it that the sniveling Mac-Gowans have left ye with yer shirt?"

"The truth, mistress?" Roderic asked, then tilted his mouth slightly. "They planned ta take that, too, but once they'd spied me . . . assets, they felt too inferior ta leave me all bare."

The old woman's cackle was definitely beginning to grate on Flame's nerves. She set her teeth and glared at Roderic, but the crone patted his back and failed to notice Flame's ire.

" 'Tis lek the MacGowans ta ruin me fun," she said, then chortled at her own wit. "Ahhh," she sighed, looking into his face, "I ken I shouldna expose me tender daughters ta the likes of ye, lad. But come on in, nevertheless." She stepped inside and bent to retrieve the buckets, but Roderic already grasped the frayed rope handles.

"None of that now, mistress. Let me get them."

Flame followed the crone, who followed suspiciously close behind Roderic.

The daughters, it appeared, had not returned to their work. They stood, all three, with their mousy hair drooping beside their narrow faces and their soft mouths gaping at him.

"Well, dunna just stand about," rasped the mother. "Take the milk and find him a place ta sit."

The buckets were taken by a blushing maid who

bobbed a curtsy before rushing away. A stool was drawn up by another. Roderic sat down, knees lax, damn him. All three daughters' eyes were as round as mushrooms as they stared at him in openmouthed admiration.

Flame ground her teeth, propped herself against the wall, and hoped the earth would open and swallow Roderic whole.

Chapter 20

By nightfall, Flame's attitude toward Roderic was a bit more charitable, for her stomach was full. He had worked all day for the Lamonts, and in exchange, the two of them had been fed and clad.

"So the steed is of the MacGowan clan?" he was asking now. He sat upon a three-legged stool, looking very large on its small seat, but somehow appearing no less manly or graceful.

"Aye," said the old woman, "the great beastie wandered onto our land and we felt it was our duty ta give it a home."

"If we could have the use of the animal, we would make certain ye were repaid once we reached our kin in Inverness," Roderic said.

The old woman swished the contents of her mug and stared lovingly into the depths of the golden liquid. " 'Tis na that I dunna enjoy a good jest, lad, but after the way ye have toiled here this day, I think it only fair that I tell ye . . . the steed is worthless."

"Worthless? He's of good size and quality."

Flame listened with only half an ear. She felt sleepy and strangely content. From outside the hut came the soft bleating of a goat to her kids.

"Aye. He be a braw one. But he willna be rode." Widow Lamont shrugged. " 'Tis lek the MacGowans ta send me such a beast." With a sigh, she finished her drink. "He is worthless, unless ye wish ta eat him. I have threatened ta do just that, but wee Wini here carries on so.'' She scowled. '' 'Tis perhaps me own good heart that keeps us paupers.''

Flame nearly smiled. Though the old mistress loudly professed her beggarly state, it seemed she and her daughters brewed a unique and potent beer somewhere in the woods nearby. Little Wini had even confessed that Laird Lamont himself had developed a taste for their special recipe.

Flame settled herself more comfortably on the bench she shared with the three daughters. Sometime during the day their names had been revealed as Ellie, Kate, and Winifred. ''My thanks for the stew and the hospitality,'' she said and found that she truly meant it. Although the old woman was coarse and the daughters jittery, there was an earthy honesty about them that comforted Flame.

They had loaned her a gown. It was constructed of the same worn, mousy-colored fabric as their own and was stretched a bit tight across Flame's torso. Still, it was a far cry better than bumbling about in a tartan that had been resurrected from the crumbled remains of a forgotten fireplace. A strip of cloth had been torn from a rag and Flame had plaited it into her hair and bound the heavy braid loosely atop her head.

She drew an easy breath and leaned against the wall now. She was comfortable. She was momentarily safe, and her belly was full. Rarely had she realized the sheer pleasure those simple luxuries could give.

''Ellie here be a foine cook,'' said the crone in response to Flame's thanks. She nodded to the tallest of her daughters, whose hair hung limply beside her face. After a day spent in the girl's presence, Flame had begun to wonder if there might not be a golden hue to the girl's oily tresses. ''And twould make a foine wife fer some strapping lad.''

Flame turned toward Roderic. Their eyes met with an unexpected clash before he pulled his gaze away. '' 'Tis the truth ye be saying, mistress, but I'm sure ye'll agree the likes of me is na meant fer any decent lass.''

"Aye." The old crone leaned closer to him and whispered, "It'll be a maid with a bit of fire under her skirts fer the leks of ye. Someone who'll burn ye raw and leave ye begging fer more."

Roderic raised his brows. "Ye think so?"

"Aye," said the crone, flitting her gaze to the mass of Flame's crinkly, auburn tresses. "Mayhap a wench with hair like fire and a temper ta match."

Flame snapped her back into a straight line. Did the old crone suspect who she was? Did she know they weren't brother and sister, she wondered. But the mistress just chuckled and tore a bit of crust from her bread to toss it to Bonny, who rested on the floor near her master's feet.

The silence seemed as stiff as ice to Flame, but Ellie spoke up now, apparently not noticing the strain. "Yer hair be as bonny as the springtime, Cara," she said softly. "As bright as a pimpernel on a sunny day."

Flame touched her hair self-consciously. She had never liked her unruly mass of tresses, for it seemed to have an unwieldy spirit of its own. As a child, she had thought her hair was a symbol of the evil that lurked within her.

"My thanks, Ellie," she said, sincerely touched. " 'Tis a bit wild, I fear."

"Ahh," said the crone, slurping a draft of home-brewed beer from her just-filled mug. "But some lads take a liking ta the wild ones, aye, Gillie?"

"Aye," said Roderic, eyeing Flame intently, "some do indeed."

The crone chuckled again as if thinking herself quite clever, but now the second daughter piped up. "Na, 'tis na too wild atall. 'Tis lovely ta behold. I only wish . . ." She touched her own limp hair and grimaced.

"Well," said Flame slowly, "it is not very late, and it would only take a short time to plait yours."

"Nay," said Ellie, but Wini, the youngest and barely past the age of thirteen, chimed in.

"Could ye? I mean, 'twould be a lovely thing ta look lek ye." She blushed and bobbed her head.

To her dismay, Flame found that she, too, was blushing. "It would be my honor," she said.

"But ye must be tired," argued Ellie weakly.

"No," Flame objected, "ye were kind enough to help . . . me brother with the chores he performed, leaving me to while the day away." It was true. The three girls had clambered around him like excited hens, fetching whatever he needed, bringing him drinks, wiping his brow, for God's sake. Still, it was difficult to resent them.

In a moment the rough-hewn table was cleared and the wooden bowls washed and set aside. The three girls lined up before Flame, looking nervous.

Eyeing the trio, Flame scowled mentally. This might be more difficult than she had suspected, for their hair seemed so . . . limp.

"Ye ken, Cara," Roderic began, "the lasses have worked verra hard this day. If they would wish ta bathe, I would carry water from the burn."

Flame turned to look at him. Who was this man, raised to command warriors and yet willing to carry water for women? Sitting, relaxed and quiet as he was, he looked for all the world like a great warlord come to rest at the end of the day, and yet, sometimes, it was difficult to imagine him as anyone's enemy, for his very presence made people happy.

"Cara," he repeated, breaking into Flame's thoughts.

"Water!" she said, guiltily tearing her gaze from him. Of course, the girls' hair needed a bit of scrubbing. "My thanks . . . Gillie. Ye fetch the water and we will set some above the fire."

"A . . . bath?" murmured Winifred dubiously. "But will we na catch the ague and die?"

"Nay," assured Flame, who unlike many of her own royal kinsmen, cherished a daily bath. " 'Tis a warm night. It will not hurt ye in the least. In fact, I bathe every—"

Beneath the table, Roderic rapped her shin with the toe of his borrowed boot.

"Month," Flame said, remembering that she was no longer the lady of the MacGowans and granted the rights allowed that title. "I bathe every month and it has not hurt me yet."

The old crone chuckled to herself. "Fetch the water, lad. 'Twill do me heart good ta see yer back flex. 'Tis just a pity Kate had ta find that blasted tartan, or I might watch more than that."

Roderic rose with a grin but leaned close to the old woman's ear. " 'Tis still some fire under *yer* skirt, is there na, mistress?"

"Aye, lad," she said with a wink. "And if I were but ten years younger I'd be setting yer tail alight."

Chuckling, Roderic headed for the door.

An old half barrel was dragged before the simple hearth. Roderic brought water from the burn and Ellie filled the kettle suspended above the fire. A blanket was strung up between the barrel and the remainder of the tiny hut for privacy, and soon little Wini had been coaxed from her clothes and urged into the impromptu tub.

Her body was as slim as a willow just beginning to bud. She stood in the barrel, arms crossed self-consciously before her.

"You must get entirely wet," said Flame.

"Ye mean me whole person?"

Flame allowed a smidgen of a grin. "Aye. And your hair, too."

Finally Wini was immersed. Flame scrubbed her hair with the contents of a small bottle said to have been given to them by the Lamont himself in exchange for their brew. By the third shampooing, a sweet-smelling lather bubbled from Winifred's small head. Thrilled with the sensation and the scent, Winifred touched her frothy halo and smiled.

So she had been wrong again, Flame realized. This

girl was not plain at all, only poor. Strange how the two could be confused.

The other girls followed. Finally the three were dried and dressed in their best gowns. Flame pulled down the blanket and set the girls in a row before the fire to begin tugging the tangles from their hair with a comb.

The evening was filled with self-conscious giggles, silly banter, and more than a few oohs of astonished delight as the little ducklings shed their down for glossy feathers.

Through it all, Roderic sat in silence. But each time Flame raised her eyes to him, she found that his gaze was upon them and his chiseled features unreadable.

His attention made her head feel strangely light and her fingers suspiciously heavy. But despite her fumbling, each girl's hair was finally combed and plaited and coiled atop her head.

They stood one by one to parade through the tiny hut like newly found princesses. Roderic rose to his feet and bowed with each one's debut.

But to Flame's dismay, there was a scowl on the old woman's face.

Wini, young and painfully sensitive to her mother's emotions, stopped the procession to bite her lip and blink into the old crone's face.

"Dunna ye think we look grand, Mama?" she whispered, near tears.

The old crone cleared her throat. "A lot of foolishness this be," she scoffed. "Will these grand airs help ye tend the brew or fetch the firewood?"

Flame drew her back straighter. It seemed as if a million years had passed since she had been as young and tender as Winifred, and yet she could feel the sting of criticism as if it were yesterday. Her throat felt tight with the memory of her father's scalding rejections. "Mayhap it will not see the work done," she began tightly, "but . . ."

"But it will surely draw those strapping lads ye spoke

of,'' Roderic broke in, stepping close and draping his arm across the crone's shoulders.

Flame's gaze darted to his eyes, expecting to see ridicule there. Instead, there was the glint of admiration and something more. Something unreadable, as if he knew her feeling and longed to share her pain. Suddenly it was difficult to draw an even breath as their gazes fused together.

"Strapping lads be well and good on a cold winter's night," rasped the mother irritably. "But good fer little else, methinks."

Roderic pulled his gaze from Flame's. "Have ye na wish for grandchildren then, mistress?"

"I have na wish ta say good-bye ta me lasses fer all time," she said. "And if any man saw ye such . . .'' Her voice broke. "Me beautiful bairns, I couldna bear ta lose ye," she sniffled and suddenly her arms were filled with the three girls she had mothered alone all these years.

"Na, Mama. We will never leave ye."

"Humph. If some strutting lad would but parade past, ye mark me words well, he would hie ye from here as quick as spit. And then where would yer auld Mama be?"

"Sitting pretty amidst a passel of chubby faced grandchildren, methinks," said Roderic. "Ye have a fine piece of land here, mistress, and if me guess is correct, a good hearty business for yer brew. A lad could do far worse than make his home surrounded by four such bonny women."

Little Wini hugged her mother's stout waist, and Ellie, seeming suddenly taller and grander, turned to nod her thanks for Roderic's words.

Roderic nodded back. " 'Tis surely time ta find our sleep," he said. "Would ye be wanting me ta bring yer goats into the hut for safekeeping?"

Mistress Lamont sniffled again and shook her head. "Even the accursed MacGowans wouldna dare take our stock with a braw lad lek ye nearby. Go on now. Get yerself some sleep."

Lifting a candle from the table, Roderic set the curled and blackened wick to a nearby flame. It hissed to light. "God's rest to ye all," he said and touching a hand to Flame's back, ushered her outside.

The walk to the barn was a quiet one. Along the way, Roderic retrieved his sporran and plaid. Bonny ambled along beside them, and her master swung the door of the slanted stable open.

Finding a lantern on a peg set into the wall, Roderic put the flame to its wick and blew out the candle. Ever so slowly, he turned to Flanna. The mellow light from the lantern shadowed and illumined her features. Her eyes were as green as living emerald. Her face seemed sculpted from purest marble. " 'Twas a kind thing ye did in there," she said.

Her gaze didn't shift from his, and though she spoke, he failed to hear her words, for her lips were rosebud pink and very near. He watched them form words, fascinated by their plumpness, their color, their soft allure.

"Roderic?"

"Aye," he said, pulling himself from his trance with a start.

"I said, ye certainly seemed appreciative of the changes."

Her throat was marvelously slim. It seemed, almost, that he would be able to span its lovely circumference with one hand, so delicate it was. And yet, she was not a feeble lass. Indeed, she had matched him stride for stride and uttered not a single complaint as they had traveled through the rain. And now the lady of the MacGowans stood in this rotting barn, ready to spend the night without mention of her fine bed and curtains. Indeed, there were barely four walls to keep out the night, for some of the timbers had rotted, leaving a hole large enough for Bonny to squirm through. 'Twas hardly a place for a fine lady to spend the dark hours, and yet she looked far more lovely and regal than all the maids he had seen at court.

"Roderic," she repeated.

"Aye," he said, again drawing himself from his reverie.

"I said . . ." She licked her lips in a nervous gesture. He watched her shell pink tongue stripe her top lip with moisture before darting back under cover. "Ye certainly seemed enraptured with the procedures."

"Oh?" He could not help but cup his hand about her neck, for it looked so irresistibly smooth, so cool and slim and delicate. His fingers skimmed beneath the fluffy softness of her escaping tendrils. "What procedures were those?"

"The girls," she breathed rapidly.

Her ears were very small with no lobe to speak of . . . or to suckle. He smiled at the thought, and without plan, leaned forward to kiss her just below one delicate ear.

"Roderic!" she gasped, pulling away, but his hand still cupped her neck, allowing her a short tether.

"Me pardon," he said, grinning slightly. "What were ye saying?"

"I said ye were staring at . . ." Her eyes were as bright as the starlight and focused sharply on his. Her teeth were straight and milky white, her tongue seductive as it swept over them. "The girls," she finished on an exhalation.

"Oh. Aye," he said and leaning forward, he kissed the pulse that raced in the tender hollow of her throat. "I couldna help but watch." Straightening slightly, he looked directly into the fathomless lochans of her eyes. Beneath his hand, he felt her throat convulse as she swallowed. "For surely 'tis the loveliest sight I have ever seen."

"I believe they were enamored with ye as well. The lasses, that is."

"Truly? *All* the lasses?" Ever so gently, he skimmed his thumb down her throat. " 'Tis glad I am ta hear that."

She nodded once. The motion was stiff. "But . . . they are young and impressionable."

"Aye." Humoring a nagging whim, Roderic kissed

the corner of her mobile mouth. "Easily wounded, though ye wouldna know it right off," he said.

He felt the rush of her breath against his mouth, but she did not pull away.

"Nay, they hide their sensitivities well."

"Aye, they do, lass."

"Sometimes"—she swallowed again—"sometimes they seem almost hardened and . . ."

"Haughty," he murmured, staring into her eyes.

"Aye," she whispered, "but perhaps they have been . . ."

"Wounded," he finished softly. "Perhaps their sire was a fool and didna care for them as a father should. And yet, if they were but cherished they would blossom like white heather upon the hillocks."

Her lips trembled. "Roderic," she rasped.

"Aye, lass."

"I will lie with you," she whispered.

Chapter 21

The world slowed to a grinding halt. Roderic blinked once, careful not to move lest he shatter the dream he had fallen into. She licked her lips again. He watched the nervous movement.

"Me pardon," he said finally. "But I almost thought ye said—"

"I will lie with ye," she repeated in another breathy whisper.

Heaven's gate! This is what he had dreamed of. What he had striven for. The answer to his tormenting fantasies. The haughty Lady MacGowan asking for his favors.

Breathlessly, Roderic bent to kiss her, to pull her into his arms, to grant her request. But errant images nagged at his mind. Images of Lady MacGowan talking with young Haydan, of the fiery Flame astride Lochan with roses in her cheeks and wind in her hair as she shouted orders to her men. Images of a girl called Cara who coaxed wispy hair atop a plain lass's knobby pate. They were all different faces of a woman named Flanna MacGowan. And he wanted them all. Not just the passionate vixen who moaned beneath his hands, not just the kind lass who could see beauty where others could not. But Flanna, the woman.

He straightened slightly. "What do ye mean?"

Her laugh was nervous, her hand slightly shaky as she placed it on his chest. "I think my meaning is clear, Forbes."

His aching groin told him not to question this gift. He should take her in his arms now, woo her with his kisses, unwrap her with his hands, love her with his body. But she was not talking about love. She was talking about copulation.

"Ye make it sound verra simple."

She laughed again, very softly. Her fingers were light and gentle against his chest. "Ye assured me it would be. That I could stroke ye and pet ye without repercussions."

"Well . . ." He caught her hand in a tight grip. It was decidedly distracting and he needed to think. "That was afore . . ."

She blinked. "Afore what?"

Before he needed her respect, her love. Before he needed her trust. Before he wanted to marry her. *Oh God!* Panic was an unfamiliar quality, but Roderic recognized it when he felt it. "Afore . . . I knew ye so well."

"So ye are saying that now that ye know me, ye no longer wish to . . . to mate with me?"

"Mate?" he said, feeling his ire rise with his panicked frustration. He was Roderic the Rogue. Why could he not act roguish. " 'Tis a crude term ye use."

She raised her chin slightly. "Are ye saying ye do not wish to?"

"Aye, that is what I am saying." It was a blatant lie.

"But I thought—"

"What? That we could just have at it like swine in the mud? That I was no more than a . . ." He backed away to wave a hand between them. Damn her for wanting to lie with him now and place the blame on him later. "No more loyal than one of yer stallions, to be bred and turned back into me stall. Is that what ye—"

She leaned forward and kissed him. Her lips were like fire, searing all thought from his mind, scattering his words to the four winds. For just an instant he remembered that he was supposed to be insulted, that he should tell her he was a man, not a coveted stallion, but . . .

He groaned as his arms encircled her of their own accord, crushing her to him. She was soft but firm, bold but trembling.

It was the tremble that made him draw back, for though she would not admit her fear, he felt it in the shudder of her fine body. Leaning back slightly, he looked into her eyes, searching for uncertainty. But there was none. She wanted him. And he needed her.

He bent slightly, lifted her into his arms, and kissed her again. When he drew his head back, her eyes remained closed for a moment. When they opened, they looked misty and disoriented. She lifted her hand, gently touching his lips. He kissed her fingertips, and she shivered. Again he closed his mouth over hers. He tasted her hunger, felt her tremble. She slipped her fingers beneath his hair, cupping his neck and pulling him closer, deepening their kiss. Her desire only increased his own, and suddenly he could wait no longer.

He strode toward the pile of hay and let her feet slip to the earthen floor. Flanna turned to face him. He felt the quick rise and fall of her breasts against his chest and knew with aching wonder that her impatience rivaled his own.

With only a few quick movements, he removed his belt and brooch. His borrowed plaid slipped away. Stepping to the side, he unwrapped it from his waist and knelt to sweep it over the fragrant mound of fodder. In a moment, his eyes met hers again.

She stood perfectly still, watching him. And suddenly, he wondered if she had ceased breathing. Ever so slowly, he rose to his feet while keeping his gaze firmly locked on hers.

" 'Tis na too late ta change yer mind," he said softly. They were the hardest words he had ever spoken, and for one hopeless moment he stood stiffly waiting for her to retreat.

Instead, she stepped forward and placed one hand against his chest. "I have not changed my mind," she whispered and kissed him with urgent heat.

His heart bumped back to erratic life, his breathing accelerated, and a groan rumbled up his throat as he reached for the ties at the back of her gown. But just as he felt them ease free, she pushed at his chest again.

"Ye said I could pet ye," she murmured.

"What?" he rasped, trying to think.

"Ye said I could pet ye," she repeated and tugged his shirt upward. The fabric slipped over his chest. He raised his arms, allowing her to pull the garment over his head. Finally, it dangled to the floor from one wrist, and there it hung, forgotten, for at that precise instant, her fingertips brushed his nipple.

Roderic sucked a harsh breath between his teeth and let his head fall back. But the sensations had only just begun, for her fingers seemed restless and curious and wandered over his body like trails of fire. They skimmed his chest, caressed his shoulders, followed a taut cord up his neck to trace the line of his jaw.

It was hard to draw breath, and harder yet to wait, to allow her exploration without crushing her to him and easing his ache inside her. But wait he did, letting her touch, letting her feel, letting the anticipation build until he felt as if he would burst into spontaneous flame.

Again her fingers brushed his nipple. He shuddered. Her touch skimmed downward, coursing a trail down the center of his chest and over his taut belly until he felt her brush the turgid heat of his manhood.

He opened his eyes, lowered them to hers, and caught her wrist in a tight clasp.

She gasped, mouth round and soft like a child who had been caught stealing scones.

"My turn," he whispered, pushing her hands aside.

In less than an instant her gown was removed. Flame stood breathlessly before him, naked and trembling. His hands were everywhere, shivering hot sensations down her neck, over her shoulder, down the arching center of her back. She felt the aching tenderness of his kiss against her throat as he took her hand in his and raised it between them. His lips were warm and firm against her palm, against her wrist, against the ultrasensitive bend of her arm. She gasped against the sharp sensations, but when he tugged at her hand she slipped onto the soft wool of his plaid with him.

They lay on their sides, thigh to thigh, belly to belly. She felt the hard thrust of his desire between them. Longing for fulfillment, she thrust her hips against him. But he urged her onto her back and made her wait as he showered her body with hot, slow kisses. They rained over her torso, down the length of her legs, and up again. She writhed frantically and moaned his name, but he had caught her wrists in his hands and kept them pinned to her sides as he kissed her breasts, her belly, the burning triangle of hair between her legs.

She gasped in shock and need as she jerked to a sitting position. Roderic eased back, finding her eyes with his own. Desire and promise smoldered between them. Her lips parted wordlessly, and then she lay back. He covered her body with his own. She opened her legs to him, wanting him, needing him.

He kissed her, slowly, thoroughly, and then, with hot, fluid ease, he slipped inside.

There was no pain, no fear, nothing but desire answered and need fulfilled. They rode together stride for stride, giving and taking, reaching for the skies until finally they burst into the clouds in a blaze of shuddering glory.

Flame gasped. Roderic growled, and finally they fell together, back to their cozy nest in the hay, where he crooned her name and stroked her lanquidly into sleep.

Flanna woke slowly, not knowing why, and for a moment not knowing where. And though the light had been doused, she knew Roderic was there. She sensed his presence as easily as she heard him croon her name.

"Flanna," he breathed, and skimmed a hand gently down her bare arm. "So ye are na a dream."

He kissed her and she felt herself fall under his power

again, but suddenly the horse outside the barn whinnied. Another steed answered.

Roderic jerked away.

"Search the cottage," ordered a gruff voice.

"The Wolfhound!" Roderic rasped.

"Troy," Flame breathed. Her gaze met Roderic's with a jolt.

"Please," Roderic whispered, "come with me."

"I cannot," she whispered. "They need me."

Hoofbeats sounded outside.

"Please," he repeated. "I canna let ye go."

She tried to argue, but warm memories assaulted her, and she knew he spoke the truth. He would not let her go without a fight.

He reached for her hand, pulled her to her feet, and tossed her her gown. They were dressed in moments. He pressed her toward the hole in the back of the barn.

Soon, they were through, squatting in the dark behind the barn.

They stared at each other, a thousand thoughts pulsing between them. "Wait here," he whispered.

She stared at him, trying to find the courage to argue.

"If ye left me I would follow ye forever. I would fight ta have ye back," he murmured.

She knew it was true, and though she tried to deny it, hope and happiness soared through her. In a moment, Roderic disappeared into the darkness. From the other side of the barn, she heard a timber drop. Hoofbeats thundered across hard-packed earth, ceased for a moment as if the horse had sprouted wings, and began again. "Hang on!" Roderic shouted.

"There!" someone yelled. "They're getting away. To yer horses!"

Men shouted. Hooves pounded.

Roderic appeared and reached for her hand.

Without thought, she went with him. They ran side by side. Dark woods loomed overhead. Bonny loped along beside them. Branches grabbed at Flame's skin and gown.

The night swept past. Their breathing became labored. And somehow it seemed that they were running for her, running from danger to save her from some unknown evil.

From behind came an uncertain noise. Roderic twisted about, still holding her hand and almost tripping. "They come," he rasped and stumbled ahead.

They splashed into a burn. Cool water washed over Flame's legs and splashed on her face and hands. In the woods behind them, a horse whinnied.

"There!" Flame gasped, pointing to a pile of brush on the far side of the river. They sped through the water and onto the smooth brownstone on the opposite bank. Somewhere in the woods, a branch broke. Flame gasped and pulled Roderic toward the tangled brush.

Brambles tore at her hands as she tugged the vines away, but in a moment Roderic nudged her aside and ripped the debris from its setting against the boulders.

Without a word, they scrambled into the crevice between the two huge rocks and turned about. Roderic dragged the brush in behind them.

From their hiding place, they could see a great, dark horse charge from the woods and into the burn. Water sprayed upward from its plunging hooves. In a moment, another horse thundered into the water. Even in the pale dawning light, they could see a white plume dance above the first man's bonnet.

"The Wolfhound doesna give up," Roderic whispered.

"What the devil be ye doing here, Nevin?" Troy asked. "Did I na tell ye ta follow the horse?"

"The horse was a ploy!" snapped the younger man. "Forbes is here. And very close."

"Aye? And how do ye know that?"

"Because I am na so foolish as ye, old man," Nevin exclaimed. "How many times will ye fall for his tricks?"

For a moment, Troy was silent, then, "Go back to the others, lad, before I make ye regret yer words."

They were close enough to hear the horses' labored breathing. She should call for help, Flame knew, but what would they do if they found Roderic? Troy would fight to take her. Roderic would fight to keep her. She could do nothing but try to prevent bloodshed.

"Do ye wish to be laird so badly that ye would let her die at the hands of a Forbes, old man?" Nevin growled.

The tension was nearly palpable, but suddenly a movement caught Flame's eye, distracting her. Bonny had been left outside, and lay now, stretching her head onto her paws to wait for her master's return.

Flame held her breath. Roderic caught her line of vision and swore quietly.

"I should kill ye for that, lad," said Troy flatly. "But for yer father's sake, I willna."

Nevin's steed fidgeted. His rider chuckled, but the sound was dark. "Ye had best not try, old man, or ye may find me not so soft as ye think me to be."

"Get back to the others."

The two remained in the river, their horses fretted at their bits.

"Do not forget that I know your secrets. Ye will not be laird and neither will your heir," Nevin warned, and turning his steed, headed back toward the cottage.

Troy's stallion tossed his heavy neck and pawed the water. Seconds ticked away until finally Troy urged his mount across the river and up onto the rock.

Flame held her breath, praying Bonny would remain immobile.

The dark destrier turned once, then stood still, his ears pricked forward as his rider scanned the distance.

"Ye'd best watch yer step and na dally where ye are na wanted, Forbes," Troy murmured, staring into the distance, "or ye'll rue the day." Turning his bay, the huge warrior splashed back into the river.

Chapter 22

*They were gone. Out of his reach. Or so Forbes
thought. But Forbes knew so little. There was nowhere safe for them. Not in all of Scotland, for he paid
his brigands well.*

The lea where they rested was quiet. Surrounded by
a thousand gnarled oaks, it rested like a smooth, green
gem in the forest's center. The sun again bathed the
earth.

Flame sat on a rock, nursing feet that burned from her
journey through the bracken.

"Why did ye do it, lass?" Roderic asked softly. He
was holding her foot in his hands and shifted his gaze
from her instep to her eyes.

"Let go."

"Ye've picked up a thorn."

She jerked her foot again, employing her very best
scowl. "I know I've got a thorn. Do ye think me so
dense that I do not feel pain?"

Ever so gently, he smoothed his fingers up her ankle
and grinned into her face. "In truth, lass, I was wondering that verra thing."

She tried to stop the shiver that followed his fingers'
slow course.

"With the way ye rush through the brambles in bare
feet, I thought surely ye were beyond physical pain."

Flame did her best to increase the intensity of her
scowl, but his fingers were excruciatingly soothing

against her bare calf. "Mayhap I be but trying to avoid ye."

He chuckled softly. "A lesser man might deduce ye dunna appreciate me presence," he said.

"A smarter man would surely do so," she countered, yanking at her foot again.

He held it still, bowed his attention to the ball of her foot and plucked out the irritating thistle.

She jerked again, but Roderic refused to give up his hold.

"Why?" he asked for the second time.

She glanced away. "I have not an inkling what ye are referring to."

"I might say, a smarter lass would. But I think ye are a smarter lass, Flanna."

She held his gaze with some difficulty, making certain her expression was haughty, though her heart hammered an erratic beat in her chest. "Do ye wish to be caught by my kinsmen, or shall we go on?"

Roderic shrugged. "Methinks I should dally here and allow ye to fend them off . . . again. For I wonder, where would ye hide me now, Flanna MacGowan? And why would ye bother?" His voice dropped to a whisper. "I was yer hostage, was I na?"

Flame pursed her lips and tried to pretend he was not stroking her ankle and causing a thousand errant thoughts to clatter into her brain. "If ye were killed there would be no end to the bloodshed." And no healing the hole in her heart.

"So ye say ye have na personal feelings for me?" Roderic asked softly.

Tingling emotions scurried from his fingertips and up her leg. Memories of the night before stole her breath, but she tried to pretend otherwise. "Aye." The single word came out on a squeak. Flame cleared her throat, pursed her lips and tried again. "Aye, Forbes, that is exactly what I am saying."

He canted his head slightly, causing the sunlight to glitter off his shoulder-length hair at a different angle and shift the shadows across his strong features. "Nevertheless, I thank ye."

His eyes were so blue. 'Twas surely a sin to have eyes like that, eyes that looked into her soul but hid his own.

"And I apologize," he added.

She knew she should try again to yank her foot from his grasp. She should rise haughtily to her feet, lift her chin in the air, and walk away.

Instead, she watched his long fingers trickle up her shin. "For what?' Her question was pathetically weak.

"It be difficult to ken where ta start, for my behavior has been less than exemplary since our first meeting."

But she had abducted *him*. Or at least, she had abducted him first.

"I . . ." He drew a deep breath and watched as his touch drifted nearly to her knee. "I admit that yer nearness puts me off me stride. Before going to Dun Ard, some people found me quite tolerable."

She held her breath for a moment, then found her voice. "Indeed?" Dear God, she wanted to kiss him, wanted to slip into his arms and beg him to stay with her forever.

"Indeed," he said. "There were even those who called me charming on occasion."

"Nay." She tried to make the word sound sarcastic but feared she achieved nothing more than a tone of breathlessness.

" 'Tis true," he murmured, skimming his hand higher still. "But with ye I find I am barely . . . coherent, for all I want to do is . . ."

Mate! Flame thought and shoved her gown back over her tingling knee. "Weren't ye about to mate—apologize!" she corrected frantically. Dear God, let the earth swallow her now.

The corner of Roderic's mouth lifted the slightest degree, almost as if he hadn't noticed her horrid slip of tongue. "That I was, lass."

"Then . . . please do," she whispered.

His smiled brightened a whit. "Do what?" he murmured.

Her lips moved. Her breathing accelerated. Her pulse sped along. "Whatever it is ye feel ye must do."

"Heaven's gate, lass, that is just the problem. I am torn between what I should do and what I must do."

God forgive her for being a weak-willed ninny. "Then do what ye wish to do."

He leaned closer. All she could see was his face, the squareness of his stubbly jaw, the vibrant blue of his eyes. All was silent. She waited breathlessly.

"I want to apologize, Flanna. I shouldna have said the things I've said. Shouldna have done much of what I have done. And I shouldna have allowed ye ta expose yerself ta danger at the burn."

"Allowed?" she echoed. "I am the Flame of the MacGowans, who are ye to allow or disallow?"

He smiled that captivating smile that haunted her dreams and muddled her thoughts. It seemed she could feel her very hair wilt from the intoxicating power of it, but she forced her back to remain stiff.

"I do love it when ye speak like that, Flanna MacGowan," he said. "All regal disdain and cool superiority." Skimming his fingers about her ankle, he slipped them lower, over her instep and onto her toes.

Her mouth fell open slightly. She tried to catch her breath and remember what she had said, what she should say next, who she was. But reality seemed so vague, and her fantasies so real. God, he was beautiful, and he would pass those fine looks on to his children. They would be fair-haired, with eyes as bright as the morning sky and laughter to make the woodlands sing.

"But mayhap ye like me just a wee bit, lass. Or at the least, mayhap ye like what I can do for ye."

Reality returned with a jolt. Flame yanked her foot from his hand. "Ye are a conceited . . ."

"Man?" he supplied helpfully. "Most are. Fortunately, I have more ta be conceited about than the others, lass."

She rose abruptly, then winced as her tender feet touched the ground.

"Sit down. I'll bandage them," he said softly.

"Nay." She stepped away, but he had already caught her ankle.

"Sit down, lass, or I'll have ta wrestle ye ta the ground and though I used ta think meself well disciplined, being near ye has changed me mind. I'd hate ta do something we might later regret."

Her gaze caught his. The desire in them was as clear as morning dew. She sat with a plop.

He grinned. "Now sit still," he said, and hoisting up his plaid, set her foot upon his bare thigh. Muscle rippled beneath the pad of her foot.

"What are ye doing?"

Tugging the end of his shirt from beneath his tartan, he glanced up with a grin. "Make me a suggestion, lass, and I'll surely consider it."

Her foot was very near his private parts. She couldn't breathe.

He watched her face, then chuckled deep in his throat. "I am but ripping off a bit of me shirt ta act as yer shoes."

Flame licked her lips. "Oh." It was all she could think to say and she felt rather silly for her lack of incriminating words. "I knew that."

His plaid dipped between his legs, showing more sculpted thigh and . . .

She snapped her gaze back to his.

His grin brightened as her face did the same. "Me apologies," he said and tugged the recalcitrant plaid a scant inch to the right. "It seems I underestimated yer effect on me yet again."

Her face felt hot and her hands clammy. "Let me go," she whispered.

"Surely ye must be accustomed ta having that effect on men," he said, still holding her foot.

She pursed her lips. "I am accustomed to choosing the time and place."

"Last night 'twas a fine time," he murmured, "but here in the lea would be perfection." Near his crotch, his plaid moved of its own accord.

She tried to keep her gaze sternly on his face, but her fingers itched to touch him and her heart galloped in her chest. "Perfection is naught but a deluded dream," she murmured.

" 'Tis na true. Ye and I tagether. That be perfection," he whispered.

Her heart stopped completely. With every fiber of her being she hoped he would reach for her, but instead he jerked his attention back to her feet and snugly bound them.

Toward nightfall, Bonny caught a squirrel. They roasted it over a well-hidden fire and shared it three ways. Roderic thought it tasted as if it had been marinated in horse sweat and left to dry in the sun.

" 'Twas a fine meal," Flame said. She sat with her back to a rough log. A bare bone dangled from her fingers.

"Now I *am* worried," Roderic said and touched the back of his hand to her forehead.

She laughed. The sound was silvery in the cool darkness. "I have always liked the taste of squirrel." She watched him draw his hand away and grimace. "I am a simple girl with simple tastes."

Nay, she was not. She was royalty—in reality and in spirit. He shifted his attention from her face to his portion of the stringy meal. "Dun Ard's greasy mutton is beginning to seem more appealing by the day."

"My people have fallen on bad luck, Forbes. Though we were never wealthy, we are harder pressed now and have learned to make do."

"Bad luck," he mused quietly. "Such as the death of yer kindred, the loss of yer stock, the poisoned well?"

"Aye. And I admit I thought it was caused by your people, Forbes," she said, but her voice was soft.

"And now?"

She shifted her gaze to the ground. "Now I don't know."

"It wasna the Forbeses, lass," he said quietly. "Therefore there is someone else who wishes ta harm yer people. But who?"

For a moment, he thought she would argue, but she sighed and looked into the night. "I can think of no one I have angered."

He watched her profile. It shone in the golden light of their campfire like a copper cameo. "Mayhap there are those who hated the MacGowans long before ye became their lady."

"Mayhap. My father was not . . . always charming."

He thought of what she had endured, alone and afraid, far from home.

"I have heard he accused many of lying with his wife. It is rumored some of those same men died suspiciously."

And Flanna had been the one to bear the brunt of the rumors and try to mold her tribe back into a family unit.

"And what of Troy?" he asked.

"Why do ye ask?"

"There are those who think him an attractive man, even in his waning years. It seems likely that the MacGowan might have accused him of a dalliance."

She bit her lip. "I think he may have. Troy, too, spent many years in France. I do not think it was necessarily because he was fond of that country."

"Yer father threatened his life?"

She shrugged. "I was far removed from Scottish politics for many years. 'Tis hard to say what he might have done."

Roderic scowled into the fire. "But if he did, 'twould seem possible that Troy could hold a grudge, would it na?"

"He is my friend, my confidant," she whispered. "All the years in Bastia, he was the only one who eased my lonli . . . who came to visit me."

Self-pity was not in her nature, he thought. But there

was pain in her tone, in her eyes. Still, he could not ignore the possibility that Troy Hamilton wished her ill, for her life was at stake.

"Mayhap he had a reason to visit ye, lass. Mayhap he hoped ta win yer confidence, and ta someday become laird himself when—"

"Nay. Ye are wrong. I—"

"Flanna," he interrupted sharply and raised his head. Something was wrong. It was too quiet. Too . . . "Run!" He yelled the word before he knew his own reasons. In the woods, a twig cracked. He wasted no time looking that way. Instead, he grabbed her wrist and yanked her to her feet.

"What?" she gasped.

An axe flew through the air and bit into the log where she had rested her back. But its thud was drowned by the terrifying shriek of a battle cry.

Chapter 23

Men crashed from the woods toward them.

Flame knew she should run. She heard Roderic's command to do so, felt him push her toward the shelter of the trees. But her legs wouldn't move.

She stood, immobilized by fear as the outlaws rushed toward them. They were armed. Roderic was not, and yet he braced his legs, swept a glowing log from the fire, and stood his ground.

''Flee!'' he yelled as steel crashed against wood. Sparks flew. Flame screamed. Jolted from her trance, she spun away. Then she saw the others.

They swarmed at her from all directions. Her next scream died in her throat. Desperation made her whirl toward the fire. Somehow, Roderic was holding the villains at bay with his flaming brand.

She reached toward the blaze. A branch came away in her hand. There was no time to think, only to swing. Fire burst in a bright arc of sparks.

A man screamed and clutched his burning scalp. But there were many more. She swung again.

It was a blazing, clashing nightmare. She felt her back bump Roderic's, and suddenly she remembered his words. He would give his life to save hers.

Something swelled in her chest. With a war cry of her own, she swung again. A sword slashed at her brand, knocking her aside.

She fell with a shriek, trying to bring her weapon to bear, to shield her face from the snarling devil who lunged at her, but her arms were weakening, her reactions slowing, and she knew she would die.

From beside her came a roar of savage outrage. Like a beast protecting his mate, Roderic pivoted about and swung for the villain's head. Blood sprayed. The man fell, dropping his claymore, and suddenly it was in Roderic's hand.

With one thrust the villain was dead. Roderic wheeled about, both hands on the hilt of his captured sword as he slashed and cut.

But there were too many.

From his left a dark man lunged at him.

Flame screamed, and Bonny leaped! The villain shrieked as the hound pierced his sword arm.

The weapon fell and Flame snatched it up.

From nowhere, another sword swung at her. She blocked the blow with a weak parry and shrieked with fear.

The sword swung again. She watched it arc and prayed for her own immortal soul.

But suddenly Roderic was there, standing over her. His claymore sang of death. Another villain fell, gurgling on his own blood.

"To their horses!" Roderic gasped. "Get a horse and ride!"

"But . . ." She could not leave him.

He gasped in pain. Blood spurted from his arm. He swung wildly about, clanging his claymore against his opponent's sword with a roar.

She couldn't stop them. There were too many. Flame stumbled to her feet. He had cleaved a path through the midst of the outlaws.

Terror drove her down that path and into the woods.

She heard her pursuers follow. Branches snatched at her face. Bracken bound her feet. From up ahead, she heard the fearful snort of a horse and then its dark form loomed suddenly before her.

Her fingers felt numb against the tied reins. The animal snorted again and tried to pull away, but she held on and soon it was free.

Behind her, a man swore and sprang through the darkness. She grabbed the steed's mane and swung upward. Hands grappled for her leg. She screamed and kicked with all her might.

Something crunched beneath Flame's heel. Her mount lunged frantically away.

But Roderic was behind her and she could not leave him. She spun the destrier about and forced him back through the woods.

From her right, men yelled and charged toward her. But she was astride now and knew what she must do.

Roderic looked up just in time to see a monstrous beast explode from the woods and fly toward him. It burst from the darkness like the devil incarnate and bore down upon him, plowing over everything in its path.

"Gawd's wrath!" he gasped and jumped aside just in time to save himself from being knocked to the ground.

"Forbes!" someone yelled.

He gathered his wits and brought his sword to bear.

"Come on!" she screamed and suddenly he realized the rider was Flanna.

"Go!" he ordered.

"Come!"

Already, men were racing toward them, swords uplifted, teeth bared.

Roderic swung his claymore as warning and yelled again for her to leave, but suddenly the stallion was at his back. In that moment, he knew that if he died she would die with him. Damn her stubborn hide. There was nothing he could do but reach for the animal's mane and swing up behind her.

Something sliced the back of his thigh. He gasped in pain and nearly fell, but Flanna's fingers twisted in his shirt. The stallion swung toward him, aiding his assent, and suddenly he was aboard and they were flying across the clearing.

They hit one man square on. He shrieked and fell

beneath the stallion's hooves, and then darkness wrapped about them as the firelight disappeared.

Behind them, men screamed and cursed and ran for their horses.

"Roderic!" Flanna's voice was raspy with fear. "Are ye all right?"

"Are ye?"

"Aye." Her voice quivered but she sat upright and steered the stallion with finesse.

"Then I am too, lass," he breathed. "And I owe ye me thanks again for saving me life." He glanced back, searching the darkness for signs of pursuit. He could see nothing, yet he knew their attackers would follow.

Beneath them, the stallion stumbled, nearly falling to his knees. "Don't thank me yet," she gasped.

From close behind, a villain's battle cry shattered the night.

"I fear it might be now or never, lass."

He saw her twist about to peer into the darkness. Her face was pale with fear and yet she didn't falter but drove the stallion onward, through the trees and out into the open.

Overhead, the moon shone upon a wide stretch of rising meadow. Again, Flame turned to look back. Judging the distance between them and their enemies, she spurred the stallion ahead.

The destrier's hooves thundered across the grass, but his breath came in great gasps and his gait was rough and labored.

"They're nearly upon us!" Roderic warned.

Flanna bent low over the stallion's neck. Though Roderic could not make out the words she spoke, he could feel the animal's desperate burst of speed.

They hit a narrow valley. Momentarily hidden from their pursuers, Flanna pulled their mount to the right. He stumbled again.

"A little further, great one," she breathed, lying flat against his neck. "Just a wee bit."

Trees loomed up and swallowed them with their darkness. Thirty strides into the woods, Flanna straightened. "He's spent!"

Roderic leaped from the stallion's back. Dragging Flanna with him, he raised his sword to send the stallion away.

"Nay! We can not leave him to them," Flame cried, jerking her head to indicate the villains and reaching for the reins.

"What the devil—" Roderic began, but a sudden noise made him push her behind him and jerk about.

From the darkness, Bonny bounded into his arms.

"Sweet Jesu!" Roderic gasped and, hugging the dog to him, turned to Flanna again.

"We cannot leave him any more than we can leave the hound," she said softly.

"Gawd's wrath!" swore Roderic. "Get the nag under cover then if ye're set on forfeiting yer life for him."

She grabbed the animal's reins and dragged him away.

The ravine in which they hid was nothing more than a green slice cut from the leaf-covered ground of the woods.

In the distance, Roderic thought he heard hoofbeats thunder past, but it was difficult to be sure. They waited in silence. Flanna held the stallion's nose lest he decide to call to his friends.

But either the stallion was not overly fond of his former companions or he failed to sense their presence, for he remained silent, his head drooping, his nostrils flared as he pulled great drafts of air into his laboring lungs.

By morning Roderic realized the truth. The animal was neither antisocial nor deaf, he was dying on his feet. Although he had managed to carry them several miles since dawn, he stumbled now, his strength spent.

Seated behind her, Roderic touched Flanna's arm. "The beast can go no further, lass."

"Then we'll walk and lead him."

"Flanna . . ." Roderic sighed. His breath fanned

against her flame-bright hair. Fatigue weighed like a sack of meal across his back and his thigh burned like hell's fire. "He's been starved and can barely walk. 'Twould be a kindness to cut his throat and leave him in peace."

Flanna dropped her hand protectively to the stallion's neck. "I hope ye will agree to spare me from your brand of compassion should I ever dawdle."

Though Roderic tried to look stern, he couldn't quite contain his weary chuckle. "Must I remind ye that ye are na a horse but a person? We Forbeses dunna usually kill our women should they lose a bit of weight. But I have seen this kind of abuse afore, lass." Sliding from the steed's back, Roderic grasped his purloined claymore in one hand. "He is used up."

Suddenly, tears shone in her eyes as she looked down at him. Yet they sparked defiance and gainsaid fear. "Then ye'll go on without us, Forbes. For he saved our lives and I will not leave him."

"He will only slow us down."

"*Me*," she argued. "He will only slow me down. Ye can go on."

Roderic gritted his teeth and swung angrily about. "Damn it all to hell!" he swore and pivoted back. "Why must I love a woman whose verra bones are stubborn?"

He watched her mouth fall open in surprise. "Roderic," she murmured, but he scowled her to silence and raised one hand to fend off her words.

"Not now, Flanna. Ye didna hear what ye think ye heard," he warned. "Just keep silent, and handfeed the crow-bait before he drops like a rock into death."

Damned if she didn't.

Roderic lay upon the grass and watched her. The back of his thigh still burned but he had felt along the gash with his fingers and decided the wound wasn't life-threatening.

Bonny lay flat out beside him, exhausted. But Flanna

remained on her feet, picking choice shoots of grass to feed to the steed.

The horse was tall and still young. At one time he might have been a handsome beast. Now, his ribs showed like the bones of a long-dead carcass, his dark coat had faded to a frizzled brown, and his eyes were sunken within their sockets.

Despite his listlessness, he managed to lap the grasses from Flanna's palm. She stroked his stringy neck and whispered soft words into his drooping ear.

Roderic stubbornly assured himself that he did not envy the wasted beast for the tender attention he was receiving. He could not feel her hands feather-soft upon his skin or imagine her breath against the lobe of his ear. "Here." He rose abruptly with a scowl, feeling restless despite his fatigue. "Ye rest, Flanna."

She refused to turn toward him. "I know this horse," she said quietly. "He was one of our own."

"MacGowan stock?" Roderic asked, eyeing the miserable beast in disbelief.

"Aye." Flanna's hand slipped to a deep hollow above the stallion's eye. " 'Tis Bruid's get."

"Bruid? That huge, ungodly beast that nearly tore ye piece from piece?"

"Aye. This lad was grazing with the other young stallions and taken in a raid."

Roderic drew a heavy breath and deepened his scowl as he realized her meaning. "So ye blame this on the Forbeses? Ye think they would tek yer beasts, then attack us both in an attempt ta kill ye?"

"Nay," she said, turning slowly toward him. "I do not." Her eyes met his with a jolt. "But the men who raided the herd those months ago were dressed in Forbeses' plaids."

Roderic remained silent as he watched her. "So we are in agreement," he said.

She nodded once. "Others disguised themselves to accuse the Forbeses of their crimes."

"Who?"

"I don't know," she said.

"But ye suspect. Who? Nevin? The Wolfhound?"

"Nay. Troy has sworn he would never be laird. And Nevin is the son of a merchant. He has no wish to rule."

Roderic shook his head. Never, not even at her most alluring, had he wished to hold her more than he did now. "Know this, lass, every man wishes to rule," he said softly.

"And does that include ye, Forbes?"

He watched her eyes, fraught with mystery and unknown marvels. "Aye," he murmured. "But some men would be content to rule the heart of a woman of spirit."

Her breath caught in her throat and he hoped it was a good sign. "To rule the *woman,* you mean."

"I fear there is na a man alive who could rule ye, lass, even if he were fool enough ta wish ta try."

She was holding her breath, he realized suddenly. "And what is your wish, Forbes?"

For a moment he had to fight the urge to pull her into his arms and tell her the truth, that he wished for nothing more than to love her as she should be loved and to receive her love in return. But with Flanna MacGowan the truth could be like a dagger at your side. It might defend you, but it might also be used against you.

Warily hiding the dagger, he sighed. "I but wish for a hot bath, lass, and me own bed in which to spend the night."

It almost seemed as if she tried to stop her words. Nevertheless, they came. "And who would be in that bed with you?" she asked stiffly. "Some mealymouthed lass who cannot say no?"

Roderic laughed aloud, so flattered was he by her anger. "It seems to me that even ye had a bit of trouble saying nay."

"I did not have—"

"Nay," he said. "Do not shatter me frail self-importance by destroying my illusions, lass."

"I'll wound more than—" she began, but his kiss stopped her words.

It seemed so natural, like breathing, like waking in the morning to find that a bright new day awaited him. Her lips were soft and warm against his. Her waist, where his arm cradled her, was as tight and small as a young beech tree. Between their bodies, his desire rose hard and fast. The kiss deepened and now it was she who made the rules, she who slanted her lips across his, who wound her arms about him and pulled him closer.

"Lass"—he drew away finally, feeling his breath rasp down his throat—"I do hate ta call a halt but I fear I must afore it be too late. We stop now or na atall."

Her face was absolutely somber. But her breasts rose and fell dramatically with her breathing. "There is something to be said for not atall."

Never had Roderic been more flattered than when he saw the stark desire in her eyes. But he would not risk her life for a few moments of pleasure. If they were attacked once, they could surely be attacked again. " 'Tis na safe here, lass," he said, managing to break the spell of her desire and his own raging need. "We must press on ta Glen Creag."

"Stop," Flame ordered.

Roderic turned. "What is it?"

" 'Tis your leg," she said. "Ye cannot go on."

"Aye. I can," he argued, but before he could turn away she had caught his arm.

"Ye will sit and let me see to your leg or I will return to Dun Ard this minute."

Roderic scowled down at her. His thigh burned like hell's own fire and he knew that she, too, should rest. But they must keep moving. "I would run ye down and drag ye the remainder of the way if needs be."

She planted her fists on her hips and laughed into his face. "You would be lucky to run down a three-legged flea in your present state. Sit down."

"Flanna!" he said sharply and deepened his scowl. He had learned the art of intimidation from his brother

Leith, and though he didn't utilize it often, he considered himself quite adept.

"Sit!" she ordered.

Bonny thumped her rump to the ground with a whimper. Behind her, the misbegotten steed that she called Great Heart snorted and stopped.

Roderic hoped to show a bit more backbone. "Ye willna give me orders, lass," he warned darkly.

"No orders?"

"Nay," he said. "For that foolish steed has surely made tracks deep enough to show a half-witted dunce our trail." Flanna had finally agreed to turn the animal free, yet the debilitated beast had insisted on following them. Although he had grazed listlessly along the way, he had refused to turn back. "The brigands may be following even now. We must move on."

"No orders?" she asked again.

He shook his head, enjoying her soft expression but a bit baffled and wary of it, nevertheless.

"Then what say you of a bribe?"

Against his will, Roderic's brows rose. "Bribe? What sort of bribe?"

Her small face was very sober. "That depends, Forbes," she said, placing a hand gently to his chest. "What would you like?"

Chapter 24

Roderic licked his lips but forced himself to remain still. What would he like? He would like Flanna MacGowan naked and dancing before his fire. He would like her hot and wet beneath him. He would like her strong legs wrapped about him like a bottle around a potent drink.

But they must keep moving.

It *was* almost dark.

Her safety must come first.

If his leg wound worsened he might be unable to defend her. He needed rest.

He did not know who the villains were and if they followed, he must be ever wary.

But the saucy wench was offering to *bribe* him.

"What be ye offering?" Even to his own ears, his voice sounded strangely hoarse.

"I am offering to see to your wound," she said, but her cheeks were flushed a rosy hue, denying the innocence of her words.

He lifted one corner of his mouth into a smile. "Somehow that doesna sound nearly so pleasurable an experience as I had anticipated."

"Sit down," she ordered again. Her eyes were sultry and her tone suggestive.

"But the wound is at the back of me leg. I would have to *lie* down."

"Then lie down."

"Na unless ye will lie with me."

He heard her exhalation of surprise but she said nothing.

"Well, lass? What is yer answer?"

Her breath was coming hard and fast now and her mouth was pursed in that characteristic expression of thoughtfulness. "What do ye mean by lie . . . exactly?"

Roderic held her with his gaze. Never had desire had him in such a tight and enduring grip. Never had he wanted to ease his carnal desires more than now. And yet, there was so much more to be discovered of Flanna MacGowan than sexual pleasures. He would not lose himself in those pleasures again until he knew that she wanted every aspect of him just as he wanted her. But he had no qualms about feeding the fire of her passions. "Ye dunna ken what I mean by the word 'lie'?" He knew she thought he was talking about sex, and was content to let her think so, for he wondered at her response. Ever so gently, he reached out to brush a wanton tendril of flame-bright hair behind her ear. She trembled beneath his touch. "What do ye think I mean, lass?"

"I . . ."

He couldn't help but kiss her neck, it looked so soft and lovely, so smooth and elegant and was made only more so by the freckle of mud that bedecked her collarbone. "Well?" His lips were very near her ear now. He felt her shiver again and closed his eyes against the barrage of desire that battered him.

"I can only imagine what ye mean," she said and shivered.

"Ah." He kissed her ear. "Let me imagine with ye, lass."

"Roderic!" She stepped swiftly back. "I must tend your wound before ye become feverish."

He grinned. Never was she more alluring than now, disheveled and flustered and needy. "I am already feverish, lass," he countered, taking hold of her arm and stepping up against her. "Canna ye tell?" Between them his desire throbbed hot and insistent.

She swallowed and cautiously raised her gaze to his face. "I meant feverish with sickness."

"As did I." He chuckled low in his throat. "What else?" He hadn't thought her face could get any redder. It was not the first time he had been wrong about her. "I only meant it would be wise of ye to sleep at my side, lest the wound festers and I tek a fever."

"Oh." She swallowed, looking as if she would die of embarrassment. "That's what I thought ye meant . . . of course."

"Naked."

Her mouth fell open. He fought down his grin and raised a hand to fend off her incriminations.

"Ye wouldna wish for me ta catch a chill. Surely 'tis a small thing ta ask that ye share yer body's warmth. I might die."

She stared into his eyes for a moment longer, then yanked her arm from his grasp. "Ye might indeed if ye don't watch your tongue," she said, stepping around him to hurry up the hill.

Roderic chuckled softly as he watched her retreat. She had intentionally teased him with the thought of a bribe, but, it seemed, she was not so bold as to carry through. Instead, she hid behind hauteur again. But someday she would not. Someday she would come to him willing and eager, without guilt or uncertainty. But for now he had prodded her into continued travel. In a matter of moments, he reached her side at the crest of the hill.

Although he looked directly into her face, she ignored him, staring straight ahead.

"So ye couldna bear ta be parted from me, lass."

"Roderic," she murmured, lifting a stiff arm and pointing downhill. "Look."

Pulled regretfully from his examination of her face, Roderic swung his attention away.

"Gawd's wrath!" he swore. Two hundred warriors headed south at a rapid pace. Upon the banner at their head waved a wildcat atop a mountain. " 'Tis Leith!"

Flame turned to him, eyes wide, air escaping in a rush. "They ride to Dun Ard?"

"Gawd's wrath!" he swore again, then, "Leith!" he yelled, waving his arms. "Leith!"

The company was nearly out of sight.

Beside Roderic, Flanna, too, yelled, joining her voice with his. But their efforts were to no avail. In a moment the troupe was hidden behind a hill.

Their cries turned to silence.

"Ye said he would not come for ye," she rasped.

"He wouldna. Na if he received the message I sent him."

"Then why?"

"I dunna know. Unless someone took my missive and sent his own."

"What will he do?"

"Gawd knows!"

"Ye said he wouldn't come!" she said again, but her tone was panicked now.

"I am his brother!" Roderic rasped, turning abruptly toward her. "Ye think he willna avenge me death?"

"Death!" she gasped.

"Yer people have na proof of me well-being. And neither will the MacGowans know of yer welfare. We must follow them. Make haste!" he said, turning downhill.

"God have pity," she begged, but instead of following him, she whirled toward the stallion.

The journey seemed endless. Although Roderic sometimes rode behind her, he spent more time running beside, holding the stallion's mane for support as they stumbled through the night.

Desperation drove them. But finally even desperation could not force them onward. Roderic fell to his knees and failed to rise.

"Forbes," Flame breathed and slipped from their mount's back to stumble toward him. "Roderic." His arm felt hot beneath her hand, but whether it was from fever or exertion, she couldn't tell. He struggled to his feet and staggered onward. "Ye must stop."

"Nay." He shook his head. "There will be bloodshed."

"I will go. My kinsmen will see I am safe. They will not fight. I'll bring the Forbeses here to ye."

"There will be battle, Flanna. And I am sworn to protect ye."

His expression was desperate. "Why?" she breathed. "I am nothing to ye."

"Ye are wrong. Ye are everything I love. I willna let ye risk yer life."

She could think of nothing to say. In all her years she had never heard those words and now there seemed no way to respond, nothing to say in return, for she knew she loved him more than life itself.

"Ye must rest. Please, Roderic, I"—she faltered and licked her lips—"I have never loved before. I could not bear to lose ye now."

He stared into her eyes.

"Please," she said again. "Rest, just for a short while so we may travel the faster."

He finally nodded and sank on the ground. "Join me."

"Aye." She nodded. "As soon as I see to the horse."

"Come rest," he insisted.

"I will," she promised with a smile. In a moment she was at the steed's side. Touching his neck, she turned back. Roderic was already asleep. "Good-bye," she whispered, and grasping fistfuls of mane, she swung onto the stallion's back.

Night stretched into day and day into evening. Fatigue blurred Flame's vision and numbed her pain, but still she could hear Roderic's scream in her mind. She had been half a league away when she heard him shriek her name.

He was following, but she must not let him catch her, for she would not risk his life. There would be bloodshed, he had said. But she would not allow the blood to be his. Not now, when she had finally found love. Flame leaned lower over the steed's neck. She was killing the horse. She knew that, but she would sacrifice his life and hers for the man who pursued them. If only she could reach the troop of Forbeses before the clans clashed. If only . . .

She felt herself slipping and grabbed Heart's mane to pull herself upright. A hill rose before them. Flame slumped over the destrier's neck, struggling to remain lucid, to soothe her throbbing aches, to keep the animal moving, but suddenly he needed no more urging. His great head rose and a nicker escaped him.

Below them was an army.

The Forbeses! Dear God, she had reached them, she thought. But in that moment she saw the MacGowan standard. She heard a roar of rage as her warriors prepared to attack.

"No! Stop!" she screamed and pushed Heart down the final hill. She saw faces turn toward her, saw arms lift to point out her arrival, but she pressed the steed onward, thundering between the two armies. "I command ye to stop!" she yelled. "I am unhurt. Roderic is—"

She heard the flight of the arrow and felt its deadly bite. The realization of pain flashed through her system, but the reality did not strike home. She opened her mouth again, trying to speak, but suddenly she was slipping. The earth dipped toward her. The horizon tilted. Men screamed her name. "Roderic . . . needs help," she rasped, but in the final moment before darkness took her, she realized she had only whispered the words to the sky.

"Ye've kilt her!" someone shrieked. Through the din of terror, Roderic heard the words. He stumbled from the woods. No! He must not be too late.

"The Forbeses die!" a warrior yelled and charged. Steel clashed against steel, but most of the men remained immobile, staring at someone on the ground between the armies.

It was then that Roderic saw her. She was lying on her side with an arrow projecting from her body and the huge destrier beside her. ''Nooo!'' he shrieked. The earth seemed to move beneath him, throwing him forward. Someone lunged at him, but he dodged, grabbing the man's sword hand and knocking him aside before running on, and suddenly she was beneath his hands. ''Flanna!'' he gasped. She did not move, but there at the base of her throat, he felt the flutter of her pulse.

''Sweet Jesu! Leith! Colin!'' he screamed in anguish. An arrow hissed past his head. His hands formed to claws at his sides. ''She is felled!''

'' 'Tis the Rogue! Dunna let him take her!'' a MacGowan shrieked and rushed forward.

''Brothers!'' Roderic screamed and gathered her into his arms.

Suddenly Leith was there, charging forward on his great white steed, knocking his opponents aside, shielding Roderic and the lady he carried. She was limp in his arms.

Behind him, men shrieked and cursed, but Roderic felt as if he were in another world where nothing existed but Flanna's pale, placid face. He raised his gaze, and there was Colin only inches away. ''She canna die, brother,'' he whispered.

Understanding sparked between them. Colin nodded, pulling his destrier close. ''Take her to Fiona. I will pray for her wisdom and skill. Take me horse. Today, I fight afoot.''

Roderic remained still for an instant more. ''The MacGowans are her kinsman,'' he reminded him.

''Then we fight for peace,'' Colin vowed.

Chapter 25

*S*he would die. He had felled her with his own arrow, had watched the barb sink into her flesh. He had done what his hired brigands had failed to do. And soon, very soon, he would rule. Then they would rue the days he had been exiled from Dun Ard.

"We have promised to return her to her kinsmen hale and whole in a month," Laird Leith said. "If she dies there will be much bloodshed."

"We needna fear the MacGowans," Colin replied. The three brothers Forbes sat in the quiet of Glen Creag's high solar. "Only cowards would advance whilst we cried peace and tried to save their own lady."

"Mayhap they didna know we tried to save Flanna. Mayhap they didna even know it was she," Leith countered. " 'Twas naught but confusion."

Roderic remained still and silent. He had finally found his soul's mate, only to have her pierced by an errant arrow. They didn't know who had fired the missile that had plunged Flanna into a fever. But to his brothers he supposed guilt looked better on a MacGowan than on a Forbes. Himself, he had no time to think of blame and hatred. He only thought of her, the paleness of her face, the stillness of her body.

"They are spineless cowards," said Colin.

A muscle jumped in Leith's lean cheek. "As many of our own men were wounded as MacGowans." The Forbes emblem of wildcat and mountain was chiseled into the high back of the rowan-wood chair in which Leith sat. His black hair showed little gray and the leg he had sprawled across the chair's arm was heavy with muscle.

"They have na the strength nor the courage of the Forbeses!" argued Colin. "If they come for her, we will be ready."

"We will be ready," Leith agreed. "But both sides will suffer nonetheless. If she dies we must—"

"She willna die!" Roderic rose abruptly to his feet, strode once about the solar, then circled back to stand before them. The days had drained his strength and had stolen his hope. She was dying and he knew it, had known it ever since he had felt the limpness of her body. Every league he had traveled with her in his arms had been like an eternity in hell. He had placed her in Fiona's care, but still she remained in an ungodly sleep. The thought of losing her nearly robbed him of all sense. "Damn ye, brothers. Ye sit and discuss her life as if she were na but a pawn in a fine game of chess."

"Roderic," said Colin, rising, but his twin turned sharply away, showing them his back.

"She willna die!" Roderic repeated hoarsely. He had spent every moment with her, slept beside her bed, prayed to be taken in her stead, but while his own wounds healed, hers stole her life.

For a moment the room was silent with regret and unspoken worry.

"The fever rages unchecked." Leith's voice was as quiet as though he had reluctantly pulled the words from his soul. "Fiona has done all she can to bring her back. I fear ye must accept—"

"Nay! I have been bred to fight, and fight I will!" Roderic roared. Turning, he slammed his fist against a timber. "I willna accept otherwise," he said, and turning stiffly away, he strode from the room.

The infirmary was a small chamber at the top of the stairs. Roderic pushed the door open with shaking hands.

"Fiona?" he said, and paused in the doorway.

"She yet lives." Fiona's voice was soft as she looked up from her place beside the bed.

"Please." He managed a step into the room. "Please, Fiona, I have asked naught of ye in the past. Please, I—"

She rose abruptly from her place beside her patient. "Roderic! I cannot promise you her life. 'Tis not mine to give."

"Ye saved the miller's son." His voice cracked.

"Roderic." She lifted a hand, her tone pleading.

"Ye saved Harlow. Auld Torquil. And . . ."

"Roderic please!"

"Malcolm!" Roderic said abruptly. "Do ye na remember when he was choking?" He knew he was babbling, but panic threatened to drown him if he did not fight. "Ye saved him. And wee Somerled, no bigger than me bonnet."

"I cannot do more!" she said in anguish.

"Gawd's wrath, woman!" he stormed, striding suddenly forward to grip her arms and shake her. "Ye saved Dora. Even that damn, stinking cur." He tightened his fingers on her arms. "Ye will save me Flanna!"

"Roderic!" Leith snapped, rushing to the door, but his brother was far past hearing.

"Please," he begged. Falling to his knees, he let his hands slide down Fiona's arms to grip her fingers. "All me life I have waited for her, though I didna know I waited. Please dunna let her leave me now."

" 'Tis na me lady's fault," Leith said, stepping forward, but Fiona shook her head and dropped to her knees in front of Roderic.

"I have done all I can," she said, squeezing his hand. "We staunched the bleeding, fought the swelling and the festering. I hoped we had won the battle. But the fever burns her without mercy." Tears of agony shone in her eyes to match his own. "She is in God's hands," Fiona whispered.

"As were ye," Roderic said. Although his voice was raspy, his fingers were gentle against hers now. "Ye were struck. 'Twas me own fault," he whispered. "But the Lord let ye live. Gave ye children. Gave ye love."

Fiona raised her gaze to her husband.

"Please," Roderic murmured. "God Almighty surely sits on yer shoulder and lights yer way, Fiona Rose. There must be somemat we can do."

Fiona drew a careful breath. "Come." Slowly, she stood, pulling him to his feet. "We will beg for God's tender mercy . . ." She bit her lip and glanced fretfully at the sickbed. "And take her to the burn."

Roderic sat chest deep in the Creag River, holding Flanna's flaccid body against him and praying. This was her last chance, he knew, for though Fiona hadn't said the words, he realized the frigid, rushing waters could just as likely kill his love as cure her.

For an eternity Flanna's body flamed with fever. His own was numb from cold. But still he remained, eyes squeezed tight against his pain, lost in prayer, aching with hopelessness.

"Roderic," a creaky voice called. He opened his eyes slowly, terrified he had imagined the sound. "I'm c-cold," stuttered Flanna.

"Gawd!" he murmured, staring into her eyes, certain he was dreaming again.

Flanna scowled and shivered. "So . . . cold," she repeated.

"Gawd!" he yelled. "Fiona! Leith! She awakes!"

People splashed into the water.

"Hurry! 'Tis na time ta lose," urged Fiona, but Roderic's muscles refused to lift him from the river, so cramped was he.

"Here. Give her to me! To me!" Leith ordered. Roderic stared transfixed into her face. His fingers remained crooked against her side. "Sweet Jesu!"

"Colin! Pull his arms free."

Agony ripped through Roderic's frigid muscles as Flanna was wrenched from his arms. He raised his face to watch her turn toward him as Leith carried her away.

Fiona hurried along beside her, wrapping her in blankets and calling orders.

"To the infirmary. Clarinda," she called to a servant, "More blankets. Bring hot water and broth. Colin, get Roderic out of the burn. Take him up to his room and out of those clothes."

"She's awake," Roderic murmured, ignoring the burning cold. "And she will heal."

"Brother," Colin said gently.

"She will heal," he repeated, lifting his gaze to his twin's.

Colin nodded. "Let us go."

"She's awake."

"Up now," Colin said and pulled on his arm.

Roderic grimaced but remained as he was. Reality slipped a notch. "She will heal. Ye will see." The cold ordered him to sleep. "Ye will see. She will heal."

"Roderic."

"She will mend."

"Roderic!" yelled Colin. "Do ye want another man ta have her?"

Roderic painfully turned his head to stare into his twin's azure eyes. "Na," he said reasonably.

"Then get yer ass out of the water before ye catch yer death, ye dolt!"

"Flanna," Roderic rasped. He stood in the doorway of the infirmary, his chest heaving. He had battled his way there, for every man he had once called friend had tried to stand in his way. Water dripped from his clothing, and his fingers would not obey his commands, though they had managed to form fists. Vaguely, he remembered hitting someone and yelling Flanna's name. "Ye live," he breathed.

"Aye." She was wrapped in a multitude of blankets. Her skin was as pale as death, and her eyes looked huge and haunted in her gaunt face. "And ye." Her voice was weak. The arm she lifted toward him was bare and thin, seeming almost translucent.

He stumbled into the room, wanting nothing more than to hold her, to pull her into his arms. But his muscles were unpredictable and Fiona barred his way.

"Ye are freezing," she said, arms akimbo and a scowl on her lovely face. Shifting her gaze from him to his brothers, who stood behind him, she asked, "Did I na tell ye to get him warmed afore he, too, sickens?"

"Aye, ye did. But he took exception ta being separated from her," Leith said, fingering his jaw. "Damn, hotheaded whelp."

"Ye came back ta me," murmured Roderic, managing another step forward.

"Ye are na . . ." Words came hard to Flanna's pale lips. "Ye are na dying?"

"Me?" Roderic almost laughed, but the sound was no louder than the scrape of a rusty knife against old leather. "Nay, lass. 'Tis ye who has been ill."

"Oh." Her eyes fell closed. "Thank the Almighty. I thought . . . I dreamt . . . ." She shuddered. "Dreamt that ye were gone." Her voice fell into a creaky whisper. "Taken from me. Just when I knew . . ."

Roderic came chest to chest with Fiona's small but impenetrable form. Instead of trying to get by her, he dropped to his knees to gaze around his sister-in-law.

"Knew what, lass?" he whispered.

Flanna's emerald eyes opened. Her frail fingers lifted to graze his cheek. "Just when I knew the truth."

The sound that escaped him was neither a laugh nor an exclamation of joy. It more closely resembled a moan of agony. "I am here." He lifted his hand toward her.

"Touch her with those freezing fingers and I'll toss ye from here meself," Fiona warned.

"She has returned to me," Roderic whispered. " 'Twould tek a strong army of men with horses ta get rid of me."

"Dunna challenge her," Leith advised. "Na when she's in a temper."

Roderic watched Flanna's eyes drift closed, watched as peaceful sleep descended on her. "I willna chal-

lenge,'' he murmured ''I but plead. Let me stay and I'll
make na trouble.''

Fiona scowled, then turned and touched a hand to
Flanna's brow. ''Ye *are* trouble,'' she said and smiled.
''But the fever is broken. You may stay.''

''How are ye faring?'' Fiona asked, stepping into the
infirmary.

Clarinda, the young maidservant who had spent the
days beside Flame's bed, had been sent away. Flame
raised her eyes from Roderic's face to the woman who
had saved her life. ''I am healed, my lady,'' she said.
''Thanks to your ministrations.''

She had slept throughout most of the days and nights.
But each time she awoke, Roderic had been there. For
a while, it had surprised her, but finally she had come
to expect to see him, hear his voice, feel the touch of
his hand. This morning he had been absent. Panic had
seized her in a choking hold, and in that moment she
had realized how needy she had become. Fear filled her,
for she knew she had done the unthinkable. She had
fallen under the allure of a man she was not worthy to
love.

Roderic rose to his feet, still holding the horn of medicine he had pressed to her lips only moments before.
''She is na healed, Fiona. Gawd's wrath, she has only
been awake these past six days. She is but being stubborn and doesna wish to drink yer brew.''

''Nay.'' Blood rushed to Flame's face. Before her
stood a lady. A *true* lady, like none she had ever met,
like none she could ever hope to be. Flame had no wish
to wound her feelings or act ungrateful for all she had
done. But Roderic's nearness and her own needs terrified
her. She could not risk the touch of his hand, lest she
lose the Flame forever and become the trembling girl
she knew herself to be. '' 'Tis not that. I simply am
healed. Completely.''

Roderic scowled down at her. ''Heaven's gate,
woman, ye are na afraid ta challenge the wrath of the

MacGowans and the Forbeses combined, yet ye quiver at the thought of drinking a wee bit of bitter medicine.''

" 'Tis not true," Flame argued, her face still burning. "I am not ungrateful for all Lady Fiona has done."

"I didna call ye ungrateful," Roderic said. "I called ye a coward." Pressing the horn toward her, he deepened his scowl. "Now drink."

Nervousness fled before his majestic command. "Is that an order, Forbes?" she asked, raising her brows at him.

"Aye." He spread his legs slightly and flexed the muscles in his back. " 'Tis."

Flame took a deep breath and opened her mouth to argue, but Fiona's laughter interrupted the impending barrage.

"I do believe ye *are* feeling better," she said. "And therefore you can forgo the herb."

Flame breathed a sigh of relief. "Thank ye, Lady Forbes."

"Call me Fiona. Or Rose if ye like," said the lady of the hall. She was, Flame thought, the most beautiful woman God had ever created. She was small and refined and possessed of a quiet dignity Flame could never hope to achieve. "But please do not call me Lady Forbes. It makes me feel five hundred years old with a prune-pinched mouth and drooping jowls."

"Nay," Flame breathed, "hardly that."

Fiona laughed again. The sound was as lovely and light as a touch of spring in the winter. Any man would love her, Flame thought. Roderic included, and he deserved someone like her. Someone who was all woman, who had been taught love at a young age and did not fight the demons she battled. She was not like the lady of the Forbes, small and quiet and tender. Only their looks were somewhat similar. But mayhap that was enough to attract Roderic's attention. Maybe he only believed he loved her.

"Ye are as bonny as the day I first spied ye in the

hall,'' Roderic said to his sister-by-law. ''And ye well know it, Fiona.''

She laughed again. ''I hope ye've had warning against his glib tongue. 'Tis said that Roderic the Rogue can charm the berries from the vines.''

''And Fiona Rose can touch the snow and make it bloom.''

They laughed in unison. Something in Flame's gut twisted in agony. She had to leave, before it was too late. Before she begged for his love, promised anything just to stay at his side.

''Believe only half of what he tells ye, Flanna, and ye will do well,'' Fiona said. She took a step nearer and settled her gaze on Flame's face. ''Your presence here is a boundless blessing to us, Flanna. I rejoice at your newfound health.''

Flame lowered her eyes. She was the quaking, hard-shelled daughter of a man who had despised her very existence. And she must not forget it. ''About my health, lady. When might I be allowed to return home?''

''Home?'' Fiona sounded shocked. ''But I thought you and Roderic . . .'' She lifted a scowl fretfully to her brother-in-law, then quickly lowered her gaze to Flame again. ''I . . .''

Flame's mind whirled. What about her and Roderic? Tearing her gaze from Fiona, she looked at him, but his expression was implacable and cool.

''That is to say,'' Fiona continued more smoothly now. ''We cannot even consider moving ye yet.''

''But, my lady,'' Flame began. Even to her own ears, her voice sounded pleading, for she could not remain much longer at Glen Creag. ''I must go back to my people.''

For a moment, Flame feared the lady would ask why. But she didn't. Instead, she settled her hands into the full sleeves of her opposite arms.

''I fear it is far too early for such talk,'' Fiona said firmly. ''God has graciously allowed ye to return to us.

I would be remiss in my duties if I let ye endanger your life now.''

Beside her, Roderic shifted his weight. Flame could feel the allure of his presence and knew she had to leave before she lost herself completely to it. ''But I cannot stay abed any longer,'' she said, grasping at straws. ''I've been here nearly a full week.''

''Ahhh.'' Fiona breathed a sigh as if relieved by Flame's explanation. ''So ye are bored is all. Roderic, I am surprised at you.''

''Me apologies,'' he said, but his tone was tight. Flame could feel his emotions, though she could not quite identify them. Anger? Resentment? ''I will try harder to entertain her.''

Fiona laughed but the sound was not so silvery light as before. ''Make sure ye do, brother. Or I will find a young man who can.''

''The cat's name is Silken,'' Roman said quietly.

True to her word, Fiona had sent a young man to entertain Flame. He was a handsome lad with a dark red mop of unruly hair that defied mastery and set off the rich color of his green eyes. He couldn't have seen more than thirteen summers, and yet his manner spoke of wisdom learned through pain. Still, despite Roman's charm, Flame could think of nothing but Roderic. Where was he? Did he hate her now, after her plea to return home?

Flame pulled her thoughts back to the lad and gazed at the wildcat that lay on the stone sill of the window. He was, without a doubt, the largest feline Flame had ever seen. ''Silken?'' she asked softly.

''Aye.''

''Does he belong to ye, Roman?''

''Nay. He belongs ta no one. But I think, mayhap, Lady Fiona belongs to him.''

The lad reminded her of Haydan, not in looks or build, certainly, for Roman outweighed the other boy by at least two stone. But they both had a quiet intelligence that touched her soul.

"I have never known a wildcat to be tamed," Flame said.

"He isna tamed," whispered Clarinda. She was a young maid of less than five-and-ten years and eyed the feline with awe and uncertainty. "He is as wild as the night."

" 'Tis true," Roman agreed. "He is na tamed, but he is my lady's protector."

"Nay."

"Aye." He nodded solemnly. "He will let none come near her unless he knows them well."

Again, Flame's stomach churned. Even the wild beasts loved Glen Creag's lady.

"She must be well protected indeed, then," said Flame. She tried to keep her tone light.

"Aye, she is that, for there is na a man amongst the Forbeses that wouldna give his life for her."

She could not stop the question. "Does that include Roderic?"

For the first time Roman laughed. "Laird Leith says that if a man be a true man he will love Lady Fiona. And amongst the Forbeses, we say that Roderic is more a man than most."

"Aye," said Roderic from the doorway. "I am indeed a specimen ta behold." Flame nearly closed her eyes against the power of his presence. When had she become so hopelessly enamored?

"Have ye been regaling Flanna with tales of me manliness?" Roderic asked, taking a seat on a nearby bench.

Roman turned solemnly toward the other. " 'Tis what ye told me ta do, is it na?"

"Ye rascal!" Roderic said, reaching to cuff the back of the boy's head.

But apparently Roman had lived a good deal of time among the Forbes brothers, for he saw Roderic's intent and had already slid from his stool and scampered away with a laugh. "As Fiona says," quoted Roman blithely, "ye shouldna think so highly of yerself."

"If I dunna, who will?" asked Roderic, still chuckling. "Now get yerself gone afore I tell yer wee sister that ye wish to play with her dolls."

Grimacing, Roman rose to his full height, then bowed from the waist. " 'Twas a pleasure meeting ye, Lady MacGowan."

She nodded at his courtly manner. "And ye, Master Roman. Thank ye for coming."

Mischief twinkled in his eyes. " 'Twas a pleasure ta tek Roderic's place fer a wee bit of time."

"Get gone," Roderic said, and Roman headed for the door.

At the window, Silken rose and disappeared from sight.

The room seemed suddenly very quiet.

Roderic cleared his throat. "He is a bright lad but can be a bit loquacious at times. I hope he didna tire ye."

"Nay." She could feel his gaze on her face and kept her attention riveted on her hands atop her blankets.

"Fiona said ye are mending well."

She could think of nothing to say.

He cleared his throat again. His gaze was warm. She knew how he would look. His eyes, blue as Highland Harebell, would be sharp and deeply set beneath his fair brows. His mouth would be cast in a straight line, and his hair, bright as sunlight, would be plaited in two narrow braids beside his ears. "She thinks ye will have full use of yer—"

"I wish to leave!" Flame said the words quickly, for she knew if she delayed, all would be lost. Lost in his eyes, in memories, in her own hopeless desires.

Absolute silence greeted her. Seconds ticked past. Flame studied the Forbes plaid that covered her lap.

"Look at me, Flanna."

"Do not call me Flanna!" she all but yelled, jerking her gaze to his. Breath left her lungs with a rush, for he was just as she had imagined, only larger and more powerful and more tempting to her woman's soul. "I am Flame," she said weakly. "And I must return to my people."

For a moment a sharp edge of unidentifiable emotion showed in his eyes, but he dulled it and said, "I willna let ye go."

She laughed aloud. "Ye think ye can hold me?"

His face was unusually solemn. "I know I can, lass."

Breathing was difficult, but it had nothing to do with the arrow that had pierced her lung. "Why?" she whispered. "It would only cause war."

His lips parted slightly. Their gazes met. He drew a deep breath and carefully let it escape. "Me brothers think an alliance would be advantageous."

"An alliance?" The words slipped from her lips.

"A marriage," he said evenly. "Between the MacGowans and the Forbeses."

Yearning as strong as the tide rose up within her, but she couldn't afford to let him sense it. Her laugh was short and unnatural. "I have na kinsmen I can spare for such a marriage."

"Gawd's wrath, Flanna!" he said, jerking to his feet. "I meant us."

Though she had known what he had meant, his words made her gasp. But she drew a careful breath now and released it slowly. "And I have told ye afore, I will not wed."

He was breathing deeply. "I know ye care for me, lass."

She lifted her chin slightly. "As young Roman says, ye should not think so highly of yourself."

With long, steady strides, he walked to her bedside. "I have felt yer fire," he said softly. "And 'tis na the flame of the MacGowans. 'Tis me own flame, kindled in me hand and set ablaze in yer body."

Her lungs hurt and her stomach roiled. "'Tis but physical lust," she said. "And easily forgotten."

"'Tis more," he countered.

"Ye imagine," she murmured, but she became caught in his gaze.

"Aye, lass. And ye imagine, too." Dropping to his knees, he leaned forward so that she could smell the scent of him, could see each fine line engraved in his face, each long, sparkling lash that highlighted his heavenly eyes. "Ye imagine what it could be like between us."

"Nay," she denied, trying to turn away from him but failing.

"Aye, ye do," he whispered, and suddenly his fingers were on her cheek. The touch was feather soft and trailed gently toward her ear.

She trembled under his hand and closed her eyes, trying to force him from her mind. But he was tracing the curve of her ear with one fingertip. Her breathing sounded gravelly.

"Ye were na meant ta be alone, lass." He pressed a kiss to her lobe. She tried to pull away, but his words mesmerized her, his touch trapped her. "Ye were meant ta be loved."

"Loved!" She forced the word out on a harsh whisper. "Men speak well of love, but they know not the meaning."

"Ye are wrong," he said, drawing back and finally rising slowly to his feet. "Ye are wrong, lass, and I will prove it."

Chapter 26

Astrangely familiar noise awakened Flame. She moaned and pulled herself from one of a thousand dreams, each filled with images of a fair-haired warrior with a jester's smile and a minstrel's voice.

"Great Heart missed ye."

The voice became reality. She opened her eyes and gasped softly, for a large, whiskered muzzle hovered above her face. The horse nickered low and nuzzled her neck.

"Heart?" she said in bewilderment, trying to place her setting.

"Aye. It seems he couldna bear ta be separated from ye and followed us here," Roderic said.

Flame tried to push herself to a sitting position, but the movement made her entire body throb. She winced.

Roderic was suddenly on the far side of the bed from the horse, easing her upright. "Lean on me."

Their eyes met, and for a moment she was tempted nearly beyond restraint. Tempted to do as he asked and more. Warm breath against her arm drew her back to reality.

She turned toward the steed that towered above her. "But . . ." Reality was strangely mixed with foolishness. It almost seemed she was still in the infirmary but . . . there was this horse . . . She placed a hand gently on the destrier's broad brow, blinked in confusion, and turned back toward Roderic.

" 'Twas the verra devil getting him up the stairs," he said, his face a serious mask.

Her mouth fell open. "Up the . . ."

"I fear he has been overeating, for I could barely squeeze him round the turns."

"Ye brought him up the stairs?"

"He was worried," Roderic said. His smile was like a ray of sunlight in the darkest night. "And I thought ye might enjoy his company."

Heart lifted his upper lip, kissing her neck. Flame couldn't help the giggle that escaped her. She stroked his head and fondled his long ears. "Ye truly brought him up the stairs?"

Roderic scowled as if confused by her words. "Of course, lass. The window was too high."

She tried to turn toward him, but the stallion was now breathing down her borrowed nightgown. "Why did ye bring him?" she murmured.

"I told ye." His voice was suddenly very soft and had lost the edge of humor. "He missed ye, Flanna, and I, better than any, understand the agony of losing ye forever."

Butterflies filled her innards. A thousand pretty words filled her head. She tried to remind herself to be stern and cool, but he was so near, so strong, so alluring. And if he thought her lovable, maybe she was. He seemed a good judge of people, and she desperately wanted to believe.

"And to prove—"

"Well, Flanna, how are ye . . ." Fiona began from the doorway, but suddenly her words stopped and a small gasp of surprise escaped her. "Roderic," she said evenly, "why is there a horse in my infirmary?"

"He was lonely."

"Ahh. And why is Clarinda lying on the floor?"

"She fainted."

"I see. Mightn't you prop her up somewhere more comfortable?"

"I fear there is na room in here, me lady."

"Aha. Leith," Fiona called, "could ye lend a wee bit of assistance?"

"Flanna! Is she . . ." Leith's voice was accented by his quick, sure footfalls.

"She is fine," Fiona assured. " 'Tis Clarinda who concerns me."

"Clarinda!" The footsteps halted. The door creaked open a bit further. "Fiona?"

"Yes, my laird?"

"Why is there a horse in yer infirmary?"

"He was lonely," said Roderic and Fiona in unison.

"Ah. And Clarinda?"

"She fainted."

"Of course," said Leith. "And ye want her out of the way?"

"If ye are not too busy. It seems a bit crowded in here."

Not another question was asked. Leith carried the poor maid away with Fiona trailing him, and the door closed behind them.

Flame blinked. "I believe I begin to understand," she said weakly.

Roderic smiled that smile that surely made lasses from Inverness to Paris swoon. "Aye," he said softly, "we are all touched. And ye, me sweet lass, would fit in admirably."

"But—"

The door swung open again and a tiny voice squealed. "Looky! There's a horse eating barley in Mama's infirmary." Apparently, Roderic had brought a bucket of grain to coax Heart up the stairs. Tiny feet pattered rapidly across the floor. "Can I ride him, Roddy? Please?

"Ohhh!" The pattering feet stopped, then resumed at a more sedate pace. "Ye're beautiful."

A wee elf of a lass appeared beside the bed, hugged Roderic's hand to her chest, and peeked up into Flame's face. The child had eyes as bright as amethyst stones and so like Fiona's there could be no doubting her heritage. And though she looked like a miniature of her mother, her father, too, was represented in her angelic features, for her hair was as dark and slick as fine sable. She blinked her wide eyes in childish wonder.

"This is Lady Flanna MacGowan, Peepsweep."

The tiny lass tightened her grip on her uncle's hand. "Good day t'ye, me lady," she said.

"Good day, mistress . . ."

"Me name is na really Peepsweep," the child began solemnly. "Roddy just calls me that because I am so small. But Papa says, 'tis na the size of the bird but the swiftness of its wing stroke that matters." The wee girl pursed her lips for a moment and blinked. "Me Christian name is Rachel. And ye are just as bonny as Mama said." The skin above her upper lip was stained red, as if she had been eating strawberries. A smile tilted the corner of her mouth. "She is a bonny one, isn't she, Roddy?" The lass lisped slightly when she spoke and turned her attention back to Flame. "Mama said ye're as bonny as a pimpernel on the hillock. Papa laughed and said he hopes ye'll stay forever, then mayhap the men will na always be staring at Mama. Will ye stay with us forever, lady?"

Flame tried to speak but no words would come.

"Will she stay forever, Roddy? Will ye make babies with her so that I may have a sister?"

Roderic smiled into the dimpled, upturned face. "Ye must na talk off Lady Flanna's ear. She has been verra ill."

"I know 'tis true," Rachel stated solemnly, turning her wide eyes back to Flame. "I am verra bright. Roddy says I am. 'Tisn't it true, Roddy?"

"Aye, lass, ye are." Love as sure as yesterday shone in his face. Something tripped painfully in Flame's chest. Dear God, what a lass could do when sheltered by such love.

"And ye must be verra bright, too," Rachel deduced, scowling slightly. "Because Mama said ye've captured Roddy's heart. And I think ye'd have ta be awfully clever ta figure how ta tek a heart without even leaving a scar. Mayhap even cleverer than Mama, though Papa says there is nobody in the world smarter than she, cuz she brought ye back from the brink of death. But Mama said it was Gawd's will, is all.'' She screwed up her face slightly, looking puzzled and rambling on. ''There isn't a scar on yer chest, is there, Roddy?''

Roderic cleared his throat.

''And ye will make me a wee sister, won't ye? Papa said he'll try his best, but he's ever so slow and all they've given me thus far is Graham. And he's all wrinkled and messy. I do so want a sister. Mightn't ye—''

Roderic raised his free hand and tilted his head. ''I think I hear yer mother calling, Peepsweep.''

Not for an instant did the ploy fool her. ''Nay. She thinks I be napping with Sarah.''

''And why aren't ye?''

The tiny elf bit her lip. ''Because I wanted ta see yer lady,'' she whispered. ''They've kept me out for ever so long cuz she was ill, ye know. And''—she scowled fretfully—''I missed ye, Roddy. Seemed forever ye were away. And I worried.''

Tugging his hand from her tight grasp, Roderic pulled the child onto his lap. '' 'Tis sorry I am ta worry ye, wee Peep,'' he said, snuggling her against his chest.

''Where were ye? Ye didna even say good-bye.''

''Be it the truth ye want, lass?'' he asked, his voice suddenly quiet as if he alone knew some great secret.

Rachel solemnly nodded, her eyes wide.

''It happened during a wilding sort of night as only the land of the Forbeses knows. Bothering no one I was. Sleeping soundly in me own bed when suddenly''—he jumped, causing his tiny listener to jump with him—''the door was flung open and Flanna MacGowan rode in.''

''Lady MacGowan?'' Rachel lisped. ''She rode a horse right into yer room?''

''Aye, for she is the greatest equestrienne in all the world.''

''Truly? Was this the horse that carried her?'' asked

Rachel, staring at the destrier. Heart raised his head momentarily from the bucket. Barley dribbled from his mouth.

"Nay, 'twas another horse. A blue horse."

"Blue?"

"His name is Lochan and I believe"—he leaned closer to the child's ear—"he comes from the deep, dark waters of Inverness."

"Where Nessie lives?" she whispered in awe.

"Aye. That is me own belief."

"And Lady Flanna rides him?"

"That she does. But when she came to Glen Creag she didna appear as she does now, for she was dressed in outlandish garb. Her legs were bound in leather and she wore a man's shirt. I awoke with a start and rubbed me eyes. Surely, I thought I was dreaming."

"But ye weren't?"

"Nay," he said solemnly. "There she sat upon her blue steed, real as rock."

"And what did she say?"

"Well, 'twas a sad tale she told. She said that the men of the MacGowan clan had weakened so that she herself, great lady of the tribe, had to don men's clothing and teach them how ta be men. But she wearied of the task and thought, if only there were a man so brave and fair that he might be a symbol to me men and teach them that which is forgot." He nodded again. In his sky blue eyes humor sparkled unchecked. "And then it was that she heard tales of a warrior so great and courageous that her heart was filled with hope. At first she did not believe such a man could exist. But in the end she was convinced. Far she traveled through the night in search of this one great man of men."

He straightened with a sigh and a shrug. "And so she came in the wee hours to fetch me."

Rachel's small mouth had formed a tiny pink circle of awe. "The great man of men, was ye?"

"Aye," he said, nodding solemnly. "None other."

From the opposite side of the bed, Heart snorted,

spraying barley onto the floor and shaking his head. Rachel exhaled softly and blinked. "Roddy?"

"Aye, lass?"

"Mama says yer tales be as wild as a Highland wind," she said brusquely. Hopping from his lap, the lass raised her hands to cradle Roderic's lean face between them. "But I love ye the more for them."

For the slimmest moment, Flame was certain she saw moisture sparkle in the great man of men's eyes.

"And I love ye, sweet Peep."

Her tiny, dimpled hands dropped away. "Someday will ye tell me the tale again?"

"Aye, lass, if ye nap now."

She turned and nodded like a tiny princess. " 'Twas the best of pleasures meeting ye, Lady MacGowan. And if ye wish, ye can listen ta the next telling of the tale. Uncle Colin says Roddy's stories age like rotting cheese, but I like them better each time."

Her narrow back was as straight as a sapling's when she turned away, and her tiny feet, Flame noticed, were bare beneath the long, embroidered hem of her gown. With a grin and an abbreviated wave, she dragged the door closed behind her.

The room was quiet again but for Heart's munching. Roderic cleared his throat. "She is spoiled beyond hope, of course," he said brusquely, but when he turned back to Flame, his eyes were still misty. "Were I her sire, I would take her firmly in hand."

Flame dropped her gaze to the blanket beneath her restless fingers but didn't resist the smile tugging at her lips. "Aye. I am certain ye would. Great man of men that ye be."

He laughed softly. "Surely yer own uncle stretched a tale a wee bit now and again."

"Lawrence, Nevin's sire, used to come to Dun Ard with his wonderful silks and ribbons. He would sometimes bring gifts for Mother and me, for he had no daughters of his own, and his wife had been long dead." Once he had brought her a small silver mirror. The handle had been engraved in the shape of a rose. She had been entranced by its beauty, and as shattered as its round, shiny face when her father had smashed it against the wall. "But that was before the MacGowan decided that only whores took gifts from men other than their husbands." She tugged at a loose thread in the earth-toned plaid of the Forbes' tartan that covered her legs. "I never saw Lawrence after that."

"I am truly sorry, lass."

"He was killed by a thief who broke into his home and set fire to the place."

"And Nevin."

"He was asleep, and barely escaped with his life. He had nothing but the clothes on his back when he came to Dun Ard. So ye see, I am far luckier than some."

"Lass, I—"

She lifted her eyes to his, and for a moment she forgot to hide her feelings. "Rachel is blessed beyond measure."

Their gazes met and melded. Roderic's face was solemn. In her mind's eye, Flame saw a lad with golden hair and laughing blue eyes.

A thousand thoughts flowed between them but none were spoken.

Heart nudged Flame's arm, snapping her from her reverie.

She drew a deep breath. Roderic cleared his throat and seemed to find their former topic with difficulty.

"Her father dotes on her shamelessly."

"She is blessed," Flame said again, but the words were only a whisper.

For a moment she thought Roderic would say more, instead he stood and took the horse away.

Chapter 27

Flame awoke with a start. The room was dark as pitch. Beside her bed, Clarinda snored on her cot.

What had she heard? She lay perfectly still, listening, and then heard the quiet creak of door hinges again. Who was there? No one had to tell her she was in enemy territory and that she was without weapons. What had they done with the dirk she always wore at her side?

"Flanna," Roderic whispered.

"Forbes!" she gasped, twisting about and finding his face in the darkness.

"Gawd's wrath, lass, ye look as if ye've seen a ghost. Did I scare ye?"

"No," she managed on a sharp exhalation.

He chuckled. "Aye. I did."

"No. Ye—"

"Shh," he said, placing a finger to his lips. "Dunna wake Clarinda. Ye've given her enough trouble, what with the horse and all."

"I did not—"

"Shh," he said again and chuckled. " 'Tis a bonny night."

She scowled through the darkness at him. Weren't wounded people supposed to be allowed to sleep? "Ye came to tell me about the weather?"

"Nay, I didna," he said, and bending over the bed, flipped the blankets aside.

"What are ye doing?"

"Showing ye a bonny night," he whispered and lifted her into his arms.

"But . . ."

"Shh," he said and tiptoed to the door as if she were no more trouble than a just-birthed kitten.

His feet were silent against the stone stairs.

"Roderic . . ."

He hushed her again. "If Fiona finds ye missing, she'll have me hide."

Flame opened her mouth to object, but they were just entering the great hall and he scowled her to silence lest she wake those who slept in the rushes. From the pile of curs near the wall, a hound rose and trotted toward them, her paws rustling through the scattered heather and herbs.

"Bonny missed ye," he whispered.

The huge hall door creaked open. He stepped through, managing not to hit either her head or her feet in the process.

"Aye," Flame said as the hound danced beside them, rapturously trying to lick the hand of the man she adored. "Bonny missed me, just like Lady Fiona would have yer hide if she found me missing."

Roderic raised his brows at her. The magical light of the full moon showed the surprise on his face. "Ye dunna believe me?"

Flame scowled. Fiona adored him as all women surely did. And she was a lady to her very soul. She would never raise a hand to him or any man. "Nay," she said, "I do not. The Lady Fiona would hurt no one. Least of all ye."

He stared at her for an instant, then laughed and continued on, saying nothing.

"Why do ye laugh?"

He chuckled softly. His hair was brushed back, showing the width of his broad throat. " 'Tis a marvel how ye can at times seem so wise only ta seem so foolish a moment later."

"I am not foolish."

He chuckled again and eased her a bit closer to his heart. "Ask ta see Leith's scars sometime," he said, then frowned. "On second thought, dunna."

"Scars? Where? Why?"

"Dunna sound so intrigued," he said, frowning into her upturned face. " 'Twas a poor idea."

"What are ye talking about?"

"Me brother has been heard to say he would rather startle a wild boar than raise his lady's ire."

Flame stared into his face. "Not sweet Fiona," she scoffed. "Ye jest."

"Sweet Fiona." He chuckled again. "Aye, lass, if ye say so. Bonny night isn't it, Gregory?"

"Aye, Roddy, 'tis indeed. Out for a stroll?"

Embarrassment scalded her so that Flame refused to look at the man to whom Roderic spoke. Surely she had sunk to the depths of humiliation to be carried about by this jesting warrior who thought himself the man of men. But his arms were strong and he smelled of fine leather. His nearness made her head light and her heart hammer.

They ascended a tower and hurried up a score of narrow stairs. He squeezed her closer to his chest and grinned. "I love tight spaces."

"Where are ye taking me?" she asked, refusing to honor his foolishness.

" 'Tis a surprise."

"I hate surprises."

"Ye'll like mine."

"How do ye know?" she asked, needing to keep him talking to quiet her jangling nerves. She had always loved the scent of leather, but he added a new quality to it. An allure. A masculinity. And he was very close, with her hale arm draped about his neck. Never in her life had she thought a man could be called beautiful yet manly.

The stairs ended. Roderic's footfalls sounded across a flat stone expanse and then halted.

"Look." His voice was little more than a whisper in her ear. They stood atop the battlements. Below them stretched a scene she had witnessed only once before—the magical Burn Glen, wreathed in mist and mystery. But now she was not racing toward the castle with hatred in her soul and vengeance within her grasp. Now she was clasped in the arms of a man who was supposed to be her enemy. A man who owned her heart.

A stallion trumpeted, drawing Flame's gaze across the burn. On a dark hillock a white horse reared, tossing his head and calling a challenge to an unseen rival. Another horse answered and suddenly, he was there. The two beasts rose on hind legs, sparring playfully. The mists swirled, sweeping up the hillside and making the scene surreal and unearthly.

"Beautiful," she breathed.

"Beyond words," he agreed.

Their gazes met and held. Their thoughts entwined. The image of the golden-haired boy returned to Flame's mind.

Roderic drew a deep breath. Against her heart Flame could feel his chest expand.

"I . . ." She should run away now. Before it was too late. "I lied about not wanting children," she whispered.

"Fear makes us hide, lass. But 'tis hard to hide from the truth. Yer daughter will have yer eyes."

"What?"

"I see her in me mind. She is as bonny as springtime."

It almost seemed as if Flame were floating in a dream where people laughed and loved, where peace reigned and she was called Mama by a golden boy with a winsome smile.

" 'Tis a lad," she said. "Just like ye."

"Gawd help us," Roderic whispered.

"Who goes . . ." someone called, then, "Ho, Roderic. I didn't hear ye come up."

The spell was broken.

Flame pulled her gaze from Roderic's. He turned slowly away.

"There be a reason for that, Cleat."

"Oh." Apparently, Cleat was not overly bright, but Roderic's gruff tone managed to alert him to the situation. "I'll be leaving the two of ye alone then."

Flame felt Roderic's gaze return to her face but refused to lift her eyes.

"Dunna draw away, lass," he said softly.

But the choices were so clear. She must draw away or lose her heart. "Let me go home."

She felt the muscles of his arms and chest tense where they touched her.

"Please," she murmured.

He said nothing, only turned and carried her back to her room.

"Ye canna keep her in here forever," Roderic said, leveling his best glare on Fiona.

She stood in the doorway of the infirmary with fists planted on her narrow hips and the light of battle in her eyes. "In case you havena noticed, the Lord has worked a miracle here, Roderic Forbes. And He has put me in charge of making certain you don't botch it up."

Intimidation worked about as well on Fiona as it did on Flanna. Roderic tried a smile instead. "When have I ever botched things up, lass?"

Her snort was, by any standards, unladylike. "I dunna have all morning as you well know."

" 'Twas me verra point," Roderic said. "I felt ye were too busy. Ye dunna have time ta help herd the beasts."

"What the devil be ye speaking of?"

"Flanna is particularly fond of livestock."

Fiona's left brow lifted over her entrancing eyes.

Roderic cleared his throat. "Isn't it true, Lady MacGowan," he asked, turning to the lady under discussion, who lay in the bed across the room. But the lady was, apparently, far too wise, or perhaps too amused to join in this particular fray.

"Are ye threatening to squeeze that lop-eared horse into my infirmary again?" Fiona asked.

"Nay," denied Roderic, trying to appear offended. "But William MacMurt's sow just birthed piglets. And of course they be too young to leave their mother. So mayhap I could simply carry the wee ones whilst ye and Roman shoo the sow up the stairs to—"

Fiona's laughter interrupted his gesticulations and commentary. "How is it that your brothers have put up with your foolishness all these years?"

Roderic shrugged and grinned. 'Twas a heady feeling being near the two women most dear to his heart. " 'Tis a wonder, me lady."

" 'Tis indeed." She laughed, then said, "Go on then. Take her down to the bailey, but no further. And I warn ye," she added, shaking a finger at him, "if she becomes chilled or fatigued, 'twill be on your head."

"Aye, me lady," agreed Roderic, employing his most boyish charm. Tucking a pair of blankets firmly to Flanna's sides, he scooped her into his arms.

Their gazes met and for a moment he thought she held her breath.

"Did I hurt ye?" he murmured.

Rosy color dappled her fair cheeks. "Nay."

"Ye are bonny indeed this morning, Lady Flanna."

Flanna blushed a bit brighter and hurried her gaze to the doorway, but Fiona was already gone. "And ye are a flirt."

Roderic laughed. "Aye," he agreed. Her hair was loose and had been brushed to a fiery glow. It flowed against his arm like a river of flame and crackled between their bodies. "Be ye ready to meet the day?"

"Nay." She blinked and found his gaze again. "I am not even dressed."

He eyed her demure night rail with a scowl. "If only 'twere true."

Flame laughed again. Roderic had long since taken her from the bailey. They sat on the sun-dappled slope of a verdant hillock. Magpies called from the woods

behind them and wild irises raised their delicate heads
to smile at the sunlight. ·

" 'Tis true," Roderic promised. Stretching his powerful legs out before him, he settled back upon his elbows. "Ta this day auld Alpin still thinks that gray mare
can talk."

His sapphire eyes looked into hers. Flame caught her
breath and pulled her attention from his face with an
effort. But it did no good, for she could still feel the
warmth of his gaze as he studied her.

" 'Tis . . ." It was difficult to think when he was so
close and nearly impossible to speak. " 'Tis a bonny
spot." He had wanted to carry her through the village
to entertain her with the wares sold there, but the thought
of others seeing her so scandalously clothed appalled
her. They had settled on this small piece of paradise.

"Aye," he said, " 'tis bonny. When I was a lad I
used ta scout the woods behind us with me brothers. We
imagined ourselves great, fearsome warriors with muscle
of iron and wills of steel."

She didn't allow herself to look and confirm the fact
that his muscles were indeed as hard and smooth as
cooled molten iron. Nor did she let herself remember
how he looked with his back to her and his arms outstretched as he battled a score of villains with nothing
more than a flaming brand of wood. He had fought for
her, risked his life to save hers. But she would not think
of that, for it weakened her will and softened her heart.
And a soft heart could so easily be crushed.

"Ye must have had an idyllic childhood."

"Idyllic?" He gazed down the hill. At the bottom, the
burn sparkled and chuckled. "I had a fine father, though
he was a wee bit hot-tempered. I had Leith ta look up
ta, Colin ta jostle, and me aunt ta soothe me hurts."

Flame knew she shouldn't ask. "And what of your
mother?"

"The birth of twins is rarely done without great loss,
Fiona tells me."

Against her better judgment, Flame turned toward

him. His expression was somber as he watched the sweeping flight of a hunting kite.

"I am sorry." The words came without bidding.

"As am I."

"Ye never knew her?"

"Nay."

How, then, had this man learned such gentleness without a mother's loving hand? "And your father?"

"Died during battle when I was a lad."

So hardships had not avoided him. And yet he viewed the world with a wondrous optimism that brightened the very day around her. Never had she been happier than during the moments she had spent with him. Never before had her heart sung.

"Ahh." His leonine head turned. "I fear me goose is fat for the fire."

"What?"

He nodded toward the castle. "Lady Fiona has sent her wee warriors ta gather ye home and pluck me feathers for taking ye so far afield."

Flame looked in the indicated direction but saw nothing more frightening than a lean lad and a tiny wren of a girl galloping across the hillock toward them.

"Roman and Rachel?" she guessed.

"Aye."

" 'Tis not too fearsome a foe for a man of men such as yourself," she chided gently.

He turned slowly toward her. The cords in his neck stood out taut and hard beneath the golden skin of his throat.

"Be ye flirting with me, lass?"

Flame's jaw dropped slightly. "Nay. I . . ."

"Dunna get me wrong, Flanna, I have na objections. In fact—"

A blast of childish woe erupted from the hillside, drawing the two from their talk. Turning in unison, they saw that Rachel had fallen and was tearfully relating her problems to her brother.

But Roman was all of twelve years old. A young man,

Flame thought, a warrior in the making, and surely not willing to ease a wee lassie's hurts. Old wounds of her own suddenly nagged, but in that moment she saw Roman squat and pull the tiny girl into his arms.

Unabashed and seemingly unsurprised, Rachel leaned her face against her brother's tunic and encircled his neck. Even from a distance, Flame could see the caring in his eyes. And though his movements were a bit awkward, he stroked her sable hair and lifted the tiny body carefully into his arms.

Tears flooded Flame's eyes. She could neither explain them nor stop them, but suddenly her throat was choked with tension and her heart stung for a love she had missed.

"Are ye hurting, Flanna?" Roderic's voice was low.

Flame swept her gaze quickly from the approaching pair to the distant burn. "Nay," she said, though she knew it was a lie, for her soul ached.

"Dunna draw away," he said softly.

She had heard those words from him before but they were even more powerful now, for she had glimpsed a different world—a world where girls were coddled and cherished, where women were loved and respected. She raised her gaze, catching his.

"Do ye hurt, lass?" he whispered.

She swallowed hard, unable to turn away. "Only in my heart."

"Is it that ye miss yer own people?" he guessed.

"Nay." She barely breathed the word past her lips. "It is that I do not."

His brow wrinkled. Every living fiber in her wanted nothing more than to open her arms, to draw him against her breast, to feel his vibrant strength and know she was loved by him.

"What say ye?" he asked.

She was the Flame of the MacGowans. And she had to be strong. "Ye are lucky to have the Lady Fiona." Her voice was admirably firm. "To tend the wounds of your people."

Roderic watched her, not speaking, not moving.

Flame tightened her jaw and turned away. "I wish Haydan were here. Under your lady's gentle hand he might yet grow strong. I would give half my tomorrows to see him healed."

Roderic's gaze was like a sunbeam on her face. She need not look directly at it to feel its heat.

A pair of sturdy boy's legs entered Flame's vision.

"I hurt my knee," Rachel said from the safety of her brother's arms.

Flame felt Roderic's attention being drawn slowly from her face. "Are ye badly hurt, Peepsweep?"

"Aye." Her small chin lifted slightly. "Roman had ta carry me just like ye carry Lady MacGowan."

Above Rachel's dark head, Roman's face flushed slightly, and though Flame felt some compassion for his embarrassment, she felt admiration with more potency. It took a strong man to be gentle, she realized suddenly. Perhaps the same could be said of women, and yet she knew she lacked the strength to show her weakness to this man beside her.

Roman cleared his throat. "Methinks ye'd best hasten ta the keep."

"Yer mother's in a fury?" Roderic guessed.

"She sent us from the room before she would speak to Da," Roman answered.

Roderic scowled. "It bodes ill."

"There was talk of a scourging."

Against her will, Flame gasped. She had known men to die beneath the lash. All eyes turned to her.

" 'Twas a jest," Roman said quickly.

"Aye, lass," said Roderic. " 'Twas a jest . . . I hope."

"What the devil were ye thinking?" Leith fumed, skirting his brothers' stools as he paced the solar for the third time.

"She is me own responsibility," Roderic reminded him. It was not the first time he had been closeted here with his laird, nor, he hoped, would it be his last. "She was as safe as a bairn in"—he jerked a nod toward where Fiona sat rocking wee Graham—"in his mama's arms."

"She was in her nightgown and naught else!" reminded Leith.

"And think ye I couldna control meself, brother? That I might lose all sense and fall upon her in the broad light of day with all of Glen Creag looking on?"

"Aye," growled Leith, "I do."

"It's happened afore," reminded Colin.

Roderic smiled. "I dunna lose control."

"But they lose their virtue."

"Well, she has na," said Roderic evenly.

"She was in her nightgown!" stormed Leith. "What be ye thinking?"

"What be I thinking?" Roderic rose slowly to his feet. "I be thinking ye are a pair of lady's maids with too little ta occupy yer minds. Will ye be worrying that her shoes dunna match her bonnet on our next outing?"

"Watch yer—" Leith began.

"Does me memory fail me?" Roderic interrupted. "Or wasna yer lady a postulate of the holy order of Mary when ye blackmailed . . . *blackmailed* her into returning with ye ta Glen Creag!"

Leith was silent for a moment, then said, "That was different."

"Aye," agreed Colin, "we were on a sacred mission."

"And, ye!" scoffed Roderic, rounding on his twin. "Dunna think yer Devona hasna told me of yer proposition to her on yer first meeting."

"Well, I . . ." blustered Colin, drawing himself straighter. "That was afore."

"Afore what?"

"Afore me own Sarah was born."

"Huh!" laughed Roderic.

"I never paraded Devona about in her nightshift!" proclaimed Colin.

"Well ye—"

"Gentlemen!" said Fiona, rising to her feet with Graham cuddled against her shoulder. "Ye are disturbing the babe. And accomplishing very little, I might add."

Colin grumbled. Leith paced. Roderic scowled. She was, of course, right again.

"The point is not that we do not trust ye, brother," she said softly to Roderic. "It is that she is the lady of the MacGowans and that her clan is a breath away from attacking Glen Creag. What if she had caught a chill? Ye know the ordinance set forth by her kinsmen. If she is not returned to them hale and whole in a prescribed amount of time, there will be bloodshed. And that time is running out."

"Who struck her with the arrow?" asked Roderic, fury causing his teeth to grind. "There is na proof that it wasna one of her own."

"Nay," Fiona said softly, "there is no proof."

"Then I willna return her," Roderic vowed, "until I know she is safe."

"Is it her safety or yer heart that worries ye more, brother?" asked Leith quietly.

"It matters naught," Roderic said. "For she stays."

"Even against her will?"

"If needs be."

"Then ye'd best fortify the castle walls," said Leith solemnly, "and keep yer hands ta yerself."

Roderic raised his palms in an expression of innocence. "Ye needn't worry about me hands," he said, "for I'll be taking them with me when I leave."

"Leave!" echoed three voices in unison.

"Aye," said Roderic, "I go tonight."

Chapter 28

The night was very still. Roderic smiled into the darkness. He had reached Dun Ard in record time and now stood in the lee of the timber palisade and listened. In the woods behind him, a chestnut stallion awaited his return.

The climb over the wall and into the village was child's play, given the great length of rope he carried with him. The climb into Dun Ard itself was a bit more difficult. Now he stood beside the stable, catching his breath and getting his bearings. And then, stealthy as a wildcat on the prowl, he crept along the palisade toward the hall.

Here, stealth would do him little good, he knew, so he straightened the green plaid he had borrowed from the MacGowans and strode inside. It almost seemed as if he had never left, so familiar was the scene. But now Bonny did not greet him and Flanna did not sleep in her private chambers on the upper floor.

But Haydan did, and Flanna wished to see him healed. 'Twas as simple as that, for he had vowed to win her heart.

His bare feet were silent across the rushes, the steps cool.

No servant lay before the low, arched door where Haydan resided. No light flickered in the hall. With a single glance in each direction, Roderic set his hand to the handle and eased the door open. The hinges creaked. He should have brought mutton, Roderic thought, but before he had time to regret his neglect he was inside and the door closed behind him.

"Who's there?" The lad's voice creaked more loudly than the hinges.

Roderic stopped in his tracks, remembering that pain often kept the lad awake and thoughtful.

"Who is every man and every woman?" Roderic asked softly, in riddle fashion. "Who does each deed and tells each tale?"

" 'Tis *I*, of course," breathed Haydan. By the flickering light of a tallow candle, Roderic could see the lad's small, quaking form. "But which *I* is it. I know of several," he said, his tone uncertain.

Roderic chuckled. If intelligence were strength, this lad could carry a hundred stone and sweep castles down in one blow. " 'Tis the only *I* I refer to as *I*, lad," he said. "But sometimes the *I* is called the man of men, the scaler of walls. And sometimes I be called . . ."

"Roderic," Haydan gasped.

In the darkness, Roderic couldn't tell if the lad's breathy tone indicated relief or shuddering fear.

" 'Tis I," said he, stepping nearer the bed.

"Ye took my lady." There was no longer any doubt about his tone. It was rife with sudden aggression.

"Aye. I did."

The room was silent for a moment as if the lad struggled to decide what to do next. "I am na man of valor," he said quietly, "or I would fight for her honor and her return."

"Whether ye are a man of valor or na is yet to be seen. But this I know, ye are a man of deep thought, young Hawk, and therefore ye would see there is na need to fight me na matter how great yer strength."

"Why did you take her?"

"Because she wasna safe here," Roderic said softly.

"I would have protected her with the last breath in my body."

"I do not doubt yer word, lad. But I know na the source of her danger, so the battle is the harder here."

Haydan drew a sharp breath. It rattled down his throat. "You have kept her safe?"

Roderic sighed and stepped closer still. "Has been a long and tiresome ride. Would ye mind if I sit?"

"Nay."

The straw-filled tick rustled beneath Roderic's weight. "She is at—"

"Nay!" Haydan's tone was suddenly panicked as he raised a pale hand to stop the words. "Do not tell me, lest I inadvertently tell those who might do her harm."

Roderic could not help but smile. "She is where I mean ta tek ye now, lad."

"Me?" The word was barely audible, the tone breathless. "Did she ask ye to fetch me?"

"She said she wished ye were there."

Haydan was out of bed in less than an instant. Standing beside his pallet in his pale nightshirt, he looked frail enough to blow away. "Then I will go with ye."

" 'Twill na be simple, lad."

He drew another rattling breath. "I go," he repeated.

The rope Roderic had secured beneath his plaid was heavy and chafed like unconfessed sin. He withdrew it as Haydan quickly dressed. It was simple to tie both ends of a blanket to the rope and toss the thing past the open shutter and into the outside air. The window in the tiny alcove was just wide enough to allow the lad to squeeze onto the stone sill. But there he stopped.

"Could I na just go down the stairs?" he questioned, his face deathly white.

"What if ye were seen?"

"I would tell them I but went for a stroll."

"Have ye ever strolled before in the wee hours of the night?"

The boy lifted his chin slightly. The movement reminded Roderic of Flanna. "There must be a first time for each new endeavor or nothing would ever be attempted."

Roderic contained a chuckle. Such pride should surely

be housed in a stronger frame. "I willna let ye fall, lad."

Haydan remained motionless for a moment then glanced stiffly toward the ground. It was far below, wreathed in mist and darkness.

"The MacGowans will worry for me safety. Troy . . ."

"I have brought a missive to explain yer disappearance," said Roderic. The note would also remind the Wolfhound that Roderic could scale the walls of Dun Ard whenever he wished. It was a satisfying thought.

Haydan drew a deep, shuddering breath. "Lady Flanna, sh . . . she as . . . asked for me?" he questioned again.

"Aye, she did, lad."

He swallowed hard. Even in the darkness, Roderic could see the sharp bob of his Adam's apple. And then he coughed. The sound seemed loud as a horn blast in the darkness.

"Please, lad," Roderic said, fretfully trying to muffle the sound with his hand. "Stealth would be desirable."

The boy nearly strangled on his noisy explosion, but he remained relatively quiet. "I swear to be silent," he assured Roderic solemnly, and with hands that visibly shook, eased over the sill and onto the woolen sling.

Roderic had wrapped the rope about a solid peg near the door. Holding it snug with one hand was no difficulty. Spreading out the blanket to secure the lad inside was harder. But finally the boy was settled. He looked no larger than a cornered hare and no less frightened.

"When ye reach the earth, climb out and tug hard three times on the rope," Roderic said.

The boy could manage no more than a nod, and in an instant Roderic was lowering the sling. Moments slipped by and finally all the length was gone and still the rope hung heavy and taut.

God's wrath! He had miscalculated the distance to the ground. With only one twist around the peg, Roderic kept a firm hold and peered out the window. Below him, coarse hemp slipped into the mist. Nothing more could be seen.

A quick glance about the room assured Roderic there was nothing else to add to the length of the rope. So, with a quick, silent prayer, he tied the end of the hemp to the peg and slipped from the room.

It seemed to take forever to escape the keep and longer still before Roderic had scaled the wall and run the length of the castle. Visions haunted him of the rope breaking, the boy panicked and fallen.

But when Roderic reached the proper side of the castle, the lad was there, dangling like a ripe apple some twelve feet above the ground.

"Hawk," he called quietly.

True to the boy's word, he was silent. Roderic winced, wondering if he had fainted, or worse yet, if the fear of being hanged from such precipitous heights had weakened the boy's heart unto death.

"Hawk?" he called again.

Above him, the sling wiggled and shook. A gaunt face, pale as morning, peaked over the side. Sharp, white knuckles gripped the blankets edge. Still the lad spoke no words.

"I fear ye'll have ta jump," Roderic informed him quietly.

The sling trembled more violently. A squeak escaped, causing Roderic to wonder if Haydan had tried to speak.

Minutes stormed by. Surely dawn marched behind.

"Lad?" Roderic called.

Rattling breath reached his ears, then, "You are quite certain she asked for me?"

"Aye, lad," Roderic said to the rocking sling. "Ye and na other."

Flame sat with her back against a pair of goose-down pillows. It had been two days since Roderic had visited her. He was gone. That much she knew, and though his family said he had but gone to make a few purchases,

Flame doubted their word and agonized over his true location.

Perhaps he was with another. He had touched her, brightened her world, showed her the strength of tenderness. Never, not if she lived for an eternity, would she forget the expression on Haydan's face when Roderic named him Hawk. Yes, Roderic Forbes had educated her, had taught her a thousand things she should have learned long ago. How to laugh—how to love.

Dear God! Tears almost won the fight against her pride, but pride had been powerful for too long.

"Flanna?" Fiona opened the door and stepped hastily into the room. " 'Tis glad I am ye're awake." She held a blanketed bundle against one shoulder. It looked no more substantial than a small sack of rags. "Agnus's bairn is coming early." Her words were rushed, but there seemed little sense to them.

"I fear I know little of birthing babes," Flame said.

Fiona laughed. "I am na asking your assistance with the birth. But I must leave immediately, and I need someone to care for wee Graham."

Flame's mouth fell open. "Surely Clarinda—"

"She's visiting her sister."

"Hannah—"

"Has a blister on her foot. I ordered her to stay off it."

"Devona?"

"She and Colin took their Sarah and Rachel to the cobbler's. I fear there is no one else," she said, approaching the bed.

"But . . ." Flame felt like a fool, but she had never held a newborn bairn. And now that the tiny, wrinkled bundle was being delivered into her arms, fear made her mouth go dry and her hands tremble. "What of his father?"

"Left early this morning."

"But surely there must be—" She was blubbering and pleading shamelessly.

"He'll be no trouble." Fiona pressed the babe against

Flanna's chest. "He was just fed and swaddled and will sleep for several hours." She was already moving away.

"But—"

"Take care, Flanna. Clarinda shall be back before the nooning."

"But that's—"

Too late. She was gone.

"That's two hours away," Flame protested to the empty doorway. Panic roiled in her stomach. She knew less than nothing about babies. What would happen if he awoke? she wondered, staring into the tiny face. She could orchestrate a midnight raid with her warriors. She could ride any steed with four legs. But to nurture a babe! The idea terrified her.

He whimpered in his sleep. Flame loosened her grip, suddenly afraid she was squeezing the poor bairn to death. Dear God, this was going to be the longest two hours of her life.

"So tell me," Flame whispered to the silent babe. "What are ye thinking in that wee head of yours?"

Little Graham lay snuggled upon the tick with the wall to his right and Flame to his left. His eyes, she had discovered, were as blue as midnight and as wise as eternity.

"Do ye lie there hour upon hour and ponder the problems of the world? Or do ye merely marvel at life at large?"

He said nothing. But his fair brows lowered slightly, causing a tiny indentation above each. He had a wee blister on the arch of his upper lip and one fist had somehow escaped bondage to be nestled near his cheek.

"I'm not good with children," Flame said, stroking his tiny nails with the back of her index finger. "I was not meant to be a mother, ye know."

The babe's scowl increased.

" 'Tis true. I have heard the rumors. Some say I am more man than woman." Something ached near her heart even as she said the words. But little Graham was not so affected, and suddenly his mouth opened in a toothless expression of glee.

It was a dawning moment of import to Flame. Never had she seen a baby smile. Her own mouth opened in surprise and then she laughed. "Oh, so ye think that's funny, do ye? Well, I assure ye 'tis not. I can ride as well as any man. Better than most. And as an archer there are few who can best my accuracy. Even Roderic . . ." Her stomach pitched strangely when she said the name. "Roderic could mayhap best me. Roderic," she whispered to the tiny babe. Her throat ached with the words. "Why has he abandoned me? He promised me he would not. But what is the vow of a man? They cannot be trusted." The bairn's smile disappeared to be replaced by a look of surprise. "Maybe ye will be trustworthy, sweet Graham. Mayhap ye will be a better man.

"But Roderic said he was . . ." Flame closed her eyes. "Roderic again. What has he done to me? I was doing well." She knew her words for a lie. "I was . . . surviving," she corrected, "in my own world, in my own way. Content enough. But now . . ." The small fist opened and four tiny, warm fingers wrapped about one of her own. The marvel of a baby's trust. It seemed like a miraculous gift from God. "I want more," she whispered brokenly. "I want love. And Roderic. And a sweet babe of me own."

"Does he answer back?"

"Roderic!" Flame jerked her attention to the doorway. The baby jumped and began to wail, Roderic grinned, and Flame felt as if she would die of embarrassment.

"Now there, Flanna, lass, look what ye've done. Ye've set him ta crying," he said, striding across the room.

"Roderic," she murmured breathlessly.

"Aye." Reaching casually across her, he fetched the wee babe to his chest. " 'Tis me." Graham wailed all the louder. "Ye look like ye've seen a ghost again." One hand on the babe's bottom and one on his back,

Roderic jostled the bairn gently. Cries turned to whimpers, whimpers to sniffles. "Were ye talking about me?" he asked slyly. "Or mayhap . . ." He moved closer, easing the babe to his shoulder where he patted its back as he seated himself close beside her on the mattress. "Mayhap ye didn't think I would return."

She couldn't speak. His eyes entranced her. His voice mesmerized her. His very nearness made her stomach pitch and her head feel light. So this was love. It felt much the same as a rough sea voyage. She decided to treat it the same, by riding it out.

Flame raised her chin slightly. "Were ye gone? I hadn't noticed."

Roderic laughed, placing Graham in the cradle formed by his legs.

"What secrets did she tell ye, wee one?" he asked.

For a fleeting moment, Flame forgot that the child couldn't talk. She almost opened her mouth to deny every word he spoke. But just at that moment, Roderic's eyes smote hers.

"I have brought ye a surprise."

"I hate surprises."

He leaned closer until his lips were only inches from hers. Breath refused to come. Her heart forgot to beat.

"Are ye sure?" His words were as soft as a caress against her face.

She tried to nod, but instead her lips parted and her soul prayed he would kiss her.

Roderic smiled and drew back. " 'Tis a wee bit late to return it after all the trouble I went to."

"Return what?"

Against her every desire, he rose. "Come in, lad."

"My lady."

"Haydan?" Flame gasped. She couldn't believe her eyes, yet Haydan stood in the doorway, looking small, frail, and very weary.

"You are sick," he said, hurrying across the room, his pale face whiter than usual as he dropped to his knees beside her bed.

" 'Tis nothing," Flame assured him. "No more than an inconvenience."

"You did not tell me," Haydan said, sounding angry and lifting his gaze to meet Roderic's.

"I did not wish to worry ye, young Hawk . . . for I know how ye love her."

The silence was heavy and long. Flame's heart hammered against her ribs as she watched Roderic's face. His eyes turned toward her. There was an unreadable expression in them, but it spoke of primitive things, appealed to instincts long dormant in her.

"You are well now?" Haydan asked.

Flame lowered her gaze to the boy's gaunt face. "Aye. Quite healed."

A corner of the lad's mouth lifted. " 'Twould seem foolish to try to fool me about illness or aches, my lady, for I know them intimately and well."

"I am *nearly* healed," she corrected. "I have been ordered to stay abed a bit longer."

"But you will be well and strong soon?"

She nodded. If her own brother had possessed but a droplet of such sincere concern, she could have loved him well. Again Flame's heart ached with loss. "Very soon," she promised. "As will ye."

He looked much older than his twelve years, and yet much smaller. "If you say so, my lady," he agreed, but even his voice was weak, and his hand where it clasped the coverlet shook visibly.

"I do," she said softly. There were tears in the boy's eyes, she realized suddenly. "I do," she said more fervently, and in sudden appeal, grasped his narrow hand in her own. "With the grace of our Lord and Lady Fiona, ye will be well."

Haydan didn't speak.

"It has been a wearisome journey for ye, young Hawk," Roderic said. "And Fiona will be furious if ye be faint from exhaustion when she arrives. I will tell Hannah to show ye yer quarters."

Flame smiled into Haydan's brown eyes. Never had

they reminded her more of a wounded deer's than now. She would give half her life to see him healed, she thought, but suddenly Roderic's words reached her consciousness. "Hannah has a blister and must rest her foot."

"Hannah? 'Tis mistaken ye are, lass, for I saw her spreading fresh basil in the hall."

Something tripped in Flame's mind. "And Clarinda?"

"She was with her," said Roderic, heading for the door. He stopped when he was nearly there. " 'Twas kind of ye ta care for wee Graham. But I always suspected ye had a weakness for the bairns."

"I don't have—" Flame protested, but her mind called her words a lie and Roderic was already gone. "I didn't have a weakness for bairns," she corrected softly.

In the quiet that followed Roderic's exit, she stared at the door and felt the trap close around her with silent, hungry teeth. Roderic had brought her against her will, but she did not try to flee. She had vowed never to bear children, but wee Graham had grasped her heart as surely as he had grasped her finger. She had mourned her parting with Haydan. But Haydan was now here.

Everything was changing. But the Flame must not be doused. For her clan's sake, she should leave and retain some pride. The trouble was, she didn't want to.

Chapter 29

"**W**e must cease these clandestine meetings," Roderic quipped. His brothers' faces were shadowed and illumined by a trio of candles impaled upon an iron stand in his own chambers. But even by that uncertain light, he could see their expressions were deadly serious. "Yer wives are becoming jealous."

"Of all the childish, immature, infantile—"

"Hawk would say ye are becoming redundant, Leith," Roderic said, pulling his shirt over his head to face them bare-chested.

"Hawk!" The room shook with Leith's wrath. "What in the name of Jesu were ye thinking when ye snatched him?"

Roderic shrugged. "The lad is sickly. Surely ye would na begrudge him yer lady's healing touch."

"I'll touch you, you brainless oaf!" Leith stormed, pacing the length of the room. "I have seen you do some feebleminded things in the past. When ye were young I thought you would surely cause yer own death. Hell! Every time ye awoke in the morn I would hold me breath wondering if today ye would fall from a roof or drown yerself in the burn. But I thought, foolishly, I see, that ye had grown ta be a man of some responsibility!"

"Well, I—"

"Well ye haven't!" yelled Leith, coming to stand before his brother. "For this be yer most foolhardy deed yet. Why didn't ye tell us where ye were going?"

"Forgive me for my naivete," said Roderic, managing to stifle a grin, "but I thought ye might voice objections."

"Objections!" shouted Leith.

"It's na too late to drown him," fumed Colin, jumping into the fray. "Let's just drown him. He's too doltish to live. And I'm the better-looking of the two anyway."

"What if the MacGowans had found ye? What if ye had been caught? Ye've abducted their lady, for Jesu's sake! Ye think they would have just inquired of her health and gone on their way? Nay! They would have hung ye by yer own worthless entrails!"

Roderic shrugged. "I am never caught, brother!"

"Hell!" Leith swore again and threw up his arms. "If ye are never caught, how did the Lady Flanna get ye ta Dun Ard? Did she but flutter her bonny eyelashes so that ye followed her down the primrose path like a panting hound?"

Roderic raised his brows. "Pretty much that."

"Colin!" Leith yelled. "Talk to him."

"Let's just drown him," Colin suggested.

Roderic remained silent for a moment, then grinned. "Ye two were worried for me safety."

"Worried!" yelled the brothers in unison.

"Worried?" repeated Leith. "We were but hoping ye wouldn't return so we could rest easy for once. Worried!"

"Roderic." Fiona appeared in the doorway. Roderic smiled and opened his arms and she came like a lithe, auburn-haired angel to hug him. "Why didn't ye tell us your destination?" she asked, pulling away to look into his eyes. "Your brothers have been worried sick."

Leith turned away, grumbling under his breath. Colin swore. Roderic grinned.

"And what about ye, sweet Fiona? Did ye miss me?"

"Like a dog misses his fleas," she said, laughing. "And ye'd best cease flirting so; yer Flanna will not stand for it."

Roderic scowled and pulled the end of his tartan over

his bare chest. "*My* Flanna," he said, feeling his stomach sink, "could na care less."

Fiona was the only one who laughed. "Humility in a Forbes!" she said, sounding amazed. "I did not think I'd live to see the day. But 'tis quite becoming on you, Roderic."

Roderic turned away, the thought of Flanna making him fretful and cantankerous. "What the hell's she talking about, Leith?"

"She's saying ye're a dolt," said Leith, not deigning to look at him. "An opinion held by most."

"I think she's saying we should drown him," Colin corrected.

Roderic turned abruptly toward them. "Flanna missed the lad," he said in sudden explanation. "She missed the wee Hawk. Said so herself."

"Sweet Jesu!" rumbled Leith. "And what if she misses her sire, auld Arthur, will ye exhume his rotted body and bring him back to life for her?"

Roderic tightened his jaw. "She willna miss *him*," he said. It seemed a perfectly reasonable statement to him. Leith, however, didn't seem to find it so.

His hands formed fists. A muscle twitched in his cheek. "Dunna speak so foolishly, lad, for ye know how the sight of yer blood upsets me lady."

It was a blatant threat. Roderic smiled. "I meself find the sight of me blood quite uninspiring. And I am wounded, brother. 'Twould na be a fair fight."

"Then why in the name of heaven did ye na think of those things before ye went cavorting onto MacGowan land to"—Leith raised a heavy arm skyward as if mere shouting weren't enough to express his emotions—"to . . . steal another of their people."

It had always been pure joy raising Leith's ire—until he started swinging. Then it took all the wits and strength Roderic had just to call it a draw. Respect and a certain amount of maturity would keep them from coming to blows this day, he hoped. "Hawk was treated more like an outsider. He isna truly a MacGowan."

" 'Tis na what I heard,'' said Colin soberly.

Roderic scowled, turning toward his twin, but the other only shrugged and added, "When the herald came with word of yer abduction, I began searching for information concerning the MacGowans.''

"And?''

"They have close ties to France.''

"That I know. Both Flanna and the lad spent a good deal of their lives there.''

"They might share more than a second homeland,'' Colin said. " 'Tis na great news that the auld laird was free with his seed, both here and abroad.''

"Are ye saying they be brother and sister?'' Roderic asked. The idea seemed farfetched, and yet not impossible, for the two shared an intimacy that could not be denied.

Colin shrugged. "The lad was born in France. Why was he brought here?''

"He was orphaned,'' Roderic said, repeating what Flanna had told him. "The lad was a cousin of the Wolf-hound.''

Colin raised his brows in question.

"Troy Hamilton,'' he explained. "Ye must see the man ta understand the name.''

"I have seen the man, or shall I call him a mountain?'' said Leith. "And I refuse ta believe that even ye would be foolhardy enough ta tek so much as the man's quill, much less his relation.''

Roderic smiled. "Where is yer fighting blood, brother?''

"And this from the man who cried 'wounded' when I but scowled in his direction.'' Leith chuckled.

Roderic considered himself a peaceable man, but talk of Flanna made him edgy. His nerves were taut and it had been long indeed since he had brawled with his brother and laird. "I didna wish ta offend yer lady,'' he said, clenching his fists. "But if ye insist . . .''

"Enough,'' scolded Fiona, stepping between them. "I fear ye have strayed from the intended track yet again.

The problem stands as it was at the beginning. The MacGowans are worried and angry. But a few days remain before Flanna must be returned to them.''

"I willna return her!" Roderic's voice quivered with the words.

"Then they will come," said Leith.

"We outnumber them five to one and outwit them tenfold!" scoffed Roderic. Celibacy, tension, and rage pressed him on. "They have na the wisdom of rabbits nor the courage of goats."

All eyes watched him. All faces showed surprise.

"Gawd's wrath!" Roderic swore, striking the wall in his fury. "Dunna look at me so. Ye dunna know her circumstances."

"I presume ye be speaking of Flanna again," said Leith. His tone was quiet and edged with humor.

"Isn't he always?" quipped Colin.

Roderic glared at them both.

"They have na the sense ta value a woman of spirit." He paced rapidly. "They sent her ta France, for Gawd's sake. Sent such a gift as she ta France!"

"The auld man is dead," Leith reminded. "And the lass leads the pack. Na wee feat. Surely they respect her now."

The truth of his words made Roderic's stomach churn. The MacGowan clan did respect her. But if he admitted such, did it not weaken his reason for keeping her at Glen Creag? "How do ye explain her wound then, if ye say they care for her?"

"There is na telling whether it was accidental or apurpose," Colin said. "One of our own men could have loosed the arrow. Or mayhap a MacGowan did not recognize her."

"Nay!" Roderic insisted. "They tried to kill her. And I willna let her go!"

The chamber was deadly silent in the wake of his exclamation.

"Then marry the lass," said Leith into the quiet.

The air left Roderic's lungs in an aching rush. The

truth was, she did not want him. In all his philandering, in all his years of flirting and flying, never had he found a woman he wished to take for his own. Not until now. And now she would not have him. The irony was not lost on him, 'twas simply that he did not find it amusing.

Everyone watched him. He turned abruptly away. "She isna ready," he said simply.

Silence again, then, "Ho! So Roderic the Rogue has met his match!" Leith said. "And found a maid who can resist his charms."

" 'Tis na that," grumbled Roderic. So what if Leith had a right arm that could fell an oak? Roderic was quicker and suddenly longed to pit his strength against the other, to vent his frustration and burn off some steam. "But mayhap I am na the kind ta force a lass ta marry me. Unlike ye, brother."

To Roderic's disappointment, Leith merely chuckled and raised a hand to Fiona. In a moment, she was nestled under his arm.

"Force is a strong word, is it na, me love?"

"Aye. Strong indeed," she murmured with a smile.

Roderic's stomach lurched again. He was not above admitting his jealousy for what they possessed. "Do I disremember, or did she na flee across the hall so that ye had ta chase her down and carry her back up the stairs by force?"

Again Leith chuckled. "I thought 'twas she who carried me."

"Damn ye, Leith!" Roderic swore. "Ye would na have let her go before the sun fell into the sea and the moon glowed red. Ye are na different than me."

Leith's gaze rose slowly from his wife's. "Then marry her, lad."

"I told ye she is na . . ."

"Ye are scairt!" proclaimed Colin with a laugh. "Finally ye have met a woman unafraid ta face ye eye ta eye and ye are scairt she will turn ye away."

"I am na scairt!"

"Then mayhap she isna fair enough ta suit ye," suggested Colin.

Roderic rounded quickly on his twin, jabbing a finger toward his chest. "If ye try one of yer tiresome tricks on her I will pound ye ta dust," warned Roderic. In years past it had been humorous to take each other's identity for a passionate night. For the most part, their women, too, had found their practical jokes amusing, for one twin was as desirable as the other. But suddenly the old trick had lost its appeal.

"I guess her fairness be na the trouble," deduced Colin.

"Then mayhap she lacks intelligence," suggested Leith.

"Ye wish ta match wits with her, brother? Be me guest," Roderic fumed.

"It must be, then, that ye are ashamed of her manly ways. After all, she acts as if she be a laird. 'Tis ridiculous. No woman can lead men."

Roderic filled his nostrils with air and reminded himself not to swing at his brother. "There are those amongst the MacGowans who would give their lives just ta see her smile. Such is her leadership, though she knows it na."

Leith shrugged. "But her heritage *is* questionable."

"In her veins, there flows the blood of kings, our own and France's."

"But what have the MacGowans ta offer the Forbeses?" questioned Colin haughtily. "Their land is cursed with rocks and their puny livestock riddled with disease."

"The steeds of the MacGowans would make our own beasts look like stunted cattle in comparison."

"But they have na men ta ride them."

"They need na men," Roderic mused, remembering how she looked astride, how her flaming hair blew in the wind, how her eyes sparkled like newly mined jewels and her cheeks glowed with health and joy. "For with Flanna, the steeds sprout wings."

The silence was as heavy as sand, making Roderic realize he had said her name like a revered chant.

"Then Colin is right," Leith said. "Ye are scairt she will refuse yer hand."

"She wouldna!" Roderic exploded. "She would tek me if I but ask."

"Then ask."

Roderic's chest ached, and his hands were clenched to grinding fists. Suddenly, it all seemed so simple, for surely no woman could refuse him. He was Roderic the Rogue, man of men. "Aye!" he growled, "that I will." He was at the door in a moment. "Prepare a wedding feast, Fiona."

"But, Roderic, think—" she began.

He slammed the door behind him and took the stairs three at a time.

"Flanna!" he yelled. The walls of the hall fairly shook with the force of his words. His chest swelled. 'Twas time he acted the part of a man. He had wooed her long enough and where had it gotten him? Weary and uncertain and aching with frustration. "Flanna!" he yelled again and yanked the infirmary door open.

The bed was empty. Beside it, Clarinda jerked to a seated position upon her cot, her eyes wide with sudden terror.

"Gawd's wrath!" Roderic bellowed.

Two brothers, a sister-in-law, and five servants stormed down the hall toward him.

"What is it?"

"Roderic?"

"What has happened!"

"She is flown!" he howled.

"Gone?"

"Where?"

"Merciful saints!"

"Hannah!" Leith yelled. "Find yer husband. Tell him the Lady MacGowan is missing. Search every nook until she be found. Julia, check Haydan's room! Roderic, for Gawd's sake, quit shaking Clarinda."

"Where did she go?" Roderic yelled into the terrified woman's face.

"I . . . I . . . I . . ."

"Where?"

"Was sl-sleeping," Clarinda stuttered.

"Gawd's wrath!" swore Roderic again and jumping to his feet, raced from the room.

The stable. She would not leave afoot, for mounted was her only hope of escape. Roderic thundered toward the horse sheds, but suddenly he remembered their night atop the battlements. She had seen the horses on the hillock beyond the burn. Would it not be like her to climb the wall and fetch one of those untamed mounts? Indecision made him halt.

No. She would not leave Great Heart behind. He knew it suddenly and raced for the stables. But just then a huge shadow caught his eye. It was near the gate and upon its back sat a rider.

Flame's hands shook. She had to escape before she lost everything, including herself. Roderic was coming to claim her for his own, like a bull might claim his mate. She had heard him plotting with his brothers, and she had neither the pride nor the will to stop him, not if she looked into his eyes, not if she felt his touch. Dear God, she must escape. She pulled the shawl more closely to her face. She was taller than Lady Fiona, but surely the guard could not tell that in the darkness.

"But m'lady," said the gate man, glancing fretfully about, "surely there be another that could check on Agnus's bairn."

Flame remembered to breathe and covered her mouth with the woolen to muffle her voice. "Please do not concern yourself on my account, William." His name was William, wasn't it? Or did they call him Willy or Walt or—"There is not a Forbes who would harm your Fiona Rose."

"Nay, there isna," agreed the guard. "But the accursed MacGowans most probably be chafing at their bits, and na woman is safe from those curs. 'Tis na right that ye travel alone at night. Might I na go with ye?''

"No. Please!'' Flame stifled the urge to rail and look frantically behind her. Heart tossed his head. "I must hurry before—''

"Before what?''

The voice was Roderic's. Breath trapped in Flame's throat like water in a dam.

Great Heart turned to nicker a greeting.

"Were ye na even ta say good-bye, Flanna?'' he asked.

"Flanna?'' the gate man gasped.

"Stand back!'' she warned.

"Flanna . . . MacGowan?'' whispered the gate man weakly.

"Nay, I willna,'' said Roderic. "I have been standing back long enough. Now 'tis time I brought ye ta heel for yer own good!''

"To heel! My own good!'' Flame laughed, but the sound was tight as she fought to remember her pride. "As though ye could judge what is good for me, Forbes.''

"I can judge,'' he said, his voice deep in the darkness. "And I am good for ye. Ye will be me wife.''

Happiness burgeoned within her breast. But in a moment, she snuffed it out. Pride! She must have pride. He could not demand her hand in marriage. Such arrogance! She could not allow such arrogance, for if he showed it now, it would only grow. He would set her aside as easily as he had demanded her. "I will not marry ye,'' she said, but her voice shook.

"Aye, ye will. And soon.''

"Ye think ye can decide for me.'' Anger was finally building within her, brewing slowly but surely. "Ye think ye can closet yerself away with yer kinsmen and discuss my future as if I am of no more import than a . . . than a fallow sow?''

"Ye were spying on me,'' he said incredulously. "Sneaking about Glen Creag like an irksome thief in the night and listening to my conversations.''

"I am not my mother!" she cried. Her heart hammered against her ribs, and each shuddering breath hurt her throat. "Ye will not decide my life. Not ye or any man." Spinning Heart away, Flame raised her chin and threw back the shawl to glare at the gate man.

"Lower the bridge, William!" she ordered. "Or ye will feel the wrath of the MacGowans and all our allies."

Behind her, Roderic chuckled. "Dunna let her cow ye, Willy. Ye were right, the MacGowans be na more than spineless cur."

"Spineless cur?" she hissed, twisting back to glare at him.

"Aye," Roderic said. "All but one. And that one I will marry."

"Not for so long as I can draw breath!" she vowed.

"Wrong yet again," he countered. His teeth gleamed in the light of the single torch when he smiled. "We'll wed in a fortnight. Ye've precious little time, Flanna. Mayhap ye should—" he began, but he never finished, for in Flame's mind she saw a young girl crying within the stone walls of a silent abbey. She would not risk love only to be abandoned again.

Spinning the steed about, she spurred him straight for Roderic. The destrier's shoulder hit him square on, but instead of being plowed beneath the animal's pounding hooves, Roderic grasped handfuls of mane and hung on.

Flame gasped in outrage.

Roderic growled something indiscernible and swung a leg toward the horse's back.

"Nay!" Flame screamed and blocking his leg with her own, forced him back down. All the while the stallion plunged ahead. They were running parallel to the wall of the keep and only an arm's length away.

"Let go!" she screamed.

"When the angels sing in hell!" Roderic growled, trying to swing aboard again.

But already she had turned Heart toward the wall. He swung to the right. Flame yanked her leg from the stirrup just in time, and Roderic's shoulder hit the battlement with stunning force.

She heard his grunt of pain, saw one hand slip from the mane. But upon impact, Heart had veered left, allowing Roderic to grapple for a better hold. Suddenly, his foot was lodged behind the saddle.

"Get down!" she shrieked, but already he was aboard, nearly knocking her to the ground as he pulled the beast to a halt.

Heart snorted and reared. Flame tried to wrest the reins from Roderic's hands, but they were like iron on the leathers.

"Ye will marry me," Roderic said, his breath coming in great gasps against her ear.

"Never!"

"Ye will marry me," he whispered, "or ye will not see Haydan again."

The strength ebbed from Flame's body. Haydan! So that's why he had befriended the boy. And that's why he had brought him here. 'Twas not out of kindness, but to gain control of her, as others had controlled her in the past. Her hands trembled and she closed her eyes.

"Flanna?" His voice was soft suddenly, his face very close to hers. " 'Tis sorry I—"

"Sorry!" she shrieked and swung her elbow with all her might. It hit his shoulder just where it had banged the wall.

Roderic's hands fell from the reins. He gasped in pain, but she had no mercy.

"Sorry!" she yelled, and twirling about on the saddle, bent her legs and thumped him full in the chest with both feet.

With a roar and a jolt, he toppled over the horse's rump, but at the last moment his hand whipped out and caught hold of her foot.

Shrieking and flailing, she was dragged after him. He yelled in outrage as he fell. Great Heart reared. Roderic's back hit the ground, and Flame, tossed from the fleeing stallion, landed with a grunt and a gasp with her bottom firmly atop Roderic's crotch.

The air left his lungs in a croak of deepest agony. But still Flame had no mercy.

Her identify had been revealed to the gate man. Her horse was gone and with him her only hope of escape. But it was not too late to exact some revenge on the man who had turned her life upside down, who had torn the heart from her chest and thought to take her to wife in the same fortnight.

Lifting her hips from his, Flame scrambled forward to thump her weight onto his abdomen.

The air left Roderic's lungs yet again. He moaned in agony, but that was an instant before he felt the prick of her dirk against his jugular.

He lay very still, trying to draw an even breath and see through the red haze of pain.

"Ye are about to die, Forbes," she warned softly.

He managed to draw a rattling breath. "Did I na say I was sorry?"

"Ye bastard!" She screamed the word. Her voice shook. "Ye think to take my life from me and ye are sorry?"

His mouth opened slightly and he shuddered as though wracked with a pain only a man could understand. "Should I have said *truly* sorry?"

"Damn ye! *Damn* ye! Ye stole my heart and then crush it beneath your heel and all ye say is—"

In an instant Roderic had wrenched the dirk from her. With his hand upon the bare blade, he tossed it aside. "I asked ye ta marry me, woman! Never, not with all the women who wanted me, have I begged for one to become me wife."

"God damn ye, ye arrogant lout!" she gasped, and jolting to her feet, prepared to flee.

A crowd surrounded them three-people deep. Jaws were lax and eyes wide. Flame skittered to a halt. But it was a mistake, for somehow Roderic had forced himself to his feet and grasped her arm in a hard grip.

She swung wildly toward him.

"Hit him again, Lady Flanna," someone called. The voice sounded like Colin's. "Just once more. 'Tis certain I am he deserves it."

Her mouth fell open. She turned her head to stare bemusedly at the people who should surely be incensed by her attack on one of their own.

"Gawd, we haven't had such a bloody fine row since Leith brought us his Fiona. Dunna stop now, Lady MacGowan."

Roderic cleared his throat. "It seems we have drawn a crowd, me lady."

She blinked, turning from his kinsmen to him.

"Roderic, I am ashamed of you," said Fiona, stepping from the crowd. "You know Flanna shouldn't be exerting herself like that. What be you thinking?"

" 'Tis truly sorry I am," Roderic said from a slightly bent position. "It seemed the lady needed a wee bit of"—he groaned in pain—"exercise."

The crowd chuckled.

"You take her inside this instant," Fiona ordered. "And if she's torn that wound open you will answer ta me."

"Merciful Gawd," someone said. "Ye got the two of them mad at ye. Ye're in for it now, lad."

Roderic's gaze never strayed from Flame's face. She watched him breathlessly.

"What do ye say, Flanna? Shall we go inside and continue our . . . discussion?"

She swallowed hard and managed a nod. She would listen to what he had to say—and then she would leave.

Chapter 30

Roderic rubbed his shoulder. The castle was finally quiet and Clarinda had been sent from the infirmary. Or, more correctly, she had scurried from the room at the sight of Roderic's face.

He was angry. Flame could see the rage in his eyes, in his carriage, in the set of his mouth. And she was glad he was angry, for now she would see who he truly was. Now she would experience his dark side, and she could hate him.

"Why?" he demanded.

She sat perfectly straight upon her straw-filled tick, trying to ignore the wild pounding of her heart. She wouldn't let him see her fear. She was not Clarinda to be frightened away by one black scowl. And yet she wished she could hide beneath the bed as she had as a child during her father's rages.

"Why what?" Her tone was admirably flat, revealing only a small bit of her numbing fatigue.

Roderic gritted his teeth and paced again, but the room was small, causing him to turn in a moment. "Gawd's wrath," he swore on a tight exhalation. "Why did ye try ta leave?"

She lifted her gaze very slowly to his and with the greatest of efforts smiled. "For ye have treated me so well?"

"Aye!" The single word was growled. He stopped his impatient strides to momentarily stare at her from close range. "That I have."

"Truly?" The arrogance of the male mind! She had witnessed it a thousand times, and yet she was always stunned by its dimensions. But she was no longer a child, and fear was fading from her mind. "Let us review your goodness then, Forbes. Ye abducted me."

"Ye abducted me—" he began, but she raised her hand and smiled smugly.

"At knifepoint if my memory serves."

His gaze dropped away.

"Against my will, ye brought me to Glen Creag."

"Ye were badly wounded. Ye wouldna have survived had Fiona Rose na nursed ye ta health."

"And why was I wounded? Because I was being forced across the Highlands without weapons or escort."

"I was your escort." His voice was deep, and if she looked she could see vulnerability in his eyes. She refused to look.

"Ye hold me here," she continued, "knowing my kinsmen will storm this castle in my name and die upon the thirsty blades of the great Forbes warriors when they come."

He stared at her. The room was deadly quiet. Anger had drained from his face.

"Ye have forgotten one thing, Flanna." He drew a deep breath as if trying to fortify himself. "That I asked for yer hand in marriage."

For a moment she couldn't breathe, couldn't think, but she marshalled her senses. "Ye do not want me," she said. "Or ye will not want me, not for long. My father—"

"Damn yer father ta hell!" Roderic's fists clenched and for a moment she thought he might strike, almost hoped he would absolve her from the guilt of being who she was, unlovable, unloving. "I am not yer father." His voice was steadier now. "And there will be na battle—if ye marry me."

She tried to voice an objection, but the thought of having him beside her for a lifetime jumbled her mind.

"It could be an amicable union," he rushed on. "A

peace between yer people and mine. Young Hawk could stay and grow healthy. Fiona would teach yer healers. The Forbeses have some fine, stout mares. We could breed them to yer stallions and lend ye bulls to improve yer beef. And yer walls. I know every chink in the timbers and stone. The Forbeses could send men. The timber could be replaced with rock. Dun Ard could be—''

''And what would ye get in return?'' Flame asked. The words seemed as if they came from another.

His eyes caught hers in an intimate spark, speaking a litany of words that never reached his lips.

Roderic paused. His face was as lean as a hunting beast's, as well sculpted as a marble bust. ''Is it the truth ye wish ta hear, Flanna?''

No. She didn't want truth. Truth was hurtful and cold. She wanted lies and reassurances, promises of everlasting faithfulness. Things she did not believe existed. She wanted to sleep for an eternity in his arms and awaken to his smile. ''Yes,'' she said. ''The truth.''

He delayed for a moment and then said, ''I want children.''

She could not help but laugh. Fatigue seemed to be tangling her emotions. ''Children!'' she scoffed. ''Surely ye jest, Forbes. Ye have probably already sired more bastards than ye can name.''

She had not thought his back could be straighter.

''I have na bastards and I never shall.''

Hope erupted in her chest like childish laughter. But she hushed it to silence, for it was only an illusion. ''The trouble is, ye forget what I know of men.''

''That they are not worth yer trust?''

''Just so.''

He took two steps forward, seeming to be drawn against his will but forcing himself to stop. His fists clenched. ''The trouble is, ye forget what kind of man I am, Flanna.''

No, the trouble was that she could not forget, could not disbelieve. And yet she tried. ''Ye do not need me to produce your heirs, Forbes,'' she said. She forced her gaze from his, for concentration eluded her when she was drawn into his eyes. "I suspect there are a good many others willing to grant ye children."

She felt him drawing nearer but refused to look up.

"Careful, lass, lest ye flatter me."

Humor had returned to his voice with characteristic speed. His eyes would be sparkling with mirth and there would be a crescent-shaped groove in his right cheek, a groove she could trace with her finger and feel the stubble of his beard. She closed her eyes, hoping for strength. She must not succumb. She must not, for the pain of his eventual rejection would be too great to bear.

He stopped and when he spoke again, his voice was deadly serious. "Ye are a fine leader, Flanna, fine and brave. And 'tis true that yer people respect ye. But they are, some of them, still uncertain." He tightened one fist. The movement almost made him appear nervous and tense. "I could ease away that uncertainty. My loyalty ta ye would secure their own. The MacGowans could prosper like never afore. Together we could bind their wounds and soothe their differences."

She stared at him in silence, barely able to breathe, and he rushed on.

"They could become a great people again, respected and honored. They could choose a clan plaid to make them proud and cohesive." His words slowed, his gaze caught hers. "Green," he said, "to match yer eyes and honor ye. I would care for them as if they were me own."

She turned away, unable to face him a moment longer without crumbling, for he talked of clans and alliances while her heart wept for love and comfort.

"Flanna"—his soft voice drew her gaze back to him—"I love ye." The words hung in the silent room for a moment. "I love ye with me heart and me soul and me body. And if ye let me, I will be a good husband for ye. Mayhap"—he clenched his fist once in a nervous gesture—"mayhap someday ye will love me in return. But until then I vow to treat yer people na different than I would mine own. Yer concerns will be mine. Yer hardships—''

"Yes."

She heard the slight hiss of his breath before the question. "What say ye?"

She had fought his charm, his allure, the laughter he had brought into her life, but she could not fight his declaration of love. God forgive her. Even if it was not honest, she couldn't fight it. "I will marry ye."

"I . . ." Rarely had she seen him at a loss for words. He took her hand and lifted it in both his own. Did they shake? But no, she was imagining. It was her own tremors that she felt. But when he brought her hand to his bare chest, she could not mistake the heat there. She felt his heartbeat strong and sure against her fingers. "Flanna, I . . ." His words stumbled to a halt again, and he drew her hand higher to press a kiss to her knuckles. Longing flooded her. She closed her eyes to it and to him but still felt his gaze on her face.

"Ye willna be sorry, Flanna." His voice was steadier now, but again she thought she felt him tremble. How silly of her. " 'Tis good," he said brusquely and released her. But suddenly, he grabbed her by the arms and kissed her with hard, aching passion. Her breath stopped. Her heart soared and she longed to wrap her arms about him and hold him forever. But in a moment he released her and backed abruptly away. " 'Tis good," he repeated. " 'Tis a wise decision," he said and bumped clumsily against the door behind him. "Ye willna regret it. It is good," he murmured again. His expression was sober, but in his eyes, emotion flared. She refused to acknowledge it. "I will"—he cleared his throat and nodded once—"I will let ye sleep now while I send the news to yer kinsmen."

Flame slept well into the morning and awoke with a lurch. He had asked her to marry him! Wild hope surged within her, but she calmed it with a desperate effort. Perhaps it had been a dream. Perhaps she had misunderstood. But of course, she had not. They would be wed. But their marriage would be an alliance and little else, she assured herself. Still, her heart hammered in her chest, and when a rap sounded on her door, she jumped.

But it was only Clarinda, come to inform her that the seamstresses had arrived to fit her for the new gowns that had been ordered for her wedding.

Halfway through the afternoon, Flame still stood on a narrow stool in the solar where she now resided. There, she was measured and turned and poked and pricked until she felt she could not bear another moment.

It was then that Roderic stepped into the room.

She felt her heart stop as her eyes met his.

"My lady." His voice was as smooth as river water. Upon his head was the bonnet he had taken from her kinsman.

"Sir." She hoped she matched his tone, but knew she failed miserably, for just the sight of him made her want to melt like warm wax onto the bed nearby. The Flame of the MacGowans indeed! she thought numbly. More like a helpless lump of pudding.

"Are you well?" he asked.

"Aye," she said, but his eyes seemed to strip her of any subterfuge.

"My lady tires," Roderic said to the room at large. "Come back tomorrow."

"But we've only a wee bit left ta—" began the eldest seamstress.

Roderic interrupted without glancing her way. "Tomorrow," he said.

The room was cleared in moments, leaving Flame alone with him.

"Ye hurt?" he asked softly.

"Nay." But she could not breathe properly when he was near.

"Then what? There is something in yer eyes. Is it only weariness?"

Every nerve in her body jangled. What could he see in her eyes? Could he read her longing? "Aye," she said, trying to concentrate. "I am weary of inactivity."

He studied her closer. "Would ye care for a ride then, lass?"

"On horse?" she breathed hopefully.

"Well!" He laughed. The sound shivered down to her toes. "I could think of other options, but, aye, horseback would seem the most . . . boring. Boring but practical," he hurried to add.

She could feel herself blush but tried to hide her embarrassment. "Fiona gave me orders to rest."

"Methinks ye are na in a mood ta rest," he said, watching her eyes closely.

"Did ye not say she had a temper, Forbes?"

"Are ye suggesting that I am scairt of her?" Roderic asked, lifting a brow as if insulted.

"I am."

He laughed, and her heart sang with the sound. "And ye are right. But she canna stop us if she doesna see us leave."

"And ye think yourself capable of such a deception?"

"Where deception is concerned, I am a master," he declared, and moving to the bed, whipped a tartan blanket from the mattress. "Sir," he said, offering it to her with a flourish, "yer plaid."

"Surely ye do not expect me to wear that."

"Surely ye dunna expect me to challenge Fiona's authority outright," Roderic said, looking horrified. "Gawd's wrath, lass, where her patients are concerned she is below God and none other. She'd have me hide. Now hurry, into the plaid."

"Ye're jesting."

"Do ye wish ta ride?" he asked.

"Aye."

"Do ye wish ta see Fiona skin me alive?"

"Nay."

Roderic breathed a sigh of relief. "That's the sweetest thing ye've ever said ta me, lass. Now hurry out of that gown before someone comes."

The thought of disrobing in front of him made her skin warm and her breath halt.

"I . . ." She was trying to remember to breathe. "Someone took my clothes. I have no shirt."

"Oh." He scowled, but in a moment, his brooch was loosened and his shirt removed. "Here." He held the garment out to her. "Put this on."

He stood before her, his chest bare and thick with mounded muscle.

"Do ye need help, lass?" he asked, stepping forward.

"Nay." She lifted a hand to ward him off. Her fingers pressed against the smooth firmness of his chest, just above his left nipple. The flash of physical longing nearly knocked her off her feet, though he didn't move so much as a hair.

"Flanna . . ." His voice was suddenly husky, the humor gone, the tone strained.

She backed away a quick step. "I'll . . . I'll wear the shirt."

He exhaled shakily, and when he turned his back, his fists were clenched.

It seemed to take forever for Flame's shaking fingers to remove her nightshift and don the shirt. It was large. The sleeves fell past her fingers, the hem to her knees, and every inch of it was warm from its time against his skin.

"Are ye ready, lass?"

"I . . . um . . . need the plaid."

He turned with the tartan in his hand and caught his breath. "Gawd, ye are bonny."

She swallowed. "I am supposed to be a man."

"Oh. Aye. Well then . . ." He walked toward her, then stopped and scowled. "Gawd, ye are bonny."

She couldn't help but laugh, for he made her feel hopelessly giddy.

"Lass, I . . ." he began, but he stopped, loosened his fists, and ran his fingers through his hair. "Ye need a belt."

"A—"

"There," he said and hurrying to the bed, untied a

braided cord that held back a velvet drape. In a moment he was kneeling before her.

"What are ye doing?" Her voice sounded breathy.

"Dressing ye, though 'tis the reverse of me desires," he said, then shushed her objections as he wrapped the plaid about her waist. His fingers felt warm and firm and when he had wound the entire length of the tartan about her, he tied the draping cord about her and folded the top edge of the blanket down to cover the impromptu belt.

"There, I am done," he said, but his hands did not leave her waist and he remained as he was, kneeling before her. His voice was deep and his eyes, when she dared look into them, were dark with unspoken emotion.

"Shouldn't I"—touch you, stroke you, make love to you?—"hide my hair?" she asked.

"Ahh." Roderic seemed to draw himself from a trance and rose finally. "Yer hair." He gathered it in his hands. She felt his fingertips graze her neck and closed her eyes to the errant sensations that seared her senses. " 'Tis so bonny." He breathed the words against her throat. She shivered, and in a moment she felt his kiss where his breath had touched her. "Flanna." He said her name like a caress.

She tried not to tremble. "I am . . . supposed to be a man."

"Right," he said, but his voice was shaky. Taking off his purloined bonnet, he tucked her hair into it and placed it on her head. But her tresses were not so easily mastered. They peeked out at odd angles. He tucked them in, smoothing his palms up her scalp. "Perfect." He stood back finally. "Now anyone would think . . ." He paused, tilting his head and grimacing. "Now any idiot would know ye're a woman."

She smiled. God, she could love him.

"Stand like this." Bracing his legs wide, he placed his fists on his hips and scowled.

She tried to imitate him.

"Nay. Ye must . . ." He stepped forward to plant her

fists more firmly on her hips. "Ye must not . . . look beautiful." He scowled, then bent to place one hand on each of her bare knees. "Here now, spread yer legs. There, that's . . ." He stood up, still staring at her legs.

"Is that better?" she asked, her face hot.

"Nay." He shook his head. A fine sheen of sweat had appeared on his forehead. "Nay, na better, lass, just . . . inspiring."

They got past the guard at the gate with no trouble, but they didn't ride far. Roderic called a halt not a full league from Glen Creag, and Flame was grateful, for the jostling caused more pain than she had expected.

He helped her dismount, watching her face as he did so. "Are ye well, lass?"

"Aye." She could not quite meet his eyes, for the feel of his hands on her waist made her head spin and her throat close up. So she lifted her gaze to the countryside. " 'Tis a bonny spot."

They stood at the crest of a knoll that rolled away into green crevices. Yellow irises nodded at the sun and prickly gorse grew in abundance.

"Aye, 'tis bonny," Roderic agreed. But he didn't turn away and when he lifted her hand to his lips, desire sparked at each light point of contact.

"Roderic." She said his name but didn't pull away. Indeed, she was not certain she could, for it seemed her bones had melted. Yet she tried to marshall her senses.

"Aye, lass?"

"What will ye ask for a toucher?"

"Ahh." He watched her eyes for a moment, before turning. Tucking her hand into the crook of his arm, they walked downhill and sat on a slanted carpet of green lichen that seemed to overlook the entirety of Scotland. "So ye've decided I want ye for yer dowry, lass?"

Her stomach cramped. Was it the way he looked at her, or worry about how he would answer her question that made her nervous? Indeed, she had spent her nights thinking, wondering. Why did he wish to marry her?

There must be a reason other than those he had confessed. "My kinsmen will arrive in a few days to discuss our union. I would know what to expect."

He turned away finally, looking over the vast glen below them. "There are two things I want," he admitted, "and I willna settle for less."

She felt the tension like a tangible thing. Now she would find out his motives. She would learn who this man truly was. "The first?" she asked.

"The wedding must take place at Glen Creag, for I willna compromise yer safety."

"I cannot hide here forever," she said, and indeed, she felt as if she were hiding, from reality, from life, from responsibility. And yet, to return to Dun Ard with Roderic at her side, somehow that, too, felt like an escape.

"Na forever, lass, but there will be a great crush of people for the festivities, and I will feel safer with ye here."

She nodded, waiting breathlessly. "And the second?"

"The second," he said, sitting very still beside her, "is yer love. But I can be patient if I have ta be."

Chapter 31

$\backsim \!\! \frown \!\! \circlearrowright \!\! \frown \!\! \sim$

Sitting about a table in the great hall, the Mac-Gowans and the Forbeses had discussed the coming union. Troy was there, flanked by elders from the villages and a few of Flame's warriors. Nevin had not come, for he had been called to Inverness regarding his father's property.

Leith had made a solemn oath to all present that his clan had had nothing to do with Simon's death and the raids on MacGowan stock. He also promised to find out who had, and that had eased the way for further negotiations.

True to Roderic's word, the Forbeses had asked for no dowry from the MacGowans. In fact, Colin had said that if they would but take his twin, the Forbeses would be willing to pay. There had been laughter then, echoing about the great hall like music. There had been laughter every day since, for Roderic was always near at hand, telling her tales, holding her hand, watching over her, or simply watching with those eyes that promised heaven. And when no one was looking he would kiss her until the world melted away and all that remained was desire.

She would have made love to him if he had but asked. Flame knew it and wondered if she should be ashamed. But he had not asked. Instead, he said that he would wait until she was his completely, with no one to dispute his claim.

Laughter welled up from the hall below. Flame could hear it as she stood in the sanctuary of the solar where she had slept for the past few weeks. Wedding guests were arriving, she thought. Panic gripped her.

Marriage! She had vowed against it, but that had been selfish. She was doing this for her people, binding them with the great clan Forbes. Flame watched her reflection in a gilded mirror beside her bed. Who was she fooling? She was doing this for herself, because she wanted him, because she could no longer resist Roderic's caring, could not disbelieve his vows of love.

Sweet Jesu! He loved her! Didn't he? But why? Her palms were sweaty. She wanted to dry them on her gown, but it was too lovely.

She slowed her breathing and concentrated on her attire. The gown was white brocade, slashed in front to reveal a silver underskirt. The neckline was cut low and softly rounded. The diamonds at her throat were a wedding gift from Roderic. The pearls in her upswept hair were from Leith and Fiona.

"My lady," Marjory breathed. She had arrived some days before to help with the preparations, but she had been jittery the whole time and now her voice shook.

"Is something amiss, Marjory?" Flame asked, turning away from the mirror.

"Nay, lady, nay. I just . . ." She stopped and glanced toward the door. " 'Tis just that ye are so bonny and Roderic, he loves ye so." Tears sprang suddenly to her eyes.

"What is it?" Flame asked, gripping the other's hands.

" 'Tis naught. Truly, I but worry . . ."

"Worry?"

Someone knocked at the door. Marjory jumped, and Clarinda's voice called out. "My lady, if it be na too much trouble, they are asking for yer maid's help in the hall for just a moment."

"Marjory, are ye all right?" Flame asked, noticing the girl's wide eyes.

"Aye. I am fine, my lady. 'Tis nothing. I will help in the hall?"

Flame nodded.

"I will return shortly," Marjory promised and closed the door, but in a moment it opened again.

"Did ye forget something?" Flame asked, not looking about.

"Aye." Roderic's voice quivered in her ear. "I forgot this," he said, and turning her, kissed her on the mouth. His lips were firm and warm and magic, searing everything from her mind but his presence, his kiss, the feel of his fingers, strong and sure as they cradled her against him. She opened her mouth to his and felt his tongue glide across her lips. A shiver escaped her. She gripped his arms for support and he held her as he kissed her into oblivion.

"My lady, they didna need me help in the . . ." Marjory stopped in the doorway and gaped.

Roderic drew the kiss to an end. "Ye must quit trying ta seduce me, lass."

Something in Flame's mind told her she should be offended. "I will try" was all she could manage.

He smiled, but his eyes spoke of flaming passions. Her knees went limp. " 'Tis only till tanight," he murmured and forced himself from the room like a wooden puppet.

They were married in the hall, for the bumpy clouds threatened rain. Hundreds of guests spilled out the doors and into the bailey. MacGowans mingled with Forbeses and Lamonts and MacAulays. Laughter was everywhere. Drinking abounded. The feast rivaled that of a royal wedding, and yet Flame could think of nothing but the night to come, for Roderic was forever at her side, touching her hand, whispering in her ear, watching her every movement, as if he feared she would be whisked away if he so much as blinked.

Finally night arrived. Sconces were lit. Their heat brought out the fragrances of the dried heather and ladies' bed straw that hung upon the walls. The music of pipers and fiddlers filled the air. But it all seemed distant and unreal. Flame 's hands trembled slightly as she lifted her gaze to her bridegroom's.

"It has been a long day," she said softly. The great double doors of the hall had been left open. Lightning cracked outside, and she jumped, feeling foolish.

Roderic tightened his grip on her hand. "And 'twill be too short a night," he said. "Perhaps we should leave the merrymakers and find our own amusement."

Heat seared her senses as his lips grazed hers. "I"— words failed her—"I will go prepare for . . ."

"Nay," Roderic murmured, "let me prepare ye."

Her face felt hot. There was an ache that spread from her breasts to her loins. "I but meant Marjory could take down my hair and—"

"Let me take down your hair," he murmured. His breath was warm against her ear.

They were in the midst of a roiling sea of revelers, and yet it seemed there was not another soul left in the universe.

"She could remove my gown," Flame breathed.

Roderic touched the bare skin of her shoulder and slipped his hand to her back. "I can remove it."

His nearness filled her senses, and yet she was scared and not too proud to admit it, at least to herself. "But . . ." Her words stopped as he lowered his lips to her neck.

"Shh, lass," he whispered. "I dunna fancy meself as a lady's maid, but there are certain things I am quite adept at. Let me show ye."

All she could do was nod. The journey up the stairs didn't seem real, but finally the door of her bedchamber closed behind them. Thunder rumbled outside. Flame gripped her hands together and paced across the room. It was dark, with not a single candle lit. "I . . . I should have asked Marjory to keep a light burning."

"I think we can start our own fire." Roderic's voice was deep and quiet behind her as he placed his back to the barred door.

"Oh," she breathed and set her fingers to her hair.

They trembled against her scalp, but in a moment he was behind her, brushing her hands aside to pull the pins from her coiled tresses. He removed the string of pearls and laid it gently across the back of her neck. They fell smooth and cool against her bare skin, and where they fell, his kisses followed, tender and hot, raining across her shoulders and back. Her breathing escalated. She shivered against his touch, and in a moment his fingers moved to her hair again. Flame felt the braid fall loose, felt his hands glide through it and up to her scalp. There, his fingers massaged as he kissed her throat, her cheek, the tender, aching hollow below her ear.

A spasm of hard desire shook her and she jumped, breathing hard as she moved away a fraction of an inch. "Roderic!" she gasped.

"Aye." His tone was husky.

"I . . . I'm not good at this."

"Was that the general consensus of all those hundreds before me, lass?" he asked, following the pearls with a single fingertip.

"Um . . ." Sweet Jesu, how could he talk at a time like this? "Yes." His fingers dipped lower, along the curve of one breast. Her breath came out in a rush. Lightning crackled outside their window, but it felt as if it were within the confines of her chest. "Yes, it was."

"Well then, let us prove them wrong," he murmured and drew her nearer.

But suddenly a movement caught her eye. A shadow reared up behind him. Flame tried to scream. Something crashed down on Roderic's head and he fell.

Terror spilled through her. She stumbled back. Lightning flared, illuminating the room for an instant eternity.

"Nevin!"

He was crouched beside Roderic with a dirk pressed to his neck. "He has a hard head," Nevin said quietly. "I didn't kill him with the rock, but one scream out of ye and I'll slice his throat, *my lady*."

"No." The word was a whimper. "Ye wouldn't."

He laughed. The sound was low and ugly. "I assure

ye, I would,'' he said and stood. "Just as I killed Simon.''

"Not Simon.'' She shook her head and backed away a step. The door behind her was barred. She would never open it before he caught her, and the revelry from the hall below would muffle any noises she might make.

"Aye. Simon.'' Nevin laughed again. A fork of lightning illumined his face, and in that moment Flame knew he was mad. "He was still pleading for his life while choking on his own blood.''

Flame's stomach roiled. "Nay.''

"Aye!'' Nevin said, advancing. "Ye thought me such a fool. Poor Nevin, the son of a lowly cloth merchant.''

"I never thought that.''

"Aye, ye did!'' he growled. "But I am not a fool. I have planned. For years I planned. For every time someone laughed at my humble position, I planned a death.''

The door was at her back now, but she couldn't escape that way. Flame sidled along the wall. "We took ye in. We shared—''

"Shared!'' he snapped. "Ye think I am content to share with a people who would take a woman as their leader? A whore? Nay.'' In the flash of lightning, she saw that he had raised the knife above his shoulder. "I was meant to be laird. But I was cheated. I was born to the wrong man, to a groveling merchant instead of a chieftain. Gregor, your brother, would have ruled in my stead. So I had to kill him, of course.''

"Gregor,'' she breathed the name.

"Aye, and cleverly. 'Twas very simple to make it seem like an accident, for I had practiced on my father.''

"Ye killed Lawrence?''

" 'Twas a delight to slit the old fool's throat and set the house afire, but only after I salvaged the few valuables he had. And then there was only the old laird left. And he was dying. Never did I think the MacGowan scum would choose a woman over me. Never!'' His knuckles were white against the dirk. "But they did. So

I tried to help them realize their mistake. But they are fools. Couldn't they see that ye were leading them to destruction? The poisoned well, the raids, the deaths.''

"They were all your doing?" Flame breathed.

"Aye. It was all part of my plan. I thought they would see the consequences of having a *whore* lead them. I tried to help them understand the error of their ways. But they would not. So I formed the brigand band and paid them with your stock and my father's hoarded money. They hide in the North Woods even now and await my bidding. They helped me trap Simon, but I butchered him myself, and cast the blame on the Forbeses. I thought the MacGowans would attack them, and I knew the Forbeses would annihilate ye. But ye decided to take a hostage instead. So much the better. For the hostage would die and then the Forbeses would sweep down upon ye like a tide. But Forbes has not died yet, has he? And ye've fallen for him.''

Flame shook her head. "No. You're wrong. I don't care for him," she gasped, but Nevin only laughed as they continued to inch around the room.

"Ye lie! Ye have fallen for him. I wish ye could watch him die, but ye must go first." Simon laughed again. The sound echoed in the room. "He will awake and find ye dead. Our honorable kinsmen will think he murdered ye on yer wedding night. Troy, that hulking fool, will give his life to avenge the daughter of the whore that bore him a child. And then this keep will be bathed in blood. There will be no one left to claim leadership of the MacGowans. No one but me.''

He was closer now. He had been content to follow her and tell her of his cleverness, revel in her terror, but Flame's time was running out, and she knew it.

"But ye want to be laird," she said. The bed was at her right, stopping her from going farther. "Surely ye don't wish all your people to be killed.''

"They betrayed me," he said. "Now they will pay. I wish I could watch them pay in blood, but I must not be here, lest I be tied to the murder." He smiled. "That would ruin my plans, and Dun Ard would be left without a laird. I couldn't allow that. I will return and show them how a man rules.''

''But ye'll have no subjects,'' she said, her back crushed against the wall, her mind churning. ''And ye'll have to wait until the fighting subsides.'' He was stalking her again, but she had nowhere to go. ''Spare Roderic's life!'' she said quickly. ''Spare it and I'll take my own. I'll leave a note saying ye should rule in my stead.''

Nevin stopped. In the unsteady flash of lightning she saw that his eyes were narrowed as he thought. ''So ye love him so much that ye would commit the ultimate sin.'' He chuckled. '' 'Tis almost tempting, but I prefer to have the pleasure myself,'' he said and lunged for her.

Flame screamed and leaped sideways. She felt the blade rip her gown. His hand clawed at her arm, but suddenly he was twirled away.

Roderic roared and dragged Nevin to the floor.

They trashed about, wrestling for supremacy. She rushed forward, ready to tear at Nevin with her bare hands, but she tripped over something and fell. In that instant, lightning flashed. Every image was etched in silver detail. Nevin, his face a mask of hatred, straddled Roderic. Light gleamed on his upraised blade.

The scream tore at her throat. Her hands formed to claws as she pushed herself from the floor. The rock was there, hard and smooth. She lifted it and swung with all her might. It hit Nevin's shoulder, knocking him sideways. He rose with a roar and lunged for her.

His fingers snagged her bodice. He yanked her toward his dirk. She could smell death, knew it was coming for her.

''Noo!'' Roderic shrieked. She saw him rise slowly, saw him raise the rock, and heard it smash with dull finality against Nevin's head.

For a moment, she saw Nevin's shocked expression defined by the crashing light from the sky. And then he fell, sliding into death with a crushed skull.

"My lady!" screamed Marjory, banging on the door.
"My lady!"

Roderic stumbled over to lift the bar and the maid
rushed in. Light from the hall fell upon Nevin's staring
eyes. She lifted her fists to her mouth. "Is he dead?"

"Aye, lass. I am sorry," Roderic said, but Marjory
shook her head. "He wasna what I thought him to be.
He wasna kind," she whispered, touching the bruise on
her cheek. "And I feared . . ." She swallowed hard and
turned to look at Flanna. "I feared for yer safety, my
lady, for sometimes he would say things that . . ." Shaking her head, she glanced at the dead body again. "But
then he was called to Inverness and I believed ye were
safe." She shivered. " 'Twas Bullock that thought he
saw him in the crowd here. And then I knew. I knew he
planned evil. But now ye are safe. There are only the
brigands to disturb our peace."

"The brigands," Flame whispered. "Nevin was their
leader. They wait in the North Woods for his command
even now."

"Then I go to the woods," Roderic said.

"Nay!" Flame gasped, but he had already turned
away.

"Stay with her, Marjory. I will send Troy ta guard
yer door."

Two days had passed since the wedding. Night had
fallen again, and still no word had come regarding the
outcome of the battle against the brigand band. Flame
paced her chambers. Fiona had insisted that she rest, but
neither her conversations with Troy nor Haydan's company had eased her mind, for worry gnawed at her.

All this time she had been a fool. Every day she had
turned away from Roderic she had wasted one more
chance at love, one more day of happiness. There were
no guarantees in life. She knew that now, but to throw
away the opportunity for love was worse than throwing
away life itself. She paced again.

If he came back alive—if God but granted her one more chance, she would grab it with both hands and not let fear rule her actions.

A noise sounded in the hallway. Flame stopped, not daring to breathe. The door eased quietly open, and then . . .

"Roderic." She said his name like a prayer and took one stilted step forward. "Roderic," she managed again.

"Lass." He closed the door behind him and leaned his weight against the heavy timbers. Their gazes met and held. "We routed the brigands."

There were a thousand things she needed to say, but none of them would come, for all she could do was stare at him and realize that he was alive, that he was safe.

He remained as he was, watching her closely. "With our combined warriors, we rid the Highlands of them."

Some numbed part of her mind realized that he must have washed, for his hair was damp and the cuffs of his shirt were folded away from his broad wrists. She searched his face, his hands, his clothing. No blood stained his person. Tears, hot and unheeded, sprang to her eyes.

"Dare I hope ye worried for my safe return?"

The tears spilled onto her cheeks.

"Flanna, lass, ye're crying," he said and took a step forward.

"Roderic," she cried and flung herself into his arms.

He folded her into his embrace and she clung to him, feeling the steady beat of his heart, the hard strength of his arms. He was alive. He was well. God was in His heaven.

"Ye did worry," he murmured, stroking her hair. "Ye did worry, lass. And I wish I could say I am sorry, but ta know ye care, means more ta me than all—"

"I love ye," she whispered against his chest.

The world stood still.

"Yer pardon?" he said softly.

"I love ye," she repeated, and drew back far enough to look into his eyes. "I've known for a long time, but I dared not admit it for I am a coward."

"Nay, lass—" he began, but she rushed on.

"There is so much pain, Roderic. So much hatred. Nevin . . ." She shook her head. "I thought he was kind. I thought he was good, like his father. But he was not. He was evil. Good does not always beget good. And evil does not always beget evil. I am good, Roderic. Ye make me feel that I am good, that there is hope.

"So many aren't given the chance I've been given. Troy," she whispered. "He loved my mother, worshiped her, and in her loneliness she turned to him. He told me the truth. Haydan is his son. Mother made him promise not to tell father, lest he kill the child. And so Troy denies leadership of the MacGowans because of his guilt. But what good does guilt do, Roderic? We're given so little time. We must cherish what happiness we can find. If ye still want me, if ye don't hate me for all the things I've said and done, then I am yours."

She saw hope light his eyes. He cupped her cheek with his hand. "Never could I hate ye, lass. Never."

"Then I am yours, tonight and always."

"Aye." Bending, he lifted her into his arms. "For always," he breathed, and in their minds a child laughed.

Avon Romantic Treasures

*Unforgettable, enthralling love stories,
sparkling with passion and adventure
from Romance's bestselling authors*

LADY OF SUMMER *by Emma Merritt*
77984-6/$5.50 US/$7.50 Can

TIMESWEPT BRIDE *by Eugenia Riley*
77157-8/$5.50 US/$7.50 Can

A KISS IN THE NIGHT *by Jennifer Horsman*
77597-2/$5.50 US/$7.50 Can

SHAWNEE MOON *by Judith E. French*
77705-3/$5.50 US/$7.50 Can

PROMISE ME *by Kathleen Harrington*
77833-5/ $5.50 US/ $7.50 Can

COMANCHE RAIN *by Genell Dellin*
77525-5/ $4.99 US/ $5.99 Can

MY LORD CONQUEROR *by Samantha James*
77548-4/ $4.99 US/ $5.99 Can

ONCE UPON A KISS *by Tanya Anne Crosby*
77680-4/$4.99 US/$5.99 Can

America Loves Lindsey!

The Timeless Romances
of #1 Bestselling Author

KEEPER OF THE HEART	77493-3/$5.99 US/$6.99 Can
THE MAGIC OF YOU	75629-3/$5.99 US/$6.99 Can
ANGEL	75628-5/$5.99 US/$6.99 Can
PRISONER OF MY DESIRE	75627-7/$6.50 US/$8.50 Can
ONCE A PRINCESS	75625-0/$6.50 US/$8.50 Can
WARRIOR'S WOMAN	75301-4/$5.99 US/$6.99 Can
MAN OF MY DREAMS	75626-9/$5.99 US/$6.99 Can
SURRENDER MY LOVE	76256-0/$6.50 US/$7.50 Can
YOU BELONG TO ME	76258-7/$6.50 US/$7.50 Can
UNTIL FOREVER	76259-5/$6.50 US/$8.50 Can

And Now in Hardcover
LOVE ME FOREVER

America Loves Lindsey!

The Timeless Romances
of #1 Bestselling Author

GENTLE ROGUE	75302-2/$6.50 US/$8.50 Can
DEFY NOT THE HEART	75299-9/$5.99 US/$6.99 Can
SILVER ANGEL	75294-8/$6.50 US/$8.50 Can
TENDER REBEL	75086-4/$5.99 US/$7.99 Can
SECRET FIRE	75087-2/$6.50 US/$8.50 Can
HEARTS AFLAME	89982-5/$6.50 US/$8.50 Can
A HEART SO WILD	75084-8/$5.99 US/$6.99 Can
WHEN LOVE AWAITS	89739-3/$5.99 US/$6.99 Can
LOVE ONLY ONCE	89953-1/$5.99 US/$6.99 Can
BRAVE THE WILD WIND	89284-7/$6.50 US/$8.50 Can
A GENTLE FEUDING	87155-6/$5.99 US/$6.99 Can
HEART OF THUNDER	85118-0/$5.99 US/$7.99 Can
SO SPEAKS THE HEART	81471-4/$5.99 US/$6.99 Can
GLORIOUS ANGEL	84947-X/$5.99 US/$7.99 Can
PARADISE WILD	77651-0/$5.99 US/$6.99 Can
FIRES OF WINTER	75747-8/$6.50 US/$8.50 Can
A PIRATE'S LOVE	40048-0/$6.50 US/$8.50 Can
CAPTIVE BRIDE	01697-4/$5.99 US/$6.99 Can
TENDER IS THE STORM	89693-1/$6.50 US/$8.50 Can
SAVAGE THUNDER	75300-6/$5.99 US/$7.99 Can

NEW YORK TIMES BESTSELLING AUTHOR

Elizabeth Lowell

ONLY YOU	76340-0/$5.99 US/$7.99 Can
ONLY MINE	76339-7/$5.99 US/$7.99 Can
ONLY HIS	76338-9/$5.99 US/$7.99 Can
UNTAMED	76953-0/$5.99 US/$6.99 Can
FORBIDDEN	76954-9/$5.99 US/$6.99 Can
LOVER IN THE ROUGH	
	76760-0/$4.99 US/$5.99 Can
ENCHANTED	77257-4/$5.99 US/$6.99 Can
FORGET ME NOT	76759-7/ $5.50 US/$6.50 Can
ONLY LOVE	77256-6/$5.99 US/$7.99 Can

Coming Soon
AUTUMN LOVER
76955-7/$6.50 US/$8.50 Can

If you enjoyed this book, take advantage of this special offer. Subscribe now and get a

FREE
Historical Romance

No Obligation (a $4.50 value)

Each month the editors of True Value select the four *very best* novels from America's leading publishers of romantic fiction. Preview them in your home *Free* for 10 days. With the first four books you receive, we'll send you a FREE book as our introductory gift. No Obligation!

  If for any reason you decide not to keep them, just return them and owe nothing. If you like them as much as we think you will, you'll pay just $4.00 each and save at *least* $.50 each off the cover price. (Your savings are *guaranteed* to be at least $2.00 each month.) There is NO postage and handling – or other hidden charges. There are no minimum number of books to buy and you may cancel at any time.

*Send in
the Coupon
Below*

To get your FREE historical romance fill out the coupon below and mail it today. As soon as we receive it we'll send you your FREE Book along with your first month's selections.
